Hurrying Angel

JONATHAN LEWIS

Cara-Heleny Book No 1
Published by Cara-Heleny Publishing 2017

First published in Great Britain in 2017

Text copyright © 2014 Jonathan Lewis
Cover copyright © 2017 Cara-Heleny Stripp
All Right Reserved

Typeset in Garamond by
Cara-Heleny Publishing

Printed by kindle direct publishing

978 1520 366 265

Cara-Heleny Publishing
Cara.Heleny.com

This is a work of fiction. Names, characters, businesses, places, events and incidents are either the products of the author's imagination or used in a fictitious manner. Any resemblance to actual persons, living or dead, or actual events is purely coincidental.

Jonathan Lewis has asserted his right to be identified as the author of this work under the Copyright, Designs and Patents Act 1988

Also by Jonathan Lewis

Into Darkness
Into Dust

For Lillibelle

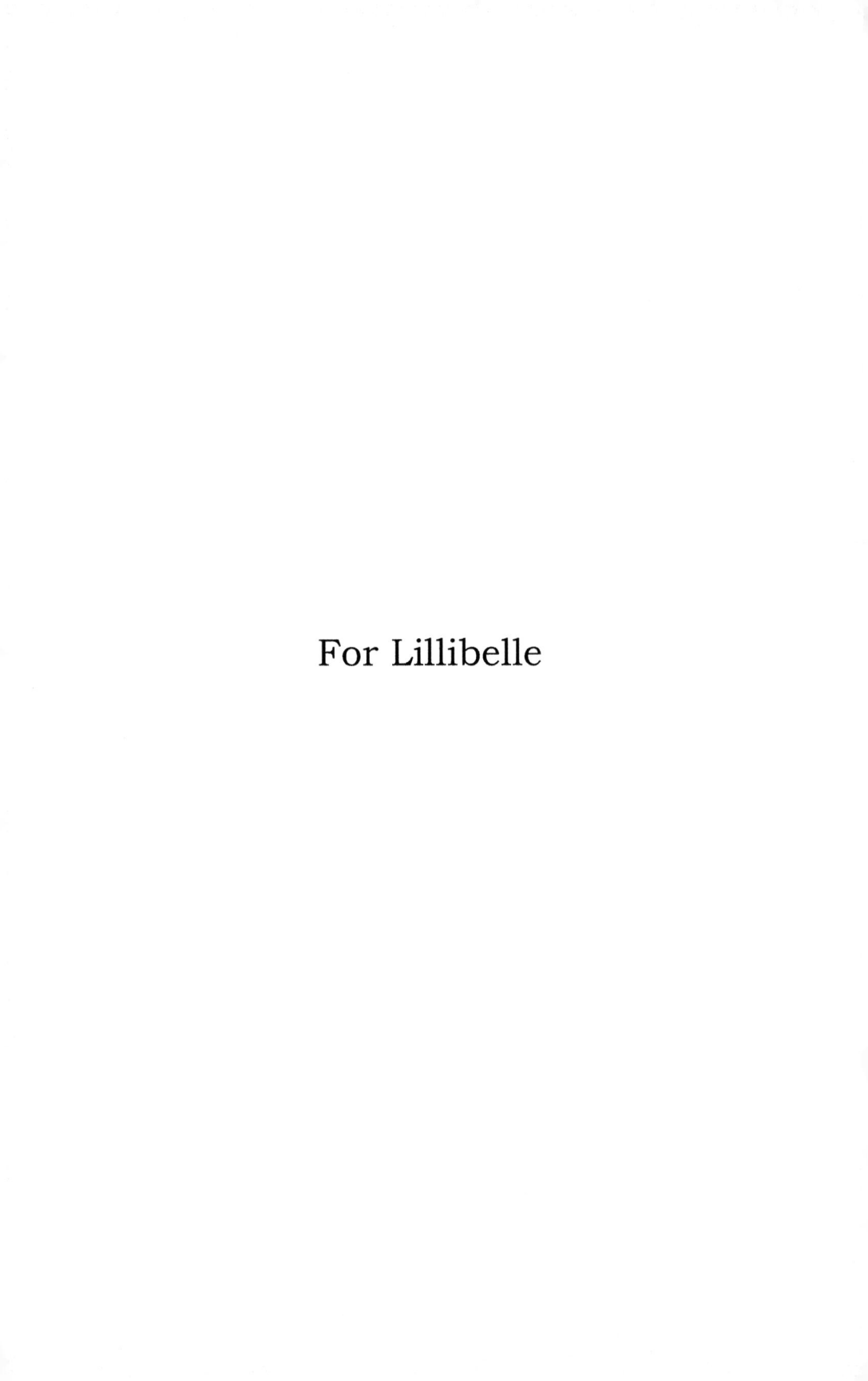

Chapter One

She stood at the top of the hill by the old water trough, staring across her little town. At its clusters of domes and minarets, its jumble of streets and alleys. At the tops of the trees in Hafiz Square, and the arched roof of the distant football stadium. At a glint of water from the drying river-bed. At the smoke from the bakery chimney. At the mountains beyond, blunted by haze. Then she looked down, with a professional eye now, at the churning mass on the slopes immediately below her.

There was no obvious path through the chins and elbows. The bales and sacks, bikes and donkeys. No safe way over cobbles slippery from spillage and the bladders of beasts. The market channelled some of the flow of people, suggesting a logical course down the back of the stalls. But the merchants piled stuff up there, and activity was frenetic between the backs of their wagons and the trestle tables. Cotton, dates, frocks, toys, onions, olives, batteries, beans, tools, underwear and pomegranates flew across the gap, and the merchants' movements were less predictable than the customers'. No, straight through the middle made sense.

'Saljan! Ready!'

Even from the street she could hear her uncle Jafar's anxious voice and the chink of crockery and glass on copper. Her cousin Hussein left with a local delivery as she dived into the cool of the coffee house to pick up her tray and orders.

'The two mint teas are for the undertakers. Not the nice ones by the well, the smelly ones. The *chai* is for Jacques in the bazaar. And the *baklava*. Have a peek behind his counter; I'm sure he's got some of our glasses. The syrups are for Mr Tubini, along with the tobacco. But you have to do the prison first – one coffee medium sweet – and the Pasha will only drink it hot! Main Gatehouse, then ask!'

And she was gone.

***

But the coffee was not for the Pasha.

The guards at the prison gate clearly expected Saljan. They rushed her to the screening area and pushed her to the head of the queue. A prison officer handed her a laminated sheet listing forbidden items. Did she have any of these about her person? It was a counter-intuitively innocuous collection of objects: pencils, pens, ink, paper, oil paints, watercolours, carbon paper, envelopes, postage stamps, note-books, telephones, laptops, scanners, printers, printer cartridges, printing presses, typewriters, photocopiers, camcorders, digital and film cameras. No problem, then, bringing in guns, knives, hard drugs, bolt-cutters, rope-ladders, and skeleton keys. Or, as it turned out, a tray of drinks. It passed through the x-ray machine triggering alarms and flashing lights. No one cared. Saljan set off another lot when she went through the body scanner. It could have been her belt buckle or a machine-pistol strapped to her thigh – no one bothered to look. Then down a corridor shiny with condensation into an iron cage. Gate behind slammed shut; gate in front ground open. Corridors, stairs, more corridors, more stairs. Then it opened out into a great grey dank cavern, with rows of cells and iron walkways and shuffling prisoners.

Saljan had never seen prisoners before. And the prisoners had never seen anything like Saljan and her swinging tray with its wake of tantalising aromas: tea, mint, apple tobacco, syrups of cherry and apricot, three different kinds of *baklava* and, above all, coffee. Around her she heard murmurs.

'Who's she? Where's she going? Coffee? Can I smell coffee?…Is that *baklava*? With pistachios?…What the hell is going on? Isn't it torture enough being in here without forcing us to smell mint tea…Aaah – apple tobacco! It's apple tobacco. Please can I have some? And some coffee, extra sweet…Make that five hundred and seventeen coffees…'

And then sniffing noses started to appear at Judas holes, rooting out oh-so-familiar, oh-so-lost and longed-for scents. Noses pulled sharply in to give eyes a turn. Who was the bearer of these delights? Saljan swished past, looking neither to left or right, aware of the tumult she was causing, determined to get the coffee to its recipient while it was still hot, desperate to get out of there. Had she been at all vain, she would have been offended by the almost unanimous re-substitution of eyes for noses. After all, women they could see at visiting times albeit none as winsome, but few had smelled real coffee in years.

And then Saljan started to hear the explanation for her presence bouncing from cell to cell, above her, around her.

'It's for him at the end... Hadn't you heard - he's getting coffee. Is he? Why? Oh... well, that's different...he deserves it. Isn't that the daughter of Mahmoud the Runner? Ah, so be it...there's nothing here for us.... Forget it...'

With that, the yearnings and agitation died away, and the last steps she took towards the isolated, heavily locked cell at the end of the walkway echoed unchallenged around the grim vault.

A sallow prison guard was sitting in a recess close by, picking his teeth. The officer accompanying Saljan nodded towards the door, which the guard ponderously unlocked with several keys on the bunch that swung from his belt. The officer went in first, said something to the occupant and then gestured Saljan to enter. She did not know whom to expect. A monster, clearly - given the seclusion of his cell, seemingly with its own guard. A powerful monster too – otherwise how had he persuaded the prison authorities to have coffee sent in? Well, she thought, I only deliver it. I don't have to approve of those who drink it. And in she went.

It was a surprising cell. Not quite as small or severe as she expected. There was a high window which, despite iron bars and steel mesh, admitted a tiny shaft of natural light. A bed, a table, a chair, a wardrobe. A shelf with just two books on it. A good rug. A lamp with a red scarf wrapped around the shade. Very plain, but almost homely. Surprising also because she was expecting bad smells and there were none. More surprising was the cell's sole occupant. He did not look like a monster. He was in his late fifties, with a fine, lined face. His hair was receding, his skin was very pale. His hands were not those of a worker, still less of a strangler. Then there were his eyes: brown and shiny like conkers. He looked very serious, but those eyes were twinkly and kind. Odd – for a monster.

He glanced up at her, and then at the tray which she set down on the end of the table. Saljan took the coffee and glass of water off the tray, placed them in front of the man and slipped out of the cell as the prison officer had told her to do. He was having a gossip with the sallow guard a little way away, but Saljan made sure she stood where she could see the prisoner. She was curious about him.

He stared at the coffee, and then gave a little shake of his head as if he did not quite believe what he was seeing. Then he took a sip and closed his eyes and smiled. Then he put the cup back on the saucer and settled himself into his chair as if he were in a coffee house. As if the chair had cushions and the sun was on his face. That was another strange thing about him. For all his paleness and solitude, he did not have the air of a prisoner. Of being beaten down by his confinement. He gave Saljan the impression that he was his own man. Not scared of the guards, not ogling her, not gulping down the coffee in case it was whipped away from him. He took his time, and yet did so without chippiness or defiance. He was a man drinking coffee at his own pace. Not just his own man - a free man.

Saljan wasn't sure what to do. She didn't want the other hot drinks to get cold but she didn't have much choice. She could hardly rush him. So she stood motionless with her face as blank as she could make it, and waited. She wasn't sure how much time elapsed – it could have been five or even ten minutes – before she realised he was talking to her, in an educated, confident voice.

'Come in, come in. I've finished.'

And he carefully replaced the empty cup on its saucer.

'Thanks – wonderful coffee. See you next week.'

And he settled back with another tiny smile, but it certainly wasn't for her benefit. He seemed utterly self-contained.

Next week? What did that mean? And who was going to pay for this week? She was about to ask him these questions when the prison officer reappeared and escorted her out.

She looked back as the door of the cell was slammed and locked on the educated man with only two books, and a window too high to reach but barred and meshed. He must be a very dangerous prisoner indeed. Just as well she had kept away from him. Anyway, he'd barely registered her existence. Well, she told herself, that's how it should be. She was, after all, just the delivery person. The coffee was the thing.

***

What is a cup of coffee? Brown dust and water - nothing really. Warm some water in your tinned copper pot. Add a spoonful of coffee and a little sugar. Stir well; you don't want any lumps. Some make a paste, then water it down, but you shouldn't need to. Low fire. Don't stir it now. Just watch and be ready to move fast. Tiny bubbles form. Not like the bubbles from stirring it cold, but shiny clusters tinged with rainbow colours. Getting hot now. Gathering, rumbling, about to erupt. Don't let it boil! Quick - off the heat, pour out the first frothing. Back on the flame. Second rise, second pour. Not as rich and thick, but still gleaming. Third and last now. Bubbles coarser, more watery. Pour it with care to keep the precious, hard-won foam intact and afloat.

There. You've done it. Not bad for a beginner. It should look as if it's an entire cupful of that first flowering from the dust and water. And so it does, more or less. There's a skill in it all, no less in the pouring than in the roasting and blending. Taste it. Any bits? A few grains is acceptable, but not a gobful of grit. You want three textures in the mouth: the crema, the coffee below that, and one or two grains for intensity.

Some add cardamom seeds ground fine. A pinch of cinnamon for others. You can do it – the ground won't open up and a horde of djinns from hell come out and munch you up if you do – but it isn't right. Not classical? Not traditional? No, neither of those two. It simply isn't necessary if your coffee is the best. Roasted perfectly. Ground fine as fine, and used quickly - the oils go stale so fast in the heat. People use cardamom to mask flaws. If you don't make mistakes, you've nothing to hide. They ask for coffee - coffee is what they should get.

Her grandfather's coffee lecture rang in her ears though she had never really listened to him at the time, and he'd been dead a decade. But it had gone in. She never forgot anything she was told, but she was no good at making coffee. Even if she followed his instructions, it never turned out perfect like Grandpa's. He became so fanatical in old age that he would add precisely three coarser grains to give just the right amount of bite.

'Did you find them?' he'd ask her, eyes gleaming. 'Three, there were. How many did you find?'

'Just two this time, Grandpa. Two. Sorry.'

For a moment he would look a little crazy, and then he'd sink back in his chair, breathing hard. When he was calm again, he'd look at her and smile understandingly.

'Can't be helped, can't be helped. Maybe next time. Whenever you want a cup, all you have to do is ask. You know that, dearest Saljan. Grandpa will make it for you.'

Next time she looked he'd be asleep. Except for the time he was dead.

Anyway, it wasn't just about coffee. It was also a question of centrifugal force. When she went round corners, the tray was almost at right angles to the ground. People would stop and watch her. Look, they'd say. It's that daughter of Mahmoud the Runner, delivering drinks. How does she do it? Is it in the tray? Or is it her wrist action? Or the grip? And they'd see the elegant first and second fingers of her right hand curled around the copper loop, swinging the tray with its cups and glasses seemingly glued in place so it looked like a shield held by a warrior, facing off the world. Bouncing the sun into the eyes of gawpers. Defying gravity. Never spills a drop, they said. And such good coffee. The best!

Mahmoud the Runner didn't make coffee and he never delivered it. He sat outside in the garden where everyone could see him, under the awning or in the arbour, with an ivory fly-swat in his hand and a cup of coffee and glass of iced water on the table beside him. He held court, but he had little small talk. He was lazy now. All those years of early morning training, pounding the cinders, exercising, dieting, running, running, running. He owed it to himself now to do nothing. He's earned it, everyone said. So he sat in the shade, and smiled and listened. It was almost as if he had been a boxer, and was brain-damaged. Except he was neither. He had just decided to become ornamental.

He was still very good-looking. Fuller in the face than when he had filled screens and dominated headlines, when he had stared almost absent-mindedly from podiums as if he couldn't quite remember why he was up there. Then he would bow his head to receive the sashes and medals and when he lifted it again he would have the same distant look. The certainty and focus he showed when he ran was never seen at other times. Then, he had something of his father's wild coffee-maniac glint, but it only ever accompanied the record-breaking moment itself. Not the world's subsequent acknowledgement of his triumph.

And then there was his hair. It was the shiniest, blackest, slickest imaginable. He had kept it short when running, but now he was strictly decorative he let it grow. His daughter made sure she never touched it, not only because she knew it irritated him, but because she hated the feel of it. His greasy carapace. He had become a little vain. Ever since a hair gel firm had paid him to endorse their product, he'd been laying it on thick, and during the day insects would land and be unable to take off again. That was why the issue of touching his hair arose. She thought he looked silly with quivering moths and daddy long legs sticking to him, but it was his problem, she decided, not hers. She was very proud of him, but she didn't really know him. He was more like a retired racehorse than a father. A racehorse covered in flies.

So there he sat, smiling and drinking coffee. His beautiful brown eyes twinkled and everyone was pleased to see him. But few went to him for facts or advice. His opinion was sometimes asked out of politeness and respect, but it was never heeded. What, after all, did he know about, except how to run faster than anyone else on the planet? They went to Mahmoud to be seen with him. To bask in his glow. And of course, to drink the wonderful coffee.

Making coffee is one thing. Making a tray with the performance of a flying saucer is quite another. Saljan was very, very fussy about her tray. She had spent days in the street of the coppersmiths, watching them work, choosing her man. At first it had seemed obvious. The old character with the wispy beard and the grey waistcoat had the most customers. But when she tried out his trays, they were too light. No ballast to them. All over the place, particularly on a sharp turn. That she decided, was why he had the queues. His trays were cheap.

The man next door was fat and had big moustaches. He looked as if he'd know about weight and wouldn't skimp on his metals. And he didn't. But they were too heavy, too clumsy. No sense of aerodynamics. And what was all that decoration? She wasn't looking for engraving and chasing, crescent moons and stars. She wanted a tray for speed and agility, not to impress the neighbours. Her tray would be judged on its performance. She moved on.

At the end of the street, where few went because a broken drain kept the ground soft and smelly, were the tatty premises of a young coppersmith. He was handsome and lean, with a scar on one arm and a bad burn on the other. At first she thought he looked angry, but it turned out that was just the face he pulled when he bashed metal. She studied him for a while. He was decidedly tactile. He'd select copper rods for his trays with great care. He weighed them in his hand. He ran his fingers along them. When he cut a length off, he'd roll it up and down his cheek. He even licked one piece of brass before hammering it into a cone, with the veins standing out on his arms and the look of a man possessed. He was clearly mad, and she slipped away before he noticed her.

But the next day, she went back. My tray, she thought, isn't going to be off-the-peg. It's not going to be made for a price, or according to old rules. So the man that makes it won't look like anyone's idea of a coppersmith. He's going to be wild, unorthodox, counter-cultural. He's going to understand things the older men don't. He's going to take risks. He's going to rise to challenges. If he fails, he's not going to despair. He's going to learn by his mistakes. Above all, he's going to listen to me. I'm the customer. I'm commissioning this tray. And I know what I want.

They sat cross-legged at opposite ends of his divan. Of course he'd noticed her the day before. How could he not? She was tall and sinuous, with close-cropped hair and a quirkily beautiful face. But he didn't say anything. He just looked into those eyes, black as coal, and listened to her talk. How someone could get so worked up about a tray, only he – amazingly – understood. At first she thought he was interested in her rather than her tray, but after a while she realised he was a fanatical coppersmith. As she chattered on, he started to sketch something on an old tea packet, and then he rummaged among his brass off-cuts, and lastly he started to fold a piece of thin tin. His fingers were grimy, but surprisingly slender, supple and quick.

'There' he said. 'Anything like this?'

'It's too early to say,' she replied. 'And anyway, that's too small for me to tell. I'll come back in a week to try out the prototype. Do you have any coffee cups? It doesn't matter. I'll bring my own.'

And she left. Nothing in writing. No order number. No deposit. He'd been warned by his coppersmithing tutor about proceeding under these circumstances. But what choice did he have? It wasn't just those smouldering eyes and that willowy body. It was the technical and creative challenge. Where was that 40 gauge pure copper wire he'd been keeping for a special occasion? Perhaps this was it.

When she went back a week later, she felt sure the young coppersmith had cracked it. Not because he told her so, eager like a puppy. Far from it. He wasn't jumpy, and he was in no rush to show her his work. He just pottered. Boiled a kettle. Made some tea. Wandered over to the old boy next door and came back with some biscuits neither of them wanted. Her instincts were to lay into him, ask him to give an account of each day's labour on her behalf, demand evidence of progress. But he was so laid-back and round-about that she could only assume he'd finished the tray. Even so, his manner threw her a little. And since she knew he'd expect her to be impatient and demanding, she decided to be neither. Wasn't going to give him the satisfaction.

She sat back on his battered cushions under his tattered canopy. He reached up to the rafters and redirected a powerful electric fan onto her. The burn on his arm was healing. The scar was bad, though. Whatever caused it must have hurt like hell. Had he screamed? Had he fainted? She nodded her thanks for the blast of cool on her face. He sold a jug. He took a call on his mobile phone. She sipped her tea. It tasted of brass cleaner. She couldn't smell the drains now. Just fire, smoke and hot metal. He drifted into the back room. She could hear him laughing at something the caller said. She took a bite of a biscuit. It tasted of charcoal. Perhaps he hadn't cracked it. Perhaps he hadn't done a tap of work on her tray all week. He wandered over and sat down on a wooden crate opposite her. She put the biscuit back on the plate with its missing arc. Right then, she said. Must be getting on. He nodded. She left.

He watched her nip down the street, dodging obstacles and vaulting the soggy bits. What was that about? He hadn't got the measure of her at all. Why didn't she ask him how he was getting on with the tray? If she didn't want to know that, why had she come to see him? Certainly not for tea and a snack. He looked at the carefully discarded biscuit, with its crescent of teeth-marks, small and very even. Did she fancy him? It didn't appear so. He'd used the business of pointing his fan at her as a chance to stare. She was like an elusive desert deer. For the moment, though, it would be safer to see her as just another customer. And failing that, as Saljan, daughter of Mahmoud the Runner. Because one thing he had done during the week was check on her. Fit as he was, her dad could probably still outrun him. And anyway, he had made some progress with the tray. All she had to do was ask.

Firstly, he had wandered the full length of the street looking at everyone else's trays. Research, he said, when asked. Some of his neighbours were flattered by the attention and mistook it for admiration. Others felt threatened. One particularly unpleasant man got so fed up with the lad fingering and staring that he told him that he had asserted his moral right to be identified as the author of his trays and if he found young Beyrek infringing his copyright he would sue him under the Berne Convention - and stick a red-hot poker up his arse. The old one-two, the livid coppersmith obligingly explained. Young Beyrek nodded, grinned, and wandered away, annoyingly slowly. He'd seen all he needed to. None of these trays were any good. None of them would meet the requirement. Saljan's tray called for a total redesign. For that, he'd need a consulting engineer. Off to the sewage works, then.

It wasn't the obvious place to find a scientific genius, but the town's entire sanitary arrangements depended on an ancient and highly temperamental pump, which sucked up bath water and bowel waste and spewed it out into evaporation tanks built down-wind of the town. When old Dumrul died, the only man in the world who understood how it all worked was his son. As a small child he'd watched his father grapple with anti-siphons and suction hoses and non-return valves, and as he grew older he'd helped his increasingly infirm parent keep the old pile of junk operational. By the age of ten he had re-designed the separator, making the new centrifuge himself. The school realised how exceptional the boy was and sent him to the Technical Institute. He soon drained the teachers there of all they knew, and by the age of fifteen he was at university. Degree followed degree and before he was out of his twenties Berent Dumrul was at Cern on the French-Swiss border: an expert in the patterns of particle movement.

Fine, said the Mayor, after yet another chief sewage engineer had handed in his notice. He's just the man we want. We've got a load of particles – he'll know how to move them. But why, asked the Clerk, would Dr Dumrul want to come back here from Geneva and live in that poky house built down-wind of the sewage works and spend his days and nights up to his elbows in...?

'His mother,' said the Mayor, 'his mother.'

No one in Mahmoud's Coffee House where the emergency council meeting was taking place wanted to look a fool by asking the Mayor what he meant. Most assumed that, for all his swish Swiss ways, Dr Dumrul was – like the rest of them – a mother's boy at heart and would do whatever the old lady asked of him. But one or two in the room with long memories, including Saljan's uncle Jafar, wondered if the Mayor intended to have Halide Hanım slowly poisoned so that Dr Dumrul would race back to nurse her. There was, after all, the strange story of the Mayor and the widow Ençand the apricot orchard...

The truth was odder even than that. Dr Dumrul wanted to come home. He wanted to gaze at the sunsets over the mountains and tend that strange, vital machine which posed more complex challenges to a physicist than anything a particle accelerator could throw at him. Besides, he wouldn't live in the poky little house down-wind of the pong. He would park an air-conditioned motorised home on the hill above, and he'd bring home with him the sassy, curvaceous Turkish girl who worked in the kebab shop down the road from his Geneva apartment and they'd have loads of kids who, like him, would grow up to the – hopefully – unceasing chorus of rumbles, whistles and belches from the sewage pump.

'Hello, Dr Dumrul.'

'Beyrek the Coppersmith! Beer or lager?'

Chapter Two

Saljan had decided to write Beyrek off, but as chance would have it she found herself in the coppersmiths' alley three days later. It was a rush order to Old Ragıp's for four coffees, one extra sweet, and a double portion of pistachio *lokum*. A deal hung in the balance. When Saljan got there, the old boy looked relieved to see her. The possible purchaser was a fat, fierce woman Saljan didn't recognise, buttressed by two acolytes. She was evidently equipping a restaurant kitchen, because a mountain of copper pans and utensils sat in no-man's-land between them while their value was simultaneously upped and downed. Poker-faced the harridan restaurateur may have been, but the sight of the pyramid of dusty, nutty *lokum* and the oily-rich sweet coffee distracted her for a moment. It was just the moment Ragıp needed. Remember me to your father, he said to Saljan, slipping a note into her palm. And away she ran from the cascading clouds of icing sugar as the balance of power behind her started to tip in the old coppersmith's favour.

Unfortunately, she ran down the alley, not up it. Yes, it was the quickest way back to the coffee house, but it led past the unbiddable Beyrek. She wasn't going to stop, but something caught her eye as she went past him. He was beating the hell out of a piece of brass: teeth clenched, veins pumping, wild look in his eye. And round his bare neck, the thing that brought her to a bemused halt. It was a disc about three inches across, with a dainty bite taken out of it. Her discarded biscuit. Round his neck. On a fine chain. Couldn't be. How could biscuit cope with all that heat and sweat? Well, one made of copper could. She couldn't believe the cheek of it.

'You! Beyrek! What's that around your neck?'

'Oh, that. Do you like it? It's my new line. Going really well. By the way, your tray will take longer than I thought. It's become highly technical… But it'll…'

She never heard what it'll, because anger at his presumption kicked her into top gear. But fast as she ran, it wasn't too quick to notice that a number of girls in the town were wearing shiny medallions round their necks in the shape of biscuits with a bite taken out.

She pounded back up the hill thinking furiously. For two pins she'd drop the whole thing. Who had the time for a chancer like Beyrek? Maybe the faster tray idea was daft. Her old one wasn't too bad. A drop of oil on the top loop, a good polish. Perhaps she should line it with a non-slip inset? Traditionalists might scoff, but… And then she walked into the back-room of the coffee house and saw her Auntie Gül Seren staring at a large sheet of paper, looking worried. She was Jafar's second wife; she had brought up his two boys as her own and been almost a mother to Saljan. She gave her aunt a sympathetic grin and knew at once what she needed. She fetched a handful of Cretan dittany – white and hairy – from the cool room, divided it between two tall glasses and steeped the mint in boiling water with the tiniest pinch of vanilla sugar. Then she joined her aunt at the table.

The chart looked very different from the last time she had seen it. The map of the town was now covered with circles of different colours. Some overlapped, some kept their distance. The main set of circles, however, radiated from the coffee house at the epicentre, like ripples in a pond. Each ring was marked with times and temperatures. Not the heat of the day, but the heat of the drinks measured by thermometer at the point of delivery, each one progressively further from the Coffee House. Saljan remembered it as perhaps the toughest work she'd ever done. In one trip alone she had taken coffees to the signal box at the railway junction and teas to stalls in four of the town's markets. On another, she'd been to the Mayor's office and the offices of the town architect and then run up the fifty two stairs of the cinema fire escape with a lemon water ice for the projectionist. Each time she got back she had reported to Gül Seren while the next tray was being prepared.

'…journey time seven minutes, twenty seven seconds. At 67° the camomile was 2° cooler than the black teas. I couldn't go straight on from there to the spice merchant because a cart had fallen over by the hairdressers and the way was blocked. I lost maybe 45 seconds going through the police station car park. It might explain why the coffee temperatures were down 1°. Next I did Abdul Bey...'

The big question was, how far from the coffee house could they deliver and still maintain the standards for which they were famous. Would the coffee still be hot? The *baklava* warm? The ices frozen? At the moment, each of the town's coffee houses had a notional boundary beyond which they dared not go. Sure, Jafar had many key destinations in his reach, and he had a bigger clientele because of his insistence on quality, his brother's fame, and Saljan's speed and memory. Her uncanny capacity to recall what was said to her was critical, because it enabled them to send out multi-destination trays without having to provide delivery dockets. But expansion with profit was the goal. Had they pushed out as far as they could? Were their rivals over-extended? Did ice melt on some sun-drenched routes, where it might stay hard down other, shadier lanes? So many questions, Mahmoud the Runner murmured from his high-backed chair by the window, as he watched his daughter re-tying her laces. So many variables.

Yeah, thought Saljan as she hared off with her fourteenth tray of the day. So much responsibility. So much sweat.

It had taken Auntie Gül Seren two weeks to process the data from that exhausting day. The more she now talked, between sips of mint tea, the clearer it became that the fate of the family enterprise depended on delivery, and the delivery system was Saljan. She traced with her finger the dotted red arc that showed how far they might reach into their rival's territory. What would it take to join up the dots? How much would she have to lop off her journey time to reach the furthest tantalising destination with the coffee still hot?

'Three minutes.'

Saljan hadn't noticed her uncle Jafar slip into the room. She smiled weakly at him. Three minutes! Was it possible? She could almost feel the tray hurtling out of her hand, almost hear the smashing of crockery. This wasn't going to be about her running - she could easily run faster. It was about getting there without the drinks sliding off the tray. How about polystyrene cups with lids? Cold boxes with ice packs? A moped with panniers? Would her uncle consider…?

Absolutely not. Theirs was a totally traditional business. That's why they were so respected. The delivery by dangling, swinging copper and brass tray was as much a part of it as the quality of the coffees and sweetmeats. In a way, given his brother Mahmoud's fantastic achievements, running was key to their success. It was their… What was that expression? He turned to his wife.

'Unique Selling Point. USP.'

'That's it. USP. Running is our Unique Selling Point. First your father, and now you… None of the others really run the coffee in the old way. The Technical Institute, the newspaper office, that clutch of travel agencies, the prison – they're on Remzi's doorstep. I've seen his boy strolling round with plastic cups on a cardboard box lid. That's not our style. People like to see the coffee and tea run. It tells them that we care about the total experience.'

'But three minutes, Uncle Jafar…'

He shrugged with an understanding, frowny little smile. He knew it was a lot to ask of her. No, Saljan thought. There you're wrong, uncle. It's an awful lot to ask of a tray.

Late as it was, she had to see Beyrek. Had to get his nose to the grindstone. She was pretty sure he lived at the back of the smithy, but it was dark when she got there. Only by luck did she avoid stepping in the damp bit. She stood in the night and smelled the banked fire in his forge, but of the coppersmith himself there was no sign. She didn't want to call his name. Or rather, she didn't want to get caught by any of his neighbours standing outside his window at night, calling his name. People are so quick to think the worst. But she wanted to do it. Had to do it. Why should he sleep when there was a tray to be made which could win or lose her family the midtown coffee war?

'Beyrek! Beyrek!'

'Beyrek's not there, little Saljan. No point waiting for him.'

It was Ragıp, walking his wheezy elderly dog Khan.

'He's up at Dr Dumrul's. Goes there twice a week and stays over. He pays my lad to get his fire going in the morning.'

'And what does Beyrek do with Dr Dumrul all that time, Ragıp Efendi?'

'Ah!' said the old man, 'I would have thought you of all people would know the answer to that.'

It was too dark to see, but the young woman could hear the smile in his voice.

***

In common with the rest of the town, Beyrek the Coppersmith did not know exactly what Dr Dumrul had been up to during the dozen years he had been away. He knew it was very scientific, very technical. He also knew that since Dr Dumrul's return, the sewage had not backed up anywhere except at the camel market in that thunderstorm, which couldn't be held against anyone, as it were. Beyrek assumed advising on the Fast Tray Project would be easier than falling off a log for the mighty scientist. In fact, Dr Dumrul was immediately struck by the theoretical complexities of the FTP, and by the way they chimed with the challenges he had faced in Geneva.

His time at the Large Electron-Positron Collider a hundred metres under the French-Swiss border had given him vast experience and understanding of how things whirl around and collide. It should be, he sincerely hoped but kept to himself, a small jump to knowing how to whirl stuff about without colliding. But it wasn't an open and shut case. A tunnel twenty seven kilometres in circumference is an awful lot bigger than a coffee tray, but at least it doesn't swing wildly around. The good thing about his Collider was, it stayed put. Would Beyrek the Coppersmith's Fast Tray Project be the final straw that would break the back of Grand Unification Theories? Time would tell. In the meantime, Beyrek the Coppersmith had found the only man within a thousand miles who understood the physics of building a faster tray.

'I really ought to correct you there, Beyrek. It isn't actually a faster tray in itself. It's a tray which can be run with faster without spilling its contents.'

'I see, Doctor. Point taken. But let me ask you: is it right to talk of this tray in the present tense, when it doesn't exist yet? All we've got in the present tense so far is an increasingly ratty customer.'

'Point taken, Beyrek. Another beer?'

***

Saljan had a choice. She could take her father's shiny four-wheeled vehicle. Or she could take her uncle Jafar's donkey Othman, who was anything but shiny. She chose Othman, because the jeep would need every speck of dust removing after the trip whereas the donkey would be happy with a quick rubdown and a bunch of carrots. Besides, Saljan loved Othman. He had enormous eyes, furry ears like the hands of a clock and he brayed with joy whenever he saw her. Added to which, he knew his way everywhere, and she'd never actually been up to the sewage works. Othman – it had to be.

'Don't you want to take the jeep, Saljan? That donkey of Jafar's is a terrible old flea-bag.'

'It's all right, Father. He needs the exercise.'

Mahmoud the Runner nodded and sat back. It was always the same with him. He never insisted on anything. It was good in a way. Left her free as she pleased. But it wasn't exactly what she wanted.

Othman lived under a big tree on the patch of waste ground at the end of the coffee house garden. In the worst of the winter weather Jafar would move him into the blacksmith's stable, but the rest of the year Othman dozed in the shade of his tree, keeping half an eye open for anything edible discarded within the forty foot radius of his tether. He shared a water trough with the Hoja's mule Safraz who was tied to the next tree. The two beasts had reached an accommodation over the years; they never used the trough at the same time. They had no choice but to be neighbours, but they were not obliged to be friends.

Saljan peered through the kitchen door at Othman. He was under the tree with his back to her and his ears at twenty to two. She always tried the same trick on him. It was a version of the old schoolyard game. She'd see if she could get right up to him without him seeing her and letting fly a peal of whinnies. As usual, he won, turning round in time to spot his little mistress as she jumped the coffee house garden fence. Then it was a question of an apple to quell the din, a blanket over his back and away. All she had to do then was get him to the edge of town where the sewage pipe snaked into the distance and he'd do the rest.

He trotted quite fast. Through orchards of walnut and quince. Over the dry river-bed. Briefly alongside the railway line as it curled round to gain height for the climb through the mountains. Dr Dumrul's pipe kept them company most of the time. Sometimes it was built up on stone plinths; sometimes it dived through embankments. Sometimes she heard it gurgling, and very occasionally she could smell it. Dr Dumrul's hill rose steeply out of the plateau, with the sewage works at its foot. She nudged Othman towards the higher ground and he steadily and carefully picked his way up the narrow track. His ears were now showing ten past nine. The clattering and sucking sounds of the old pump receded as they climbed. The view just got better and better. The mountains which, from town, were lost in haze were serried and distinct. And it was true – you couldn't smell the sewage works from up there. In the distance was the gleaming motor-home she had heard about, with its streamlined elegance and air-conditioning. Two children played in its shade while a very handsome pregnant woman hung out washing. That must be Scheherazade Dumrul. But no sign of her husband, or that Beyrek.

They sat in the cool of the shaded sitting area on cushioned divans, drinking *ayran* and eating nut moon biscuits. At first it seemed to Scheherazade that Saljan was overly adamant that Beyrek was purely her contractor in the matter of coffee trays – not her boyfriend. But the more they talked, the more she saw the almost daunting seriousness in Saljan. This was no flirt on an impulsive dash. It was someone who, bearing responsibility for her family's survival, was worrying that she was being let down - and one of the people doing the letting down was Scheherazade's own husband. Except he wasn't, and neither was Beyrek.

Come, said the woman to the girl. Let me show you something. She scooped up her daughter and, with her son scampering ahead, led Saljan up a path behind the motor-home. It wound between steep rocks and then opened into a clearing. The sight was a little bizarre. Stuck into the ground were four wooden posts with pulley-wheels bolted horizontally on top. Hanging from one spoke on each wheel was a coffee tray. An endless cord ran round all four pulleys, then off to a winch with a flywheel bolted to the rock. And the ground between and around the four posts was strewn with broken crockery.

On close examination, each tray was slightly different. One had a weight hung below it on four short lengths of chain. Another a gyroscope. The third had a base about an inch thick. The fourth just looked like an ordinary tray.

'That's what Dad calls the "control". He uses it to measure the others against. Watch!'

He went over to the winch and turned the handle, and the trays started to swing around. Slowly at first, and then they rose higher and higher. Saljan noticed a saucer had survived on the tray with the thick base, but when the boy stopped turning and the trays slowed and sank, the saucer slid off and smashed.

'How have they done – the others?'

Kazan took her to the tray with the hanging weight. That didn't work at all. And the one with the gyroscope didn't want to swing up in the air, and then when they got it up, it didn't want to come down…

'Besides,' Saljan interjected. 'I don't see how I could put either of those trays down with that stuff on the bottom.'

Kazan's eyes widened.

'You? You're the person the tray's for? Who's actually going to use it?'

Saljan gave a modest grin.

'Wow! I wish I were you. It's going to be amazing…'

Had any of them worked, Saljan wanted to know. The boy nodded.

'Yes,' he said, 'the ball-bearing one. Sort of. But…'

He took hold of the tray with the thick base and shook it.

'It's a little noisy, isn't it?'

Kazan nodded.

'That's what we thought. But your one will be silent. It'll be brilliant, when Beyrek's made it more of a cone inside, and Dad's got the mercury…'

Then he looked quickly at his mother as if he had said more than he ought. Saljan pretended she hadn't noticed, and bent down to pick up a cup-less handle.

'We've got a few left. To test what Dad calls the final proto…top…or something.'

It was Saljan's turn to nod. So they had been working on the tray. She'd got that Beyrek a bit wrong. She squatted down next to Kazan.

'Would you like a ride on my donkey? He's called Othman and he's very gentle. He likes little boys. And carrots. But not in the same way!'

Scheherazade watched as she took Kazan by the hand. It was the first moment she'd seen Saljan relax. High time Berent got back with that mercury and Beyrek produced the perfected cone thing. Then she'd cook them all a celebratory dinner and everything would be fine. She popped Fatima onto her shoulders and went off to fetch some carrots.

***

The next week was uneasy all round. Jafar took the plunge and went into the red dotted sector on a marketing mission. He pressed the flesh and handed out flyers and made promises he didn't know if he could keep. Gül Seren had insomnia. She'd done the sums and redone them and still couldn't see how the coffee house could survive without working Saljan into the ground. Mahmoud the Runner took to his bed after a sharp exchange with his brother in which Jafar pointed out how few of his cronies ever paid for their coffees. Scheherazade Dumrul spent two days in the hospital after a routine check-up revealed sky-high blood pressure. The mercury cost Dr Dumrul twice what he'd estimated – a far cry from wandering into the stores at Cern and strolling out with a drum of the stuff. The Hoja's mule decided to sleep by the water trough and Othman went thirsty rather than risk his neighbour's foul temper. And Saljan's trainers finally fell apart, forcing her to spend a third of her savings on a new pair. New tray or not, she had to be able to run without twisting her ankle.

Only Beyrek had a good week. He sold his entire run of copper bite necklaces to a buyer from a chain of accessory shops, who also ordered a bracelet and anklet version for evaluation. And, at three one morning, he finally finished a tray base he was satisfied with. He'd got the thickness down, so the finished item would be virtually indistinguishable from run-of-the-mill, subsonic trays. And they'd cracked the deceleration problem. The idea – which was Dr Dumrul's - was to give the tray a smoother descent from higher angles of inclination by making sure the mercury didn't rush back to the base of the cone. An elegant notion, but its realization would push the copper-smithing envelope to the limits. Eventually Beyrek found a way of bending tiny rivulets into the cone, alternated with minute baffles. Together they would slow the mercury both in take-off and landing.

Last of all he inserted a tiny threaded filling collar flush into the base, with a screw cap that fitted like a dream. At first the Chief Designer of the Fast Tray Project had talked in terms of filling the cone with mercury and then simply brazing on the round base, sealing it in forever. But Beyrek pointed out that hard solder only melts above 430°C, a temperature which would boil the mercury inside. And Dr Dumrul, increasingly sure that Beyrek had missed some higher scientific calling, realised that the quantity of mercury in the tray might need trial-and-error adjustment, so a removable filler cap made perfect sense.

Thus it was the next evening, after the hospital had given Scheherazade Dumrul the all-clear and the coffee house was closed, that Dr Dumrul and Saljan met at the mouth of the alley, both on their way to Beyrek the Coppersmith. They guessed who the other was: the man clutching his precious container of mercury, the girl with brand new trainers. They exchanged polite greetings and walked together past the shuttered emporia of those coppersmiths who shunned experimental work and closed at seven sharp. All save Old Ragıp. He had an avuncular regard for Beyrek and had stayed on for the big night. His boy Turgut was with him; he hero-worshipped Beyrek and had begged his master to let him make the teas and coffees for the test-runs of the tray. So four people it was who walked the final yards to Beyrek's together.

The smithy was dark where they expected light. And instead of the roar of fire and the tap of hammer, there was deep snoring. Dr Dumrul flashed his torch around, its beam eventually alighting on a sprawled shape in a hammock hanging from the rafters. Only one of the four onlookers jumped to an optimistic conclusion. The boy Turgut immediately assumed his hero had fallen asleep exhausted by triumphant labours. Old Ragıp, who'd known Beyrek since his childhood, reluctantly feared he was hiding under his blanket as he used to do when he didn't want to go to school. Dr Dumrul, aware of how tricky the task was he'd set the coppersmith, concluded it was the sleep of failure. Regrettable, but completely understandable.

Saljan alone spoke her thoughts:

'Beyrek, you idler! Where's my tray?'

The snoring stopped instantly, but the shape didn't answer. It just surreptitiously flipped a switch it had rigged up to the hammock last thing before it crashed out two hours before. Beams of light suddenly shone down on the anvil, which had been draped in a piece of red velvet. And dazzling in the glow was the tray. Its copperwork gleamed. Its brass carrying ring stood up invitingly. The three rods which joined cap to base were beautifully curved, their ends finely splayed and pinned with perfectly domed rivets – no tell-tale flats from hammer blows. The chasing around the lip was elegant and restrained. The inner recess in the base had been consummately fashioned, all signs of trickery concealed. Even without its secrets, it was a tray among trays. The visitors gasped in awe. While they moved in for a closer look, the shape above pulled on a shirt, ran fingers through unruly hair and crunched a few breath-sweetening cardamom seeds, before resolving itself into Beyrek the Coppersmith. He jumped down and joined the admirers below.

Old Ragıp was the first to speak.

'I would be proud to make a tray like that now. To have made it when I was your age, Beyrek...'

And the old boy shook his head before turning slowly away.

Dr Dumrul caught Beyrek's eye and threw an inquisitive glance at the base. Beyrek nodded reassuringly. Then Turgut piped up.

'Can we try it out now, Beyrek? Can we?'

It was a potentially embarrassing moment. No point testing the tray without first filling the hidden reservoir with mercury, but Beyrek and Dr Dumrul had agreed to keep the design an absolute secret, in line with a request Saljan had made after seeing the copper bite necklaces all over town. She didn't want to find Beyrek churning out fast trays for her rivals. It was a one-off for her and her alone. So they couldn't exactly start pouring mercury into hidden chambers in front of Ragıp and Turgut without giving the game away. Certainly the old boy knew that given Dr Dumrul's involvement this was no ordinary tray, but he was discreet. The same could not perhaps be said about the enthusiastic Turgut...

'Come on, young Turgut. We'd better get over to our place and fire up the samovar. Can't try out a new coffee tray without coffee...'

He bundled the boy out, then turned and gave a broad wink to the three standing around the tray. Whatever secret it contained, Old Ragıp didn't want to know.

When they had gone, Beyrek turned the tray over, removed the filler cap and inserted a funnel with a slender spout. Then Dr Dumrul opened the canister and, using a measuring jug, poured in exactly 275 millilitres of mercury. Saljan had never seen mercury before and was utterly fascinated by the slippery silver liquid. Dr Dumrul placed a drop in a small brass ashtray. Such was its surface tension that it remained an almost perfect gleaming ball, where the base of a water drop would have spread flat.

'That' Dr Dumrul explained, 'is because mercury has 13.5 times the density of water.'

Which wasn't much of an explanation as far as Saljan was concerned, but she didn't care. It was just such strange, fascinating stuff. She watched it swirl around as if it were alive. And the thought that her tray had a secret compartment full of it was even more fantastic.

Then Beyrek screwed the little cap back and ran a bead of low-melt solder around the seam. A buff with a polishing cloth and the tray was handed over to its new owner.

It appeared to Saljan to be an ordinary coffee tray. A bit heavier, perhaps, but that was all. Then she started to move around the smithy. At first it was a little reluctant to lift as she turned corners, but the more she swung it, the more the mercury inside was forced to the outer edge of the cone. She suddenly felt the tray alter its pitch as if with a life of its own. Dr Dumrul saw the look of surprise on her face and realised it had just done the tray equivalent of Concorde smashing the sound barrier. He expected her to slow down, but she just speeded up. Around the anvil, past the fireplace and chimney, weaving in and out of tubs of copper rod and bronze pipe, bales of wire and the posts that held the roof up. And the faster the girl went, the higher the tray rose until it was flying around at over 100° to the ground. She felt it strain against her; the joints in her first and second fingers were white where they coiled around the copper loop.

Beyrek watched her slip around his smithy like the ball of mercury in the ashtray, and started to laugh with pure pleasure: pleasure in his creation, pleasure in her. Soon Dr Dumrul too was grinning from ear to ear, and still Saljan whirled on. She swung it high and low. It skimmed within a cigarette paper's thickness of precarious stacks of brass sheet. It orbited oil lamps. It slipped out the back and in through the front. And nothing fell. Nothing was dislodged but dust.

She and the tray only came down to earth with a knock on the door and there were Old Ragıp and Turgut bearing cups of coffee and glasses of tea. Saljan slowed and the tray followed her, the tiny baffles and folds in its hidden cone delaying the descent of the magic liquid so the tray almost seemed to hover for a second over the anvil before settling on its red velvet throne.

Saljan sank onto a tatty old rug, her head bowed in relief and momentary exhaustion. Beyrek stared at the nape of her neck, the lazy curls of hair nestling in that perfect hollow. Luckily Turgut handed him a glass of tea with two lumps of sugar, which was not at all what he wanted but very much what he needed. Then Saljan looked up with a broad grin on her face which told the FTP designer and constructor all they wanted to know.

Then they tested the tray all over again, and Saljan found it more controllable with the coffees and teas on it. Dr Dumrul said that was because it was designed to work at its optimum under load, and Beyrek thought that was a bit pompous, so had a go at telling him that it was just a tin tray after all. Old Ragıp tried it out and broke a glass and then Turgut smashed two cups, and the tray was handed back to Saljan forever. As they walked home together by the moonlight they all agreed it had been one of the best evenings of their lives.

***

So it was that Saljan could run all the way to the prison without the coffee cooling and without spilling a drop, no matter how high the tray swung, how sharp her turns.

After all, the prison monster would only drink it hot!

Chapter Three

The coffee was İsmet Turali's first privilege in seven years. Getting to that first sip had taken a terrible tussle with his conscience, and then months of waiting. That's the thing about making pacts with the Devil. You never know if he'll keep his end of the bargain, and how do you enforce it? Had İsmet lacked all power, the gamble would not have been worth taking. But he had two things going for him. He knew his own strength, and he knew the Devil's weakness.

The Devil was the Governor of the prison: Osman Reşid, known to all as the Pasha. He was very dapper in an old-fashioned way. He liked watch-chains, cuff-links, tie-pins and cigarette-holders. He was fussy at his tailor's where he favoured three-piece suits in dark blue pinstripe, cut to conceal his stockiness. Sometimes he wore English-style tweeds. His shoes had built-up heels. His hair was dyed to remove the grey and his nails manicured. His face was a little pasty. His long nose grew out of a moustache clipped to keep it just short of extravagant. His teeth were implausibly white. His eyebrows were trimmed into circumflexes. He had import-export eyes.

His prison contained no thieves, murderers or rapists. To enter the Pasha's world you had to have committed crimes not against the person, but the state. In practice, of course, there were one or two in his custody who had killed or stolen, just as there are in any football crowd or railway station, but that was not why they were there - conventional criminality was a side-line they kept to themselves. It was much more rarefied to be locked up for one's ideas, which was why there were prisons up and down the country for those with unacceptable behaviour - for the violent and the crooked - but just the one for those with unacceptable views.

The rarity of his constituents conferred exclusivity on the Pasha. At the annual conference of prison governors, he begged to be excused having to have an opinion on this challenge or that initiative. I'm afraid it simply doesn't apply to my lot, he would say sadly but with the faintest note of pride in his voice. That's not the sort of thing my lot get up to. Oh no. Would that they did, would that they did… And the Pasha would shake his head as if close to despair. Easy enough for other governors to electrify their fences, or double the number of dogs at the outer perimeter. But how very difficult to prevent the escape of ideas. And to avoid the creation of martyrs! Not just national martyrs – international ones!

At this, the other prison governors would nod their heads in respect. They didn't like being patronised by the Pasha, but the last thing they wanted to do was point out that he had it easy. That his 'lot' rarely rioted or smuggled in hard drugs or raped new arrivals. Wiser to agree that his job was undo-able except by him, or else they might find themselves having to do it. The truth was, they felt a lot safer with mass-murderers and bank-robbers. Men of conviction were too damn dangerous.

The Pasha would walk out of the Ministry after these events like the cock of the roost. Once in the sunshine, he'd drop the pretence of beleaguered worry in favour of smug superiority. His lot could run rings around their toughest thugs any day. How much greater did that make him, the Pasha: the man who controlled these violent thinkers, these anti-social artists, these rabid politicos, these intellectual delinquents? They might be some of the country's smartest and most articulate, but he had the measure of each and every one of them. That must mean he was cleverer than they were.

Some days – days when he wore tweeds - the Pasha saw himself as the provost of a university, presiding in seminars and at High Table over fine but unruly minds. A queue of professors outside his door, learned discussions in the quadrangle, a dash to the bookshelves to prove, yet again, he was right. On other days – three-piece suit days - the Pasha was more of a lion-tamer. Chair in one hand, whip in the other. All his beasts where he could see them: on their stools with tails tucked in and not a growl to be heard, let alone a roar. Either way, pinstripe or hacking jacket, he ruled his prison with fitful cruelty and constant arrogance. Herein lay the secret of his weakness: monumental intellectual pretension. Manipulate that, İsmet worked out, and he'd be tasting coffee again.

Crucial to this long-term plan was the fact that the Pasha occasionally saw İsmet one to one. He would suddenly have him brought to his office. Ah, there you are İsmet Efendi, the Pasha would say peering over his silver-rimmed spectacles, as if there might have been some doubt as to his whereabouts. As if İsmet Turali were not a Category A* prisoner in a maximum security gaol, but an absent-minded professor who had mislaid himself in the library stacks or perhaps allowed the questions to go on a bit after one of his lectures.

'Sit down, sit down, İsmet Efendi. No need to stand on ceremony with me. We are, after all, old friends by now, are we not?'

İsmet responded to this repellent notion with a smile whose faintness and brevity he masked by slightly bowing his head as he sat. The Pasha's office was decidedly that of the university provost, with heavy wooden furniture, old prints on the walls, brass reading lights and copper ink-stands.

'We are stuck with one another, are we not?'

And the Pasha would laugh at his own wit, on the basis that it encouraged laughter in others. While politely going through the motions, İsmet would think just how very stuck he was. At his last - closed - trial the judges had used the dread phrase 'detained indefinitely at the state's pleasure'.

'I hope,' İsmet would generally say at this point, 'that when you retire you will have the goodness to take me with you.'

And it would be the Pasha's turn to pretend to laugh before straightening his face into one of his viciously insincere looks.

'Would that I could, İsmet Efendi. Would that I could…'

Then the Pasha would launch into a diatribe about the system's inherent inflexibility, the increasing bureaucracy of the Prison Service, his own terrible workload, the ridiculous demands by the Ministry for transparency and accounting and good governance – as if the Pasha needed lessons in that!

'The trouble is, between you and me, İsmet Efendi – and it must go no further than these four walls…'

At which İsmet always nodded – it was, after all, an easy promise for a man in solitary confinement to make.

'…these people are intellectual pygmies. I sometimes think you and I are the only ones in this whole country capable of real, original thought.'

The Pasha would often rise at this point and idly run his finger along the spines of the many books on his shelves.

'You see, old friend? Al-Ghazali, Descartes, Proust, the great Hafiz, Dostoyevsky, D'Annunzio, Henry Corbin, John Berger, Naguib Mahfouz… Men you and I understand. Our kind of men. Men we could talk to, bat ideas around with…'

On one occasion, the Pasha was silly enough to take a volume of Imru Al-Qays's poetry off the shelf and make as if to riffle its pages. Unfortunately the book was uncut, and did not riffle so much as flop from first page to last. Not wanting the Pasha to realise he knew the books were unread, İsmet had to make a quick choice between a coughing fit and looking for his glasses. He plumped for coughing fit, as that allowed him to slip some giggles in unnoticed between gasps for air.

'The thing is' the Pasha would say gesturing at his stage-set of an academic's study, 'I have no choice but to be an intellectual. My colleagues who run prisons for violent criminals are doubtless handy with their fists and knives. I, by the same necessity, must wield logic and criticism. They exchange physical blows; I am obliged to swap bon mots and airy concepts. Set a thief to catch a thief, and all that. It takes one to know one, does it not? So, if I am not to be out-witted by all you clever chaps down there…'

[Vague nod towards the seething misery below]

'…I have to think as you do. Yes, even subversive, anti-social thoughts – not…'

[Supercilious chuckle]

'…that they could ever gain a toe-hold with me! Indeed I see it rather like homeopathic medicine. I protect myself against dissident notions by allowing the occasional one to flit into my brain…and then I usher it safely out again. Thus I am ready at all times, not to fight, but to understand. Otherwise...'

[Alligator smile]

'...you would all run rings round me, no? Ha!'

İsmet had a particular self-deprecating shrug-smile combination for these moments. It said: how could we ever flatter ourselves we could do that, even if we wanted to - which we don't. Of course.

'...not that I would dream of lumping you, İsmet Efendi, in with those others. There are some distinctly second-rate artists and intellectuals in this prison, I'm sorry to say. Would that I could choose who we let in...'

The Pasha as university provost pursed his lips and gave a little shake of his head, wishing he could require potential inmates to sit exams or show evidence of significant, peer-reviewed publication before granting tenure.

'...but you are different, İsmet Efendi. In another league. Which is why I so look forward to our little chats...'

In this, for once, the Pasha was unquestionably right. İsmet Turali was different. After all, how many prisons boast an Oscar-winner who also had the *Palme d'Or*, the Pulitzer, the *Prix Goncourt, the Chevalier de la Légion d'Honneur* and honorary doctorates from the Sorbonne, UCLA, Columbia, Oxford, Rome and Bombay on his CV?

***

İsmet, and his first film *Kanli*, came out of nowhere. The equipment was borrowed, the crew as ignorant as he was, the budget not just low but microscopic. Yet the story – about a sheep herder whose flock strays into an old minefield - was gripping and brilliantly told. Kanli was played by a real-life shepherd boy who proved to be a screen natural. The only other performers were his own dog – old, scrawny and wise – and the sheep, played by his own flock. The casting ensured that the relationship between boy and animals was utterly convincing. By the end of the short film, audiences felt they knew every sheep and lamb as individuals, and had come to share Kanli's anguish as he and the dog try to guide them from lethal ground to safety.

This empathy between Kanli and the audience lay at the heart of the film's success. It was almost unwatchably tense, as calamity overtook calamity, as lambs bolted, as an old sheep tumbled into a dry river-bed and broke a leg, as no sooner have Kanli and the dog managed to herd them together than the flock is buzzed by a vulture and scatters. No safe moment is lasting. While Kanli is heartstoppingly rescuing one sheep, a group of others blithely munch their way into danger. The beauty of the idea was that if Kanli panics, they'll run, so he has to force himself to keep outwardly calm. His concern for the safety of the dog as it makes huge arcs through the minefield to come up behind the sheep was unbearable. Some audience members couldn't take any more at this stage, and left the cinema.

The film contained one outstanding, arresting shot: a close-up of the boy biting his screwed-up fist in the pure agony of fear. When *Kanli* won the Oscar for best short film, this was the image that was flashed around the world, helping to push İsmet Turali into the limelight. Limelight which had grown brighter, not dimmer with the passing of the years, no matter how hard the state tried to hide him from its glow.

So where had he come from?

It wasn't, of course, nowhere. He came from a city in the east of the country. The city had a university, old and distinguished. The university had a fine library, the library a chief librarian, the chief librarian a son, the son İsmet. His French-born, English-educated mother was a professional translator. He was brought up surrounded by books and manuscripts and speaking three languages. He went to the university he had grown up in. He studied behind walls he had kicked his football against. He sat in his father's library, trying not to catch his eye for fear the old man would make him laugh, which he could always do. His father was anything but dry. Quick to question, to argue, to rethink, to joke, to cry. He was the most passionate person İsmet had ever and would ever meet in his whole life. As a small boy after school, sitting quiet as a mouse at the chief librarian's desk, folding paper aeroplanes and drawing, he could never reconcile his father's character with his work: patiently cataloguing, quietly answering questions, re-arranging shelves, rubbing out pencil marks in books, re-binding the frail, labelling the new, and always reading, reading, reading.

Of all his father's paradoxes, submitting himself to the library's injunction to silence was the strangest. Outside it he was downright noisy. He roared with laughter, he sang, he recited verse, he whistled, he waved his arms around, he even breathed heavily. But across that threshold he became economical of movement and mute. As İsmet grew older he wondered if his father was all pent up in his library like a desperate genie in a bottle, or if he had some sort of split personality. At one point he took to being in the library at closing time to see the moment of transformation between silent days and loud evenings. The strange truth was that his father didn't change suddenly upon locking the library doors. He wouldn't speak at first. Then maybe a short question or two. A terse, almost whispered answer to a query put to him. By the time they reached home his father might have fallen silent again, but then he would greet İsmet's mother in a long and not exactly platonic embrace, and that seemed to be the pilot light for the passion which would enliven their evenings and, İsmet guessed, their nights.

His parents had always been very physically demonstrative with one another. It was only when he himself started to have sex that he realised that his parents must often have been conjoined under the bedclothes when he went into their room as a toddler and they were at a particular angle to one another which looked as innocent above the waist as it turned out to be pleasurable below. They weren't brazen; it was just how they were with one another. He could see as he got older that they tried to temper their mutual desire so as not to embarrass him. And it was possible that this coincided with or was overtaken by the natural erotic diminution that age and familiarity can bring to the most loving relationships. The truth was, the older they got, the more skilled they became at giving one another pleasure. It didn't matter that they made love perhaps only once a fortnight - when they did it was so consuming, so intense, so utterly satisfactory.

But İsmet had left home by then. Despite their endeavours, they did embarrass him; besides, he wanted to seek out some passions of his own. The first one that grabbed him was story-telling, and it never let him go. At university, studying first French and English and then doing an MA in Modernism, İsmet started writing – something neither of his parents did. Surprisingly, for someone young, he found he had things to say. He didn't know why since he had experienced very little, but he had a good eye and a keen ear and a volcanic imagination which kept throwing stuff up. Bright, burning, powerful stuff. He wrote *Kanli* first as a short story. The process of putting it on paper made him visualise it in such detail and with such vividness that he decided others had to see it as he did. This turned him into a film-maker.

With barely any dialogue *Kanli* entranced film festival audiences around the world. Awards arrived by the sack-load. And İsmet couldn't believe how much rubbish was being written about his film. Critics praised the way the young film-maker created such tension without a score – but İsmet couldn't afford music. They delighted in the chiaroscuro use of black and white film – but İsmet couldn't afford colour. So clever to use a 'real' boy – but İsmet couldn't afford actors. Certainly the film wouldn't have been any better if he'd had more money. It would almost certainly have been worse. But that wasn't the point. The point was that they interpreted constraint as choice. They wanted to see him as a discerning prodigy. None of them really believed in the existence of a 'poor cinema'.

That, at any rate, was how they wrote. How they thought was another matter. İsmet had a sneaking suspicion that, however good his film may have been, it wouldn't have been greeted with honours and acclaim had he not been an unknown kid from a minor Central Asian country with a parched history of film-making. But *Kanli* had created a wave, and İsmet knew he'd be a fool not to ride it. One of the most prestigious film schools in Europe offered him a bursary with all expenses paid to study advanced film-making techniques. There he could hone his self-taught skills, make films and forge vital industry contacts. The unknown from nowhere was on his way.

The night before he left the country, İsmet held a screening of *Kanli* at the university for family, friends and those who had worked on the film. He was in the gallery fussing over the projector when he noticed his parents making their way to their seats in the auditorium below. He hadn't seen them for a while. Two tall, handsome people, being greeted with warmth by old and young. Everyone knew them. They had a word for everyone. Their progress was slow, so that by the time they had found their seats, İsmet was at their side.

'I'm so proud of you, İsçik,' his mother whispered.

His father just gave him a huge, slow wink before being claimed by two professors from the science department, the athletics coach and a small knot of students.

When the lights came on at the end and a reluctant İsmet was summoned onto the stage to answer questions, he could see that the audience looked shell-shocked. All except his parents. His mother was grinning from ear to ear, and his father was crying. Again, he felt that familiar wave of love and embarrassment in equal portions.

Afterwards they all went out for dinner: İsmet, his parents, the crew, various friends and Adnan, the shepherd boy who had played Kanli. He was accompanied by his father, who had helped with the sheep during the filming. They had travelled by bus in their best clothes; first time in the city for son, first time for father. Everyone made a fuss of them, and asked why they hadn't brought the dog. They grinned and said, well – you know. Someone has to stay behind and keep an eye on those sheep... you know what sheep are like. Out of deference to the film's absent stars, they ate no mutton or lamb that night.

When İsmet got a quiet moment he asked Adnan why his mother hadn't come with them. Not knowing how to answer the question, he looked to his father.

'She could have come, İsmet Efendi, but she didn't want to. She said everyone would laugh at her clothes. You know women.'

Actually, İsmet barely knew women at all but he remembered this woman, with her high cheekbones, her sun-beaten skin and her penetrating gaze. He had met her when he went to ask permission to use Adnan in his film. They lived in a shack at the edge of a village, and the father stood in the doorway while İsmet went in to ask the mother. She was making bread. İsmet trotted out his little prepared speech, and only when he finished did she stop kneading the dough and look him straight in the eye.

'What will happen to my son after this filming of yours?'

It was the one question İsmet hadn't been prepared for. One for which he had no answer. Was he, he wondered, responsible for what would happen afterwards? Was it like his friend Murat said it was with virgins? Did you have some sort of perpetual obligation towards them for altering them and their lives? Surely that would only apply if force were used, or if they did not know what they were letting themselves in for?

'He will return to you, Birsen Hanım, and to your family. He may come back a little swollen-headed from all the attention, but he's a sensible lad...'

'That isn't what I meant, İsmet Efendi.'

'No... I can see that. I don't know. I'm sorry...'

At the dinner after the screening İsmet asked Adnan's father why the mother had agreed. As he asked the question, he wasn't sure that she had the power in the family to say no, but it was clear from the man's answer that she did.

'She said it might change him for the good, or the bad. But it was important to give him the chance to make something different for himself. The sheep, she said, will always be here.'

He would recall that evening till the end of his days. The sense of relief that the projector didn't break down. Wonderment at the audience's stunned reaction. Happiness at seeing the mix of people he loved eating together. The shepherd loosening his tie and then his belt as more food and wine came. His parents grinning at İsmet with, they told him, pride now based on fact not hope. Catching the eye of his petite friend Reyhan who had organised the film's business and legal side and smiled enchantingly back at him. Tingling inside with excitement at having settled that night's sleeping arrangements. The boy Adnan teaching the Professor of Cognitive Science and the Senior Lecturer in the History of Art how to make the correct noises to get a dog to round up sheep. Adnan's father judging the results with delightful mock seriousness. İsmet's best friend Murat ensuring the flow of food and wine as diligently as he had organised the filming. The smoky, spicy air filled with sheep-calls and whistles and laughter.

Afterwards İsmet walked on air with Reyhan by his side. She smelled of lemon and had the prettiest ankles he had ever seen. He was just breaking to her his plans for smothering them in kisses when she asked him if he felt he had automatic power over women, now he was a big film director. He said he didn't and he wasn't, but his electric fire was broken and he was cold and she had that big bed with a lovely eiderdown full of duck feathers. To say nothing of those ankles. And she said that was all right for him, but what was in it for her? It was another unanswerable question. He went to his student room alone.

That was the last time he saw his parents before he flew away - before the regime changed and the university was turned from a haven into a hell and the Ministry of Internal Affairs did what İsmet had refused to do for the shepherd boy Adnan: take absolute responsibility for changing their lives. For mangling them.

Chapter Four

Going to the foreign film school turned out to be a little weird. It wasn't any kind of a surprise to find almost all the students came from the over-educated middle class. İsmet was, by the standards of his own country, fairly privileged himself. No, what shocked him was the banality of the films they were making. The only talent seemed to be among the animators, who kept busy creating witty animals. The others were technically slick but totally unimaginative. What they were really good at was talking about film-making. One whole seminar hinged on a hair-splitting distinction between "films" and "movies": the difference between European and American cinema. It had something to do with the fact that American directors apparently worked sitting down, whereas Europeans directed on their feet.

İsmet listened for a long while, wondrous at their total ignorance of – or disinterest in - the cinema of other countries. Finally he spoke up. He said that where he came from, directors didn't sit or stand - they ran. From cast and crew not unreasonably wanting to be paid, from local villains wanting protection money, from the police, from the censors. Ah, said one of his more benign colleagues, you're so lucky, İsmet, coming from the Third World. How many directors can there be in your country? You'll have a job for life.

This remark provided the clue to why the students' films had nothing to say that hadn't already been said. They were desperately positioning themselves to slot into the existing film business, an old industry that feared innovation and polemic. They would probably spend their days filming safe, well-loved books several centuries old – or their modern equivalents. They needed to know how to stage a country-house party, or a court-room scene. There were, it must be said, a few who went in for imitations of non-narrative modern European cinema, but İsmet saw them as bridegrooms at their stag-night; they'd soon settle down to a beginning, middle and an end with a hunt and a game of billiards somewhere in the middle. And presumably one of those sex scenes where the sex is tastefully substituted by a tracking shot up stairs over discarded underwear.

İsmet knew none of this would work for him. His country's backward, state-controlled industry was in no shape to make cinema out of what was going on around it. The veer to the right. The steady elimination of freedom. From time to time he met people who had just got out – heard their worrying stories. But he learned most about what was going on back home during his fortnightly telephone conversations with his father. Not from anything he said, but from the fact that his father was whispering as if from the library, not booming with life and gossip from his study at home with a glass of wine in his hand and İsmet's mother on his knee. From his increasingly joyless voice. From his lengthening silences. From all that he did not say.

İsmet wondered whether to go back. The Professor of Cognitive Science to whom Adnan had taught dog-whistles at the dinner, was in town for a conference and rang İsmet up on his last day. İsmet went with him back to the airport and they had a drink in a plastic, neon-lit bar. The Professor said things were getting a little tighter back home, certainly, but it was nothing that hadn't happened before. These things swing one way, and then after a while they swing back. He'd seen İsmet's father only the week before and he was absolutely fine. A bit under the weather with a cold, but fine. Everyone seemed to have colds back home at the moment. İsmet shouldn't worry. The most important thing he could do for his family and for himself and, yes, for his country, was to get as much out of this wonderful, well-deserved opportunity as he could. And then go home and cheer them all up with his films. There, he said. That's my flight. Must go. Goodbye, dear boy.

İsmet was on the bus back into the city before it dawned on him that the flight that had been called was non-stop to Boston. Didn't MIT have a Center for Cognitive Research? If the professor was turning tail, it was time for İsmet to return. There was just one thing he wanted to do first, and that also involved crossing the Atlantic. The success of *Kanli* had led to an invitation for İsmet to attend an intensive workshop for film-makers at an old railway magnate's pile in Vermont. He'd never been to America. It sounded like fun. So he went.

Years later, in one prison cell after another, İsmet allowed himself few nostalgic journeys into his memories. In time the happy ones became more painful to recall than the sad. But he made an exception for the ten days he spent at that gilded mansion.

The sense of suffused gold wasn't just triggered by the opulence of the surroundings, though they were grander than anywhere he'd ever been. It started on the journey from the airport. It was fall in New England. The light was glowing, the leaves every shade of red, yellow, umber, silver. Coming from the Garden of Eden it would still have been a remarkable sight. But coming from a country where trees have a tough time of it and go into winter shrivelled rather than blazing, İsmet was transfixed. He wound down the taxi window and stared and stared. Vales, ridges, forests - gilt uplands shimmering against great mountains of granite. And everywhere the leaves. Swirling, falling, clinging on, dazzling.

'It's the carotenoids.'

With the wind in his ears and his sight totally hijacked by the view it took a moment for İsmet to realise the taxi driver had spoken.

'How do you mean?' asked İsmet, not wanting to tear himself away.

'The colour of the leaves – it's the carotenoids. They're the pigments, you know, the colours in leaves which help the process of photosynthesis by grabbing specific wavelengths of sunlight during the year. Come fall the leaf starts to die, and as it does you get to see all these pigments again. Clever, huh?'

Amazing, thought İsmet. The leaves hoarding sunbeams, and then giving them up so gloriously in death.

'You a botanist?'

The man laughed.

'No sir! Just a cabdriver. But I got curious every fall and looked it up. My mom used to say that fall in New England proved the existence of God, but turned out it was just the carotenoids.'

İsmet ducked the issue of why the driver saw it as either/or, and sticking his head back out of the window, wallowed again in the alchemy. By the time he reached the great house it was getting dark. Coach lights twinkled down the drive, fires roared in grates and everywhere he was welcomed. Welcome packs, welcome drinks, name tags to enable him to welcome others, welcome dinner, speeches of welcome, more welcome drinks, a welcome square of chocolate on his pillow. He felt very welcome when he went to bed that night. He felt even more welcome when he went to bed the next night.

Her name was Anna. She had made an extraordinary documentary about a group of children living in a Bolivian necropolis. She had a darting, questing mind. She preferred to talk about the next film, not the last. She had no time for twaddle. She didn't look for praise and didn't gush at others. She asked awkward questions. She played a mean game of table tennis. She laughed. She looked like a Modigliani nude: huge eyes, fine nose, full lips, long neck, languorous body, close cropped auburn hair. The hair was all of a piece with the autumn palette outside and the glowing fires inside, reflected in the walnut panelling and oak beams. He told her about the carotenoids, she said she'd had the same taxi driver and they took it from there.

There wasn't much doubt in either of their minds that they were going to sleep together that first night. Sleep in the same bed together, that is. It was the logical extension of not wanting to be apart. Neither of them wanted to end the evening, neither of them wanted the other to end it. So they sat by the huge fire in the old hall drinking brandy and talking and talking, while the noisy gaggle dwindled to a quiet handful, and then there was just them and a Professor of Anthropological Film from Houston. Old and wiry with a goatee beard, he joined them for a while, but then something about how Anna and İsmet were with one another, the angle of their bodies and heads, a sense of segue in their verbal exchanges, awakened memories of his post-graduate fieldwork among the courting youth of New Guinea. These people, he realised, are like two musicians tuning up. They want to be a couple. As I recall, they don't need me. Right, said the Professor, I'm off to bed. So are we, thought Anna and İsmet simultaneously.

His place or hers was settled in an instant, because she was sharing with an exceedingly serious Finnish woman, not – as she said - that it would have altered things if she'd been flippant, and no one had turned up to claim the other bed in his room. The door closed and they kissed. Kissed long. Kissed deep. Then they fell on the bed and kissed some more, and held one another tight. Then they got up and pulled the two beds together, and remade them so they were like a double because, as he said to her, you never know. Then they took it in turns to have showers and try to improve on what the other already thought was fairly perfect. Then they got into bed, he in the one he'd been sleeping in, she in the other.

He wasn't wearing anything, and he didn't know if she was below the waist because he'd used the bathroom second and she was already in bed by the time he got out. But she had kept on a little white t-shirt. They stayed apart for a while, heads together but bodies in different beds. Then she sat up with an exquisite sigh of willing resignation. Crossing her long arms she lifted the t-shirt over her head and tossed it away. She did not then dive under the bedclothes but looked at him with that clear, open gaze that Modigliani's subjects have. Then she slipped slowly down into his arms. She wasn't wearing anything else and the two beds definitely became one, proving İsmet absolutely right. Because you never, never know.

The table tennis was a whole thing in itself. Between sessions a group of them would race for the tables in the conservatory built on to the back of the mansion. There was something compelling about the lightness there after the dark of the screening room, the frenetic activity after the sedentary passivity. Something mindless and classless amid the intensity of the conference and the elitism of the surroundings.

It was always doubles. Sometimes İsmet would partner Anna, sometimes they'd be on opposite sides. While others continued the elevated discussions, delineating filmic nuances over coffee and cigarettes, they'd be smashing the little white balls at one another, bouncing them off the bottle-glass windows, desperate to reach a result before the next masterpiece began. Then they'd dash back into the gloom, perspiring and elated, ready again to watch and discuss. Sometimes they sat side by side, sometimes they'd cut it so fine there were no longer two places together. Sometimes they chose to sit apart, as if intensifying a pleasure by postponing it. He didn't know if the others knew about them, and he didn't care. It was a thoroughly grown-up, idyllic ten days, and he didn't want them to end.

He was in his room packing and thinking about Anna, when a member of the table tennis gang put his head round the door to say goodbye. Dan was a big jolly character with a senior commissioning job in US public television. He wanted to know if…well he assumed, in fact, that he'd be seeing İsmet at the festival in Phoenix at the end of the following week.

'But I'm not invited…'

'Don't be crazy, İsmet. I invite you. They'd love to show *Kanli*, there are some great films there and then we can drive down to Third Screen First in San Antonio. *Kanli* will fit real neat into their "Frames from the Field" segment. There's a whole load of us going from here.'

İsmet knew one person who wasn't: Anna. She was flying to Alaska to start work on her next film. That was what he had been thinking so hard about before Dan pitched up.

'Then we have like a two week break before it's back up to Montana for the Dreaming Film Workshop.'

'Not invited to that either…' said İsmet, almost under his breath.

'Lookit, İsmet. You know Astrid? Who played table tennis with us? She only schedules Dreaming Film and she is totally into *Kanli*. It's like her favourite film ever.'

An impatient voice hollered Dan's name from the lobby below.

'Gotta run. See you in Phoenix. Don't be late…'

İsmet flopped onto his bed. He didn't know quite what to do. He wasn't greatly looking forward to going home, but he wasn't sure how much of the film festival circus he could take. Particularly without Anna. And he couldn't follow her to Alaska, though the thought had crossed his mind.

'One film, carefully used, can last you a lifetime…'

İsmet looked up. The man opposite had wandered over. He was something in documentaries at the BBC and İsmet had taken him for a bumbler, but now he saw a sharp, discerning look in his eye. He leaned against the door-frame shining one of his shoes. Cracked brown leather with caked mud in the sole.

'Pity. I was curious to see what you'd come up with after *Kanli*.'

And he drifted back to his room.

He waited for Anna in the lobby, but she was apparently still in her room on the phone to someone in Anchorage. Vermont did not look so burnished on the drive to the airport. It was starting to look dead. He waited for her in flight departures as long as he dared, and then he went through. As he boarded the plane he tried to recall when exactly it was that he had seen her for the last time. He couldn't work out if it was at the Grand Farewell, or when they all dived out of it for a last game of table tennis, or after that when they went back into the hall. But did she go back in with them? Or was that when she went up to her room to make the call to Alaska? Why couldn't he get the order of events straight? What was his last glimpse of her? For some reason he just couldn't remember, and he started to cry. He cried all the way to New York. Then he went home.

Chapter Five

'You should never have come back.'

The door was only open a crack. Not a position İsmet associated with his parents' front door. He gave it a gentle push but his mother must have had her foot against it, as if İsmet would take the hint and head straight back to the airport. But he didn't and something in her gave way and she jerked the door open and flopped into his arms. They stayed like that for a few moments, and then she suddenly lifted her head from his chest and stared into the darkness behind him. Then she pulled him inside and slammed the door.

He barely recognised the place. Stuff everywhere, drawers open, filing cabinets emptied, picture frames smashed. Apparently the police kept barging in and ripping it apart, initially on the pretext of looking for incriminating evidence, but latterly, his mother thought, just to be cruel. The bookshelves were shockingly empty.

'That's their whole case against him. The books. They say he's polluting the minds of the impressionable student body with "filth, blasphemy and anti-state propaganda." He says he's just carrying out his duty to make available respected works of scholarship and literature for academic study. They say he is subverting the country's youth by exposing them to decadent Western ideas. He says the library's acquisition policy is a direct function of curriculum requirements; he gets in books appropriate to and necessary for the courses taught. They say he goes way beyond the set texts. He says that lateral reading leading to lateral thinking distinguishes university from high school, that…'

'Where is he?' İsmet interrupted. 'Where's Baba?'

'They've taken him off for questioning again. Oh İsçik, your poor father. Your poor father.'

She sobbed in his arms for a long while, heaving and damp, mumbling about how İsmet wouldn't know him now, he was so changed. Then she broke away and resumed the daunting task of tidying the mess. He looked at her as she knelt on the floor, her back to him, her clothes dusty and faded and her hair in a bun. She could have been his grandmother. He remembered Maminou, also on her knees, cleaning the grate in the farmhouse in the Doubs and he recognised her now in his mother: the bun, the distressed shoulders, the hole in the stocking.

When İsmet was young she never wore her hair up. He once came down the stairs and saw his father at the foot, kissing her, holding her head with both hands, his fingers woven in and out of her luxuriant mane. He couldn't push past them and he didn't want to be embarrassed. So he crept silently back to his room. That dark cascade was almost scrawny now, and entirely grey. She looked exhausted. She looked terrible. They had been doing so well, the pair of them, growing old gracefully, cocooned in books and old friendships. But it's hard to stay graceful with the police smashing your cocoon.

He squatted down beside her and tenderly lifted her.

'You go to bed, Maman; I'll wait up for him.'

She suddenly looked wild.

'I can't sleep if he's not in! I won't sleep!'

'Doesn't matter if you sleep, Maman, or if you just lie there. But it's really important to rest.'

The crazy look subsided and she nodded. Kissed him on both cheeks and started up the stairs. Then she stopped and turned.

'I'm really sorry, İsçik *chéri*, I never asked you about America. How was it? Did they all love you?'

Her old voice again. He smiled.

'Yes', he said. 'They all loved me. I'll tell you about it in the morning.'

Well, he thought to himself. I'll tell you about some of it. He was halfway to the kitchen when he heard her disembodied, heartfelt voice again.

'It was so good of you to come back, *chéri*.'

He lay on the sofa with a mug of tea, thinking about Anna and about how one can fly overnight from bliss to trauma. He couldn't see a way to get back to her. Wasn't sure how to reach her. Anyway, he had his hands full here. Wanted to be there, but had to be here. He went upstairs to check on his mother. She was fast asleep.

The sofa was as comfortable as he remembered. Now, the thing that would make sense of his coming home would be if he could do something. What? A petition? Of past and present students and colleagues? That might work. But maybe it should be something more radical. Maybe there was no point in standing and fighting. Maybe they should all…

He was woken up by a screech of brakes. Slamming doors. Revving engine. Squeal of tires. Silence. He got to the door just as his father did. They fell into one of their old hugs. He felt like Baba. He smelled like Baba. But İsmet could get his hands right round this Baba's waist. İsmet hadn't been away that long. How could his father lose so much weight in that time?

'What are they doing to you, Baba? Are they using torture?'

His father shook his head. No. Not torture. Fear. But it couldn't go on forever. They'd soon see how mistaken they were, and they'd leave him and Maman alone. But, his son asked tentatively, suppose they don't? Suppose they just keep on with their crazy accusations? Suppose things get worse? What then?'

His father shook his head.

'Academic freedom must be defended, İsmet. You know that. We've all seen what happens in other countries when they lurch to the extremes of right or left. When rabid politicians or megalomaniacs or clerics or generals decide they want the country to be run according to their fanatical rules. So they silence alternative voices, they control the media, they allow police and the courts summary, grotesque powers. They use thugs to intimidate, beat up, kill opponents. If the regime is fundamentalist then they force women to leave education and employment, cover up and stay home. Either way, ignorance and brutality take over, and ordinary people are oppressed – that's on top of the poverty and hunger and worrying about the children which already weigh them down.

You know all this, İsmet. You know these catastrophes often begin with something small – or someone small. Here in our university it's begun with me. They are always suspicious of Western influences and values, even if they are just sitting on a library shelf, unread.'

'Do you think there's a problem with Maman – being French? Being a foreigner?'

His father raised his eyebrows. Was it possible the thought hadn't occurred to him?

'No. Maybe. I never think of her as being foreign. If they have a problem with her, then they'll have a problem with half a dozen more in the Faculty. Including the Principal's wife who is from Canada, and the German husband of the Professor of Physics.'

They sat in silence, and then his father stirred.

'Perhaps it's impossible to stop it. Maybe it is...'

Baba was now on his feet. He started to stride about in declamatory mode. It was like old times.

'...but the best chance of stopping it is early on, before too much momentum has built up. Before everyone becomes cowed. When there isn't yet so much at stake that people who aren't particularly brave or moral will be too frightened to say, we don't like the look of this. We don't want our country to go in this direction. Enough!'

He sat down with an emphasis that sealed the argument. It was good to see the fire in his father again. And İsmet couldn't really take exception to his words. He'd heard them often enough and agreed with them. The walls of that house had echoed with these arguments for as long as he could remember, whenever the country was at a crossroads. Over big dinners and late suppers, across the kitchen table or by lantern light in the garden. Fine food, flowing wine, tobacco smoke, laughter and liberal arguments. In fact they weren't really arguments, because friends, students and faculty all agreed: that the lessons of history and the dictates of a sound moral conscience required resistance as early as possible in the face of repression or the strong threat of it. İsmet would have to try a different tack.

'Fine, Baba, fine. That all makes a lot of sense. But let's look at it another way. Why don't we just get out of here? I mean, if you can look ahead and envisage a time when you'll think back and say: that night İsmet got home from America – if only we'd all just walked out of the house that night…if you think that's any kind of possibility then we have to leave, right now. You, me and Maman. Now. OK? Let's just get into the car and go. We can drive all night…'

If İsmet expected his father to chastise him for his spinelessness, to upbraid him for his selfish flight from moral, civic duty, he was dead wrong.

'I'm afraid, son, they've taken the car away. And today I had to hand over our passports.'

It was a faster turnaround than his father's old switches from library silence to domestic ebullience.

'OK Baba, what about Kenan? He's got a car. And Rahmi will do anything. They've known us forever…they're like family.'

His father shook his head.

'I can't ask Rahmi and Kenan,' he said matter-of-factly, 'and that's that.'

'Why, Baba? Why can't you ask them?'

'Because I don't want them to say yes. If they are seen to be lifting even a finger to help us, they'll get into the most terrible trouble. And then…'

His father rubbed his hand across his face, across his eyes.

'…suppose they said no? I couldn't stand to hear that: my two oldest and dearest friends telling me: no - we can't help you. I couldn't bear it.'

'But you'd help them Baba. If it was the other way round, you'd help them. You know you would.'

At that his father looked at him with the saddest smile imaginable.

'I hope they love me too much to ask, İsmet my son. It's safest if the question is never put. And better by far not to know the answer.'

Baba shrugged and took himself into the remains of the kitchen to make them both coffee.

Right, İsmet said to himself. I'm going to sort this out. It's my kind of problem, like making a film. We'll need money, transport, a friend with nothing to lose. But first: the schedule, the timings. How far to those mountains where we went hiking that year? The high pass at the top of the valley leads straight across the border, and it was never guarded. 100 miles, maybe 110 to the point where the road peters out. Then maybe another 5 or 6 miles to the frontier itself. Hmm. Hope the skies are clear in the mountains. Lucky there's a bit of a moon tonight. 5 or 6 miles…Maman and Baba will have to take it carefully. Rest five minutes, move on, rest, move on…pace themselves. Particularly Baba. He looks so weak. He's lost so much weight… I could almost carry him. That's what I'm going to have to do when he gets tired: carry him.

We'll need warm clothes and stout shoes. A thermos flask of hot tea. Something to eat on the way, something sweet for energy, raisins, dates. I'll get Maman up in a moment so she can get the stuff ready. They won't be able to take anything except the clothes they stand up in. Still, there's nothing much left here anyway. Let's hope Baba can dig out some maps. Right. Who's got a car? Deniz has, and Murat. Murat's closer, he's crazy enough, and he's always loved them. So. Give him, say, half an hour to get here…That's…five hours, six at the most. We could be across by dawn - safe!

He had started to dial Murat's number when his father walked in with the coffee. Seeing his son on the phone he almost dropped the tray. Eyes wild, head shaking, hurtling across the room to replace the receiver. Click! Then he sagged in a chair. When he spoke it was, as before, strangely calm. Parent, perhaps, to child. Kanli to his sheep. Mustn't cause panic.

'You can't ring anyone, İsçik. The phone is bugged. And if you go off and see someone, you'll be followed. Think of it as if we have the plague. You breathe on someone, touch anyone, and you've given it to them. It doesn't matter here, in the house, inside. We've already got it. We can't get it any more than we already have.'

Father and son sat in the still, dusty air of the up-turned plague house, drinking sweet coffees in the little white cups with the yellow handles. Good coffee, although İsmet preferred it medium sweet. Maybe his father had forgotten, or more likely couldn't be bothered making coffee twice. Anyway, as İsmet had thought to himself earlier, they needed the energy. Whatever was going to happen, they'd need energy.

They woke the next morning and if anything, the situation felt worse. The three of them sat at breakfast together for the first time in ages. İsmet had all those feelings you get when someone has died: from the knotting in the pit of the stomach to not wanting to be the first one to talk about banalities in case it looks like you don't care. Then his father said, out of nowhere, that he had done nothing wrong. And he looked at them, first at his wife and then at his son. Maman's eyes filled with tears and she raced over and wrapped her arms around him. He saw his father's shoulders quiver and İsmet too got up and put his arms around the pair of them.

Oh dear, thought İsmet. Is this how it is going to be from now on?

But it wasn't.

For some reason, the police left them alone for a while, and when they did return it was too late. İsmet and his parents had had time to come up with a plan.

It was born out of near-despair. Baba was caught between defensive indignation and the fear that he had somehow put his family in jeopardy. İsmet had lost all momentum since hearing his father's clincher arguments against flight. From being the fearless rescuer, he'd become the third prisoner in the cell. So it was left to Maman to say, 'we're all supposed to be clever, aren't we? To be able to think on our feet, to spot flaws in argument, to outwit others? And the whole point of being educated and well-read is that one has the critical tools to analyse a situation and look for ways through, or round. So that's what we have to do.'

The two men couldn't see a problem with that, and in fact they both brightened up a bit.

They decided to split up and use their brains to come up with ideas for a way forward. They should draw on anything they had experienced or read or learned in their lifetimes. They could research the problem with whatever materials remained in the house. They'd meet over meals and compare notes and maybe separately or together they would light on a plan. They all agreed that was better than waiting for the axe to fall. So İsmet went up to his old room, closed the door, glanced for reassurance at the beloved old quince tree outside his window, and then lay down on his bed. Maman climbed the ladder into her study in the attic.

Baba stayed in the kitchen. What he had to do first didn't need research tools. It needed brutal honesty. So he put the kettle on, and confronted himself. He knew, which his wife and son did not, how he had been responding to the police interrogations. It was the way he'd been in argument as long as he could remember: the big man waving his arms about, grandstanding, booming, charming, taking positions, being clever, sarcastic, superior. And how well did that work? Well, he'd not lost any friends over the years – they all loved a robust argument, and Maman had a way of smoothing ruffled feathers. Hold on a moment…there was that girl Rahmi brought round to dinner a million years ago. She'd wound up throwing a jug of water over him. Rahmi had tried to calm her but couldn't. And then Maman had taken her out into the garden.

They'd sat on the bench under the quince tree, and the girl had cried a little. When she stopped she became very lucid about Baba. She said it was cruel of him to let other people know he thought they were stupid. They may be stupid, or they may seem stupid alongside him, or they may be having a bad day, but that didn't make it right to tell them so. If you know you have a spot, and even if you don't, you don't want someone to say "you've got a spot", least of all in front of others. Beautiful women aren't allowed to go around telling other women they're ugly. So why is it OK for clever people to tell other people they are stupid?

It isn't, Maman said. I love that man to pieces, but he can be a little cruel. And stupid. The girl nodded. And then she asked Maman to get Rahmi to drive her home. She didn't want to go back in there and have all those people look at her, and she didn't want an apology. "Sorry I said you're stupid" doesn't, she said, make the spot go away.

For what it's worth, Maman told her, I think you're pretty damn clever. And when everyone had gone, she sat her husband down and told him verbatim what the girl had said. He spluttered at first and tried to downplay it. She'd overreacted. Perhaps they'd all drunk a bit too much... But Maman simply repeated a second time what the girl had said and went to bed, leaving him to stew in it. And in a way he'd been stewing in it ever since. He'd never found a way of hiding his cleverness, or of stopping it from being aggressive. He'd never really tried. Never had to. But now he faced more than a night on the sofa with sodden hair.

So. What's the lesson? Baba made himself a cup of tea and sat where he'd been sitting when she poured the water over him. I may not have lost any real friends, he thought, but I may not have made all the ones I could have. I never got a chance to make friends with her, for example, and she can't be the only one over the years. No good arguing that my manner is just a way of weeding out people I wouldn't want to spend time with, because I'm not a great judge of character. I may have scared away the wrong people. Now. Apply this to what's going on...

I haven't exactly made friends among the policemen who've been asking me questions. And they aren't sitting around my dining-table eating my food and drinking my wine. I'm at their table – in fact I'm potentially the bill of fare. So it's no good winding them up, letting them know what I think of them. Letting them know what I'm thinking full stop. I mustn't show off. I mustn't have a quick reply to everything. I mustn't talk as if there's an invisible jury present awarding me points for neat blows landed. There's only me, and them. And they probably already hate me. That can't help my position one bit.

The best thing I can do is...keep quiet. Like when I'm in the library. İsmet always said he had two fathers: the one in the library and the one at home. Well I've been letting these policemen see the wrong one. So stupid! Why give them grounds to wonder if there's any more to me than a dull man who puts books back on shelves? The aim must be to have them say, he's just a librarian – let him go.

The police had, of course, raided the attic, carting away most of Maman's books. But in their obsession with the evils of the printed word they had ignored her manuscripts: the handwritten texts of books she'd translated. She knew as she was climbing the ladder that there was one she could think of that might help them. About ten years ago she had worked on a dense but fascinating academic work entitled Inter-Jewish Conflict in the Ghettos of the Second World War. It contained descriptions and analysis of the arguments that had raged in places like Lódz and Warsaw in public meetings and within families, with often the younger generations urging active resistance while the older counselled docility. Make ourselves useful to the oppressor, went the argument, and they'll leave us alone. As long as we stick together and don't antagonise them... Some of the material was heart-breaking, the issue becoming not if but how you are going to die: on your feet, or on your knees. Maman sat on the floor, turning the yellow pages, making the occasional note, shedding the occasional tear.

The trouble was, this was by no means an exact parallel. What she was reading about was a late stage in the long, desperate process towards mass extermination. What Baba and she and İsçik were facing, so far, was vicious but personal harassment. She was just thinking that there might be more to learn from those who had decided to leave Germany in 1933, not that Baba was in the frame of mind or body to flee, when she heard the distant wail of sirens.

Climbing on top of the filing cabinet she could just look out of the dormer window towards the university campus on the ridge beyond. Most of the houses in the woods between were the homes of faculty members. At least two were on fire and she could see smoke rising from the building that housed Law, History and Modern Languages. The sirens were from police cars hurtling up and down the narrow lanes that connected the academic community - not going anywhere, but just making intimidatory circuits. There were no fire engines in sight, and somehow Maman didn't think any would be showing up for a while. So it wasn't just about Baba and his books. The university itself was in the line of fire.

İsmet didn't hear the sirens at first. He'd fallen asleep. But not before he'd decided what he had to do, which would pretty much determine his mother and father's course of action. If they'd agree.

The three of them didn't agree or indeed talk about anything when next they met. They were too busy filling buckets with water, joining together lengths of hose, removing paint and white spirit from the cupboard under the stairs, putting clothes and their few treasured items into a suitcase and generally preparing for the worst. Then they sat down at the kitchen table and it was like playing a game with İsmet when he was little. He wanted to begin.

'I think if anyone's got a plan, then he or she should just say it. Before they start banging on the door.'

'That, İsçik, means you've got a plan.'

His father was looking at him with a little smile.

'At the height of Stalin's terror, the secret police arrested the son of the poet Anna Akhmatova. She spent seventeen months queuing outside the prison in Leningrad, hoping to get news of him, trying to get them to accept food parcels and warm clothes for him. One day she was in the queue as usual when someone recognised her - a woman in the crowd. She sidled up to her and said in a whisper, "Can you describe this?" And Akhmatova said, "I can."'

No one spoke for a moment or two, and then his mother smiled wanly and nodded. His father gave his son's cheek a little pinch.

'You see, Maman. All that education wasn't wasted after all!'

He left that afternoon, making sure the men in the car outside heard his furious parting words with his parents. For safety's sake, İsmet needed the illusion of a family rift. Over the next five years he made a fiction film depicting the minutiae of life in a university under an increasingly repressive and vicious regime. At the heart of the film was the university librarian and his wife, who were both witnesses and victims. Their intense, whispered conversations, often under the bed-clothes, about the latest arrest or denunciation, became the film's leitmotiv. And what gave it such power and authority was its believability. Audiences almost felt they were watching a documentary, so convincing were the characters and what they said and did. So horribly plausible the tearing apart of a close, liberal community as friends and colleagues picked sides and prospered or suffered accordingly. The witch-hunts, the betrayals, the breakdowns, the suicides.

It took five years to make because it was slow, difficult work getting hold of Maman's copious notes of conversations and events, made with a translator's devotion to accuracy. It took five years to make because İsmet had simultaneously to direct a string of pot-boilers, a part of whose resources and budget he quietly diverted to make the secret film. It took five years to make because that was how long Baba kept going before his heart gave out, before Maman was deported to France clutching Baba's ashes in his old blue tobacco jar.

Two months later, İsmet's friend Murat smuggled a print of *The Librarian and his Wife* out of the country just in time to be the closing night's film at the Cannes Film Festival. İsmet was in the mixing theatre at the State Film Studios dubbing the latest pot-boiler when the secret police came for him.

İsmet's trial dragged on because every time he refused to reveal the names of his collaborators, the Judge adjourned the case for "deeper questioning". İsmet had no illusion that he could have withstood physical torture – had they hurt him enough, he'd have told them all they wanted to know and a lot more besides - but his interrogators stopped short every time. Not that they were squeamish or principled; they tortured many who had done much less wrong than İsmet, and a few who had done no wrong at all until their finger-nails were ripped off, their teeth thinned out with pliers, their bodies broken. Then it turned out they had done little in their lives that was not wrong, because one will say anything to stop the pain. In their cases that meant making it all up.

İsmet, of course, had no idea he wasn't going to be tortured. He knew he was guilty as charged and expected the worst. When it strangely did not come, he set himself the task of working out why. If you know what it is that's keeping you safe, it helps you stay safe. But he couldn't fathom it. He thought it was his backward country's pathetic and involuntary respect for her Oscar-winning son. It wasn't. It was the regime's love of those potboilers he had been making as a smokescreen for subversion: love stories, comedies, several musicals and – most popular of all – a string of what had become known as "Steppe Westerns" starring the country's three biggest heart-throbs as high plains drifters bringing justice to men and jut-jawed romance to women amid the waving grasses, wild horses and black tents.

The President himself had given İsmet the Golden Ram – the country's highest artistic honour – for his latest Steppe Western. İsmet Turali's films promote, he said in his speech, a sense of national pride. They tell us and all foreigners who we are. In Cannes just a week later *The Librarian and his Wife* filled out the picture perhaps a shade too much, particularly for the country's ambassador to France. His Excellency had proudly shown up at the Festival in his white tuxedo with no idea of the film's content, sat in deepening anger through a searingly brilliant indictment of the regime to which he owed everything, remained seated through the ensuing standing ovation, and then found himself very much on his feet being chased for a quote down the Croisette by the world's press.

The Minister of Internal Affairs argued for İsmet being given a quick trial and beheading. The Minister of Culture said why bother with a trial. But the President wasn't so sure. He had the foreign press comments on *The Librarian and his Wife* translated for him. He marked some passages in blue highlighter and others in red. Then he had the Chief Statistician do the maths. The result was that only 4% of the international column inches registered concern at his country's foreign rights record. 74% rejoiced in the birth of a cinematic messiah.

Besides, as the President told his cabinet of obsequious ruffians, İsmet Turali was so good at these Steppe Westerns. Tell the Chief Executioner to take the rest of the day off; what young Turali needs is seven years in gaol.

Chapter Six

So it was that İsmet's twenty-eighth birthday found him neither having his head lopped off nor being wooed by Hollywood producers on bimbo-garnished superyachts. Instead he celebrated it butt-naked in a sweltering hot prison reception room, forced forward across a table, being strip-searched by men passionate in their wish to hurt. It was the sort of thing you want to forget, but your memory won't oblige. And yet, amid the indignity and the embarrassment, the anger and the pain, he found himself relaxing. It was very strange. He had spent five years watching and documenting his parents' and his country's suffering. Living an exhausting double-life, shooting a musical during the day and then editing *The Librarian and his Wife* most of the night. Striving to lift the pot-boilers high above the Studio's expectations. Worrying sick about the safety of his secret collaborators. He was shattered by the stress and the distress. He had barely had a moment to mourn the death of Baba, or wonder how Maman was coping alone in the mountains. For the first time in as long as he could remember, he was being given time to think without having to act. A quick going-over by a bunch of psychopaths seemed a small price to pay for that.

İsmet was assigned to the prison kitchens. He had of course, and with utter naiveté, applied to work in the library. The authorities invariably staffed the library with illiterate gang bosses. They knew one another; they could transact their ugly business in clean, hushed, secluded conditions. Their blood-stained hands need never be sullied by honest work, and – on the positive side – no library books ever went missing. Not one was ever defaced. No pages torn out to provide paper for cigarettes or messages. A perfect arrangement in every way. Not so in the kitchens. Anyone with food preparation experience arriving in the prison was assigned to the plumbing and sewage system. Except for Ahmet Erdal. Chef Erdal had spent much of his life behind bars, and had learned at induction to keep quiet about his culinary skills and request a job in the library. He was generally preparing dinner within the hour.

İsmet was thrust into the inferno of the dungeon kitchens. They were almost impossibly hot and dangerous places. Flames, angry men and sharp knives made for a volatile work-place. Chef Erdal was tall and thin and could see trouble coming a mile off, though that instinct clearly let him down on the outside. He was generous to those he liked, and he liked İsmet from the start. He saw him struggling with a cauldron of boiling water, hastened over to show him how it should be handled, and kept him at his side the entire shift. When he realized how much this polite, open-faced young man liked food, he took him under his wing. He later explained to İsmet that many of his protégés were now cooking in the world's finest restaurants, and that the ability to turn out a better-than edible meal had kept many a delinquent from the noose. He never told İsmet why he himself was in and out of gaol, and when İsmet asked him, Chef Erdal taught him the first lesson for prisoners: never ask what the other man has done.

The second lesson Chef Erdal taught him was to treat everyone as fellow human beings. Against his own liberal, egalitarian instincts, İsmet could not, at first, stop himself from thinking he was a cut above the thieves and rogues around him. But as Chef put it, if we all thought that, we'd eventually drown in one another's bile. İsmet's education in this matter was hastened by the fact that his third day in the prison kitchens was the first day of Ramadan.

Chef Erdal used to refer to Ramadan in prison as "the poisonous shark". As if prison were not bad enough, plunge men with little to look forward to other than the next meal into a month-long fast… There was always the option of regarding the whole situation as one of emergency, in which case there would be no obligation to fast. But pressure from family and one another made this the tougher option. For some prisoners Ramadan imposed a greater sense of acceptance and self-discipline. Some felt more at peace; the numbers at prayers increased significantly. But tensions also rose. Tempers frayed, as hunger gnawed stomachs and thoughts of home filled minds with self-reproach for letting down loved ones.

Chef Erdal's answer was a combination of small touches and big helpings. For *sahur* – the meal taken before dawn – he would somehow scrounge extras like dates, nuts, fruit and milk. And he would make sure everyone was awake for it by insisting it be delivered to every cell in the prison. One of İsmet's tasks was to push the trolley down the dim corridors. The coughing, the yawning, the stale smells. But there were also the smiles in the dark, his hand held for a second in gratitude, bidding *salaam 'alaykum* – peace be upon you - at every cell, and the return chorus of *wa alaykum as-salaam* – and upon you be peace - following him like a progressive, embracing echo through the prison. A month of that, and İsmet no longer wondered – let alone cared - if he was handing food to a rapist or cleaning the ovens with a cannibal.

Chef Erdal took the preparations for Şeker Bayram, the festival marking the end of Ramadan, as seriously as he had done the weeks of fasting. Difficult as it was to provide, the men must be reminded of that childhood excitement at having a sweet taste in their mouths after the weeks of deprivation. It was good, Chef Erdal insisted, for all our souls. İsmet took his turn stirring the pot. Water, lemon and orange juice, sugar, gelatin were brought to the boil and then simmered. Then chopped nuts added. Mostly almonds, with just a few precious pistachios. Then the pot was taken from the heat and allowed to cool, with occasional stirs, until the temperature dropped to that of blood. Then Chef Erdal and İsmet took a handle each and poured the thick liquid into square tins which were then placed in pans of cold water. When the mixture was set, it was cut into cubes and dusted with icing sugar: *lokum* – Turkish Delight!

The laughs and smiles and thanks which greeted İsmet as he pushed the trolley of sweets and dates into the grimmest corners of the prison would stay with him all his life.

Gradually, like a diver, İsmet decompressed. He took the time to assimilate the tumult of the past five years, and he acclimatised himself to prison life. Oddly, his thoughts did not turn to another film project. He did not hunt around for ideas, and they did not seek him out. Except, perhaps, for one.

He had been in that first gaol ten months, and had just finished helping to prepare the evening meal. In the summer Chef Erdal used to change the shift just before food was served, to give those who had been roasting in the dungeon to get it ready the chance for some fresh air after supper. So İsmet took a turn around the sports field and went to his cell for a quiet read. His cell was a good one: high up on a corner. He shared it with two others, neither of whom he would have chosen for friends but both of whom were civilised compared to some. As he climbed the last flight of stairs to his cell he was surprised to find his way blocked by a queue. Ahead was the sound of jostling, and mild argument. He waited a bit, not wanting to get involved. The man in front turned and recognised him. They had worked together in the kitchens a couple of weeks before.

'That's your cell at the end, isn't it, İsmet?' the man asked, gesturing up the stairs.

İsmet said it was.

'Well you can go straight in. No need for you to queue. Lucky man!'

İsmet, increasingly puzzled, tried to make his way to his cell, but was stopped several times and accused of barging. On declaring the cell to be his, the most frightening-looking of his obstructors stepped politely aside. The scene in his cell was bizarre. The furniture had been stacked along the window wall to create a platform. Standing on the platform were six men staring out of the long window. In the cell itself, the older of his cell-mates who was clearly in charge was taking money from the queue. His second cell-mate was arranging the men on the platform and those waiting by height, fitting the shorter ones between the taller. The older man immediately ushered İsmet to a position on the end of the platform. He looked out through the bars to spot what they were looking at. He could see nothing. Just the apartment block opposite. He asked the man next to him. You'll see, he said. Can't miss it. The only cell in the prison with a view of it.

The older cell-mate kept looking at his alarm-clock. The younger had now arranged two more rows of six prisoners each waiting behind the next, and was making sure everyone understood they had to move, on the word of command, in a clock-wise direction. Clock-wise only. Another six or seven who had paid much less were allowed to stand at the back. And no shouting out or whistling allowed. The queue outside was then told "no more!" which elicited considerable discontent and grumbling. Try again next year, the older man said as he closed the cell-door.

Nothing happened for another five minutes. Someone said maybe they'd got the wrong day. Someone else said perhaps she'd got married and her husband won't let her. Then the lights went on in the balcony room of the central apartment on the top floor of the block opposite. A corridor led off the room into the distance beyond, and someone was moving in silhouette down that corridor towards them. When the figure reached the room İsmet could see she was a woman with long dark hair. And she was totally naked.

'Dead on time,' İsmet's older cell-mate declared with the pride of a showman.

Music began playing and the woman started to dance.

It was totally surreal.

She moved very well, like a classical belly-dancer. The distance was close enough to see her reasonably clearly, but İsmet had no idea how old she was. Perhaps late thirties. And was she doing it in joy or sorrow? İsmet could not tell. Either way, it felt very, very sad. He didn't want to watch, didn't want to be part of that ogling line of frustrated men, but he was trapped up there on the platform until the shift changed. İsmet had no idea why she was dancing, or for whom. And neither, it turned out when he quizzed his cell-mates later, did anyone else. The best guess was that her husband or lover had once occupied this cell, and maybe today was his birthday. Or their anniversary. Or the day before his execution.

Anyhow, she danced naked for as long as the song played, which was a few seconds over six minutes, allowing two changes of audience. This was conducted with balletic precision, although there was always one in each row who needed prising away. İsmet felt nothing but relief when his turn was up and he could leave the platform and its depressing view. Those at the back had to make do with the music and a running commentary from the younger cell-mate, who actually made rather a good job of it. It occasionally descended into filth, but that was inevitable.

İsmet couldn't leave the cell, so he sat on his bed with four men he did not know, listening to the commentary and hearing the distant music. The shift changed again. Men with faces alive with anticipation replaced the crestfallen. Then the music ended and the lights went out, and no movement would be seen in that apartment for three hundred and sixty four days.

When everyone had gone and the cell was back to normal, the older man divided up the audience take. İsmet refused his share on the grounds that he'd just been a spectator. The other two looked at him as if he was mad. After lights out, as they lay in their bunks thinking their different thoughts about what they had seen, the older man spoke.

'We've all of us made a pact, İsmet', he said. 'If after getting out of here anyone finds out who she is and why she does it, he's not allowed to pass the information back to us. It's probably some sad story, and who needs that? We don't want to know. She's just the naked dancing girl. That's good enough for us.'

İsmet vowed that night that when he got out, he'd learn the story of the naked dancing girl. There must be a great film in it. But as the months passed, the less curious he became. The explanation was bound to be more banal than her dance. Buttressing it with a beginning, middle and end must make it ordinary, must remove the mystery. It was the strangeness of the moment – its utter impenetrability – which made it so extraordinary. Every man who watched her from the cell had a slightly different interpretation of what they were seeing. Why stifle the imagination with the truth?

A year later to the day, the audience of prisoners in İsmet's cell had to be given their money back. The naked dancer did not appear. A watch was maintained on the apartment on that date in the calendar for years to come, long after the cell's original occupants had been released or transferred. It became a prison myth that no one really believed. But the subsequent tenants of the cell always looked out on that particular day, until the elapse of time was so great that no one knew what it was they might be going to see - but they stared out of the cell window all the same. The anticipation was not to be compared with those moments of voyeurism their predecessors had queued for, but it was better than no hope at all..

***

İsmet was released from prison on his thirty-fourth birthday. To his surprise, the State Film Studio sent a limo. He didn't think it could be for him, and kept walking. But the car purred along beside him, a window slid down and the uniformed driver called out his name. İsmet recognised him from location recces on the high steppes, and climbed in. It was all so out of place: the leather, the polished walnut, the pile carpet. The smell of delousing carbolic on İsmet hardly masked the prison cocktail of stale tobacco, urine and sweat. Özkan talked as if no time had passed, least of all in prison. As if he had just collected İsmet from the VIP lounge. As if the great director were wearing cashmere and smelling of sandalwood. İsmet barely listened to him. What was going on? Why the chauffeur-driven car? Next thing he knew he was being ushered into the studio head's office. How to play it? Injured innocent? Defiant freedom fighter? High and mighty artist? No. Years in prison had taught him to play a longer game.

Balık Bey was a wizened survivor of regime change and studio coups. Around the walls were photos of himself with the stars, home-grown and international. Filling the glass-case behind him was an array of gongs he had awarded himself. On his desk was a Colt 45 he told visitors John Wayne had given him. In his eye was a very steely glint.

'So, little İsmet. You've paid your price?'

İsmet allowed that he had.

'And how, little İsmet, do you feel about it? This price of freedom you have had to pay?'

'Nothing.'

Balık Bey tried narrowing his eyes but they wouldn't go any more, so he opened them wide instead.

'How so, nothing?'

'Just that, Balık Bey. My time in prison is nothing compared with the contrition I feel. Nothing whatsoever.'

Balık Bey fixed him with a long stare.

'Contrition, eh?'

İsmet nodded.

'You're saying, little İsmet, that prison works?'

'Definitely, Balık Bey. Prison works. No question. Look at me.'

To Balık Bey's credit, he stopped himself from laughing, which would have been a problem because that might have set İsmet off and the room was bugged. As it was, the old survivor risked a smile. While İsmet had been out of circulation, he explained, several directors had tried stepping into his shoes, but they'd tripped badly. So the cinemas had been running prints of İsmet's old films until there were more scratches on the screen than images. The audiences had even started shouting out the lines in chorus with the actors. It was time to give them something new. He handed İsmet a contract for two Steppe Westerns and a romantic comedy. That way, he figured, the studio would make a ton of money and if it turned out in time that little İsmet was slightly less than totally contrite, it wouldn't matter as Balık Bey was not long off retirement.

A week before, Balık Bey had told the President he wasn't sure İsmet Turali would accept the assignment. Perhaps he'd want to leave the country. Hollywood's doors were wide open to him. The old monster shook his head. He knew a patriot when he saw one. Hadn't Turali already turned his back on the foreigners when he returned home from America? Besides, the propaganda value of the country's sole international creative figure being seen to re-enter the fold was too great to miss. What a message to the world! And beyond that, the President just adored the Steppe Westerns. Watched them over and over again. That was him in his fiery youth: swooping down ravines, reins in his teeth, stallion's nostrils flaring, doe-eyed women flushed with desire gazing up at him from their tents. Get Turali back, the dictator told Balık Bey.

So get him back Balık Bey did. But the old survivor was anything but reckless. He told Studio Security to watch İsmet like a hawk. They were to check every foot of raw stock to make sure he was diverting none for subversive ends. The camera and sound gear had to be locked away every night. They must make sure İsmet's actors went home to learn their lines for the next day, and not nip out the back for some treasonous moonlighting. And just in case, Balık Bey kept in his safe the President's note asking the studio to take the unruly genius back providing he emerged from prison a changed man. Together with the secret tape recording of İsmet proclaiming his contrition.

The studio snoops were wasting their time. İsmet knew he could never make another subversive film by stealing resources from the pot-boilers; he had to find another way. There'd be no time to think about it once he started work on the films, which were to be shot back-to-back. The schedules were so compressed, the locations so remote. But Balık Bey had given him time to write and prepare the scripts. Time to devise a new plan. He had Özkan drop him at the bus station. Özkan offered to drive him to his door, but İsmet wouldn't hear of it. He wanted to go home the slow way. The old way.

It took him a while to realise why the journey in the bus felt so particularly timeless. At first he thought it was because of the unchanged landscape once they were out of the suburbs: the dusty plains with their vast skies, the ramshackle villages, the waving children and barking dogs. The hills with their birch groves giving way to pine forests. The jagged snow-tipped mountain ranges in the distance. But the answer lay not beyond the bus, but inside it. There wasn't a single foreigner on board. Before the repression, back-packers and tourists had been regular sights on that route between the capital and İsmet's home town, with its white-washed minarets and blue-tiled domes. For a while as the regime tightened its grip, the country continued to appear the exotic, "oriental but safe" place it had always been. The foreigners kept coming – not in such numbers, and not the same sort. Inquisitive liberals and adventurous retirees sunned themselves and rode camels elsewhere. Then it got a bit dangerous and no one came.

It was rather nice in the bus without foreigners. İsmet knew he shouldn't think that, but he felt the need for the familiar. It was a lovely journey. İsmet sat near the back, sometimes holding a baby for someone, or their shopping. At one stop, an old woman with a huge bundle got on and sat next to him. Almost immediately and without words she handed İsmet the bundle. Inside it was a baby goat. It had huge black eyes and the softest fur, and it smelled a good deal nicer than İsmet did. He assumed it was just a temporary arrangement while she settled herself, but evidently it was so she could get on with her knitting. After a few miles she leaned towards him and sniffed.

"Just out then?"

İsmet looked a little defensive for a moment. Then he smiled and apologised. The old woman said it was nothing. She herself had a son and a grandson inside. The smell was reassuring.

'It's good to know they actually let people out.'

Apart from this exchange, İsmet was surprised and delighted that life in the bus seemed to ignore the shadow that lay across the country. People talked without lowering their voices or their eyes. As twilight fell, a flagon of amber wine was passed round. A basket of figs almost bursting their black skins. A sheaf of paper-thin breads. From a bag at her feet, the old woman produced a quivering mound of fresh, snow-white, muslin-bound cheese. 'Her mother's finest' she said, nodding towards the plump spiral of fur on İsmet's lap. There was laughter on the bus, and occasional song. He tried to stay awake to see the Amal Gorge by the light of a dazzling moon, but relief to be free and a few gulps of unaccustomed wine closed his eyes long before the bus reached the summit and began its descent to the high plateau beyond.

He woke as the bus was pulling into the square at the end of its journey. The old woman and her goat were gone – he had no memory of when or how they had slipped away. He got out, smelling even stronger than the day before. The sunlight had that brilliant sharpness that gives headaches. Murat was sitting on the bumper of his car. Murat with the big blue eyes and greying beard and beaming smile. Murat his oldest friend. Murat. As they hugged one another, there was a commotion behind from the direction of the bus. Three of İsmet's travelling companions were being led away by men in suits. The man who had sung an old ballad about the snow leopard and the mouse. The woman who had contributed the figs. And a thin-faced man in his forties who, as İsmet told Murat in a whisper, hadn't spoken or joined in during the entire journey.

'That'll be the informer, then,' said Murat as he turned İsmet firmly away from the scene. 'They always make a show of arresting the informer. They think we're stupid.'

İsmet was home again.

Murat left his friend to get clean and rested and then returned at twilight. İsmet was lying on the bench under the quince tree, his head on a cushion, asleep. Murat fetched a blanket from the house and laid it over his friend. He looked for a moment at İsmet to see what marks age and confinement had left. His boyish face now seemed a little gaunt, yet oddly untroubled. Short, prison-cut hair. He was thinner than Murat remembered. He probably just needed a good meal. Murat went off to the shed to fetch charcoal for the *mangal*. By the time İsmet woke, it was dark and the air in the garden was full of barbecue smoke and the smell of grilling lamb, onions, peppers. Murat had found and filled the oil lamps which he'd hung in the branches of the quince just as Maman used to have them. When young Murat would come over and eat his fill, and then race İsmet round the garden, chasing the cats, collecting fireflies in jars, stubbing toes, grazing knees, darting back to the table for dates and chocolate *halva*. When, long after bedtime, the boys would wrap themselves in goat-skin rugs and peep down from upstairs windows into the garden trying to listen to the grown-ups. The same smells wafted up to them, and that tantalising, soporific sound of distant, easeful talk against a background of cicadas.

İsmet lay on his side, on one elbow, chin in palm. Murat had his back to him, drinking beer from the bottle, wielding tongs and a goose feather for basting. And beyond him, through the blue smoke, under a lamp's glow, was a woman. A woman İsmet knew. A petite woman with shoulder-length hair. It was too dark to see her ankles, but İsmet knew he'd thought them the prettiest he had ever seen. Reyhan. He was about to say something to her - he didn't quite know what - but then Murat leaned down and gave her something from the barbecue to try. He blew on it for her as she looked into his eyes, and then she popped it in her mouth and did that quick, sucking-in air and hand-waving movement you do when you've eaten something hot. Then she raised her lips and closed her eyes and they kissed, after which Murat must have said something to her because when he stood away from her to return to the grill, she was looking straight at İsmet.

'İsmet Efendi. It's good to see you again. And to see you free.'

'Just İsmet, Reyhan. I am just İsmet. Welcome to my garden.'

They ate at the old table and talked: the grown-ups now. Murat had brought dates and *halva* and made coffee. Sweet for Reyhan and himself and medium sweet for İsmet. Murat didn't have to be told. He remembered everything. When the glow from the *mangal* started to die, İsmet could see the fireflies flashing at one another in the dark of the garden. Five seconds apart for the male, then two seconds later a gleam in response from the female. Murat and Reyhan, it turned out, were husband and wife.

They had got married a month after Maman had died in the farmhouse high in the Jura, at the age of sixty-five. She had spent the previous seven years mourning Baba, missing İsmet and refusing to live somewhere more sensible. Murat was going to tell İsmet about himself and Reyhan at his next prison visit, but Maman's death made it impossible to talk about anything else. Besides, Murat had adored both İsmet's parents, and wasn't quite sure what İsmet still felt for Reyhan, although he knew he had wanted to sleep with her after the *Kanli* screening. So nothing was said, tears were shed, and Murat left assuring his old friend that he would continue to look after the family house and garden ready for İsmet's eventual return. Then they would eat and drink and catch fireflies and remember Baba and Maman.

İsmet fetched the goat skin rugs and a bottle of Baba's oldest plum *rakı* and told Murat and Reyhan how happy he was that they were together. He thanked Murat for tending the place so well. And he asked them both a favour. A huge and dangerous favour. He needed their help making the next film.

The plan had come to him just before he fell asleep on the bench under the quince tree. He wouldn't make another subversive film. Others would do it for him. He'd provide the script and a detailed set of notes for each scene, and his secret collaborators would do the rest. It should be made abroad. Much better and safer. Finance? Easy. The revenues from *Kanli* and *The Librarian and his Wife* had mounted considerably in a foreign bank account, and the pot-boilers gave him a good income at home. But someone would have to act as go-between. Who? Murat. He had his small trucking business. He could come and go, even abroad, without attracting attention. That was how he had taken *The Librarian and his Wife* to Cannes. All Murat would need to do was to carry İsmet's script and ideas to a freer, neighbouring country where the film would be made according to İsmet's blueprint.

'I don't have to direct anything, İsçik? I couldn't do anything like that.'

'No, Murat. I promise. You just have to follow the plan. It's like being the vehicle, not the driver. And you Reyhan, I want to give you power of attorney over my foreign assets. To finance the film. To get it made.'

She nodded and said she would be honoured. İsmet went on a bit about did they really understand the risks they would be running, until they both put their hands over their ears. Then they drank some more of Baba's *rakı* until they couldn't tell the male fireflies' flashes from the females', which, though none of them knew it, was Baba's test that he had drunk too much and that it was time for bed.

'What's it about, İsçik, this film of yours. Of ours...' Murat mumbled as they negotiated the steps up to the house.

A bus journey, İsmet replied. A whole country, packed into one bus journey. Lives, song, a little goat, food, friendships, stories, betrayals.

'And at the end of this journey İsçik, do some people get arrested?'

'They do, Murat old friend. But not us.'

İsmet was right about Murat and Reyhan, but wrong about himself. He would spend most of the rest of his life in gaol.

***

Thirty five years, a dozen films, a book and several prisons later, İsmet Turali sat in his cell with the taste of the coffee Saljan had brought him still in his mouth. The pact he'd offered the Devil was that he would write the Pasha's contribution to the Annual Prison Report in exchange for one cup of coffee, medium sweet, to be brought in from the best coffee house in the town to İsmet's cell every Monday at 11am for a whole year - at the Pasha's expense. The Pasha said that sounded a little steep; all he needed İsmet to do was to check over the Pasha's draft. Perhaps insert a little scholarly joke or two. He'd have to think it over. Months passed, with no sign of the speech in draft. And then İsmet had one of those sudden summonses to the Pasha's office.

'Ah, İsmet Efendi! Been wondering where you've been. Haven't seen you for ages. Look, I might be able to help you out with this coffee thing, only I need a bit more from you to sweeten our little arrangement, so to say. I've been asked to deliver the keynote speech at this year's Prison Governors'

Conference – fearful bore but, I suppose, an honour in its way. I came up with the title <u>Inside the Mind of the Dissident</u>. Rather catchy, don't you agree? They thought so. Jumped at it. Anyway, naturally I had you in mind - that you would write it for me. Together with my contribution to the Annual Prison Report.'

The Pasha sat back with a shameless smile, nobly giving İsmet time to think it over. İsmet already knew his answer. The Pasha's brazen proposal intrigued him. It gave him a superb opportunity to mislead at quite a high level, and if it got him his coffee, delivered in the traditional way... But he didn't reply immediately. He didn't want the Pasha to see the coffee as anything more than a whim, and he knew the old Devil would expect to see İsmet weighing the moral arguments, overcoming his scruples. So İsmet screwed his face up a bit and shifted uneasily in his chair, while the Pasha cleaned his nails with a letter-opener and pretended not to notice the fêted artist wrestling with his conscience.

All right, İsmet eventually said to the Pasha. We have a deal.

It was the Pasha's idea that the coffee be taken to İsmet's cell. His instinct was to have it served in one of the interview rooms, which were all bugged. But then it would take extra staff to move him there and back each week, and the chances of him somehow passing stuff out in the process would be increased. İsmet's cell was not wired for sound as he was in solitary and didn't talk in his sleep, but as long as the guards made sure the runner was given nothing by the prisoner but waited patiently outside the cell while the coffee was drunk, where was the risk?

Then word came to the Pasha that the lissom young woman who brought İsmet Efendi his coffee was being whistled at and subjected to unseemly catcalls while she waited to collect the empty cup. What was odd was that the prisoners hadn't yelled and whistled at her the first time, but for some reason they started the next. It was terrible to see her so embarrassed and scared. To make matters worse, it turned out she was the daughter of Mahmoud the Runner, mighty Olympian and national hero.

The Pasha had his office ring the coffee house and ask for the prison run to be carried out by a boy, but the well-spoken woman who answered said that the delivery schedules had been worked out on a scientific and commercial basis and absolutely no changes could be made. Might not the empty coffee cup be picked up the following week, obviating the need for the girl to do more than deliver? Out of the question, apparently, on grounds of hygiene: Mahmoud's Coffee House cups could not loiter behind bars for a week before being washed up. Perhaps, the Pasha's secretary asked hesitatingly, the prison kitchens could be asked to… The snort of derision from the well-spoken woman drowned the end of the question. Hard on the snort's heels came a diatribe about health and safety, about government directives on the temperature of washing-up water in establishments selling comestibles, about E.coli…

Fine, said the Pasha when this was relayed to him. Let the daughter of Mahmoud the Runner wait quietly in İsmet Efendi's cell while he has his precious cup of coffee. Not close enough for her to be handed anything, mind. The door must be left open so the guards can hear what they talk about. If they talk - after all, what could an ageing intellectual have to say to a slip of a girl doubtless obsessed, like all her sex and age-group, with landing a good husband?

The whistles and catcalls had been a little tricky for İsmet to engineer. The problem wasn't getting his wishes known, but obeyed. Once a week he was allowed to attend the prison mosque. 'How can we do that, İsmet Efendi?' said the veteran political cartoonist whose turn it was to pray near him, and give him news and receive requests. 'She's the daughter of Mahmoud the Runner. It isn't respectful to him – or to her. They say she's a very serious young woman.'

'You have to, Metin Efendi. You see…imagine I've taken a liking to the girl. I'm not saying I have, mind you, but supposing. How can I know if there is any hope for me if I am not granted time alone with her?'

The old cartoonist didn't think for one moment that İsmet Efendi had suddenly fallen in love with a girl a third his age, but he'd been behind bars for long enough not to give voice to his curiosity. Besides, it was İsmet Efendi's first request in years. The catcalls started the next Monday. A week later the guards told Saljan to stay in İsmet Efendi's cell while he drank his coffee. They kept the door open. They heard no talk of escape or undermining the regime. They saw nothing pass between prisoner and delivery girl. It is how it looks, the prison officer reported to the Pasha with a shrug. İsmet Efendi likes his coffee.

Well, İsmet Efendi did like his coffee but that was not what this was all about. He had been kept apart from the other prisoners for years for fear that he would find a way of smuggling out a film script or a novel - again. The Pasha wasn't going to let himself get caught out as other governors had been – hence not allowing him to share a cell, hence the fine mesh over his barred window, hence the guard outside his door. İsmet Turali was allowed no paper to write on, and no writing implement. No water pipe ran through his cell into the cell next door on which he could tap in Morse for his neighbour to transcribe. He had run rings round his governors in previous prisons, and the Pasha was determined to box him in.

Hence, İsmet thought, the need to get a new ingredient into my life: coffee. Properly made, traditional coffee. A simple, innocent little pleasure. But coffee doesn't float into a prison of its own accord. Someone has to bring it. Maybe a willowy girl with a penetrating stare, a tiny mole on her right cheek and an odd necklace with teeth marks. Wonder how tough a search they give her, she being the daughter of the great Mahmoud the Runner? And then there's that shiny tray of hers. Interesting things, trays. They look so open, so innocent, but they must be riddled with potential hiding places: hollow caps, tubes instead of rods, false compartments...A tray like that is crying out for a good idea to smuggle out – and by chance I happen to have the very thing!

It was an idea for a film which İsmet had been thinking about for twenty years. Ever since his second prison spell for making the film about the bus ride. And it owed its conception to a series of conversations behind bars with three men of God: a Jew, a Christian, and a Muslim.

Chapter Seven

The Chief Rabbi of Bessarabia was having a bad day.

Most of his breakfast was stone cold, and the bits that weren't were inedible. Then one of his neighbours was carted off with some ghastly coughing, vomiting bug – a neighbour to whom he'd just lent a rather precious book. He'd not see the book again for ages, and he wasn't sure he wanted to. Next he proved he was going senile. When he turned sixty a few months before he set himself the task of remembering something he hadn't thought about for a while. Last week it was his mother's recipe for *chulent* plus variants. This week it was family, and today it was the names of all his cousins and their children. He'd done really well until he got to Menahem's oldest boy's second daughter. Total blank. What made it worse was that the more he thought about it, the less sure he was that Raphael had a second daughter. Shaken by self-doubt he went off to give his afternoon talk on the Babylonian Gemara, only to find just five people in the audience, two of whom slept all the way through it.

On top of all this, he was in prison.

According to the cliché, everyone in prison is, in their version, innocent. Many claim innocence even when they are guilty as charged. But some political prisoners see innocence another way. They might happily admit to publishing the pamphlet, singing the song, telling the joke, organising the meeting, posting the blog. But they do not believe they have done anything wrong. They hold that laws which restrict freedom, discriminate against the weak and protect ruling elites are themselves criminal and so are the secret policemen who enforce them. It is such prisoners' right, even their patriotic duty, to speak out against social and political injustice. They certainly did "do it", and the minute they get the chance they'll do it again.

Then there is a third class, peopled by absolute innocents. They really did do nothing. Unfortunately secret policemen have arrest quotas, and someone in chains is always better than no one. Crammed holding cells and queues for the torture chamber create the illusion of productivity and down that blood-spattered corridor lies promotion. So people are picked up in the street for no reason. Front doors are kicked in arbitrarily. The fear that churns the stomachs of their families, the collateral shiver that passes through their communities are intentional, debilitating side-effects. They are the saddest inmates, because in prison their innocence is a stigma. No one wants to hear about it. No one knows if it is true. No one cares.

The Chief Rabbi of Bessarabia had been arrested after leading a protest against state persecution of the country's tiny Jewish community. So he perhaps best fitted the second category.

As did His Eminence, the Patriarch of Aleppo. An older man than his Jewish cellmate, this Orthodox Christian priest was permanently near the end of a two year sentence for officiating at a religious service without a licence from the Office of Faith Affairs. As soon as his release date approached, it receded. No reason was given. A world authority on damnation, he was quick to realise it was not bureaucratic error, or the result of his behaviour - which was exemplary. It was an integral part of his punishment. Had he been a Neo-Platonist, he would have seen himself as if in Tartarus at the very depths of Hades, with King Sisyphus of Corinth for company always pushing his stone up the slope down which it would unfailingly roll back. After months of tantalising hope and stomach-churning frustration, the Patriarch applied his great brain to the problem and emerged a realist. He told himself he was never going to get out of gaol alive, slipped his calendar with its scatter of circled but unfulfilled release dates to the trio of tax inspectors in the next cell and relaxed for the first time since his arrest.

He had been in the cathedral in the capital celebrating the feast of Epiphany when they came for him. He had made few foreign trips in his life, and had not been looking forward to this one but felt it important to support the Orthodox Church in her beleaguered outposts. In the event, his host the Bishop was a decent man, the food wasn't bad and the Cathedral was surprisingly well-attended. He was in the middle of blessing the holy water when the doors were flung open and a dozen unshaven thugs burst in brandishing guns and shouting orders and threats. As he was frog-marched down the aisle he heard the Bishop raise his voice in protest and then heard a dull thud. The faces of the appalled congregation supplied the rest. He was bundled into the back of a van that smelled of vomit and excrement. He set himself the task of not adding to the stench, and almost managed it, but the drive was long and thugs are easily bored.

If there were attempts by his own country to have him freed, the Patriarch of Aleppo never heard about them. If his staff made numerous applications to visit him, he knew nothing of it. If his seventy year-old sister travelled privately and alone – a woman who had rarely left the confines of Aleppo's citadel – and pitched up at visiting time only to be told that her brother was dead before being bundled back to the airport, he was not told. After that, he was moved from prison to prison so that no one outside the country could know where he was, and even those inside who should have known, somewhat lost track of him.

The same could not be said of the Mufti of Naples, who fell into the third category: the genuine innocent. His arrest had almost caused a war. On his way home after attending a conference in Ürümqi his plane flew into a monstrous sandstorm and was forced to land. The Bureau of State Security loved these ill winds and regularly scanned the passenger lists of overflights, hoping for a nicely non-lethal emergency. This time the Takla Makan Desert answered their dark prayers. The Mufti was among the crowd of relieved passengers filing into the transit lounge when four men in shiny suits walked in, each with a photograph of an elegant, turbaned man in his late forties. They walked like automata around the room, holding the picture up and comparing it with the faces before them. They didn't distinguish between men and women and children. All were studied with an unblinking gaze: the fat, the small, the blonde, the bald, the pig-tailed. It was an oddly effective message: we are as systematic as machines when confronting a djinn with many disguises.

They reached the Mufti of Naples almost last of all, sitting in a corner reading the Qur'ān. He was anything but a djinn and looked just as he did in the photos. By then everyone was staring at him, so that when he glanced up from his beloved book he found several hundred eyeballs drilling into him. The crowd's curiosity gave way to recognition, then shock as he was aggressively searched, stripped of his turban, deprived of his Qur'ān. As they escorted him out, he saw soldiers with machine-guns standing beyond each panel of the lounge's glass walls. They hurried him down the corridor with its ratty carpet and lurid folkloric posters, while the soldiers ran ahead in orchestrated, leap-frogging moves, successively coming to rest with their muzzles trained on him. His captors evidently knew their quarry not a jot, because the Mufti of Naples had never run away from anything in his life.

He was an unimpeachable authority on the Qur'ān. Softly spoken and without agenda, he had become the scourge of politicised clerics around the world who justified repressive dictats by claiming their roots were to be found in the Prophet's holy words. When asked if it was true that such and such a Sūra proscribes such and such a thing, the Mufti of Naples simply gave an honest answer. He didn't look around for ignorant or malicious judgements to challenge; he did not seek controversy, but controversy found him.

He first came to fame when a Naples newspaper consulted him after a young woman with severely impaired vision was forced to walk home with her seeing-dog late at night, and was mugged and raped. Some Muslim taxi-drivers in the city had been refusing to allow passengers with dogs to travel in their cabs. The Mufti told the journalist that nowhere in the Qur'ān does the Prophet – God bless him and keep him - say dogs are unclean. Indeed, he told her about the devout seven youths in Sūra 18 who, persecuted for their Muslim faith, hid in a cave where they slept for 309 years 'with their dog stretching its paws on the threshold'. And he read her the fourth verse of Sūra 5 in his clear, gentle voice:

> 'They ask you what is permitted to them.
> Say, "Permitted to you are all good things;
> and those hunting beasts that you teach,
> training them, teaching them what God has taught you
> - eat what they catch for you,
> mentioning God's name over it
> and fearing God.'

Within a fortnight of the article appearing, the *Associazione Tassisti di Napoli* announced that henceforth none of its members would refuse to carry passengers accompanied by bona fide working dogs. The editor, sensing the birth of a popular hero, promptly sent his fashion correspondent to ask the Mufti what exactly the Qur'ān said about how much women should cover themselves in public. His answer to that – modesty in dress was ordained but hiding the face was not - turned him into a national celebrity. Next, a delegation of feminists asked him why, according to Islam, angels can only be male – to which he suggested that in the spiritual world as well as the secular, appearance might not necessarily be evidence of gender. The Mufti went global when, on the eve of three-way talks at Camp David on the future of Jerusalem, he outlined the Prophet's heaven-sent teachings on Jews and Christians. In time he became as revered by some as he was reviled by others, and the distinction had no neatness about it. It did not break down into East/West, male/female, ayatollah/liberal. The only country on earth which proclaimed a supposedly unanimous consensus against him was the semi-secular one to which he was blown by that malevolent, sand-laden wind.

İsmet went to the Chief Rabbi of Bessarabia's talk on the Babylonian Gemara in search of a quiet place for a doze. There were only four others in the Self-Improvement Room off the library. A slim man in his forties exuding elegance even in grey prison clothes, an old chap who looked like a biblical patriarch – both of whom were listening intently, and two grubby and unshaven men in their early thirties - both of whom were fast asleep. İsmet tried to emulate the latter pair. He slumped in his seat and closed his eyes, but somehow the smiley, scholarly-looking speaker was more than a match for İsmet's tiredness. Ideas kept getting past his defences, sneaking in around the edge of his fatigue. He sat up, and started to listen. He even asked a question at the end.

After the Chief Rabbi of Bessarabia's talk, the three older men ate together in the prison refectory as they always did, except when they had a falling out. Then two would sit at one table, and the third would find a seat as far away as possible, even if it meant breaking bread with bandits and stranglers. Twice they had all disagreed with one another and then they sat alone at three points of the compass, heads down in books to make sure they didn't catch the eyes of the others. The first time it was caused by a disagreement over the findings of the First Council of Nicaea in 325AD regarding the divinity of Christ. The second followed a disputed umpire judgement by the oldest during a game of Batumi marbles in the exercise yard. The sporting schism lasted a great deal longer than the doctrinal.

So the three men ate together as usual and talked. And what they talked about was the sixth man in the room. Or, as the Chief Rabbi put it, the fifth. How so, five? asked the Mufti of Naples. You are not excluding yourself, are you? The Rabbi thought for a moment, then advanced the notion that from where he stood there were five men in the room. Five men in his audience. But, the Patriarch of Aleppo suggested gently, as God looking down saw the room, there were six men present. The Mufti looked uncomfortable, started to speak, then pursed his fine lips. The Chief Rabbi murmured something about being fairly sure He had better things to do than that. At this, the Patriarch too looked uneasy, but said nothing.

For a while they ate their savoury slop in peace, until the Rabbi told himself it would be a shame to allow a chill to descend on them at the exact moment when they had the chance of being joined by a fourth man who favoured thought over brawling. But the Rabbi knew that his fellow theologians would not be able to move on unless they got off their chests what was so obviously bothering them. Reluctantly the Mufti admitted that he was slightly troubled by his friend the Patriarch referring to Allah – the Merciful and Compassionate - as 'looking down' on the room. It was a short step from this to saying that there was more than one Allah.

There was silence at the table. The Rabbi abandoned the savoury slop for the sweet one, which tasted the same but sweeter. The Patriarch of Aleppo racked his brains. He had no idea how the Mufti could make that jump. Maybe when he was younger he could have worked it out, but now... He shook his head. Hold on. Could it be to do with anthropomorphising God? No, because Allah in the Qur'ān is sometimes described as having a face, and faces have eyes, so... Unless...it's that old *Kalam* chestnut...

'My dear old friend, I am sorry. Clearly the notion that Allah – the Merciful and Compassionate - possesses sight is to suggest that he has a second uncreated attribute alongside His essence. But how can there be two uncreated attributes without there being more than one God? I apologise for offending the Good Lord, both yours and mine.'

Whereas mine, you assume, thought the Chief Rabbi of Bessarabia, is game for a laugh.

The Mufti of Naples smiled graciously and inclined his handsome head towards the Patriarch of Aleppo. The old man was endearingly pleased with himself for solving the theological conundrum and relieving his dear friend's distress, but not so pleased that he forgot how the Chief Rabbi of Bessarabia had offended him.

'What did I say exactly, your Eminence?'

'Words to the effect that you thought God had better things to do than peer down from Heaven at your lecture.'

Hmm. Where to start, wondered the Rabbi. On the one hand, it would be a sin of great vanity to believe that He would be the slightest bit interested in my musings on the ancient East Aramaic commentary on His Word. It's all a bit removed, and besides, He knows it already. But that isn't what's getting Aleppo hot under the collar. It's something more obvious. Something like…

'Old friend, if I were to say the words "Jeremiah 23" to you would that unfurrow your brow?'

The Patriarch thought for a moment, and then nodded and smiled.

And what, the Mufti wanted to know, was to be found at Jeremiah 23? His Jewish and Orthodox colleagues spoke in duet:

> 'Can a man hide himself in secret places so that I cannot see him? says the Lord.'

Although, the Patriarch went on, I was thinking more of something from the New Testament, from Hebrews 4:13:

> 'Nothing in all creation is hidden from God's sight. Everything is uncovered and laid bare before the eyes of Him to whom we must give account.'

'Same meat, different gravy', replied the Rabbi. 'The point is, the Lord our God sees everything regardless, including a humble room in a squalid gaol. In the room: three men of the Book, one talking, two listening. Two men of the flick-knife, both sleeping. And one man of the unknown, listening and then asking a rather bright question.'

The Mufti proposed that they should each try to find out who the unknown man was. And if it turned out that he was…reasonably innocent of whatever crime he was said to have committed, then they should invite him to lunch.

Hmm, thought the Rabbi. He'd probably like to go to Ronisch's Restaurant in Chișinău. Who wouldn't? They might start with the *borscht* and then maybe some fried *fogasch*…

Supposing he is in fact guilty, the Patriarch mused, rocking back on his chair with his eyes closed, but guilty of a crime of which we approve? At which point they plunged into a conversation about acceptable levels of wrongdoing which, even by their own standards, hit new depths of philosophical hair-splitting.

Meanwhile, the man of the unknown, by [now] common consent the sixth man, was trying to find out who they were: these three gentle, distinguished men of God.

There are protocols for learning about fellow-prisoners, particularly for new arrivals. Asking bald questions is not one of them. That is the way of policemen and their informers, and no one behind bars can afford to be mistaken for either of those. The trick is to put yourself where information is to be had without appearing to elicit or register it. Also, it's a bad idea to be seen to be in any kind of a hurry, as time in gaol creeps so slowly and emptily that even the tiniest hint of pace or purpose draws attention – and attention carries risk. So İsmet left it a while before taking himself to the poky Administration offices.

The clerk at the front desk was himself a prisoner. He was very fat and very pale, like a slug under a stone. İsmet waited while he vented his irritation on the queue of men ahead of him. The clerk was totally unsympathetic to anything that smacked of evasion of responsibility, so attempts to switch from hard jobs to soft met blank refusal to pass the supplicant on to the organiser of work duties. He had little sympathy for those requesting medical appointments, except in one case where the prisoner was genuinely ill. Requests for parole hearings elicited furious eye-rolling, although one older, well-spoken man was treated with respect and given a form to fill out. Gradually İsmet formed a picture of the clerk as a peevish, petulant snob, but with a heart buried somewhere in all that lard. When it was finally İsmet's turn, and with no one in the queue behind him, he stepped smartly up to the desk, noting the name on the plaque: Sıtkı Güneş.

'Yes. What do you want?' the clerk asked without looking up from his writing pad.

'Good morning, Güneş Efendi.'

The big head lifted slowly and fixed İsmet with two deep-sunk, rheumy pink eyes.

'I don't know you. Who are you?'

The questions were no less abrupt, but the tone had changed. It had softened. No one had addressed him as "Mr" in a long while. İsmet gave his name. The clerk started to thumb through the prison register, but long before he had reached the T's he put the lever-arch file down and slowly looked up at him.

'İsmet Turali?'

İsmet nodded.

'What can I do for you, Turali Efendi?'

İsmet replied that he hoped to start a chess circle, and was wondering if he could book the room off the library. The clerk replied that he would need to clear it with the Self-Improvement Officer, who was on leave for another fortnight; no bookings could be made without his authorisation. İsmet said he understood completely, and would make application to him upon his return. But in the meantime, could he possibly get an idea as to how booked up the room was? So he could have a few times and dates with which to start canvassing interested fellow-prisoners - no point clashing with other pursuits. The clerk gave an understanding shrug, and produced a scruffy red exercise book from a drawer. When, he asked İsmet, did he have in mind? İsmet named the exact time and day of the week when the wise and cheery theologian had given his talk.

'Not possible, Turali Efendi. The room's taken'.

İsmet looked suitably disappointed. How about same time, a week later. The clerk shook his head. Not possible, he said. It's a regular booking. He turned the exercise book round so İsmet could see. Against that time, against that day, were the words "The Politans – cell 677". İsmet did a tiny, taken-aback look with a questioning furrow of his brow. The clerk fell for it.

'It's my name for them. The Politans.'

He was clearly dying to share the joke, so İsmet obliged by looking interested.

'Well, Turali Efendi…'

At which point İsmet interrupted him to say that he much preferred being called by his first name.

'If you really prefer it…?'

'I do. I'd much prefer it.'

'Well, İsmet Efendi…'

'İsmet, please.'

'Well, İsmet…'

And so İsmet's new friend Sıtkı told him. There were in fact three Politans. They all shared a cell, and they were men of God. Not that they were particularly bad men of God, the clerk thought. At any rate they were no worse than any others. They just happened to get caught, that's all. And, as he'd said, there were three of them. The oldest was the Patriarch of Aleppo. Apparently the Orthodox Christians give such senior holy men the title: "Metropolitan". So His Eminence the Most Reverend Theodore Mopsuestia II was, if you like, the first Politan. The second was a very learned Jewish gentleman: the Chief Rabbi of Bessarabia, Professor Josef Abramovici. Naturally, being Jewish, he was "Cosmopolitan". At this the clerk paused for audience reaction, so İsmet smiled obligingly.

'Last of all, is Dr Zahi Suyuti, the Mufti of Naples. A very considerable scholar of the glorious Qur'ān - a world expert, in fact. He's not Italian, of course, but he carries himself with great…I like to think, Italianate elegance. I believe he's originally from Egypt. No matter. So, İsmet, you can guess which Politan he is. No? You're teasing me, I'm sure. Give up? "Neapolitan"! So there you have it: Metropolitan, Cosmopolitan and Neapolitan. Sorry. You'll have to find another time.'

İsmet had to think what this last remark referred to, then remembered his pretext of booking the room and said he would be back when the Self-Improvement Officer returned. The clerk told him that was the way to play it. And then he glanced quickly around the empty office, before confiding in İsmet that for her birthday treat, he had taken his mother to see *The Knot Girls*, İsmet's romantic comedy about rival carpet-weavers in a remote village. She absolutely adored it. So did he. In fact, they'd seen it five times. Then the clerk's demeanour changed. He returned the red exercise book to the drawer and slammed it shut. He put up a "Gone to Lunch" sign, and waddled away. Then İsmet turned and, seeing that two prison officers had entered the room behind him, realised why Güneş Efendi had suddenly reverted to type.

So. Cell 677 it was.

Such were the rigours of prison life - İsmet was again assigned to the kitchens, which included the extensive vegetable garden – that it was two days before he had a free moment to pay a call on the Politans. As he was about to leave his cell, a guard handed him a note from the Governor of the Prison. A request had come in for İsmet Turali reference a marital visit. Madame Turali would be arriving at ten in the morning in a week's time. The conjugal facility had been reserved for them for one hour.

Madame Turali. İsmet's wife. He had almost forgotten he had a wife. And she was coming to see him. In prison. He did not visit cell 677. He lay on his bunk and thought.

Chapter Eight

It was four years ago. Murat had met him in the square; he and Reyhan had agreed over dinner to act as midwives for *The Bus Ride*; they had then made themselves scarce so as to arouse no suspicions. İsmet had sat in the garden writing the scripts for *The Knot Girls* and the two Steppe Westerns. It had gone well. He'd carried his father's old wing-backed chair into the garden, under the quince tree. He had a jug of lemonade on the table and a bubbling *nargileh* at his feet, filling the air with apple smoke. After lunch – bread, cheese, olives, a hunk of *bastourma*, a glass of beer – he went for a stroll in the web of lanes he had known since childhood. The lanes the police cars had roared up and down that awful day when his family's cloistered world caught fire. Sometimes he borrowed Saladin from next door. For some reason, he had more and better ideas taking the old sheepdog on his walk than when he went alone. On this particular day he had just returned Saladin to his kennel and was ambling back down his drive, when he saw a silver limousine parked in front of the house. As he drew near, a uniformed driver opened the rear door. A very striking woman slid out. Peered over her expensive sunglasses. Proffered a gloved hand. Smiled a devastating smile. İsmet had been in jail seven years, and out of it just a fortnight.

Her name was Talya Begüm Demir. And, she told him, she would be his producer. Balık Bey had asked her to look after him. Balık Bey wanted İsmet Efendi to be utterly secure. To be free of all worries. That was why she was there. İsmet Efendi could have complete faith in her professionalism. She had worked four years in Hollywood. She had produced the Steppe Westerns that were made in his absence. She had looked after several huge international co-productions filming in the country. She rattled off famous names. She was utterly confident. She had a low, husky voice. She had a mane of lustrous, jet-black hair. She had well-turned calves. She had a compelling bosom. She wanted fresh mint tea. She did not like coffee.

İsmet went off to pick the mint, his mind full of conflicting thoughts. He clearly had no choice. She wasn't asking, she was telling. Presumably she had been put in by Balık Bey to make sure İsmet didn't get up to his old tricks. On the other hand, he needed someone who knew her way around. He'd been out of circulation for seven years. For their own safety he had severed all contact with the people with whom he'd made *The Librarian and his Wife*. Three films on a short turnaround called for tight organisation and, given the state of the country, considerable autonomy. She would clearly brook no nonsense. Heaven help a local official who refused her filming permission. She'd be terrifying if crossed. She was terrifying enough just sitting in his garden reassuring him of her credentials.

He steeped the malachite-green leaves in boiling water. Wondered if she liked sugar in it. Decided he didn't want to risk it, and put some into a bowl. Went back out into the garden. She was sitting in his wing-backed chair. She had taken off her gloves and her sunglasses. She was reading the script for *The Knot Girls*. She didn't look up when he put the tea down by her side. She didn't say thank you. She didn't, in fact, say a word for forty minutes. Until, that is, she turned the last page and looked up at him.

'It's a masterpiece. Simple as that.'

'Well let's hope I don't mess up directing it.'

'You won't, İsmet. I won't let you.'

She smiled a devastating smile. Put on her sunglasses. Stood. Put on her gloves. Shook him by the hand. Left. She hadn't touched her tea.

She came back a fortnight later to read the scripts for the Steppe Westerns. She loved them. They talked about casting and locations. Her ideas were sensible and safe. She wore blue instead of black. Again, she left her mint tea untouched. But this time when she was leaving, she did not put her gloves on until after she had shaken his hand.

They slept together six weeks later.

They had hardly been out of one another's sight since he returned to the capital. No bus, this time; she sent him a plane ticket. The minute he landed he was plunged into meetings. Casting meetings, budget meetings, schedule meetings. Meetings to select the heads of department: photography, sound, art, wardrobe, hair, make-up, editing and then meetings with the people he had chosen. She was always there, even when she had left the room. That was the sort of person she was: a lingering presence. He had never deferred to anyone creatively in his entire life, and he didn't defer to her exactly, but he agreed with her a lot. It was partly because he did actually often agree with her, and partly because he needed the potboilers to run smoothly so he had time and space in his mind for the secret film. But that wasn't all there was to it.

He noticed that it gave her pleasure when he agreed with her. Her eyes crinkled almost imperceptibly at the corners, but more telling was something she did with her legs. She often sat with them crossed; when he went along with something she said, she'd tighten the cross with a tiny, squeezing, slithering action. Not every time, but often enough for him to rule out coincidence. In fact, during the period when he was testing out this theory he consented to a number of suggestions he had no intention of following, simply to see if she'd do the slithering thing. And she did. With the theory proved, there was no need to continue the experiment. But İsmet still found himself agreeing with her more than he needed to. He obviously wanted to give her pleasure.

So when she held a drinks party in her huge apartment for the principals and key members of the production team after which everyone left except for İsmet, and she told him it was time for them to make love – he agreed.

He did not, he had long realised, think about sex every moment of the day. Given that some men did, he perhaps helped provide the necessary statistical balance. What he did was think about sex when it occurred to him, and then he thought about it very happily. In between, he wasn't just abstinent. It was rather as if sex were a country he had never heard of, and which therefore it could not cross his mind to visit. He was in that respect, he supposed, rather well-suited to prison. Some of his colleagues turned their attention to other men. Others, of course, had no turning to do – they already faced that way. Many more lay alone under coarse blankets making the best of what was to hand, hoping that the memory of a woman's breathing and her cries of pleasure would cram their imaginations and crowd out the sounds of fellow prisoners' snores and nightmares.

Being faced with others' frustration never put İsmet in mind of sex. He did not find it contagious or suggestive. What turned him on was sex itself. Its imminence, closely followed by its reality. Then he remembered how lovely it was, and made up for all that lost time. Given the oddly amnesiac mechanics of his sexual drive, it was surprising he'd slept with as many women as he had in his life. But most of that was down to a particularly fervid phase in his early career, when he was directing the first potboilers. The remainder constituted what Murat would have dismissed as a low score, but İsmet saw rather as a precious collection. Though maybe collection wasn't quite the right word. And if he was being honest with himself, he wasn't sure it had all been equally precious. Certainly, Anna in Vermont had been, but she was in a league of her own.

And now here was Talya Begüm Demir, kissing him backwards into a marbled bathroom and running the bath and taking his clothes off and giving him a big towel and pouring aromatic oils, hyssop and magnolia, into the water's vortex and once he was in, standing a little way off so he saw her fitfully through the steam as she slowly removed the clothes from her superb body. She didn't do it with exaggerated provocation, but it was anything but matter-of-fact. She did it as she seemed to do everything: with almighty confidence and more than a touch of 'this is as good as it gets – take it or leave it'. It was as if, had he just dressed and gone she would neither have chased him nor wasted a second feeling offended. She would just have thought "more fool you" and continued with her life. But he did not go. He stayed to wash her and be washed by her. To dry her and be dried by her. To climb together into her huge bed as white and soft and cradling as a hammock of clouds.

The sex, though, was something different.

She looked gorgeous, she smelled great, she felt sublime, and she was absolutely passive. She received him when and where and how he chose. She renounced control, abdicated power, surrendered. It was only when he thought about it later that it occurred to him that, once they were in bed, had he made no moves she would probably have lain where she was and fallen asleep. At the time, he wanted her so much, his memories of sex were so powerfully awakened, that he misread her passivity for sensuous malleability: she would take, she appeared to be saying, whatever shape or position he desired. Whatever he wanted to do, she was his. And given his passionate arousal and her absolute acquiescence to it, they had a great time. Well, he had a great time. He wasn't sure she had. They had done whatever he wanted to do, but were there things she wanted to do? If so, then he was sure he could manage a bit of languorous passivity, and perhaps she'd have a great time. And after that they could try sharing the initiative. They'd clearly have to sleep together again.

It took six months before İsmet realised that how it was that first time was how it was. And of those six months, they had been married for three. He knew he should talk to her about it, but he didn't know how to without hurting her. And once the moment early on is missed, you can't go back to it. It's like forgetting the name of someone you see every day. You can't ask them a year later what it is.

They were a golden couple. They made hit film after hit film together. He turned down amazing offers to direct abroad. When Balık Bey retired, Talya succeeded him as head of the studio, reporting directly to the Minister of Culture himself. They were the most important creative figures in the country. Through it all, she never grew casual, never allowed her looks to slip. He thought back to those frustrated men in prison; how they'd kill to have a woman who'd allow them to take such control in bed. Beyond "such". All control. But it wasn't sexy. İsmet was reminded of something Murat had once said about a girl he'd slept with at college: that she wasn't even a witness. Sex with Talya Begüm Demir was like making love to the dead.

***

So İsmet lay on his bunk with the note from the Governor on his chest. He felt terrible about her. Terrible about the way he had treated her. Because she was not the only one to hold something back. Through their courtship, their marriage, their work, on holiday, at the quiet times of the day, he had never once breathed a word to her about *The Bus Ride*. He didn't trust her. She was the regime's person, not his. In fact it was worse than that. He had not merely not trusted her. He had used her.

She had unwittingly provided cover and legitimacy for him while he made a film behind her back via Murat and Reyhan which would tell the world that his beautiful country and its decent, humane people were being governed by monsters. And being part of the elite, the nomenklatura, made his wife a monster, however minor. So *The Bus Ride* was more important to him than she was. He used to wonder how to soften the blow, but he couldn't think of a way. As with the sex, as the years went by, he couldn't take her aside. Couldn't get it out in the open and make it good. He couldn't let her in on his secret.

The world premiere of *The Bus Ride* was at the Sundance Festival. Reyhan had taken the print to Utah herself. The night of the screening İsmet went back to the old house, leaving Talya a note saying he'd gone to pick the quinces. He put the light on in Maman's old study in the attic: his sign to Murat that he was at home. In the morning he went round to see Saladin. Tucked in the usual place under the kennel roof was a message: "Triumph at Sundance. Standing ovation. Distributors queuing."

İsmet didn't pick any quinces. Knowing his arrest was only hours away and not wanting his father's wing-backed chair to be left outside for years, he sat on the bench. He thought, not about his film's success on the other side of the world, but about the news of that success arriving in his backward little country: the clattering teleprinter in an ugly government building at dead of night. The traitor named. Not just that loose cannon İsmet Turali up to his nasty old tricks, but İsmet Turali, husband of the Head of the State Film Studios. Her career would presumably be dashed. Would anyone believe one half of the golden couple hadn't told the other? What would she think of him? What would she say to him when they met?

She didn't attend the trial. Having no defence for his actions, he offered none. They didn't let him see newspapers or hear the radio. They never spoke about her to him and he didn't ask. He had done her enough damage already. Yet here she was coming to visit him in prison. For a conjugal visit, of all things. It was grotesque. He reached for the Governor's note and took another glance at it. There was some small print at the bottom he hadn't read, so he read it and immediately wished he hadn't: "Nothing must pass between visitor and prisoner and vice versa that is not a natural product of the human body. Visual proof may be required."

Knowing the dangers of brooding, and with seven days to go before Talya Begüm Demir Turali's visit, İsmet climbed down off his bunk. From the time on Farouk the Forger's alarm clock there was still forty minutes to go before the end of free association for Category B prisoners. Time enough to go visiting.

İsmet was in a general wing, where politicals lived with criminals, human rights activists with safecrackers. For the moment he only had Farouk the Forger in his cell, but until a few days before they had shared it with a grim, wiry individual who had terrified everyone. He had been docile within the cell, reassuring them after beating someone up in the exercise yard that he didn't like fouling his own nest. But he clearly liked fouling any other nest he could get into. They hauled him away in a straitjacket after he threw a guard off a balcony, breaking his back. Farouk and İsmet assumed he was on the criminal, rather than the dissident spectrum, but the difference can be a fine one.

İsmet knew there were corners of the prison which were comparatively free from rough stuff, because the word was that was where they housed senior members of the regime who had fallen out of favour – and their relatives. He supposed he sort of fitted into that category, but preferred where he was. More room for manoeuvre. Besides, Farouk was a delight, with a fund of knowledge about the life and times of Bihzad, being personally responsible for a quarter of the thirty-two miniatures declared by experts to be the genuine work of the great Safavid master.

Within the wing for white-collar, "soft" criminals was a particularly quiet cul-de-sac, and at its very end lay Cell 677. İsmet knocked and receiving no answer, glanced round the half-opened door. It looked very cosy inside. Shelves laden with books. An icon over one bunk. A good prayer rug. A shaded reading light. A neat row of slippers. Simple food waiting to be prepared on the table. The only Politan at home was Cosmopolitan. He was standing with a fringed shawl round his shoulders and a *yarmulke* on his head, rocking to and fro while reciting something in a murmur that dwindled to a whisper, then swelled into a rumble. The Chief Rabbi of Bessarabia was saying his prayers.

During one pronounced rock backwards, he noticed İsmet in the doorway and without missing a mumble, gestured him in and pointed to a chair. But İsmet did not feel comfortable sitting while a man old enough to be his father stood in prayer, so he remained on his feet and listened. It was pleasantly soporific. And it was intriguing, too. Were the louder bits accompanying text which called for particular emphasis? Or was it arbitrary, and owed more to the vagaries of the Rabbi's lung power and breathing? In the event, prayers ended on a whimper, not a roar, and the two men shook hands.

They spoke in English. Apparently the Politans had been expecting İsmet. They were hoping he might have come to the talk the week after on the Palestinian Gemara; they had looked out for him, but couldn't see him. As there were only – the Rabbi had to think about this – three people in the audience this time, they knew they hadn't missed him. İsmet explained that he had wanted to attend but his kitchen shift had been changed. That was why he was there now, to introduce himself. Professor Abramovici gave a graceful little bow of his head and made them both a cup of tea. While he did so he apologised for the absence of his colleagues. They were engaged in pastoral duties around the prison. His Eminence was hearing confession, while Dr Suyuti was visiting the sick in the prison hospital. When they came back, they would eat together. It was his turn to prepare the evening meal. Smoked fish which they had been kindly given, sliced tomatoes, some bread. Nothing heavy; at their age, they had to think of their digestion. Not Dr Suyuti perhaps, who was of a younger generation, but they had learned during their incarceration to live together.

It turned out that they had come into prison die-hards in their own faiths. They had barely met people of other religions, let alone had to share a slopping-out bucket with two of them in a confined space. At first it had been tense, uncomfortable. Dr Suyuti didn't like His Eminence putting up his icon. Five times a day Professor Abramovici couldn't get past Dr Suyuti while he blocked the floor in prayer. Neither Dr Suyuti nor His Eminence wanted the Professor to screw a *mezzuzah* to the door jamb outside their cell for fear they'd be mistaken for Jews. The clash of rituals made life almost impossible. One would be celebrating when another was doing penitence. One fasted while the other two filled their bellies. There'd be a solemn prayer for the dead being spoken in this bunk, a happy canticle being sung in that one, and a vow of silence hanging over the third. As for the dietary differences… Professor Abramovici shook his head slowly, and looked slightly queasy.

'We weren't talking to one another. Not helping one another. Never smiling. It was as if we had built three little prisons inside this big one. Horrible! And then, one night, last thing before I went to bed, I recited the *Shema* as usual. It's the prayer you make "when you lie down, and when you rise". So I sang it, in Hebrew of course, and got into my bunk. There was silence for a few minutes, and then a voice came out of the darkness. Dr Suyuti's voice. He wanted to know what it was I had just said. So I told him in English – the one language we have in common:

"Hear, O Israel: The Lord our God is one Lord;

and you shall love the Lord our God with all your heart,

and with all your soul, and with all your might."

Then His Eminence spoke from his bed – in that quiet, clear voice of his. He said: "Deuteronomy, Chapter 6, Verse 4. We have that." And then Zahi – Dr Suyuti said, "But we also have something similar in the Qur'ān, Sūra 2:

"Your God is one God;

there is no god except Him,

the Merciful and Compassionate…

Those who believe have greater love for God."

No one said anything else that night, although we all must have thought a lot of things. Because in the morning you could feel the change.'

The Professor rubbed the thumb of his right hand against the tips of his fingers. His next gesture was half-shrug, half-smile.

'Now I hear his confession, he joins our prayers, we say grace together, we eat the same, we fast the same, we share what we can and respect what we can't. Naturally, we still argue over the slightest thing, but that's theologians for you. It's done without malice. Is that the time? They'll lock you out of your cell if you aren't quick. You might see the others on your way down. Please take the blame for their supper not being on the table.

Oh, and next time you come back - and make it soon, please - you do all the talking.'

The Chief Rabbi of Bessarabia gave İsmet a twinkly grin and started to slice the tomatoes. İsmet did indeed meet the other two Politans on the stairs. Metropolitan had stopped for breath, and Neapolitan was keeping him company, with his arm around the older man's back. The introductions were brief, but welcome. When İsmet looked up from the foot of the stairs, the Patriarch of Aleppo and the Mufti of Naples had reached the top. They leaned over the rail and waved down with grace and elegance respectively, before turning towards the warmth of Cell 677.

The conjugal facility was even worse than he imagined. It was a lofty ceilinged, window-less room decorated some time ago like a teenage girl's bedroom. Now the pink paint was flaking higher up and mouldy lower down, the lampshade was full of dead wasps, the plastic flowers thick with grime. The solitary picture on the wall was a faded photograph of the Taj Mahal, cut from a newspaper. It was hanging crookedly. İsmet started to straighten it, and then something made him turn it over. On the reverse someone had taped a pornographic photo of an athletic couple in the position Murat used to describe as "man supine, woman superb". İsmet turned it back. A mausoleum for a dead wife seemed more appropriate.

Then there was the bed. It was made to look like ornate brass, but was in fact just plastic-effect. The bedspread had a polythene cover, the way some taxi-drivers covered their seats. The idea was presumably to catch moisture born of impatience. The blanket was thin and tattered. The top sheet was real enough, particularly in its stains, but the bottom sheet was made from something like industrial strength kitchen paper, evidently sold to correctional facilities in wide rolls. Under that was, inevitably, more polythene sheeting.

The only other item of furniture was a bruised white dressing table. Its drawers had been locked shut with their handles removed, and all three of its mirrors were cracked. One of its legs was missing and another was split. Had it not been propped against a wall, it could not have stood. It looked as if it had tried to intervene in a severe marital dispute. Impact marks on the walls reinforced the impression that the room had hosted more conjugal division than coupling. Or perhaps one followed the other, depending on whether reconciliation or retribution was the initial priority. Either way, chances were the likeliest natural product of the human body to be emitted in that room was tears.

He heard her coming from afar. The sharp alto of high heels amid the bass of prison guards' boots. The sound of a powerful, busy woman with her escort. İsmet looked to the doorway in time to see his wife and attendants trot past. It was a place she had never been and yet she was in front. They called, she turned, İsmet composed himself. He still did not know what he was going to say to her. She stopped for a moment at the threshold to give some instructions to an assistant İsmet had not seen before. Then she nodded in dismissal. Flunkies evaporated. She drew a little breath and, sucking her already slender waist in so as to touch nothing, entered the room. The door closed behind her.

Disconcertingly, she did not look around the room. She wasted no time as İsmet had done, horrifying herself with its seediness. She simply gazed at him. It took İsmet a moment to work out what sort of gaze it was. He quickly dismissed adoration, closely followed by admiration. No, it was a species of wonder. Wonder how any man could have been so idiotic as to throw away career, luxury, respect and, most of all, Talya Begüm Demir Turali herself. She was as striking as ever, this time in grey. Her high heels were grey. Her slender legs were encased in grey silk stockings. Her suit was grey pinstripe. At her neck was a string of grey pearls. She wore a silver grip studded with more grey pearls in her raven hair. She was dressed not to kill, but to rule.

The trouble was, İsmet was not one of her subjects. She had thought he was, but then there was this ridiculous business at the American film festival.

She looked around for somewhere to sit. The bed was the only place. She took a grey linen handkerchief from her bag, carefully spread it on a corner and lowered her taut, shapely behind onto it. He didn't want to sit on the bed. He didn't think the dressing-table would take any more pressures. So he stood, a little way from her. And then she spoke.

'I had such a nice note from the President. Some people feared for my position, but he told me it was obvious I had no idea what you were up to or else I would have stopped it dead in its tracks. He is so sympathetic.'

Why, she went on, did İsmet have to go on making these – she couldn't think of a word for it – these "private" films? She said the word "private" as if it were a euphemism for "lavatory". He had a public forum. Why wasn't that sufficient for him? She couldn't see why, if he had wanted to make a little film about a bus ride, he hadn't he come to her - his producer? They could have got it made in between bigger projects. She didn't sound angry. She sounded puzzled.

'I just don't understand you, İsmet.'

She had not of course seen this bus film but the Ministry had had a full report from the embassy in Washington. It sounded like a fantasy. A figment of his imagination. There could be no basis in fact for the events he depicted in the film.

He thought about saying that, on the contrary, it was more documentary than fiction. It was a film of record. But why bother? She wouldn't believe him. Her next remark showed how right he was.

'They only arrest the guilty, İsmet. Never the innocent. Otherwise, what sort of people would that make us?'

She knew he blamed those in power, but who was it doing all those bad things he said were happening in their country? The little people. It was the little people he was always going on about in his "private" films who were actually the rotten apples. Not those at the top. That was precisely what the people at the top were trying to do: get rid of the bad lots lower down. How İsmet could side with them was beyond her imagination.

She shook her head gloomily, and then brightened a shade. She was flying to Paris next week for a special screening of *The Knot Girls*. There was going to be an all-day seminar on the film with contributions from top critics and academics, and then in the evening the President of France himself was hosting a gala dinner at the Élysée Palace at which she was to be given the *Légion d'Honneur* on his behalf. İsmet wondered how the French could do this given he was behind bars for making what were called "films of conscience". How Maman would have laughed at his naiveté.

'You have such talent, İsmet Efendi. Such international recognition.'

It was strange to hear his wife address him so formally. A little shocking.

'Look. I have something to show you.'

She reached into her bag and pulled out a glossy coffee-table book. It was titled called *'Spaghetti to Steppe – the Western from Leone to Turali'*.

She held it up for a moment and then put it back.

'How can you waste yourself?'

She waited but he didn't reply. So she stood, brushing imaginary dirt from her immaculate rear which had touched only spotless linen. Then she straightened up and faced him, hair cascading over her shoulders.

'And how can you waste me?'

He shook his head a little, looking miserable and feeling it inside, but only for the hurt he was causing her. Not out of any regrets. Abandoning her grey handkerchief on the bed, she turned on her grey heels and went to the door. Knocked twice. It swung open. Only when Talya Begüm Demir Turali was well clear did the guards escort her husband back to his cell. They were ready with a leer but one glance at their charge's face told them there'd be no need to change the paper sheeting on the bed. Not only had İsmet not touched his wife; he hadn't said one word to her.

***

It was Farouk the Forger's idea. He could see how closed-in İsmet became after the conjugal visit. When he was not working in the kitchens he spent most of the time lying on his bunk. Occasionally he took himself off to see the three men of God they called the Politans, and he always came back from them in a better state. But it didn't last long. İsmet soon started brooding again. He needed to get out of himself. Become involved in other people. Farouk had just the thing.

For some time, Farouk had been writing letters for prisoners to send home. It had started with a barely literate man wanting to give the family he had let down the impression that he had been bettering himself in gaol by improving his skills of penmanship. So he showed Farouk a sentence it had taken him ten laborious minutes to write, and in half that time Farouk completed the page so you could not tell where forger had taken over from burglar. News got around, and soon Farouk had a queue at his cell door. Most turned out to be illiterate; Farouk's skills of imitation were much less in demand than his simple ability to write. That would not have been a problem, except that many prisoners wanted to send letters, but had little idea what to say in them. And Farouk's difficulty was that, whereas he could dream up a dangerously plausible fifteenth century Persian miniature, he had no imagination whatever for creating believable narratives for prisoners to send to loved ones. Or to ones outside, those inside wanted to be loved by again. It was a tall order, and Farouk was tiring of it. One day he suggested İsmet accompany him to the room off the library where it all took place, for an hour once a week before lock-in. See it as a change of scenery, he told his depressed cell-mate. Besides, Farouk added as they were walking over to the Self-Improvement Wing, there were always a few laughs to be had at letter-writing sessions.

The first half dozen prisoners dictated their letters to Farouk the Forger without hesitation, while İsmet sat off to one side. But next in line was one of the gaol's legendary characters: Big Berk. A bear of a man, Berk lived up to his name which meant "hard". No one knew what crimes he'd been convicted of, but the assumption was they involved unspeakable acts of violence, and for that reason doors were held open for him and kitchen servers loaded extra dollops onto his plate. He accepted these acts of kindness not as his right, but with slight surprise, which confirmed people's impression of a man who was as stupid as he was strong. More open doors; more dollops. The truth, as so often, lay elsewhere.

İsmet's involvement with Big Berk began when Farouk the Forger turned to him for help constructing the giant's first letter home. Berk was so inarticulate, and Farouk pretended to be so unimaginative, that İsmet was invited to lend a hand. Perhaps, Farouk suggested, handing İsmet a pen and some paper, he would like to take Berk Efendi over there and work with him, while Farouk attend to the rest of the queue. The guards by the door saw the writing implements being passed over, and summoned their superiors. Prison rules forbade the subversive İsmet Turali from possessing any materials for communication. Nothing to fear, Farouk the Forger said when the officers arrived. He'll be taking nothing out of this room. He's only helping Berk Efendi with a letter home. The officers looked at Big Berk, who nodded and gave an affirmative grunt. Feeling he should add something to the general reassurances, İsmet invited the guards to search him on leaving, and the officers said that was just what they were going to do. The officers left. The guards returned to their positions by the door. İsmet led his first customer to a quiet corner.

Big Berk had not the slightest idea who İsmet was. But he looked kind, and was clearly prepared to help, and contrary to popular misconception, the big man took no kindness for granted.

'To whom', asked İsmet, 'do you wish to write?'

'To my wife', Big Berk replied.

'And what is her name?'

'Yazmira.'

'And how,' İsmet wanted to know, 'do you address her?'

Big Berk looked totally blank. İsmet explained to him about terms of endearment. That some couples had pet names for one another. It took a while before the big man decided the best way to start the letter was "Dear Yazmira". He watched İsmet writing the words with huge interest, as if he had never seen anything like it. And maybe he hadn't. İsmet turned the page round so he could see what "Yazmira" looked like written down. He stared at it for a long while before reluctantly handing the page back to İsmet. And what, İsmet wanted to know, would you like to say to your wife Yazmira.

'Ah', Big Berk replied, his huge forehead furrowing at the difficulty of it all. 'Here's the thing...'

There was a long pause while the big man stared at İsmet, searching him out. Berk's eyes were like those of an elephant. They seemed much smaller than such a big beast would need, but they had an acuity about them.

'...I've never met her.'

'You've never met your wife, Berk Efendi?'

'No. I've seen her from afar, but never met her.' He shook his head sadly. And then he looked down at his feet, and went very still. When he raised his head, he had made his mind up about something.

'I'll tell you something else…'

He leaned in, like a giant İsmet remembered from a film he had seen as a child. The giant had suddenly appeared at the upstairs window of a house, terrifying the children inside. İsmet held his breath.

'My name's not Berk.'

He shifted his great weight back in the chair, as if, giant-like, to take in better the spectacle of shock he had created. At which point the first buzzer for lock-in sounded. Letter-writing was over for the day. The prisoners hurried off, some with what they had come for, others empty-handed. As the guards searched İsmet, he saw Big Berk – or whoever he was – leave the room clutching in his huge mitt the sheet of paper bearing only the words: "Dear Yazmira".

Chapter Nine

The minute Saljan walked back in after making her first delivery to the prison, she realised something was up. Something more than the usual coffee-house rush. She put the tray on the counter, handed Auntie Gül Seren the money she had taken, popped the tips into the communal jar by the big urn and then bent down to loosen her laces. The new trainers were a little stiff, and she assumed she wouldn't be going out again immediately. When she stood, her aunt peered at her around the till and, mouthing the word "undertakers", gestured in the direction of Saljan's uncle Jafar. He was pacing up and down, the wire from the wall-phone at full stretch. He was handling a complaint.

'…So, Toprak Efendi, you definitely received the two mint teas?'

Jafar looked at Saljan who nodded furiously back.

'I'm just trying to get it straight in my own mind, Toprak Efendi, …You got them, but you're saying they weren't hot…?'

Jafar held the phone from his ear. The undertakers weren't happy.

'They were stone-cold. I see. No, that isn't right at all. In fact it's totally wrong. We're very sorry. We are sending you another two mint teas, Toprak Efendi, right now, without any charge and with a refund for the cold ones…'

Jafar gestured to Tarık, the coffee and tea maker, to get on with this new order. Saljan re-tied her laces.

'…a refund for the "stone-cold" ones. Exactly. That's what I meant. They'll be with you shortly.'

Jafar rang off and, reaching past his wife into the till, put the price of two mint teas together with a twist of apple tobacco in a saucer on Saljan's tray.

She started to apologise to her uncle: the man in prison took his time, she couldn't leave the cup, she'd run as fast as she could… but then her aunt broke in and seized the blame for herself. The orders were down to her. If there was a next time – which Saljan said there would be, every week apparently – then she'd make sure there were no other deliveries on Saljan's tray but the one to the prison. Jafar nodded. The problem was solved.

'Now then,' he said to his niece with a grin as Tarık placed the steaming teas on the tray, 'let's see if you can't scald the little bully's tongue for him.'

It wasn't until they all sat down for supper that the family had a chance to puzzle over the identity of the mystery man in solitary. First there was the question of his age. Saljan thought he was older than Father and Uncle Jafar. He was probably in his late fifties. His face was a little lined, but fine. He must once have been very handsome. In a way she supposed he was still handsome. She didn't know. It was difficult to say. He had brown eyes, and a lovely voice. Very educated. He didn't sound like a criminal. Not all criminals are ruffians, her aunt said quickly. Saljan thought about it and nodded.

She really knew nothing about any of this. Before that day she'd never given a moment's thought to the ugly sprawling building in the middle of her town. Not thought about all the people in there, behind those tiny barred windows. Now she had seen some of them, and one in particular, it would be hard not to think about them.

What was he doing now, the man in the cell? Had he eaten? And eaten what? Can't have been as nice as they were having: chicken *çerkes* with spinach *pilav*, followed by her favourite: little dough balls dusted with sugar and cinnamon. Did he have a daughter her age? A brother? A wife waiting for him to get out? Had they switched his lights off already? What was it like, lying there in the dark? Did he have nightmares about the terrible things he'd done?

Her father interrupted Saljan's broodings to make sure that this man had behaved absolutely correctly. Funny, she thought, it was rare for him to worry about her. She assured him that the man hadn't taken the slightest notice of her. Because, her father went on, he's probably not used to being in the company of women. And does he know whose daughter you are? She said it was most unlikely. Mahmoud the Runner wasn't sure whether to be relieved or offended, so he went back to his dinner.

'It must be very easy for prisoners to become institutionalised,' Jafar said. 'Particularly lifers.'

Saljan nodded.

'I don't know if he's in for life. But he certainly looks as if he's been in jail a long time. His skin is very pale. I don't think they let him see the light of day very often. But the odd thing is…he doesn't seem beaten down. He isn't angry or tense. He's…he acts as if his conscience is clear.'

'Well', said her father, in another uncharacteristic intervention. 'Perhaps it is.'

They all thought about this, and then Gül Seren asked a question which made them think some more. Who, she wanted to know, had paid for the coffee? She'd totted up what Saljan had given her and could see it was paid for, but by whom? Are prisoners allowed money? Saljan shrugged. She had no idea. All she knew was that when she left the man in the cell, the officer with her asked if she had a bill for the coffee, and when she said she did, he said she had to present it to the Governor's secretary for payment. So he took her up to the office and they kept her waiting, which is another reason why the undertakers' teas were so cold. Eventually the secretary, who was really attractive, took the bill in to show the Governor. Saljan didn't see him, but she could hear him huffing and puffing. Then the secretary came out and realised the Governor had given her the exact money. No tip. So she went straight back in, and then Saljan heard what sounded a bit like cursing. Then the secretary popped back out with a nice tip and a big grin.

'Why would the Pasha pay for a prisoner's coffee?' asked Jafar.

No one knew the answer to that, and then Hamid from the coffee wholesaler rang about the extra sack of beans Jafar had ordered and Gül Seren remembered that Minoş the cat hadn't been fed and Mahmoud the Runner took himself off to play backgammon with the Hoja. But Saljan continued to think about the man in the cell while she washed the dinner things. Supposing he was innocent? What sort of dreams do you have in prison if you are innocent?

The next week when it came time for the second prison delivery, Auntie Gül Seren, true to her word, gave all other orders to her stepsons Hussein and Salih. Jafar placed the cup of coffee and glass of iced water on the tray, and away Saljan ran. But then something strange happened. As she hared over Hazreti Halit bridge she became aware that someone was running after her. She quickened her pace – and she was already moving fast. Whoever was chasing her fell back, because when she reached the end of the bridge and turned up the street of the butchers, she glanced round and saw no one. But skimming across Hafiz Square, weaving round the strollers and idlers, she heard the pounding footfall again. And someone shouting her name. But she couldn't stop suddenly with the tray in high elevation, and she didn't want to. Only when she neared the gates of the prison did she slow down. And only then could her pursuer catch up with her. It was Beyrek. He had something important to tell her, but was so breathless he couldn't get the words out. Saljan, on the other hand, looked gloriously fresh. She also looked impatient.

'Well, what is it you want, Beyrek the Coppersmith? I don't like being chased and I've got a delivery to make.'

'That's why,' he said between gasps of air, 'I've been running after you. When you take him his coffee…the other prisoners will make a big racket. Don't worry…not for real. But…very important…you look upset, look frightened…'

Saljan started to ask him how he knew this, how he knew about the man in solitary, but Beyrek was in no shape to say any more and she didn't want the coffee to get cold. She nipped up the prison steps, leaving him in a heap at the bottom.

He was waiting for her when she came out, but he wasn't in a heap. He had put his head under the fountain, tidied himself up and was drinking a glass of pomegranate juice from Zeki's handcart, oasis for visitors to the prison. That Beyrek's quite good looking, she thought, but he can't run as fast as I can. They sat on the wall by the fountain. He offered her a swig of his drink, which she accepted, and an explanation, which she welcomed. He spoke softly, particularly when anyone went by.

It seemed that Beyrek's neighbour, Old Ragıp, had a younger sister who was married to a prisoner. As chief cartoonist for a radical newspaper, he'd upset a lot of big people so they put him inside. Well, he managed to get a message out to his wife to say she should find a way to warn Mahmoud the Runner's daughter that there'd be a lot of noise today, but not to worry. It was part of a plan to push the authorities into letting her wait inside the cell while the man drank his coffee.

'Metin Efendi said especially to tell you that this coffee-drinker is absolutely no threat to you. He just wants your company for a few minutes a week.'

Saljan must have looked suspicious, because Beyrek quickly said he'd checked with Old Ragıp and he knew Metin Efendi to be an honourable man. His words were, that none of them wanted the daughter of Mahmoud the Runner to feel a moment's fear. But she had to look it for the plan to work.

'And did you, Saljan? Did you look scared?'

She nodded. She didn't have to pretend much. It sounded as if they were going to break out of their cells and smash the place down. But she thanked Beyrek the Coppersmith for warning her. And there was one more thing he might know the answer to.

'Do you have any idea who this man is I deliver the coffee to?'

Beyrek did not.

'Does Metin Efendi know his name?'

If he does, Beyrek replied, he's kept it to himself. He certainly hasn't told his wife.

Saljan nodded and stood. She had to run back to the coffee house. She could go past the end of his street, if he wanted to keep her company. It's all right, he replied, still panting a little. I'll walk back.

Sure enough, the next time Saljan delivered coffee to the prison, she was allowed to wait in the man's cell. But she asked him nothing and the only words she heard from him were "hello", "thank you" and "goodbye". But later that week, on her first run of the day, she saw Scheherazade Dumrul dropping Kazan at school. They didn't talk long, but Saljan did mention the mysterious man in solitary. Then Scheherazade asked her if the tray was living up to her hopes. 'Just watch', Saljan said, and away she flew, circling the newspaper kiosk twice – just to show off - with the tray at a disaster-defying angle to the ground.

A few days later, just as the coffee house was closing, Dr Dumrul popped in to pick up some *baklava* and give Saljan a book he'd found it in a box he'd brought back from Geneva and never unpacked. He had put it in a discreet brown paper dust jacket, and he spoke in a lowered voice.

'I wonder, Saljan, if this is your man. There's a photograph of him on the back. Obviously taken some time ago, when the book was published.'

Funny, thought Saljan. What is it about this man that makes everyone go into a whisper? She turned the book over and lifted the wrapper. It was more the face of a boy than a man. Half the age of the man in prison. Rounder in the cheeks and with a full head of hair. But those eyes were unmistakeable even in faded black and white. She looked up and nodded. So the coffee-drinker's name was İsmet Turali and he was a writer.

'Actually, he's rather more than that. I heard he was in the prison here - in solitary. He's famous, though it's not a wise idea to talk about him these days.' At this point Dr Dumrul touched a finger to his lips. 'He has somehow led two lives: as a popular artist, and also as a dissident. He started off making films. Your father and uncle would remember: like cowboy movies, but set on the steppes. And he made one Scheherazade and I saw in Geneva, about groups of girls competing with one another to make the best carpet in the village and marry the handsomest boy. We loved it. But the reason he's in prison is because of some films he made in secret and books like that one: critical of the regime. They would say subversive, seditious.'

Dr Dumrul shrugged. Either way, Turali was a brave man paying the price for being outspoken. And honest. Saljan should read the book and make up her own mind. He'd wondered whether to leave it behind in Switzerland, as Turali was banned over here. Saljan should keep it hidden. Not flash it about.

'But he's not a killer, or anything horrible?'

Dr Dumrul shook his head.

'No. Definitely not'.

She lifted the wrapper to look for the first time at the book's battered cover. The image was of a sheet of paper on which someone had started writing a letter, but had only got as far as the two words: "Dear Yazmira".

'Who is Yazmira?'

Dr Dumrul smiled, and didn't answer.

***

İsmet had to wait a week before he could sit down with the man who was not Big Berk and learn his secret. It took the whole hour because the giant left giant-sized gaps between his sentences, presumably to give him time to find the right words for the next bit. The result was that he talked, with a quaint verbosity, in slow-firing bullet points:

His name was not Berk, but Kerem.

He was not Yazmira's husband.

He was entirely innocent of the charges which had landed him behind bars.

The real Berk, her husband, was not the man Yazmira had taken him for, being in fact a hardened professional criminal.

Kerem had, while working as chauffeur for the real Berk, overheard many things which made him feel very sad about the state of his beloved country, in particular regarding the improper relationship between thugs like Berk and government officials, some very senior.

This Berk had capped a lifetime of crime by absconding abroad with his plunder, together with a belly-dancer: one Nazli the Supple.

Berk had engineered his flight from justice by having Kerem sent to prison in his stead - a callous and wicked substitution.

Berk had been assisted in this cruel deception by tier upon tier of corrupt officials, policemen and judges who had for years been the recipients of his villainous largesse.

Kerem was prepared to put all this behind him and hold no grudge, if Yazmira would only allow him to reap – in time - the connubial benefits of said substitution.

Given the length of his – or rather, her husband's - sentence he was able to give her as long as she needed to come to terms with his suggestion.

If Yazmira had originally found her husband attractive, then he could reassure her that he – Kerem – looked sufficiently similar to him to have lent the switch a degree of plausibility.

If, however, Yazmira preferred not to be reminded of one who had betrayed both their trusts, then he had the time to make some adjustments in respect of his weight, muscle tone, hairstyle etc.

It was entirely possible - given the risk of exposure and embarrassment for tier upon tier of officials, policemen and judges were his story ever to become known - that he might never be allowed to emerge from his present confinement, in which case he begged to be forever remembered by Yazmira as a devoted admirer.

Kerem asked İsmet if he could get all these bullet points into the first letter, but İsmet persuaded him that for love to grow out of such unorthodox beginnings, adopting the pace of a snail stood the best chance of success. In the end, it would take İsmet and Kerem nearly four years and a hundred and seventy two letters. And a large part of their charm, and of the subsequent book's charm, lay in the fact that İsmet retained many of Kerem's quaint ways of thinking and figures of speech. Indeed, they secretly shared the royalties from the book, and would have had joint authorship were that not to have risked inviting accusations of subversion, slander etc., thereby tarnishing Kerem's record as a genuinely innocent prisoner.

But before he and Kerem could write the first letter, İsmet had two obstacles to surmount. He somehow had to get the correspondence past the prison censor, which given its unpatriotic revelations about state functionaries on the take, seemed unlikely. Then, he would have to secure Yazmira's cooperation: keeping the letters safe; passing them on from time to time to İsmet's emissary; maintaining strict silence about the arrangement now while allowing publication when and where it became possible. But how could an emissary explain what was required of Yazmira promptly enough to prevent her throwing any letters into the bin, without spilling the whole story in one go?

The answer to the first challenge was proposed by Farouk the Forger. A world-class dissembler, he knew that the best way to get the letters past the censor was to make sure they in fact went round him. The key to this plan would be the corpulent clerk, Sıtkı Güneş Efendi, gatekeeper to both the prison records office and the Bureau of Postal Intervention. İsmet chose his moment carefully, arriving as the queue thinned before closing time. He had prepared his pitch carefully, to appeal to Sıtkı's innate sense of fair play but via his pettifogging mania for crossing t's and dotting such i's as require dots.

After exchanging warm pleasantries, İsmet suggested to his slug-like friend that there might be an anomaly in the prison records. The clerk looked concerned and a shade defensive. What anomaly? It concerned a prisoner by the name of Berk. Sıtkı reached for the prison register. Did İsmet have in mind the Berk who nobbles horses or Berk the Yoghurt Maker or the one they call Big Berk? The one they call Big Berk, İsmet replied. Only he says he isn't. His name is Kerem. He has been falsely imprisoned. The clerk relaxed a little. This was a familiar device. Was he saying it was a case of mistaken identity? No, İsmet replied. That he was framed. And what made it look less like a gambit was the fact that this had come to light not because Kerem was publicly campaigning for his own release, but because he wanted İsmet to write privately on his behalf to the real Berk's wife. To win her heart.

At that, Sıtkı the clerk almost went from prison cynic to gooey romantic. But he did not quite lose all his deductive reasoning. So, given that he could not alter or correct the prison records, why had his friend İsmet come to tell him this story?

'Because, Sıtkı, it is a very good story.'

As he said this, İsmet raised his eyebrows and gave a little nod, inviting Sıtkı to read as much as he possibly could into his words. It took a moment or two before the reply revealed that the message had been understood.

'And would, for example, my mother appreciate this story, in the same way she loved *The Knot Girls*?'

İsmet believed there was an excellent chance she would. But long before that could happen, the prisoner's letters would have to get to their destination - intact. The corpulent clerk nodded. Thought for a moment. Glanced around. Then turned in his swivel chair and scooted himself over to the table outside the prison censor's door. On the table were an in-tray and an out-tray. There followed a little mime. First he wrote something on a sheet of paper, then folded the page in two and placed it in the in-tray with his left hand. Then, with his right hand, he lifted it out, slid back to the front desk, pulled a rubber stamp from a drawer, pressed it into a purple ink pad, stamped the outside of the folded paper, signed a squiggle across it, rolled back to the censor's door and placed it in the out-tray. Then he turned his face to İsmet with a look of cherubic innocence, before retrieving the folded paper and showing him what was written within: "My mother will be so proud of me".

İsmet was almost at the door when he remembered something; he had found some lost property. And he placed on Sıtkı's desk a greaseproof paper parcel of *kadayıf* which had been left over from a visit by the Examiner of Prisons. The delicious syrupy pudding had thereby ventured much further into the gaol than the Examiner, whose inspection did not extend beyond the Governor's private dining-room.

'Very civic-minded of you, İsmet,' his large friend replied, pink eyes all agleam. 'I shall file it away immediately. Always a pleasure to see you.'

The answer to the second challenge was also a gamble, but in a different way. If İsmet's emissary to Yazmira was not told anything about Kerem's story, then he could not jump the gun. It would simply be down to him to enlist her support in safeguarding some letters she would be receiving from prison. As she read them, she would realise for herself the need for secrecy, the delicacy of the material, the ambition to publish them to overturn a grotesque miscarriage of justice. And she would either go along with it or not. It was down to Yazmira. Then there was the matter of her replies. If she decided to write back then her letters would also have to bypass the prison censor – another task for Sıtkı.

In the event it was Reyhan who went to the address on the envelope: a comfortable little house in a prosperous southern town. The woman who opened the door was decidedly handsome. In her early forties, with oval green eyes and a good figure, well-dressed if a trifle threadbare. She sounded educated. Reyhan told her they both knew people in the same gaol. The woman hurriedly invited her in away from nosy neighbours. It turned out she was indeed called Yazmira, she had received the first letter, and was intrigued. It hadn't felt like the sort of thing her husband would write to her. She wasn't sure why he had changed, unless it was out of remorse, but she hoped he'd write again. If Reyhan wanted to see the letters after she'd read them, that shouldn't be a problem. In fact, if there was anything fishy going on, better someone else have them. She looked at that point, Reyhan later told Murat, as if she was not unaware that wherever her husband went, the smell of fishiness was never far behind.

***

Reading *Dear Yazmira*, with its minute dissection of the over-lapping worlds of criminals and corrupt government officials alongside its epic love story, made Saljan realise how much she'd been burying her head in the sand. She knew the regime was cruel and intolerant - had seen the arrests in the street, heard the hatreds whipped up, felt fearful of informers, learned to mistrust outsiders - but she had suppressed within herself the enormity of it all. An easy thing to do, partly because this was all she had known; she had nothing to compare it with. But it was mostly because her own immediate world felt so safe. For the first time in her life, she started to wonder why that was. Making coffee threatened no one, certainly. But it wasn't just that. Her father's shining reputation was like a shield. It didn't matter, she could see now, that he was so idle around the coffee house. Just being Mahmoud the Runner insulated him and his family and their business. Not from economic pressures, maybe, but certainly from suspicion and hurt. She'd had proof of that with Metin Efendi's message being passed, at some risk she assumed, from behind bars via intermediaries to Beyrek the Coppersmith.

At the same time she was aware that something within herself was changing. It had come to her during one of those almost dizzy moments she spent at the top of the hill before diving down with her tray into the swirling mass below. Dodging the obstacles used to make her feel earth-bound. That complex of transactions and emotions - the waving arms, the laughter, the anger, the sorrows, the worries, the lives – seemed so stolid and mortal. But she had started to feel she was skimming over it all, moving so fast that nothing rubbed off on her. As if she were not of the world. Almost flying over it, like a winged messenger.

When she had finished *Dear Yazmira*, Saljan passed it to Auntie Gül Seren. She could tell what her aunt thought of it and of the man who wrote it, because a little something on a saucer started to appear on the tray bound for the prison. One Monday a couple of cubes of dusty *lokum*. Next, a generous spoonful of rose petal jam. Slivers of candied orange dipped in chocolate. Caramelized hazelnuts. Dragées. Jafar frowned at his wife the first time, and asked her what she thought she was doing. She replied that Mahmoud's Coffee House often gave regular customers a complimentary sweetmeat. Yes, he said, but after all, this man is a convict. His wife replied by handing him *Dear Yazmira*. After he'd read a chapter, Jafar not only raised no further objections, but outdid Gül Seren in saucer-sized generosity.

The security guards at the prison were a little worried when Saljan arrived with a third object on her tray. She explained to them what her aunt had told her uncle: that it was something they did for regulars. A natural accompaniment to coffee. And by chance – Auntie's clever forethought – she happened to have some extra *lokum* with her which the guards might like to sample. Purely for reasons of security, of course. Well, said the guards, we may have to send it out for testing. Entirely up to you, said Saljan, as she slipped by into the prison. But when she passed them on her way out, they all had a dusting of icing-sugar on their moustaches.

Then, one Monday, at Jafar's suggestion, Gül Seren put out two slices of quince, poached in its own syrup. For the first time Saljan saw tears in İsmet Turalı's eyes. He didn't say why, and she didn't ask. But she could see it had something to do with the quince. Don't give him quince again, Auntie, Saljan said when she got back. Didn't he like it? Jafar wanted to know. Sami makes beautiful poached quince. Saljan shook her head. It wasn't that. It must have reminded him of something.

Or someone, Gül Seren suggested.

Or somewhere, Mahmoud the Runner thought to himself from the comfort of the high-backed chair by the window.

Chapter Ten

'How is your father?'

People had been asking Saljan that question all her life, so she answered it automatically. But she registered the guards outside breaking off their chat to listen to the first conversation between Turali Efendi and the girl from the coffee house. And she wondered how a man in solitary knew who she was.

'...I remember seeing him at the athletics track - must have been at least thirty years ago. The university turned out the best it had, but he left them all standing. In fact from where I was, it actually looked as if the others were running backwards. He can't have been much more than twelve years old....'

When the guards realised the subject was Mahmoud the Runner they nodded admiringly, and returned to gossiping. İsmet had already earned his gaolers' respect for the dignified way he endured his incarceration, and because they had been brought up on his Steppe Westerns. Nothing unpatriotic about a trio of high plains heroes killing scum and seducing beautiful girls against the stunning backdrop of the Amal Gorge. By banning his subversive work, the regime ensured that no one in the country would have any idea what İsmet Turali had done wrong.

But İsmet's running track reminiscences upped the ante. Not only was Mahmoud a totally innocent subject; talking about him helped undermine the stigma attaching to political prisoners. What kind of traitor can this Turali really be, the message was, when he clearly follows sport, and saw his country's greatest ever athlete run before the rest of us had even heard of him? İsmet had artfully slipped himself under the great man's protective coverlet.

For his part, İsmet had wondered what the willowy girl with the immaculate tray would do to check him out. That was the reason he'd asked Metin Efendi to pass the message on via his wife without giving away his name. Much better if the girl discovers it for herself. But did the fact that she had a pedigree mean she had more to lose? Or did it give her the useful aura of respectability? And then there was the question: when she knows who I am, will she be sympathetic?

The answer came on a saucer. The *lokum* was more than İsmet had hoped for. Pistachio crammed and meltingly chewy, it also told him she knew who he was and that she approved. And then when other delightful accompaniments to the coffee followed, he deduced that she must have her father's backing. With this, İsmet spoiled his run of good guesses. The family didn't exactly conspire to keep its figurehead in the dark about the prisoner's identity, but they knew it would worry him. So Jafar did not pass *Dear Yazmira* on to his brother. Besides, all Mahmoud ever read was the cartoon page in the newspaper. He'd stopped looking at the sports pages when his record-breaking triumphs no longer dominated them. It wasn't so much wounded vanity, as the fact that he'd moved on. Now he was strictly ornamental, and that was a full-time occupation. It required taking great care of one's appearance, accepting a lot of flattery, smiling, drinking coffee and staying above the commonplace. In that last sense, Mahmoud the Runner had never really got down from the winner's dais.

İsmet was wrong about the father, but it didn't matter. It was the daughter who was critical. He had to make her trust him. Not just trust, but invest in him so that his proposition, when it came, would have the greatest chance of being accepted. She would need to be steely, cool and brave. Absolutely discreet. And with more than her fair share of luck. But before all that would be put to the test, he had to pull off a daunting trick. It would be a bit like directing a film in which the actors have no idea they are in a film. He would have to so engineer his meetings with Saljan that they submerged themselves into the commonplace life of the prison. From being unusual events – the cause after all of a near, albeit fictitious, riot – they would have to become utterly unremarkable. İsmet would have to create a norm so unchangingly dull that it would totally camouflage the smuggling out of his next and possibly last great work.

Initially Saljan suspected İsmet was up to something, although she didn't know what. Then, as uneventful Monday succeeded uneventful Monday, she realised she'd been mistaken. All he wanted was a cup of coffee and a chat. Having decided this, she started to relax, which was part of İsmet's plan. He and Saljan would talk banalities while the guards progressively lost interest in them. Changes would only be made incrementally. For example, İsmet realised that the more relaxed he and Saljan looked from where the guards sat, the less it would seem as if they were conspiring. So, one day before she arrived, İsmet arranged his cell so that he could sit on his bed, and she could sit on the one chair. The gaolers noted and approved; not fair to keep the girl on her feet. Nothing to worry about. But they remained watchful.

One guard was particularly vigilant: Şevket the Bald, who more often than not brought Saljan up from the screening area. He felt responsible for her. He suspected the man in solitary not of subversion but lust, and he didn't want to be delivering her into the clutches of an old goat. Not just because of who she was, but she being so innocent and pure looking. The Pasha's orders were to make sure nothing passed between prisoner and coffee house girl, and Şevket had come to the conclusion that the only risk of this was from him trying to grope her. As long as they sat apart with the door open, all was well.

The cell door was a tricky element in the scenario İsmet was creating. It would obviously have been much easier if the guards simply closed it and left him and Saljan to their devices. But that was never going to happen, and the door was too heavy to swing shut by itself. The plan would have to be constructed around the door remaining wide open. It wasn't perhaps so much like directing a film as performing a conjuring trick. One of those where the magician comes right up to your dining table and produces a live white goose from under a napkin before your very eyes. Except in this case, İsmet would have to make the goose disappear. And unlike film directing – which he'd done, albeit not actually in person for two decades - İsmet had never been a conjuror.

It would definitely require sleight of hand. For the plan to work, something had to pass from him to her. Or rather, from her to him and back again. She would have to bring him in pencils and paper; giving him a sheet one Monday for him to fill up on both sides during the week, so that the next Monday she'd swap it for another fresh sheet. And again, and again, and again. Maybe fifty pages in total. Given that his deal with the Pasha was for one year of coffee, they'd have to start very soon or they'd run out of time. He didn't have a clue how they were going to make the exchanges without being seen. But he'd started to work out how to smuggle the paper in and out.

Saljan's gleaming tray had caught his eye as a possible hiding-place the first time she'd brought him coffee. The next time, he realised something about it didn't add up. The items on the tray seemed to stand higher off the table than the thickness of the copper sheet that formed its base. The cups from Mahmoud's Coffee House had gold circles running round them. When İsmet idly placed one by the tray's edge, he could see that the tray top was level with the second ring. And the second ring was nearly two centimetres above the table. It looked as if, for some purpose İsmet couldn't guess, the tray had a false bottom.

And then, the day he had steeled himself to risk all and ask the girl as quietly as he could if she would help him, she brought him a saucer of quince. When he first saw the two crescent moons in a tiny puddle of syrup he wondered fleetingly if they could possibly be slices of persimmon, or poached sand pear. But then he lifted the saucer to his nose, and the smell yanked him back to childhood. Gathering the windfalls while Baba worked the lower branches. Carrying the baskets into the kitchen, but keeping the best and the biggest out on the table, ready for the final judging. Following Baba around the tree as he attacked the tenacious ones high up – the unbiddable ones that resisted branch-shaking and thrown sticks. Then İsçik would have to watch his head as Baba toppled them with the picker he had made by tying an old knife to the end of a pole, with a net slung below that missed as often as it saved. The boy would try to catch them himself, and they were always honoured with their own pile on the table.

Meanwhile Maman would be doing the dull bit: the peeling, coring and slicing. But then, when the harvest was declared over, she would come outside, her apron stained as if she had been applying gold leaf to some great dome. Then the three of them would vote for the winners in six different categories: the biggest; the smallest one with the finest leaves; the one with the fluffiest down; the finest of those İsmet managed to catch; the most heavily scented, and the overall champion, defined by Maman as the one Paul Cézanne himself would have chosen for a still life. These six would not go the way of the herd, but would remain intact and glowing in the bowl on the kitchen table, filling the air with their unique perfume.

İsçik loved the next bit: warming up from the garden's chill on a stool by the kitchen range while Maman poured a cascade of sugar over the fruit, and added twists of lemon peel, a cinnamon stick and half a dozen cloves. Then they'd toast the harvest with wine for her and Baba, and blackcurrant juice for İsçik. Over supper they'd regale Maman with tales of quinces caught and missed, of wounds received, of branches wiggled and recalcitrant fruits brought to heel. Lastly, before bed, İsçik would be allowed to stir the huge saucepan. It was like being a alchemist, with a whole cauldron full of priceless, bubbling pink gold.

They never managed to pick all the quinces from the tree. After Baba and Maman died, and the house and the garden and the quince tree were his, he wondered if Baba used to leave the lingerers behind on purpose, the way farmers keep back seed corn. Or perhaps as sentinels to delay the onset of winter. Whatever the reason, İsmet would look out from his bedroom window the evening of the harvest and always see a couple they'd missed, hidden from below by the clustering leaves. Sometimes, days later, he'd be playing in the bushes on the far side of the garden and he'd notice another, gleaming like a defiant dwarf sun. Out would come the long pole and another chance of a catch. Then there'd be the one which suddenly appeared on the ground weeks later, finally fallen. In İsmet's mind these were always the real winners: the bruised survivors who'd clung on alone.

He lowered the saucer from his nose, and instead of taking the bold initiative to recruit Saljan, he fell apart. She left him with lips clenched white and tears rolling ever so slowly down his cheeks. Next week she steered off fruit and brought him in three squares of almond paste, but he didn't get a chance to eat those because of the riot. And this time it was a real riot. The guard on İsmet's corridor was sitting as usual with Şevket the Bald, working one another up over the heartless inadequacy of the prison service pension, when they heard a clamour in the distance and then the alarm bells all around them. The phone rang at the guard's station and the next thing

Saljan knew, the cell door was slammed shut and the key turned. She reached the Judas hole in time to see the two guards haring off to join the mêlée. She was locked in.

She wasn't aware of it, but she looked petrified as she turned away from the door. She could see the shock in İsmet's eyes at the fright in hers. He suggested they both sit down and wait it out. He reassured her that she was in the safest place she could be, which was why Şevket had locked her in there. The guards would come for her only when it was absolutely safe to move her out. So there they sat, on either side of the plain wooden table, with the tray between them. He had a sip of the coffee, she had a sip of the water. They didn't touch the almond paste, in case the riot went on for days. He said he had a cucumber and a bit of smoked sausage somewhere, but Saljan said she rather hoped it wouldn't come to that.

And then, realising the chance might never come again, İsmet seized the moment. He told Saljan he needed her help. He had an idea for a film, but the only way to get it made would be if he could smuggle the script out of the prison. And she was his best hope of doing that.

So her original instinct had been right. The old man in the cell was up to something. And it was something that would put her at considerable risk. She should tell him to get lost. But instead, for some reason that had something to do with *Dear Yazmira* and something to do with the gentleness in his eyes, she heard herself saying instead:

'How big is this script?'

She couldn't quite believe she had asked that, but his answer was even more surprising.

'I don't know – I haven't written it yet.'

He had the script in his mind, but he had no paper, nothing to write with. She would have to bring it all in, and take it all out again – a sheet at a time. He would fill a page between Mondays, when they'd make the exchange. Somehow.

Saljan wrinkled her nose.

'You haven't really got this worked out, have you?'

He had to admit that some of the details were still a little sketchy. He was, he said, waiting for her input. And where, exactly, did he suppose she would be able to hide all this where it would not be discovered? Because although she'd not been searched thoroughly so far, it must only be a matter of time. There were female guards in the screening area who conducted body searches on the visiting wives, mothers, daughters and girlfriends.

'I was thinking about your…your tray.'

Saljan tensed a fraction.

'You see, I've been looking at it during your visits…' he went on, trying to ignore the fact that her eyes had narrowed. '…and the base seems to be a shade…er…thicker than it needs to be. A bit deeper. I don't know if you've noticed this. Only I've been wondering if, by chance, it might in fact be hollow…'

İsmet's voice tailed away. She looked distinctly unamused. The din of rioting seemed to have abated a little. The guards might return at any moment. He drew breath, and carried on.

'If I'm right, then wouldn't that make the perfect hiding place? You don't mind if I have a look, do you?'

But as he was reaching forward to turn the tray over, her hand slammed down on the cap.

'A thing may be hollow, but it doesn't mean it's empty. It doesn't mean it's not being used.'

Her huge black eyes were flashing. She really was quite daunting. İsmet sank back onto the bed. Impasse.

They sat motionless and wordless. The riot took on a new lease of life. İsmet racked his brains, trying to work out what on earth the base of a coffee tray could be filled with. Saljan, meanwhile, reviewed the situation. It was one thing the old man wanting her to risk her freedom getting caught smuggling stuff in and out of a prison. Monkeying around with her tray was another thing altogether. Apart from anything else, Beyrek the Coppersmith had soldered the little filler cap up, so if the guards ever did turn the tray over in a routine search, they might realise it had a secret compartment but they'd know it wasn't something she had access to. If Beyrek removed the solder so she could stuff paper and pencils in there, then the guards would just undo the cap themselves and she'd be for it. She thought about having to take out all that precious mercury and those tiny baffles to make room for the old man's script. The words "diabolical liberty" came to mind. She wasn't about to sacrifice her tray's performance, her own competitive edge in the cut-throat world of coffee delivery, for anyone's creative ambitions. Even a man with eyes like conkers.

'I am sorry, Saljan. Forget I said anything. I've really come to look forward to our meetings. The coffee. The little somethings on the saucer. Our chats. It's perfectly true I engineered the whole thing because I thought it would give me a chance to get the script out, but I now realise that it's not worth jeopardising your safety and our Mondays.'

Conkers be blowed. Saljan wasn't having any of that.

'But it isn't really up to you, is it, Turali Efendi? As long as I don't give you access to any secret compartments I may have, then there's nothing for you to jeopardise.'

He now looked really rather miserable. As much to cheer him up as anything, she reached into her purse and, glancing at the Judas window to make sure they were not being watched, handed him the stump of a pencil. His eyes widened. He hadn't seen a pencil for years. Not since the Pasha became Governor. It was, at that moment, the most precious thing she could have given him. He held it, as you would a new-born chick. And then he handed it back.

Now it was her turn to look surprised.

'The riot will end, Saljan, and they'll come for you. After you've gone, they'll strip search me and turn the cell upside down. Almost certainly you'll also be given a full body search. If they found your pencil in my possession, you'd be in big trouble and we'd never be allowed to meet again. No more coffees, no more *halva*, no more happy moments in my life. But if they find your pencil still in your possession, then they'll be convinced our meetings are utterly innocent. And we'll be perfectly free to carry on as we have been.'

She removed her hand from the tray and sat back in the chair. The old man was certainly no fool. And she had to admit that she too enjoyed their time together. He seemed interested in her without being seedy. And that book of his showed his heart was definitely in the right place. But there was nothing much more she could do for him.

İsmet was thinking pretty much the same thing, and decided to normalise the situation. There was, he said making conversation, something else he'd noticed. When she first visited him, she'd had lots of other drinks on her tray. Now she just had what she was bringing him. Yes, she said. She had started off trying to fit the prison run into her other deliveries, but stuff had got cold and ice had melted and customers had complained. Quite rightly. They had decided to separate his coffee from the rest. That first tray was pretty full, he remarked. He had been surprised. That's nothing, she replied. Sometimes she had a dozen places to deliver to. Isn't it difficult, he asked, remembering where it's all got to go?

'I didn't see any piece of paper on your tray saying who was expecting what. As you can imagine, I notice paper these days.'

They both smiled. No, she never wrote anything down. She never used that pencil. She just remembered what she was told. İsmet nodded politely and said it was starting to sound a bit quieter out there and they'd probably come for her soon. They must be worrying about her at the coffee house…

But she wasn't listening to a word he said. At least, she wasn't listening to a word he was saying now. She was listening, in her mind, to something he had said weeks before. And, having heard it again, she closed her eyes and said it out loud.

' "I remember seeing him at the athletics track. It must have been at least thirty years ago. The university turned out the best it had, but he left them all standing. In fact from where I was, it actually looked as if the others were running backwards. He can't have been more than twelve. I'd never been particularly interested in athletics – football was more my sport – and then I saw your father flying round the track. I don't know…it was like seeing an apparition. Something almost supernatural. But when he reached the finishing line, and looked back and saw the rest miles behind, puffing along, he just gave this huge grin. He became a kid again. It was lovely." '

It took İsmet a minute or so before he could understand what she'd just done, and to get his breath back. And then they heard the guards approaching. They only had seconds. Best not be heard whispering.

'So, Saljan,' he said in normal tones as Şevket's bald head filled the Judas hole, and the key turned in the lock. 'You'll remember what I say?'

'Every word, Turali Efendi' she replied, with the same winning grin İsmet had seen lighten her father's face thirty years before.

And she was gone.

***

What with the royal going-over the guards gave his cell, and a summons from the Pasha, İsmet was given no chance to think about his script for days. The meeting with the Pasha was an odd one, because for the second time in twenty-four hours, he was offered a pencil.

'Not to keep, İsmet Efendi. You'll have to jot it all down here, I'm afraid. Can't take any risks with a man of your conviction - so to say. Ha!'

As usual the Pasha laughed loudly at his own joke and as usual İsmet politely kept him company. But he had absolutely no intention of doing what was being asked of him.

Apparently the World Film Institute in Geneva had sent a request to the State Film Studios, which they had passed on to the Department of Penal Correction which forwarded it to the Pasha. The WFI was updating its records and, "given the unique significance to world cinema of İsmet Turali's remarkable films with their unerring sense of humanity and their luminous mastery of genres commercial and artistic, popular and political", had decided to make him the inaugural recipient of their new and ever-so grand lifetime award. In order to ensure the absolute accuracy of the citation, they would need a comprehensive filmography for him. The Minister of Culture himself had been consulted, and approval given for Prisoner Turali to comply with this important request – the security aspects being left to Governor Osman Reşid – the Pasha.

'See, my old friend? I've cleared a space for you on my own desk, and put out exactly ten sheets of paper and one pencil. Together with a questionnaire from the WFI for you to use as a template. I'll just sit over here and get on with my work.'

The Pasha took his newspaper to the easy chair by the window, while İsmet sat at his desk and wondered which bit of this, if any, did not stink to high heaven. The WFI questionnaire looked genuine enough. The route by which it had reached him was, however, suspicious. İsmet's address was given as c/o The State Film Studios… which meant that it was bound to have been through the manicured hands of Talya Begüm Demir, and she did not wish him well. Then there was the approval of the Culture Minister. That old rogue positively hated him, and his xenophobia was legendary. Why would he want to help an international organization honour one of his prize bêtes noires?

And then there was the questionnaire itself. It asked for full details of production dates, running times, synopses, versions, alternate titles, full cast and crew lists, principal locations, budgets, schedules, cross-plots, music, music cue-sheets, contracts, clearances, insurances, waivers, indemnities, financing, completion guarantees, distributors, box office receipts, credits, awards. Then, as if all that was not enough, it wanted to know what archival arrangements were in place for cut negatives, dupe negs, CRIs, director's cuts, show prints, digital masters, scripts, subtitle texts, post-production scripts, trailers and publicity materials. What was ultimately and terminally suspicious about all this, İsmet decided, was not the request from the WFI itself, but the fact that the State authorities wanted him to fulfil it. And the reason for that, he deduced, was buried deep in the questionnaire, contained in the innocuous phrase: "crew lists".

The years may have passed, but the organs of State Security had lost none of their curiosity about the identity of İsmet's secret collaborators. They had even considered inviting him to make a Steppe Western or two from behind bars in the hope that he would stick to his old, clandestine network because it had already proved itself more than capable of proxy film production. Then all the secret police need to have done was pitch up and arrest the cameraman puppet and the puppets of make-up and costume and all the other movie-making marionettes whose strings somehow led into the cell of Turali Efendi, where he lay on his bed, pulling them and twisting them - all the while laughing at the pygmies who sought to stem his creative flood. That was how the great and the good in the Ministry of Internal Affairs saw it. It was not İsmet's view of things.

Nothing kept him so awake at night nor so often, as worrying if Murat and Reyhan were safe, along with all the people whose names he did not, and perhaps would never know. Not just skilled crew-members but people who slipped pages of script and schedule under doors at dead of night. Who processed precious rushes on the graveyard shift in the film laboratories. Who midwived and suckled İsmet's babies from idea to birth to maturity. Without, as the film industry would say, credits. So when a raft of his opponents wanted him to satisfy a third party request to supply, *inter alia*, the names of all these up-till-now unknown people, İsmet smelled a giant, stinking rat.

'Well, İsmet Efendi? How are we doing?'

The Pasha spoke with a schoolmaster's hint of tetchiness. Interesting, thought İsmet: if the regime really had no special interest in the WFI request, then why the irritation? Receiving no answer the Pasha lowered the newspaper to find the ten sheets of paper still virginal, the pencil where he had left it, and İsmet standing by the door. The Pasha's circumflex eyebrows reconfigured themselves into question marks.

'I can't help these people in Geneva, Reşid Bey. Sorry.'

The Pasha was a little peeved with himself for allowing that note of impatience to creep in. But he was too cunning to allow his voice to register disappointment now.

'No matter, no matter, my old friend. But if you should ever change your mind, I will be happy to act as simple intermediary.'

The Pasha smiled his serpent smile and pressed the buzzer to summon the guard.

'By the by, İsmet Efendi, how are you getting on with my little speech?'

'Oh, I think it's extremely good, Reşid Bey. Very well written, and so very well informed.' He had not, of course, read a word of it yet, otherwise he would not have been able to lie so well. 'I'm hardly having to do anything to it. Just a tiny scrub here and a polish there…'

'And the coffee? That's all going well?'

'Very much so', İsmet reassured him. 'Thank you'.

'Young Saljan seems a responsible young woman', the Pasha went on, the surveillance camera footage of her strip-search fresh in his mind. 'I know her father, of course. I might ask him in, one day, to talk to you chaps about the art of winning…'

At which point the guard arrived to escort İsmet back to the simplicity of solitary confinement. He now had just four clear days before Saljan showed up again, swinging her tray into his cell, thirsty to sponge up his new script with her extraordinary memory. The script İsmet had been thinking about for twenty years but which he would have to tell Saljan in the time it takes to drink forty seven cups of coffee.

Chapter Eleven

The idea had crept up on İsmet in the prison where Talya Begüm Demir had visited him, where he met the three Politans, and where his cell-mate Farouk the Forger wisely suggested he try a little letter-writing to take his mind off things. Working with Kerem gave İsmet human contact and new purpose. His life slipped into a more settled routine. He did his shifts in the kitchens. He paid a call on Sıtkı the clerk once a week. And he saw the three Politans. Occasionally, when the rota permitted, he'd join them at mealtimes. More often he would meet them in the exercise yard: the Mufti of Naples – Neapolitan - jogging. The Chief Rabbi of Bessarabia – Cosmopolitan - strolling. The Patriarch of Aleppo – Metropolitan - sitting in the sunlight. And they talked. After a while, İsmet heard something in their talk which intrigued him.

It wasn't that, up till then, he had found them dull. They weren't. But they were not always easy to understand. Much of their discussion concerned the abstruse and discordant theologies of three religions. True, they had a lot in common: monotheism, Moses, Abraham, Ishmael and Isaac. Mary and Jesus featured in the Qur'ān. Indeed, the Archangel Gabriel who had announced to Mary that she would bear the Son of God, had also appeared to the Prophet and revealed the Holy Qur'ān to him. But the shared factors provoked as much as they united. Occasionally the Chief Rabbi would roll his eyes at İsmet, which İsmet took as meaning "what are these two on about?" only to find Cosmopolitan following his look with some quiet remark to stop Metropolitan and Neapolitan in their tracks and send them into arcane, nitpicking argument.

İsmet, ever a listener rather than a talker in their company, would try to keep up, but it was a bit like his occasional runs with Kerem: fine for a lap but not much more. Then, early one evening in their cell over a card game, the three Politans started to talk about something İsmet had no difficulty understanding, and about which he was curious to know more. It began with a chance remark by Cosmopolitan while he was shuffling the pack. He said that whenever he read the New Testament, which he now did rarely but very carefully, he never understood how Jesus could treat his own mother so badly. Perhaps it wasn't so surprising, if we think how impatient we can so often be with our own mothers. And we don't have the excuse that we are redeeming the human race. But, even so, he wasn't at all nice to her.

A pained look flickered across Metropolitan's brow. Neapolitan looked puzzled and cut the deck. İsmet - surprised - dealt and listened. Cosmopolitan saw the Patriarch's evident distress, and apologised for raising the subject. No offence at all, Metropolitan replied, arranging his hand. It is not a new thought. Maybe not, thought İsmet, but it looked as if it still had the power to wound. They played a round or two. Neapolitan won the first. İsmet the second. The others seemed to have lost a little concentration. Cosmopolitan had to be reminded which suit was trumps, and Metropolitan trumped his partner's ace. Then it was İsmet's turn to shuffle. Neapolitan got up to make some more tea. What exactly, Metropolitan asked Cosmopolitan as casually as he could, did you have in mind?

The Chief Rabbi of Bessarabia rocked back in his chair. It was difficult to know where to start, he said. Hard to think of any communications between mother and son that do not have an edge – on his part. But if the Patriarch of Aleppo wanted specific examples, how about the wedding at Cana in John's Gospel? To the best of his recollection it went something like:

> "On the third day there was a marriage at Cana in Galilee, and the mother of Jesus was there; Jesus also was invited to the marriage, with his disciples. When the wine failed, the mother of Jesus said to him, 'They have no wine.' And Jesus said to her, 'O woman, what have you to do with me? My hour has not yet come."

İsmet stole a glance at Metropolitan. The old gentleman had removed his glasses and was cleaning them on his shirt cuff. He looked a little vulnerable. But when he spoke, it was with Socratic authority and method.

'And how do you read this and the other Mary-Jesus exchanges? How should we, do you think, understand them in the light of Jesus's dual divine and human identities? How do they help us answer the question posed by the pre-Cyril theologians of Alexandria: "Did the Word of God die on the cross?" What light do they cast upon the *Theotokos* argument? Have you considered the teaching of Severus of Antioch on the mother-son dialogue at Cana? And how viable is it, do you think, to extrapolate Jesus's private feelings for his own mother from public statements in which he is teaching, leading, winning over the masses? Do you see those as normal filial duties? Or are you saying that Jesus must be a son to his mother, but a Father to everyone else? Are you – either as a man of faith or as a son yourself, Josef - being entirely fair?'

Metropolitan slipped his glasses back on his nose. It was Cosmopolitan for whom İsmet now felt sorry. Then three things happened at once. Neapolitan returned with the tea. Cosmopolitan brought his chair back to earth with a clunk. And the first buzzer went. No question of drinking tea or finishing the game, let alone hearing the Chief Rabbi's answer. İsmet barely had time to borrow a Christian Bible from Metropolitan and say goodnight before hurrying away, the lock-up warning buzzer screaming in his ears.

İsmet reached his cell just as the second buzzer went. He had the place to himself; it was the evening Farouk the Forger had a ticket of leave to teach a class on Safavid art to students at the local college. He lay on his bed with a crust of bread he had brought up from the kitchens and started to read the Gospels.

In retrospect, İsmet would have renounced all he knew about his parents' sex life in exchange for a single definite clue about what they believed in. He certainly had memories of praying with his father, and of the family fasting during Ramadan. He had no idea if Baba paid *zakat*. As a young man he had apparently gone to Mecca on *hajj* with his own father who was very devout. Indeed, it was Old Baba who had whispered *shadada* into the tiny soft folds of İsmet's ear shortly after he drew his first breath: *"There is no god except Allah, and Muhammad is the prophet of Allah."*

For her part, Maman went to Midnight Mass, and helped with the tiny Roman Catholic congregation's church bazaar when cornered. And he remembered as a boy going with her and his French grandparents, Maminou and Gran'papa to the little wooden church in the Doubs to celebrate Lady Day - what Maminou called *L'Annonce Faite à Marie*. It was the coldest he could ever remember being in his entire life. He sat on his hands to keep them warm and to soften the effects of hardwood pew under skinny bottom. The odd thing was it looked as if it should have been warm in there, what with the steam issuing from the mouths of the congregation as they sang and smoke pouring from something swung on chains by a red-headed priest around the gilt statue of a young woman. She, alone, was glowing. From the expression on her face she looked as if she was humbly accepting some huge prize. İsmet had no real idea who she was, beyond the fact that her name was Marie, and she was the mother of the dead man on a cross opposite her. The man was carved out of wood and polished, but he had what looked like real blood pouring from a gaping wound in his side. İsmet couldn't look at this man; he was so frightening. And why wasn't his own mother trying to help him? How could she look so calm? Every now and then Maminou would catch his eye with a look that said "isn't all this wonderful fun?" İsmet tried to smile back at her, but his face was too frozen to remember how.

It was a shame, because the day had started well. Gran'papa had woken him before sunrise, tickling his cheek with his moustache and, wrapping him in a blanket, had led him to the window. The stars shone clear against the lightening sky. 'You see,' the old man had said, eyes agleam. '*Vraiment Notre Dame de prospérité*! It'll be a good year, P'tit Ischou. We'll get a little row of vines in, you and me, when we get back from church. That'll give us something to drink together when you get a bit older.' Unfortunately, Gran'papa was on the far side of the aisle for the service, otherwise İsmet would have taken shelter under his army greatcoat, with its smells of tobacco and hay. After lunch he sat on the window-seat and watched Gran'papa attacking the soil with his old entrenching tool the way he had once laid into *Les Fridolins*. He longed to help him but Maman and

Maminou said it was far too cold for a child to be outside, although it felt warmer to İsmet on that sun-glanced hillside than in the icebox where they had spent the entire morning.

At bedtime Maminou supervised his prayers. İsmet was blessed with a seriousness which made it all look very convincing. But he was only doing it to please. Maman would watch from the doorway, with an expression of concern. The same face she had when she took him to the doctor. Her 'don't hurt my little boy' face.

So religion in his family was observed – to an extent - but İsmet had no idea if it was felt. If it was lived. And then, when he thought really hard about it, the picture that came into his mind was of praying with Baba in the library with everyone else, never in the privacy of home. He could not remember saying grace before Maman's meals as they had done the month they spent – without Baba - in the smoky old French farmhouse. At first İsmet was bewildered when, on the happy brink of tucking into potage santé – leeks, potatoes, sorrel, butter, broth, egg yolks, cream - and *pain au levain* hot from the bread oven, everyone instead broke into sombre murmurs. By the end he was expected to say grace loud and clear and all by himself, albeit with Gran'papa mouthing it at him, hand cupped so Maminou couldn't see. Lying on his prison bunk, İsmet could still see the miming moustache. Still remember the words:

> Béni soit le Seigneur,
> pour le moment de ce repas,
> pour la joie d'être ensemble à partager le même pain.
> Rendons grâce à Dieu.

Looking back, İsmet realised that in those days a three-way tug of war was being waged over his soul. Maminou had decided he was being brought up a heathen, and determined to use the little time she had with him to secure his salvation through Christ. Baba's father took the same view – only he thought it was the French lot who were the heathens - and did all he could to make a good Muslim out of İsçik. But there was a third force at play: a rational agnosticism in the ether at home. Unlike the other two, it wasn't rammed down his throat; it didn't shape his little hands in prayer. It didn't bid him kneel, or fast, or serve. And its very passivity may have given it the winning edge.

Up to that point when he started to read Metropolitan's Bible, most of what İsmet knew about Mary the mother of Jesus came from the Qur'ān rather than the Gospels - which was why Cosmopolitan's remarks surprised him. Because, as he remembered from Hoja Yıldız's crammed, baking schoolroom, the Qur'ān was unfailingly respectful of Mary, mother of Jesus. The Hoja told them a story from the Hadīth – the collection of the Prophet's sayings and actions – which gave a definitive picture of her prominence. One day, Muhammad summoned his favourite daughter Fātima and said something which made her cry, and then something which made her laugh. After Muhammad's death, she was asked what the weeping and the laughing had been about. Fātima replied that God's Messenger had told her he was going to die, so she wept. Then he told her that, apart from Mary, she would be the most important woman in paradise. At that, his daughter laughed in happiness.

So İsmet settled back to see what the Testament of Mary's own son made of her. And the more he read, the more surprised he was. Cosmopolitan had been right. According to the Gospel writers, Jesus never had a kind word to say to his mother. Even Luke, who seemed to İsmet to have been sympathetic to Mary, described Jesus snubbing a woman who publicly praised his mother:

> "…a woman in the crowd raised her voice and said to him, 'Blessed is the womb that bore you and the breasts that you sucked!' But he said, 'Blessed rather are those who hear the word of God and keep it!'"

And then there were his words to another multitude:

> "If any one comes to me and does not hate his own father and mother and wife and children and brothers and sisters, yes, and even his own life, he cannot be my disciple."

At which point Farouk the Forger was returned to the cell. He waited till the prison officer's footsteps had died away, before giving İsmet an orange and a handful of plump raisins. At first he wasn't sure why Farouk had agreed to do the teaching; he would find it unnerving to be allowed out but have to return to gaol. Then Farouk began bringing back tastes of outside and it started to make sense. The week before he had smuggled in a small jar of rakı. But İsmet wasn't sure he didn't prefer the fruit. He lay back on his bunk with the orange peel like a moustache under his nose. He would go to sleep smelling sunshine.

Somewhere in all this Mary stuff was an extraordinary, untold story. A story as much about real people, as about remote divinities. The Politans would have the answers. But one at a time or they'd go into their private language. He'd start tomorrow.

***

İsmet was up early. He was on the breakfast shift in the kitchens, so he had several hours of mindless washing-up in which to work out the best order in which to see the Politans. He decided early on he would leave Metropolitan till last. That way he could put the questions raised by the other two to His Eminence the Patriarch of Aleppo. It made sense to start with Cosmopolitan, because Mary may have been Jewish, but the Old Testament stopped long before she showed up. Arguably the Chief Rabbi had already performed his most useful service by setting the ball rolling and presumably had little more to offer. İsmet considered not troubling him, but thought he might be offended when he realised İsmet had spoken to the other two and had left him out. So get him over and done with first. That left Neapolitan in second place, which made good sense. Mary was a conspicuous figure in the Qur'ān with a Sūra named after her, and the Mufti of Naples might have some useful insights from the Islamic perspective. Of course he could always go back to any of them later for more information, but it was always good to start with a plan.

In the event, the plan stood no chance against chance itself.

When İsmet went into the exercise yard, the only Politan in sight was Metro. He was sitting on the far side on his usual bench in a splash of sunlight. İsmet could hardly ignore him, even though he was literally the last of the three he wanted to see. And yet as he drew nearer he realised he hadn't been seen; the old churchman's eyes were closed. In thought? In prayer? In sleep? Perhaps İsmet should turn on his heels and leave him in peace. He slowed, but did not retreat. There was something about the face of the Patriarch of Aleppo that he found compelling. It had a simple openness that suggested power, not vulnerability, as if he calmly accepted the consequences of his actions, driven as they were by unswerving conviction. It was like looking into the face of a saint.

'İsmet, my young friend. I'm sorry, I had no idea you were with me - how long have you been there?'

İsmet told him he had only just sat down. Metropolitan smiled and looked around. It was such a beautiful day, wasn't it? Given the time İsmet had just spent in the cockroach-infested prison kitchens the thought hadn't occurred to him, but he supposed it was.

'It's sometimes difficult to remember to think that a day is beautiful.' Metropolitan said. 'But it is especially important to in a place like this.'

They watched the prisoners trudging round the yard. Some had a worrying blankness to their faces. Up on the balconies of their watch-towers the guards smoked and spat.

'How you must regret the day you came to this country.'

Metropolitan shook his head. He had spent enough of his life in the safety of churches and monasteries. He now knew that a priest's place was as much behind bars as in front of an altar. Did İsmet know what he had been thinking about? Ah! He could see that İsmet assumed he was asleep. No, he had been thinking about hell. Metropolitan had spent most of his life thinking about hell, and this spell in prison was very useful. It was giving him first-hand experience of punishment, retribution, repentance, the reformation of some souls, the difficulty of cleansing others, the despair born of hopelessness, the terrible pain of loss, the cruelty of devils.

Before his time in gaol, he had been so curious to see if hell was as he'd come to imagine it after half a century of study and thought, that he had started to wonder how small a wrong would be needed to consign him for the briefest possible spell to Purgatory. Indeed, might this curiosity itself with its attendant hubris constitute sufficient sin? But how much of the rest of hell can be seen from Purgatory? It would be a terrible thing to commit oneself to all that tribulation for the faint smell of sulphur coming up from a vent. The alternative was to live as devout and sin-free a life as he could, and hope that if granted admittance to heaven he might be allowed to absent himself from the beatific vision long enough to make a brief research trip below.

'That would indeed be fascinating,' İsmet said, 'but it might be an idea before you go to make sure you have full diplomatic immunity and an open return ticket.'

The older man grinned and nodded slowly.

'Thank you, my dear young friend. I hope, in all the excitement, I shall remember your wise advice.'

They sat in silence for a moment or two, and then Metropolitan started to talk to İsmet about a prisoner who had been coming to him for confession and pastoral care. Well, the other day this prisoner had invited Metropolitan to accompany him at visiting time to meet his family. He had happily consented and he and the family had stood together, as together as the ceiling to floor grille between them would allow, to say a prayer or two and receive a blessing. The man himself, his wife - and their baby.

Metropolitan was deeply shocked to see a baby inside a prison. He hoped he hadn't shown it. He didn't think he had. But it made him very sad, and a little angry. İsmet wasn't sure why he was angry. Surely it was better to let the man see his baby? It might give him some purpose, some hope. And the baby would have no memory of seeing his father in gaol, assuming the man's sentence wasn't too long. Metropolitan shook his head. He hadn't been cross with the wife for bringing her baby in, or with the prison, or with the man for getting himself into trouble. He was cross with the Roman Catholic Church. İsmet looked puzzled, and Metropolitan explained.

'The week before I received the Bishop's invitation to come here, I was in Rome to address a papal commission which had been convened by Pope Pius XII in 1946 and whose successors are still deliberating the question of what happens to the souls of babies who die before they are baptized. You see, İsmet, the Catholic Church believes that without baptism there is no admission to heaven. It holds that these poor dead babies are sent instead to a place on the edge of hell they call the Limbo of Infants. We in the Orthodox Church of the Levant do not believe that there is such a place, and I personally do not believe our Lord God would so penalise unbaptized babies. If our beliefs do not accord with what we know of God's grace and mercy, then – I told our cousins in Rome - the burden is on us to revise our beliefs. And we cannot allow a grief-stricken mother burying her baby to think the little mite will be denied the beatitude of heaven for the want of a few words from some priest and a drop or two of water. I told the Cardinals that there is much that has not been, and may never be, revealed to us. But that does not give us the right or the excuse to make it up.'

The whistle blew. End of exercise time. İsmet helped the Patriarch of Aleppo to his feet and gave him his arm to walk him back to Cell 677. It took a while not just because the old man was a little unsteady on his legs, but because he had more to tell İsmet. And oddly, it reopened the subject which İsmet had been wanting to discuss with Metropolitan, only preferably not yet. He had, he feared, responded a little robustly the other evening to his friend and brother in God, the Chief Rabbi.

'Josef was, in many ways, right. The Gospels do not depict Jesus as a loving son. Worldly concerns, family ties - everything takes second place to His mission. We are perhaps surprised that He is impatient with His mother because of what Mary became over the subsequent millennia. We do not understand how He can be curt with the very embodiment of goodness and purity, the benchmark of humility and devotion for Christians and Muslims. But this Mary, this "Mother of the Church", this "Mother of God" is largely man-made. And the work started almost immediately. What Josef said to us the other night about how Jesus treated her, the Fathers of the Church saw in their time and it didn't suit them. Nor were they comfortable with the idea that Christ was born to anyone other than a virgin free of the taint of sin. The work of back-tracking, revising and adding to her persona and rôle began while the Gospel writers' ink was still wet.'

By the time they reached the cell door, Metropolitan was tired. He decided he would like to rest on his bunk a little. İsmet helped him off with his shoes and settled him in. But the old priest's mind was still racing.

'My guess is that the real Mary was more interesting, more extraordinary than the one the world has been at such pains to create on top of those tantalisingly enigmatic foundations in the Gospels. We have come to see her as some kind of spotless receptacle in which to culture divinity. Not surprisingly, since she agreed with the Archangel Gabriel to accept the burden of carrying the Son of God Himself. But for all that perfect trust and submission, she never renounced her human right to worry, to fear, to doubt. Remember Luke, describing the Archangel's visit:

"And Gabriel came to her and said 'Hail, O favoured one, the Lord is with you! Blessed are you among women!' But she was greatly troubled at the saying, and considered in her mind what sort of greeting this might be."

Most important of all - never for one moment did Mary pretend to understand what was going on. This young, uneducated woman knew instinctively what those Cardinals in Rome with two thousand years of sophistication still cannot grasp: that what is beyond understanding is not beyond acceptance and belief.'

There was a long pause, and then Metropolitan thanked İsmet for looking after him, and closed his eyes. İsmet was tiptoeing out of the cell when the Patriarch of Aleppo murmured a last thought.

'Imagine, İsmet: she came to terms with something unimaginable: the realization that her own child would become divine.'

***

Over the following days, İsmet started to sympathize with Mary's reaction on meeting the Archangel Gabriel. He felt puzzled, anxious. He wondered what it all meant. So he tried to take his mind off it. He threw himself into writing Kerem's letters to Yazmira. He twice called on the corpulent clerk Sıtkı. He asked Farouk to teach him how to draw. He did not go looking for Neapolitan or Cosmopolitan. But one day, he returned to his cell after the lunch shift in the kitchens, and there was the Chief Rabbi of Bessarabia, waiting for him.

'Nu, İsmet. You never phone. You never write.'

İsmet made tea, and they talked. Apparently His Eminence had been worrying that he'd bored İsmet with his religious ramblings. He'd asked Cosmopolitan, if he saw İsmet, to apologise to him and to express the hope that he might visit the three of them once again for a game of cards and some strictly secular conversation. This unwarranted apology forced İsmet to confront why he had been avoiding the occupants of Cell 677. It was not out of boredom, nor out of resistance to religiosity, nor out of fear of conversion. It was more like the rearing of a horse being broken. Or the wriggling of a fish when it is hooked. It was a reaction he recognised in himself, after reading a script, but before committing himself. It was the last twist and turn before submission.

Chapter Twelve

Beyrek knew something had changed.

For two weeks running, Saljan had stopped by his smithy after delivering coffee to the man in prison. It was the only time in the week when Jafar didn't fret if she wasn't back promptly, and Beyrek was the delighted beneficiary. He was, of course, besotted with her, and his heart leaped to the rafters the first time she broke her journey from gaol to coffee house to make the detour up the alley. He didn't see her arrive; he had his goggles on, welding a broken axle on the Hoja's mule cart. When a particularly spectacular shower of sparks had cleared, there she was, stretched out on his divan. She had kicked off her trainers, and lay with one endless leg hitched over the back and the other crooked, with bare toes peeking between cushions. Her eyes were closed. The expression on her face was hard to read. It was closer to languor than torpor. A lock of hair had fallen across one eye. Her mouth was very slightly parted with – Beyrek fancied - the tiniest, almost sated smile hovering at its corners.

'I love you, Saljan.'

He didn't mean to say it. He hadn't planned to. He wasn't thinking. It went a great deal further than he intended at this stage. It had crept up on him. He was talking to himself. He was trying it out in his head to see how it sounded. He had been wondering how she would react if he said it, and now he had betrayed himself. Let himself down. Set himself back weeks, maybe months. Perhaps dashed his hopes altogether.

'Do you have a cold drink for me, Beyrek the Coppersmith?'

Saljan spoke without opening those huge eyes like lumps of coal about to catch fire. She spoke as if he had not. As if she were opening the conversation. Maybe she hadn't heard him. Maybe he had only thought it after all. Thank the heavens. It was like being given a second life. He fetched a flagon of Zeki's pomegranate juice from the fridge, poured her a glass, and added ice cubes. He went back and squatted by the divan. She did not stir. He held the glass against her forehead. She gave the tiniest murmur of pleasure, then reached up, took the glass and drank. Her eyes remained shut. She had the longest lashes. And now she had the coolest lips.

Beyrek the Coppersmith forced himself to stand up and walk away. He put the small hearth between himself and the divan. He must get that fire going. It looked almost out. He pumped the bellows till the flames started to revive and then leap. He had absolutely no need for the small hearth, but he had to do something that wouldn't land him in trouble.

'I've been roughly totting up the miles you've done with the tray, Saljan, and I reckon it's probably time for its first service. Nothing major, just a check all round, touch of oil on the loop. Examine the fastenings. Make sure the filler cap is tight. That sort of thing. Don't worry, there'll be no charge. It was built in to the original price.'

'How long will this first service take? I can't afford my tray to be out of commission for any length of time.'

Still the eyes shut.

'If you brought it in this time next week, I could have it done in the time it would take you to lie on my divan and have a glass of pomegranate juice. And some *börek* with stuffed vine-leaves and a little bean *plaki*.'

She smiled again and, opening her eyes, swung her beautiful, rangy body round, sat up and slipped on her trainers. Then she stood and slid around the small hearth and right up to him. He stopped pumping the bellows. Getting the fire going didn't seem particularly important any longer.

'Do you do that for all your customers, Beyrek the Coppersmith? Or only those you love?'

And she was gone.

The next week Saljan brought in the tray for its first service. She lay on the divan, drank icy pomegranate juice and ate the titbits Beyrek had set out on little interlocking blue and white dishes around a vase of wild flowers he'd picked early that morning from the ruins behind the town. He concentrated on the tray and said nothing of his inner feelings. She took pleasure watching him tighten a copper pin and buff out a scratch. He was quick and confident and careful. He gave it a final polish as she swallowed the last golden *börek*. Then, just before slipping into the midday crowd thronging the coppersmiths' alley, she gave him a smile he would remember all the days of his life.

Which was why, the week after that, Beyrek knew something had changed. Because Saljan was not to be seen.

He left it an hour or two, and went next door to see if his neighbour had heard of any trouble at the prison. Old Ragıp had not, and reassured Beyrek that Saljan was more than capable of looking after herself. Beyrek agreed and went back to pummel some brass. Then Old Ragıp started to worry, and sent young Turgut down to ask Zeki at the kiosk outside the prison. Zeki hadn't noticed Saljan arrive but he definitely saw her leave. It was around 11.45am. A racing camel being led to the market had knocked over Pelin the flower seller's stall. Just after that, Zeki noticed Saljan dart round the edge of the gathering crowd and disappear up İskender Street. He assumed she was returning to Mahmoud's Coffee House.

Turgut told Old Ragıp, and Old Ragıp sent the lad straight round to repeat it all to Beyrek. Beyrek then stopped worrying if Saljan was safe, and started worrying if he had done or said anything stupid which might make her avoid him. Then he remembered that last smile, and stopped worrying about her not liking him, and started worrying if Mahmoud the Runner had heard about Beyrek the Coppersmith's interest in his daughter and had laid down the law. He may have slightly over-pummelled the brass as he fretted over this possibility.

Zeki was right. After seeing İsmet, Saljan went straight back to the coffee house. But it was not at her father's insistence. She had told him nothing about Beyrek the Coppersmith, mostly because she hadn't told herself that much about him - yet. But also because she knew that, however her father responded, it would disappoint her. He might mumble some platitude about "that being nice..." or show stupid concerns about social differences. Or he could just not say anything. He certainly wouldn't be genuinely happy for her. Auntie Gül Seren was another matter. She'd be thrilled. She'd hug Saljan, and ask a lot of questions. She would probably start sketching wedding dresses in the corners of the ledger. Saljan wasn't sure about that. She had no thought of marriage, and did not want the enthusiasm or the indifference of others to push her towards it. So, even the little she knew, she kept to herself. The reason she went straight back to the coffee house was that she was carrying something precious she had to keep safe. And loitering around Beyrek's smithy was just the way to lose it.

She had barely sat down after placing the cup of coffee in front of İsmet, before he started talking to her. It took her a moment to realise that it had started: he was dictating his script to her. Except it wasn't exactly dictation, because she wasn't writing anything down – not on paper. His tone was conversational, so as not to alert the guards. She sat on the wooden chair, and tried her best to look relaxed. He sat on the edge of the bed, occasionally leaning forward for a sip of coffee or a taste from that day's saucer: poached pumpkin in tahini syrup with a pinch of finely grated coconut.

Her task was made a little easier because the script was broken up into numbered scenes. The first was set in a small, dusty town on the edge of a desert, a long, long time ago. A girl of about ten is running errands for her mother. Wherever she goes, whatever she does, she is being watched. She buys bread from the baker, and is watched. She stops at a street-seller for some thread and needles, and is watched. You can't see who is watching her, but they can see her. Sometimes many of them. She goes to a small, empty square to draw water from a well, and there are perhaps twenty pairs of eyes on her - with not a person in sight. It feels eerie. Uneasy. But the girl is oblivious. She does what she has been told to do, without loitering or stopping to gossip with friends. She is neither timid nor self-conscious. She has dark hair, and a long straight nose, and oval brown eyes. She wears a faded blue dress, held at the waist with a simple cord belt. Her feet and head are bare. Her name is Mary.

And then the time was up, and Şevket the Bald was escorting her back down to the screening area. They didn't search her, and if they had, they'd have found nothing. It was locked in her memory. But how safely, Saljan wasn't sure. It felt a little precarious. She didn't know if it was better to keep on repeating to herself what İsmet Efendi had just told her, or to make her mind a blank, to block out rival, invasive thoughts. But it was hard to close everything down. She'd already decided to give Beyrek the Coppersmith a miss to reduce distraction, and then she stepped out of the prison into a major scene in the street. An overturned cart. Flowers scattered everywhere, with stems broken and heads crushed. People shouting. Pelin the florist in tears. A huge camel, eyes staring and beads of foam at the mouth, being restrained by several strong youths. The owner of the beast insisting the damage had been done by its hind legs, because that would excuse him from paying reparations. According to custom and rule, only Allah - the Merciful and Compassionate - and the camel itself bear responsibility for what a camel will do with its back half. And no man, of course, can ever hold them to account. 'No, it was the front legs…Pelin must be reimbursed', Saljan heard people call out as she skirted round the throng, wishing she had earplugs.

In the event, she decided to run home as quickly as she could. Faster even than if she were making a delivery. Not to reach pen and paper sooner, but because the faster she ran, the more she could disconnect from the world. Float over it. People who saw her that day said they had never seen her move as fast. Never seen anyone move that fast since her esteemed father hung up his spikes. She saw no onlookers. She was, as ever, unaware of anything or anyone. She avoided obstacles as if equipped with radar. The tray, lighter by virtue of İsmet having consumed coffee, water and pumpkin, flew higher than any had seen before. Round the hairpin turn it was, according to the weighbridge staff watching in amazement, at 110° to the ground.

The last part of her journey led up through the market on the hill. Fit as she was, she never took it at more than a jog. There was no point, on the return. But on this occasion she ran all the way. Past the stalls, and the crowds and the beasts. Past the sellers of *simit* with their laden poles. Past the man with the cages of song-birds. Past the nice undertakers who didn't smell, carrying an empty coffin for the approval of an ancient, bed-ridden customer. Past the blue-shuttered coffee house. Over the wall, into the patch of waste ground at the end of the garden. Othman the donkey was lying under his tree. Saljan collapsed to the ground alongside him, resting her head on his shoulders. It was the first time she had ever managed to sneak up on him unobserved. He looked round at her, reset his ears in pleasure to show midday, and sank back again. Then, when she had got her breath back, she told him the entire first scene of İsmet Efendi's script, without getting a word wrong.

For some reason, when the cell door slammed shut that day, İsmet felt more than usually alone. He had wondered what it would be like, the day he started to smuggle out the script he had been thinking about longer and harder than any he had written. When starting a new project in his distant days of freedom, he'd have opened a bottle of wine with Murat and Reyhan. The fire would have been lit, Baba's *saz* taken from its peg, tuned and played. Music and smoke wafting up through the branches of the quince-tree, into the night. It would have been the occasion for celebration.

Even in prison, he thought he'd feel elated. Happy and relieved to have kept faith with the godfathers of the idea: his old friends, the Politans. Perhaps he would sense their approval and, through that, their presence in his cell. But instead he felt as solitary as a man in solitary can feel. It was the pain, not so much of seeing no one else, but of not being seen himself. Mary in his script and, though he didn't know it, Saljan on her way home were observed. Their existence affirmed by those who watched them pass. But İsmet was like a beggar in the street people look through and do not see. Like a beautiful woman when her youth is gone and, with it, the stares that tell her she is alive.

The worst of it was, he had no idea if it had all been worth it. Could he honestly say that the exchange of his freedom for what he had created in prison had left the world or himself better off? Was there any likelihood this new script would wave a magic wand over his life and pronounce it totally, creatively justified? Perhaps he had got it all wrong. Perhaps he should have played the game with Talya. Made *Son of the Steppes* and *Daughters of the Knot Girls* until he died of praise. Or answered the calls from Beverly Hills and gone abroad to direct movies sitting down, not films on the run. How do you judge what you have never seen? He knew about some of the awards he had won; he knew about his revenues from foreign sales. They were, after all, how he had funded the secret films. But he had no way of judging his work himself. He was a deaf man singing.

He lay on the narrow, hard bed, staring up into the darkness. This was the triumph of solitary confinement: he was trapped in his own loneliness.

It sustained itself, fed off itself, filled the entire cell like a nightmare. He really was alone. After Maman died, İsmet's one source of faint comfort was that he need never again dread the news of the death of a parent. He'd often wondered if he would have felt differently if he had had a sister. For some reason, he never thought about having a brother. But a sister, to grow old with in tandem, who'd remember the names of all the family pets in order, and keep the moths from the white table-cloth with the tiny coloured squares. A sister to love. A sister who really knew him. Someone to share the burden the memory of Baba and Maman had placed on him.

And maybe she would have children, as he had not. Small persons who would lessen the weight of old memories by starting new ones of their own. Then he could adopt their baby words for water and toast, remember the names of their puppies and kittens, see things through their eyes, not his tired old ones. He probably wouldn't be aware of the past being steadily displaced, and if he were, it would be a cause for joy, not regret. In time, small persons grown bigger might take over responsibility not just for the house and garden, but for Maman's little gritty kitchen knife with the wooden handle, which had to be found else all would starve. Baba's *saz*. The white table-cloth with the tiny coloured squares. The cooking of the quinces. And if some or all of those old memories were lost as the baton was passed, it would no longer matter. But there was no sister. No small persons.

Worse than the loneliness, he thought before closing his eyes, was the mawkish self-pity it evoked in him. He went to sleep thoroughly ashamed of himself. And then, after a terrible night and like a sick joke, he had a message from the Pasha's office. The Minister of Culture was coming to see him. But the Minister did not want to talk to him about culture. She wanted to talk to him about divorce.

He had not seen Talya Begüm Demir Turali for twenty years. Not since she had swept into that wretched conjugal facility in his old prison and harangued him before sweeping out again. She must now be in her late fifties. He wondered if she had kept her looks. She had clearly increased her power: a cabinet minister! He had no idea; solitary confinement is as good a place as any for keeping a man in the dark. Of course, the Pasha had known for years that Prisoner Turali's wife was a mighty person in the land, but he had kept it a secret from İsmet, lest he try to taint his Minister wife with inappropriate pleas for intervention on his behalf. As if Talya Begüm Demir Turali would have lifted a finger to help her husband.

There was no question this time of them meeting in a room with a bed - plastic-sheeted or not. The Pasha vacated his office for the occasion, having first gone down to the front gate to meet her. He was wearing his full three-piece pinstripe suit, and was at his most oily. He found her very, very attractive. For a start, she came in an armour-plated limousine with motor-bike outriders. For another, she had over-exercised calves, which made the Pasha feel slightly faint with desire. This wasn't, he assured her as they mounted the stairs, a "correctional" centre so much as "self-correctional". Minister Demir cared not a jot if her husband did it to himself or had it done to him, just as long as it and he were no longer part of her life. His name chopped off the end of hers. She said nothing, and that, unusually, made the Pasha fall silent.

She really was very scary. As usual in a totalitarian regime rife with euphemisms, no one knew where culture ended and repression began. No one knew the pecking order at the very top. Was she in fact the Pasha's boss's boss? Or the next President? She certainly had the power to damage the Pasha, whether directly or via cabinet colleagues. And then there was her wasp-waist, and her jutting, lace-cosseted breasts, and the diamond brooch in the shape of the national flag. And those muscular legs scything up the stairs in front of him. Why was she in front of him? It was his prison, after all. Or maybe it was hers, and he just didn't know it. For a variety of reasons the Pasha would need a little relief after this.

The Pasha showed Minister Demir into his office. She dusted the spotless seat of his revolving chair with a paper tissue in her gloved hand, dropped it on the floor and sat down as lightly as possible. He pressed a buzzer on his desk. A moment later İsmet was escorted in with prison officers on either side of him. As if self-correction had made him savage. The Pasha was about to make a little joke of introducing husband to wife, thought better of it just in time, and left the room to book two hours with Soraya at Arzum Hanım's discreet establishment off Atabay Street. No need to call his wife to tell her he would be late home. After all, he was tied up with a Government Minister. The accommodating Soraya was always up for a little role-playing.

İsmet stood before his wife, noting the fact that she chose to sit behind the Pasha's walnut desk. Exercising authority, craving distance. Her hair was now a wiry grey. Her cheeks gaunt. Her shoulders looked excessively padded. She scanned him up and down.

'You look terrible, İsmet. I want a divorce.'

She spoke as if the demand were a consequence of the statement. So, İsmet thought, that's been the problem all along: me looking terrible.

'Fine. Where do I sign?'

She pursed her lips at his indifference, and pulled the papers from her briefcase. He signed where indicated.

'Since you cannot be trusted with paper, your copy will be filed with your personal effects. For when – or if – you are released.'

He gathered from her tone she would be a hostile witness at any parole board. She stood to put the papers away.

'So - Minister of Culture! My congratulations.'

He said it with plausible sincerity, but she accepted the compliment without grace, as if advancement were her natural right.

'Yes, for the moment…'

She snapped the brief case shut.

'You haven't asked what the grounds were. Aren't you even curious, İsmet?'

He shook his head. What did the grounds matter? The marriage had been dead at birth. But she was determined to tell him, anyway.

'Mental cruelty.'

She did not need to tell him on whose part.

'…and there is another, unstated, reason which I suppose you deserve to know.'

My God, he thought. She's found someone to marry. A necrophiliac who can be trusted with paper.

She had stopped by the door, unable to deny him one last glimpse of paradise lost.

'There is a law, preventing a sitting President from having a spouse with a criminal record.'

He was speechless. She really was a monster.

Talya Begüm Demir misread his silence. She took it as his final, overdue realization of her true worth. A good a moment as any to leave. She turned, opened the door, and marched away. The Minister's once svelte figure, her ex-husband couldn't help noticing, had settled into a certain stateliness, which she had evidently been fighting with exercise. Those slender calves were now decidedly beefy. My, she has let herself go, İsmet thought. And now, thank heaven, she has let me go.

He went back to his cell a freer man.

***

'Where, İsmet, does it say in the Bible that Mary, mother of Jesus, died a virgin?'

Cosmopolitan, holding forth in the prison refectory, twenty years before. It was like being back at university. İsmet had, by now, read the New Testament and re-read the Gospels. In common with countless others, he'd become beached and stranded on the issue of Mary's virginity, and sought guidance. The old Rabbi curled strands of his beard between his fingers, his eyes dancing with the thrill of the chase as he answered his own question.

'It doesn't say anywhere she died a virgin. On the contrary, the Gospel according to Matthew, Chapter 1 Verse 25 is unambiguous: Joseph "knew her not until she had borne a son; and he called his name Jesus." Mark's Gospel, written barely forty years after Jesus's death, actually names his brothers: James, Joses, Judas, Simon, and refers to sisters as well. One, according to the second century Gospel of Philip, was also called Mary. Now, some people who can't live with the idea that the mother of Christ ever had sex, will tell you that when the New Testament says Jesus had brothers, what it meant to say was, he had cousins. The trouble is, Greek has a perfectly good word for "cousin" but the ancient scribes consistently chose to use the word for "brother". My wise and beloved old teacher, Rabbi Ya'akov Lev ben Z'vi – God rest his dear soul - used to say through a cloud of pipe smoke, that you should always give your author credit for meaning what he says.

The New Testament does not pretend Mary died a virgin, and neither should we. In fact, according to a number of sources, both biblical and secular, her son James went on to be an important leader of the early Church, before being stoned to death around 63AD. With, some say, a rather beautiful prayer on his lips.

> "My God and Father,
> who saved me from despair,
> who gave me life through the gift of His great glory,
> do not let my days in this world be prolonged,
> but let your light, in which no night remains,
> shine upon me."

And was she a virgin, İsmet wanted to know, when she gave birth to Jesus? Cosmopolitan rocked back in his seat and gave a little smile. The person to ask about that was surely the Patriarch of Aleppo. İsmet had talked to His Eminence, had he not? Why had he not raised the subject with him? There was a pause. A pause long enough for İsmet to finish his lunch, and for several prisoners and a guard to come up and pay their respects to Cosmopolitan. The Rabbi did not chivvy İsmet, but waited patiently for his answer.

The truth was, İsmet couldn't bear to offend Metropolitan.

'The Patriarch of Aleppo is a Christian, is he not, İsmet? A very great Christian. He cannot be that without having pondered deeply on the circumstances of Christ's birth, can he? Are you, an outsider in this, likely to be able to unsettle him in ways the Biblical accounts – with their gaps and mysteries - do not? Not if you are civil, which you are, and if you genuinely wish to understand, which you do.'

And then Cosmopolitan explained some things İsmet had not understood. His Eminence's Orthodox Church of the Levant traced its lineage back to the very beginnings of Christianity: founded by the

Apostles, blessed by St Peter himself. Ever since, the Patriarchy of Aleppo had resisted both absorption into other Orthodox Churches and the suzerainty of the Church of Rome. His Eminence's Church did not share all the beliefs of Roman Catholicism. And one of the differences, which would work in İsmet's favour, was this: in common with other Orthodox Churches, the Church of the Levant saw itself as the modern bearer of the original apostolic message. Rome had no compunction about adding layer upon layer of new doctrine when it saw fit, ordering the faithful by papal bull to swallow fresh-minted dogmas. But Orthodoxy derived strength and faith from its direct, continuing line back to those men two thousand years before who had heard the word of Jesus Christ, lived it and then died for it.

Yes. İsmet could picture that in Metropolitan. His old head, like that of an ancient apostle's statue, heavy with knowledge, wedded to truth, guided by belief.

'In fact I might come along myself and listen, if he and you don't mind. I promise to keep quiet. And not to look in the slightest bit sceptical.'

Cosmopolitan had on a most serious look, but couldn't sustain it for more than a few seconds before his eyes twinkled into laughter.

His Eminence was duly asked and duly consented. And, yes, he would be honoured if his old friend and brother in God wanted to *kibbitz*. And there was absolutely no need for him to keep *shtum*. It turned out that both Metropolitan and Neapolitan were learning a little Yiddish, the inevitable consequence of ecumenical openness within a cheek by jowl existence. In the event, Cosmopolitan did keep fairly *shtum*, as they all did, listening to Metropolitan speaking frankly and personally about one of religion's great puzzles. He sat at the head of the table, with the others around him. İsmet had brought up from the kitchens what was left from the Governor's lunch: half a loaf of fresh bread, a small slab of *beyaz peynir* made from ewe's milk, some pink Süslü olives, the precious remains of a lamb *pilav*. First Neapolitan said grace. Then they ate. Then Cosmopolitan made tea. Then His Eminence the Most Reverend Theodore Mopsuestia II, Patriarch of Aleppo, began.

He started by talking about the Gospels of Mark and John. Surprisingly, because neither had a word to say about Jesus's birth, choosing instead to open their accounts with his baptism. How, he wondered, should we understand this? Did they feel no need to make the point that His mother Mary was a virgin? Had they no duty to report the miraculous circumstances of His birth? Not just the gynaecological marvel, but the visit of an Archangel to a young girl to inform her she will give birth to the Son of God, the angel that tells Joseph in a dream to accept Mary even though she is pregnant, another angel who tells the shepherds that the Saviour is born that day, the heavenly host which then appears praising God, the star in the east that guides the three wise men, the angel who warns Joseph in a further dream to gather his wife and child and flee from Herod? On all this, Mark and John are silent. Did they not know these things? Or did they know of them, but not believe them to be true? There was silence in the cell, while the others pondered not just these issues, but Metropolitan's reason for casting such heavy doubt so early on. The old Patriarch then told them that he would leave these questions hanging, before coming back to them at the end. Perhaps then there would be some answers to them. Or perhaps they would no longer be questions.

Metropolitan went on, seemingly to condemn his case still further. Noticing that İsmet had brought with him the borrowed Bible, he asked İsmet to read some lines from Matthew, one of the two Gospel writers who described the extraordinary circumstances of Jesus's birth.

> "All this took place to fulfil what the Lord had spoken by the prophet: 'Behold, a virgin shall conceive and bear a son,
> and his name shall be called Emmanuel'
> (which means, God with us)."

He then asked İsmet to turn to the Book of Isaiah in the Old Testament, to the original prophecy itself.

> "Behold, a young woman shall conceive and bear a son,
> and shall call his name Emmanuel."

The Mufti of Naples shook his head ever so slightly. The Chief Rabbi was motionless. İsmet read the two again to himself and looked up at the Patriarch.

'So, İsmet, which is it? Young woman, or virgin? The Hebrew word used in Isaiah is עלמה – *almah*, which simply means "a young woman of marriageable age", not *betula* which is the precise word for "virgin". But the Old Testament in the Christian Bible is based not on the Hebrew version, but a Greek translation. And when these Christian translators came to the Isaiah reference in Matthew and found the Hebrew word *almah*, they chose to render it using the Greek word παρθένος - *parthenos*, which can only mean "virgin". I wonder why they did that? And if the birth of Christ was the fulfilment of Isaiah's ancient prophecy, why was he named Jesus, and not Emmanuel? Perhaps it is time for another cup of tea.'

The break in tension, with the boiling of kettle and clatter of mugs, only increased their impatience for Metropolitan to resume. And so, in his own good time, he did.

'What other evidence is there that Mary was a virgin at the time Gabriel appeared to her, the moment of the Annunciation? In Matthew, Joseph discovers she is pregnant "before they came together". His instinct is to divorce her quietly. But the angel tells him he should have no fear to take her as his wife because "that which is conceived in her is of the Holy Spirit." Luke, alone among the Gospel writers, explicitly states that God sent Gabriel:

> "to a virgin betrothed to a man whose name was Joseph, of the house of David; and the virgin's name was Mary".

So what does Luke know that the others do not? And how does Luke know it?'

It was growing dark in the cell. Neapolitan lit a candle and they sat in its glow, for all the world like apostles themselves in some great oil painting. The almost painfully handsome face of Dr Suyuti as he blew out the match. Professor Josef Abramovici, his round head wreathed with white curls and crowned with his black *yarmulke*, leaning forward in anticipation. Theodore Mopsuestia II sitting back, his eyes closed in thought or prayer. Or maybe just waiting for his tea to cool. İsmet himself: candle flame dancing in those brown, deep eyes, savouring the moment but impatient for more.

'And what,' Metropolitan asked - granting İsmet's wish – 'of the genealogies of Joseph, husband of Mary? Luke gives one, and so does Matthew. But they are not the same. If corroboration were the priority, if the Gospels were a unified, clever construct, then they would at least agree on the name of Jesus's earthly grandfather. But they do not. Was it Jacob? Or Heli? And why risk giving a genealogy of the male line, if the message is that Jesus is the Son of God? Some say it was in fulfilment of another prophecy: that the Messiah would come from the House of David. Indeed, Paul writes to the Romans that Jesus "was descended from David according to the flesh and designated Son of God". According to both genealogies, Joseph has King David himself as an ancestor. But what is this worth, unless Joseph is Jesus's biological father?'

İsmet caught Cosmopolitan's eye. The Rabbi seemed as puzzled as he was. İsmet had expected the Patriarch of Aleppo to make the case for Mary the Virgin, for Christ the Son of God and woman. But he appeared to be doing his hardest to undermine it. Presumably he had answers to these damning points. He would build the enemy's argument and then refute it, like a medieval Schoolman. But he had not yet exhausted his opponents' ammunition.

Why, Metropolitan wanted to know, did John baptize Jesus? He paused and looked around at his listeners. İsmet thought the question as rhetorical as the others, and could not, anyway, see the connection to Mary. Cosmopolitan, however, ventured an answer. It was, according to Matthew, to "fulfil all righteousness". The Patriarch nodded his agreement. That was indeed what Jesus told John. But only after John told him it would be more fitting if Jesus baptized him. If baptism is, as John the Gospel-writer states, for repentance, to cleanse impurities in the soul, then how can Jesus benefit from it, if he is born without any taint of sin? Is that not, after all, the basis, the purpose, the meaning of His conception by the Holy Spirit and His birth to a blessed, pure virgin? What indeed could baptism add to that? Perhaps, Metropolitan ventured, they should consider Jesus's own words on the subject:

"Why do you call me good? No one is good but God alone."

The first buzzer went, and no one stirred. Metropolitan waited a moment, and then turned to the question of Mary's virginity until death. We know, he said, how very important this issue has been for our friends in Rome. Let us for the moment ignore the arguments as to whether Jesus had brothers or cousins. Let us note, but not rest our case on, Matthew's statement that Joseph "knew her not until she had borne a son."

Cosmopolitan caught İsmet's eye at this ground they had already covered. But Metropolitan was going further still.

Let us rather, he went on, see what Luke gives as the reason why baby Jesus was brought to Jerusalem to be presented to the Lord.

> "It is written in the law of the Lord, 'Every male that opens the womb shall be called holy to the Lord'."

'There is no doubt that had God wanted to, He could have brought Jesus Christ into the world through the body of Mary and left her in her blessed virginal state. Without, as the Bible so graphically puts it "opening her womb." But that is clearly not the impression Luke wishes to give of what happened. And Luke is, of all the Gospel writers, the one who perhaps had links to Mary herself. Certainly he is her greatest advocate. So if Luke chooses this explicit turn of phrase rather than concoct a medical miracle, we should take serious note. What then, of the midwife telling Salome that Mary remained a virgin after giving birth to Jesus, and Salome refusing to believe her? Daring - may I be forgiven the indignity of the thought and its expression - to probe Mary's private regions.

> "And Salome made trial and cried out and said: Woe unto mine iniquity and mine unbelief, because I have tempted the living God, and lo, my hand falleth away from me in fire."

Here you see the foundations of the edifice of perpetual virginity under their very construction. But this is not in the Bible, but from a text a century later. A humble teenage Jewish girl chosen by God Himself to provide His son Jesus Christ with a human mother is being revamped into the miracle-working Mother of God herself. Which almost, does it not, make her a Goddess? What a strange thing for a monotheistic religion to go on to do.'

İsmet remembered Cosmopolitan's words. Could now almost see the thread leading from the Patriarch back to the Fathers of the Church themselves. His uncompromising refusal to be side-tracked or misled by the agendas of those who came after. The second buzzer went, and still no one stirred. İsmet had never missed lock-in before. He assumed Farouk would do as they had long agreed: use spare clothing and pillows to construct a pretend body asleep in İsmet's bunk, and hope it would stand up to a guard's fitful torch-beam. Either way, it was too late now to go back, and he would never hear anything like this again.

'You know, by the way, that it isn't just the idea of perpetual virginity? Look in the Bible for the words 'Original Sin' and 'Trinity'. You will not find them. Not in the Hebrew or the Greek or the Vulgate. Not in the Roman Catholic or the Orthodox or the Protestant. They are not there.'

The Patriarch looked round at them, with a little smile.

'All this, you may think, has the whiff of heresy. But how can the Bible itself be heresy?'

No one answered.

The great mind continued its analysis and dissection into the night. Always with questions. Filleting out the paradox. The heresies, and wisdom, of Tertullian, Arius, and Nestorius. The dogmas forced upon the Councils of Nicaea and Constantinople. Gnosticism, with its virtual rejection of the Old Testament and its mythic fantasies overlaid on the New. The inconsistencies. The ridiculous. The unbelievable. He talked, and they listened, wrapped up now in blankets against the cell's clammy cold. Occasionally İsmet slept for a bit, and he assumed the others did too, but every time he awoke, the old man was still speaking. It was a theological tour de force, but it was also in some way the longest confession in history, as he unburdened himself of every reason he could think of to doubt, to undermine his own faith. Only when dawn eventually strained through the bars of the arched window did the Patriarch of Aleppo declare himself done, and fall silent.

The three other men were wide awake, looking at one another in amazement and speaking in whispers. How could he be done? That couldn't be all. There had to be more. They had to know his conclusion, but His Eminence had been talking non-stop for nearly twelve hours. He must be exhausted. His eyes were closed. He was asleep. Anyway, were they right to think there must be more? Had they missed something? Perhaps he had already given his message. What had he said early on? That he would leave his questions hanging, and that maybe, by the end, they would no longer be questions. But there was one question outstanding. A question as big as a cathedral. But who dare ask it?

Metropolitan was not, in fact, asleep. He was resting his eyes. He heard the whisperings, and let them flutter about the cell a while, tracing question marks in the stale air. Then he spoke again.

'You want to know, given all I have told you, how I call myself a believer. My answer comes, fittingly, from Luke's Gospel. From Mary herself. You remember that Gabriel appeared first to Zechariah telling him that his barren wife Elizabeth would bear him a son, a son who turned out to be John the Baptist. Zechariah asked Gabriel "How shall I know this? For I am an old man, and my wife is advanced in years" and Gabriel struck him dumb. Then Gabriel appeared to Mary and told her that she would bear "the Son of the Most High." Mary asked "How can this be, since I have no husband?" And the angel Gabriel told her. Why did the Archangel punish Zechariah, and reward Mary with the answer?'

It was a final, rhetorical question. İsmet couldn't see the difference and the others were too tired to work it out.

'Because Zechariah does not believe. How, he asks, shall he know this? But Mary believes. If Gabriel says it is so, it is so. She is not unreasonably curious about, if you like, the mechanics: how, given her virginal state, will the Holy Spirit enter her? But her belief is instinctive, immediate and absolute. She doesn't ask Gabriel to prove a thing to her. She just believes, and so do I – a mere insect at her feet. And the older I get, the less I care about the mechanics. I simply believe.

Just as I believe we are not guilty of the crimes they say we committed which brought us to this prison. I do not know a single fact to prove the innocence of any of us, but I believe in it with all my heart.

So it is with me and Mary and my Maker. Only much, much more so.'

And with that the Patriarch of Aleppo really did fall asleep, and so did the Mufti of Naples and the Chief Rabbi of Bessarabia. For İsmet, sleep would have to wait. He could hear the guard working his way closer unlocking the cells, and İsmet was on the breakfast shift in the prison kitchens.

Chapter Thirteen

Twenty years later, almost to the day, Saljan asked her aunt for an hour off. Gül Seren naturally assumed she wanted to see Beyrek the Coppersmith. She knew that Saljan and Beyrek had stayed friends after he'd made her the tray. Jafar had been at school with Dr Dumrul, and Dr Dumrul always bought his ground coffee, leaf tea and pastries from Mahmoud's Coffee House, so it was only a matter of time before Gül Seren met Scheherazade. Talk of Saljan led to talk of Beyrek, which led to talk of Saljan and Beyrek. Scheherazade told her what a very positive impression Saljan had made on her in the short time they had known one another. She added that Beyrek seemed a very pleasing young man, and both women agreed that they would make an excellent and remarkably handsome couple, with as much chance of happiness as any they knew. Though they conceded that, given the strengths of both young people's characters, no one could hope to have any authority over their feelings or actions. Particularly Saljan's. No point trying to arrange her marriage. In fact, to the best of Jafar's recollection, this Beyrek was the first boy she had ever allowed to give her a second glance. The two women agreed that the best thing they could do with their approval of this potential liaison was to keep quiet about it. So Gül Seren gave her niece the hour off without asking what she was going to do with it.

But Saljan did not intend to spend it with Beyrek the Coppersmith.

She wanted to buy some paper and pencils. That was why she needed time off, because Fahir the Stationer was on the other side of the town near the stadium, firmly in the fiefdom of Seljuk's Tea Garden. She never delivered that far so it would have to be a special journey, not a detour. And anyway, she wanted to linger. Saljan loved stationery.

She started off by walking, to see what walking was like. It felt very strange, going so slowly. Everything was in her sight for so long. True, she saw stuff she had never noticed, like a new harness shop by the camel market, and that Çinar the bike repairer had gone bald and how the flowers on the tiles outside the *hammam* in fact turned out to be birds. But these were fairly dull things. Before she knew it, she was jogging.

Something didn't feel right. Her tray. She didn't have her tray. She felt a bit undressed. And what do you do with your hands, if you aren't swinging a tray? She held her arms in by her side, the way she remembered her father running, with a forward and back movement like the pistons of an old steam engine. By the time she neared the Fire Station, she was sprinting. There was a horse cart just ahead of her, laden with copper, brass and tin, with sheets, tube and wire. She recognised Old Ragıp and his boy Turgut on the seat. They must have been stocking up at the wholesaler by the railway station. And on the back of the cart, one leg dangling and the other up, was Beyrek the Coppersmith. She'd have drawn level with them anyway, but a policeman was holding up the traffic to let the fire truck back into the station. So she stopped, just behind the cart, her face almost in his. It was a little embarrassing. Partly because she hadn't been to see him, and partly because, with people all around them, he couldn't ask why she hadn't. So they smiled like strangers, and said nothing. He fiddled with a piece of brass, and she tightened her laces. When she stood up, she heard a shout from the front of the cart. From Turgut.

'Look, it's Saljan! Right in front of you, Beyrek! Hello Saljan! Where's your tray?'

She told him it was at the coffee house, having a rest.

'It's Saljan,' Turgut said to Old Ragıp. 'She says she hasn't got her tray, because it's at the coffee house having a rest.'

Old Ragıp turned round and, grinning at her, offered her a lift. He was sure young Beyrek would move over to make some room. She thanked him, but said she was going to the other end of town. And then the policeman lowered his hand, Ragıp flicked his whip and the cart moved off. Just as Saljan was about to overtake it on the inside, Beyrek looped something over her arm. She didn't look at it immediately, assuming it was some Beyrek nonsense, but accelerated past the cart with a wave to the old man and boy on the front. Only when she turned down the alleyway that led to Fahir's did she realise it was brass rod Beyrek had beautifully shaped into a heart. She slipped it back on her arm as if it were a bracelet, and entered the shop.

It was like walking into a treasure trove. Saljan didn't know whether she liked the look more than the smell, or the feel more than the colours. Boxes of pencils, tins of crayons, reams of paper, notepads, hole-punches, tags, bottles of ink of every tint, sticky labels, rubber stamps, files, balls of string – they filled old wooden racks and glass-fronted cabinets. Fahir was now a very old man, and the shop was run by his granddaughter Yaprak. Everyone thought Yaprak would bring it up to date and ruin it, but she had kept everything just as it was. Even the gas lighting and the cat snoozing in a box file on the counter by the ancient till. It was said that, in the back and out of sight, she had a photocopying machine. And there were even rumours concerning computer consumables, whatever they were, but Saljan dismissed such scaremongering. She and Yaprak had known one another since they were babies, and the shop looked exactly the same as it had done when they went back there after school. Then Fahir would give them a tray of paperclips to sort into different sizes, or a bag of different coloured rubber bands to loop into bundles of twenty. Saljan loved going home with Yaprak, as much as Yaprak loved going home to the coffee house with Saljan. Envelopes and sealing wax. Honey-soaked pastry and clotted cream.

The two girls were as different as could be. Yaprak was round where Saljan was slender. Yaprak was sedentary, not active. Her curl-fringed face was forever on the brink of a smile, with none of the other's earnestness and caution. Indeed, the two girls looked as if they had been accidentally switched at birth. Anyone set the task of correcting the error would have instinctively placed the cot containing Yaprak within reach of a tray of sweet, whiskery *pişmaniye*, while the natural place for serious little Saljan's crib was wedged between boxes of carbon paper and the display of geometric instruments.

They fell into one another's arms, and in the process Yaprak first felt, and then saw the heart Beyrek had just given Saljan.

What does it mean, Yaprak asked her. Saljan shook her head. She didn't know. Is it from a boy? Yes, it was from a boy. Saljan clearly wasn't about to say which boy. What, Yaprak said carefully, would you like it to mean? Saljan frowned. That was the bit she knew least of all. Yaprak looked at her friend and took her hand, with its long, slim fingers and perfect nails.

'You are funny, Saljan.' Yaprak said. 'You are so serious. You could have any boy you want, but you never seem to do any wanting.'

'Yes I do', Saljan replied. 'That's why I'm here – as well as to see you, of course. I want paper and pencils. They're better than any boy. I want very handsome paper, and pencils that are ever so faithful and will never let me down.'

Yaprak smiled, and slipped from friend to master stationer. What were they for? The coffee house? No, Saljan said, shaking her head. She needed to write something down. Write what down? Again, Saljan shook her head but didn't answer. Yaprak explained that she wasn't being nosy, but she had to know so she could be sure Saljan was buying the right pencils and paper for her purpose.

'I'm writing a story.'

Yaprak's eyes widened. How exciting! Was it a love story? Saljan said she didn't know yet. In a way. Was it autobiographical? No. It wasn't her story. She was just the person writing it down. Yaprak shook her head in wonderment. How amazing! She'd always thought Saljan would do something extraordinary. Yaprak led her friend to the reams of paper, and pulled down a packet of medium weight in white. There were 500 sheets in a pack, and they always kept some in stock. In case it turned into an epic. Yaprak opened it carefully, slid out a sheet and handed it to Saljan. It didn't feel flimsy, and it wasn't too stiff. It was nicely in between. The sort of paper you could write a story on. Or a film script, but she wasn't going to tell Yaprak that.

Next, the pencils. It felt incredible, after all those years of looking at them, and sometimes being allowed to sort them by colour and size and hardness for old Fahir, that she should now be buying some with her own money and taking them home. Rather than leaving them in their compartments on the varnished wooden rack. Saljan already knew exactly which pencils she wanted. They had always been her favourites; she loved their special look and feel.

'You can't have those.' Yaprak said adamantly.

'Aren't they for sale?'

'Of course they're for sale, but they're for builders. That's why they're flat. So they don't roll. You need something like a 2B. They're over here. Hexagonal in section. Red, yellow or blue?'

But Saljan didn't want a hexagonal 2B in red, yellow or blue. She wanted a flat pencil that wouldn't roll, that you could build something with. In her case, a film script. She picked one out of the box and held it in her hand. It felt positive and supportive, as if it wouldn't slip away somewhere under the table and never be seen again.

'I want this one, Yaprak. In fact I want four of them. To start with.'

Yaprak took them from Saljan and put them into a paper bag. She looked a little put out: her professional advice ignored.

'How do you sharpen them?' Saljan asked with a carefully constructed little frown. 'Do you have flat sharpeners?'

Yaprak's face was never that far from a smile for long.

Carrying the paper and pencils home in their bag was odd. It felt the same sort of weight as the tray, and they were connected. If İsmet Efendi had had his way, she'd be smuggling the one out of his prison hidden in the other. As it was, they were part of the same secret. She'd made Yaprak swear not to tell anyone that she was writing a story. Saljan said it was in case she didn't turn out to be any good at it. It was an excuse, but Yaprak believed her. Before she reached the coffee house, Saljan slipped Beyrek's heart into the bag, hidden under the packet of paper. She didn't want Auntie Gül Seren or Uncle Jafar wanting to know where she'd got it. Who had given it to her. She knew her father would never ask.

The more she thought about her excuse to Yaprak, the more Saljan wondered if it explained why she hadn't told Yaprak what she wanted Beyrek's gift of the heart to mean: in case she turned out not to be very good at it - at loving someone.

***

Twenty years before, two days after his all-nighter with the Politans, İsmet joined the Chief Rabbi of Bessarabia on his morning constitutional around the exercise yard. İsmet hoped His Eminence had recovered from his spiritual marathon. Cosmopolitan said he had lain in bed a little longer than usual, but was up in time to go on his pastoral rounds. Both agreed he was an incredible gentleman. And had the incredible gentleman referred in any way to that extraordinary night? Cosmopolitan smiled. Only to say that, at home in Aleppo, he had a splendid view from his study window of the Mosque of Zechariah, where John the Baptist's father was said to be buried. And how glad he was that the Archangel Gabriel had restored Zechariah's power of speech after the birth of his son; after all, it is so easy for old men to say foolish things in the presence of angels.

And how, Cosmopolitan wanted to know, was İsmet getting on with all this religion? Oh, all right, İsmet replied. It's pretty difficult…but very interesting. The answer wasn't quite enough for Cosmopolitan. The Politans had had a discussion, he told İsmet, to work out why a talented young film-maker with a Catholic mother and a Muslim father and no discernible faith himself should be so curious about a nice Jewish girl all those centuries ago.

'His Eminence half-wondered if you were turning to God. And Dr Suyuti said you were probably just being polite. I, on the other hand, believe you are gathering material for a film.'

İsmet laughed, and did not give his blessing to any of the three theories. Instead, he asked something that had been puzzling him. What did the Chief Rabbi himself make of the wedding at Cana? Of Jesus's abruptness? Of addressing his own mother as "woman"? Cosmopolitan gave İsmet a nod of approval at questions worth asking.

'This passage in John was much debated by the early Church fathers, partly because they wanted to interpret it in a way which didn't make Jesus come across as being so rude, and partly because they saw it as a chance to see Mary as having semi-divine attributes: she seemed to anticipate Jesus's actions in turning the water into wine. This, they argued made her a prophetess… You know how keen those old boys were to elevate her out of the human herd. Make her miraculous in her own right.'

Cosmopolitan gave a telling little shake of his head.

'Their problem was not just that they had an agenda; they didn't really get the meaning of the story. Because by then, they were thinking like Christians. The secret to understanding what happened at Cana is to think Jewish. Picture the situation, İsmet. A Yiddisher wedding in the hills of Galilee. A big, big day for two families, cartloads of guests, trestle tables groaning with *gefilte* fish, chopped liver, potato *latkes*, loaves of *chollah* – and suddenly the wine runs out! Calamity! Maybe the hosts were relatives of Mary, maybe she just felt the pain of their shame. So she turns to the only person she knows who might be able to work a miracle: her own son. "They have no wine," she says to him. And Jesus answers like any boy embarrassed and irritated by his Jewish mother wanting him to perform a party trick. He says: why are you asking me to do this – I'm not doing miracles already. You can tell from this that he's still a kid; he hasn't taken off yet. He's got his disciples with him, sure, but they must have been kids too. And here's the thing that is so characteristic of the Jewish mother, İsmet. She doesn't argue the toss with him. She simply turns to the servants and tells them to do whatever her son says.

Now it isn't just between him and his mother – now he's got a bunch of servants waiting for his instructions. Now the spotlight is on him. So what does the boy do? What can he do? He goes for it. He gives them their orders. So they fill the jars with water, he says abracadabra, wine flows, honour is saved. The Jewish mother has got her way. And, as John says, this was "the first of his signs". She's got him to start small, with a helpful little secular miracle among friends and family. It is his first taste, not only of his own powers, but of the experience of being believed. Now he'll start to turn his gang of kids into disciples. Now he's on his way.'

Seen like that, the story sounded utterly plausible to İsmet. Here were Mary and Jesus behaving like mother and son. Like real people. They walked on without speaking, and then İsmet asked the Chief Rabbi how he knew so much about Christianity. How, for example, did he happen to know the dying prayer of Jesus's brother James? Cosmopolitan stopped strolling and smiled a little. Then they sat down on the bench where Metropolitan had talked to İsmet.

'I have always been interested in that time when, if you like, the Old Testament met the New. When there were Jews and Christians and Jewish Christians and Christian Jews. As well as pagans of all kinds. When people really had to ask themselves what they believed in, and on the answer could depend their life and, they believed, their salvation. Why did some Jews who, after all, had been hoping and praying for the Messiah, reject Jesus Christ while others got thrown to the lions for him?'

Cosmopolitan shrugged a very Cosmopolitan shrug.

'As to brother James…that's a funny little story. You know, İsmet, about the Dead Sea Scrolls found at Qumran in 1947 and before that the discovery of Gnostic writings at Nag Hammadi, in Egypt? Well, when I was a younger man with Hebrew and Aramaic and Greek and Latin fresh in my mind and my brain cells intact, I was part of a multi-disciplinary team assembled in Princeton around a tiny, precious collection of ancient texts that had come to light in Egypt in the mid-1950s, after Nag Hammadi and Qumran. There were experts on conservation, dating, history, theology, and, of course, translation. That was where I came in, as the most junior in a team that had the luck and responsibility to work on an extraordinarily intact *Book of Esther*. The oldest that's ever come to light. And all the more precious because it was the one book of the Bible not found among the Dead Sea Scrolls.

One quiet week, while the *Book of Esther* was being photographed, I was asked to look at a single page of Aramaic. It was on a sheet of papyrus and had been provisionally dated by the technical people to around the middle of the first century CE. I recognised it as the prayer that ends the second century *Revelations of James* which had been found among the Gnostic texts at Nag Hammadi. But here it was on its own, and unlike the Coptic version, the text was completely legible and without any later Gnostic slant. When I'd finished, it read very differently. It had never felt quite right to me – or possible - as something uttered while being stoned to death. It was clearly a reflective prayer in anticipation of death. I wondered whether, given its dating just twenty years after the crucifixion of Jesus, it could in fact have been James's record of something uttered by his brother. But what did I know?

Anyway, it was an extraordinary find. Two lads known only as Boy A and Boy B had been exploring the hills behind Asyūṭ in Central Egypt. There were old tombs there and they apparently hoped they might find a treasure trove, Pharaoh's gold or whatever. Instead they stumbled on a cave containing these ancient texts, none dated later than around the middle of the first century. As well as the *Book of Esther* and James's *Prayer*, there was a very fine copy of the *Didache*, all of Paul's letters in remarkable condition and a unique copy of *1 Esdras* in Aramaic. There was also – apparently - a page from a very early document, possibly near contemporary, recording the sayings of Jesus, but I never saw it.'

İsmet was gripped. He asked Cosmopolitan a host of questions: was anything discovered, for example, about Mary? Did they excavate the cave? Did the boys ever tell their story? Did His Eminence know about the find?

Cosmopolitan could only definitely answer the last: yes, the Patriarch of Aleppo did know about it, but whether he had seen any of it, Cosmopolitan had no idea.

'Then I'm going to have to go back to His Eminence.'

Cosmopolitan shook his head.

'He's not the man you want to ask about this.'

İsmet gave him a questioning frown.

'The man you want to talk to, İsmet, is Zahi.'

'But Josef, the Patriarch of Aleppo is the Christian theologian around here, not the Mufti of Naples.'

'I know, İsmet. But thirty odd years ago, His Eminence wasn't "Boy A". Zahi Suyuti, on the other hand, was.'

***

Dr Suyuti was the one Politan İsmet did not really know.

Cosmopolitan had become a friend, Metropolitan a mentor. But Neapolitan was a closed book. It was time to turn the pages. Part of the problem was that Dr Suyuti was effectively the prison Imam. Nominal responsibility for the pastoral needs of inmates lay with the Deputy Leader of Prayers at the New Mosque, whose precincts touched the prison perimeter at its south-western corner. But that gentleman's interests inclined towards the city's power-brokers – and in particular the inner well-being of their fashionable wives. The presence on his doorstep of a dirty, volatile pressure-cooker filled, as he saw it, with his country's vilest scum, was not so much a reproach to his calling as an embarrassment. His salvation came with the news of the latest addition to that cess-pit: the dangerous international cleric the Mufti of Naples. Whatever terrible crimes Dr Suyuti has committed, he told the Mosque's Committee of Duties and Directions, we must give him a chance to show his remorse through charitable works. Such as, for example, shouldering some of the burden of pastoral care within the prison. For does it not say in Sūra 3?

> "…those who, when they commit an immoral act or wrong themselves, remember God and seek forgiveness for their sins……the reward of these will be forgiveness from their Lord…How excellent is the reward of those who work."

With which pious remarks the Deputy Leader of Prayers effectively cleared his diary of all dates with convicts, leaving ample time for Tuana Hanım and Mme. Simay and Hatice of the silken thighs. Odd that - for does it not say in Sūra 24?

> "The fornicator and the fornicatress,
> scourge each one of them with a hundred lashes.
> Let not pity for them slacken your obedience to God,
> if you believe in God and the Last Day."

So Dr Suyuti became very busy. He took prayers. He arbitrated disputes. He acted as advocate for the prisoners in their doomed petitions to Governor Ümit, a thuggish bully of a man. He comforted distressed families. He conducted marriages and for one fractured couple mediated *khul'* – divorce instigated by the wife. He accompanied prisoners to and from floggings, and to execution. This man for whom the sublime, whispered Word of God was all, now lived his life deafened by the screams and cries and whimpers of His children.

The one thing İsmet had on his side was time. He waited and he watched. He had decided that he did not want to talk to him in front of the others, so that pretty much ruled out a meeting in Cell 677. Zahi was not a lingerer at meal-times. They gave prisoners too many opportunities to beard him with their problems. İsmet knew that he was friendly with the clerk Sıtkı. Once a week they played chess in the room off the library: the fat man and the thin. The round pink face and its tanned, elegant opponent. The men got on well, and were evenly-matched. Both, after all, were playing the system in deeply hostile environments – a challenge for which it was essential to think many moves ahead.

There were as many ways to survive as go under in the prison. İsmet tucked himself away, and was not a little helped by his association with Kerem. Kerem hid inside Berk's terrifying persona. His Eminence floated above it all. The Chief Rabbi was his open generous self with everyone. Farouk was a master of deception. And Zahi and Sıtkı had chosen – or been chosen – to serve the system. In some ways theirs was the most dangerous route of all, because no one likes a collaborator. It was a mark of the two men's decency that, for all their tiny badges of authority, they retained the respect of their fellow-prisoners. Their decency – and their mastery of game theory.

That left the exercise yard. And here the problem lay with İsmet. If he wanted to talk to Neapolitan he would have to start running in earnest, but İsmet was unfit. It hadn't always been so. At school he'd been an avid football player with Murat and the boys. Making films in the early years was anything but sedentary, and when it came to the first – pre-Talya - Steppe Westerns, stamina was essential. İsmet learned to ride, he climbed four of the six Yurt peaks, he swam the Amal Gorge with two stuntmen - standing in for the three stars. And he was having regular sex. With actresses, young ladies from film magazines, beauties from the art department, continuity, hair and make-up. Or perhaps it would be more accurate to say he was having sex regularly. You can't do all that and start gasping for air after a minute. But that was then.

Farouk was hugely amused when his cell-mate started doing sit-ups and press-ups. He was less amused when İsmet stopped bringing sesame seed pies and *lahmacun* from the kitchens, in favour of salads and fruit. Not that Farouk was greedy, but he had an impatient metabolism. İsmet then took pity on him, intensified his own self-control, and resumed Farouk's supplies of extra-curricular carbohydrates, while sticking himself to rabbit food. And he ran regularly with Kerem, when he was sure Zahi was busy elsewhere. It suited Kerem; Yazmira had confided to him that she found her husband Berk's great girth rather unappealing. Gradually, İsmet found he could keep up with Kerem for a full lap. Then two. And then four.

So Neapolitan found himself with a jogging companion. And it was only a matter of time before they started talking. At first, Zahi spoke about his two cell-mates. Like İsmet, he had come to love them both: the funny, golden-hearted Rabbi and the gentlemanly, saintly Patriarch. The Jew and the Christian. *Ahl al-kitab* - "People of the Book" - both. Favoured sons of the two other great monotheisms, but still *dhimmi*: protected, but of lower status than Muslims. Living in Naples, he'd met many People of the Book, but had only come to see them as equals since meeting Josef and Theo. It was a terrible admission, but religion is not always fair or generous. And from the start, Theo and Josef had been both to him, whatever the history of their faiths told them about how to treat infidels.

'And then,' said İsmet, waiting the moment, sensing the mood, 'there's the history of Boy A.'

He had no idea how Zahi would respond. He certainly didn't guess that the demure and refined Mufti of Naples would stop, shake his fists in the air and yell out.

'Aagh! That *verkakte* Rabbi! Why couldn't he keep *shtum!*'

The guards in the watch-towers leaned over their rails and stared at the two men. İsmet must have looked horrified, particularly after all Zahi had said about the People of the Book. Neapolitan burst into laughter and told İsmet that the Jews didn't have a monopoly on bad jokes. He waved reassuringly up at the guards and led İsmet to the bench. The bench he had sat on with Metropolitan and then Cosmopolitan.

'Josef told me ages ago you wanted to know about Boy A. What took you so long?'

Chapter Fourteen

It seemed Zahi's shout was close to the truth. He had not wanted to talk about the cave. Indeed, he had never spoken about it to anyone since until, on his first day in Cell 677, Josef asked him where he was from in Egypt. He replied a place no one had ever have heard of, called Asyūṭ, and the Rabbi said: ah! – where the boys found the *Asyūṭ Scriptures* in a cave. Then Josef told him he had worked on the translations of the Aramaic texts in Princeton. Whenever he got really stuck on a squiggle he would stroll down Mercer Street to clear his brain, resolutely resist the attractions of PJ's Pancake House, and then plunge back into the basement gloom of Manuscript Room No. 7. And he would wonder what it must have been like for those Egyptian boys to stumble, a bit like him, out of the light into that cave. Into that ancient, precious past. He would love to have known. Well, it would have been churlish of Zahi not to put his hand up and tell him.

But Zahi did not tell Josef much. And he didn't want to tell İsmet anything. Not because he didn't like İsmet. It was more difficult than that… He didn't want to break his word. His word to whom? İsmet asked him, but instead of answering, Zahi stood up.

'Let's run some more.'

They did another five laps of the exercise yard in silence. The sun never penetrated that cold, grey place so late in the day, but even Zahi was bathed in sweat and wanted to stop. They sat again on the bench, and İsmet said nothing.

'What use will you make of it? Josef says it's material for a film. Is it?'

İsmet said he wouldn't know, until he'd heard the story. He was certainly intrigued by the idea of a family slowly realising that one of its members has a divine destiny, and how they come to terms with it - each in his and her own way - or not. So he was very interested in Jesus and his relationship with Mary and Joseph and his brothers and sisters. And interested in any indications of their own personal beliefs. Zahi nodded, and looked troubled. İsmet said he and Boy B had found the cave over thirty years ago. Was the person he had made the promise to still alive? Was there anyone living who could cause hurt, or be hurt, if it became known that Zahi had spoken? There was a long pause. Zahi shook his head. But he had given his word. He looked at İsmet. And looked away. At the gaol looming over them and the prisoners trudging in its shadow.

'I will tell you as much as I can, but it will not be all I know. If you can live with that, fine. But if you think you'll be dissatisfied and start pressuring me, then I would rather not speak of it.'

İsmet didn't have to think about it. He would be happy with what he was given, and would simply make up the rest. That was what film-makers did. Zahi smiled and nodded. And then he started to talk.

When he was fifteen, he and a boy a year older named Abanoub Da'oub decided they would go into the limestone hills behind Asyūṭ searching the old tombs for a mummified wolf. In ancient Egyptian times the city had apparently been defended by wolves and had worshipped Osiris in the form of a wolf. Whoever or whatever they valued in those days, they embalmed. Every now and then, one of these four legged mummies turned up, and Zahi and Abanoub decided they wanted one. They didn't know what they'd do with it. Perhaps have it for half a year each, or else sell it for a fortune. As Zahi said, they were just kids.

The time seemed right for finding mummified wolves because there had recently been a series of earth tremors in the valley and they were known to dislodge the stone slabs which sealed the tombs. The weekend before they had scoured the lower slopes without success; this weekend they were going high. It was a remarkably hot day, and his friend Abanoub was overweight. He found the climbing hard. It was slow work getting above the honeycomb of ransacked catacombs to the places they hoped no one else had reached. They spent the night in one of the highest tombs on the upper slopes. After a day drenched in sweat, Abanoub was now shivering with cold. Zahi made a fire to keep them warm. And to keep away the wolves that hadn't been mummified. They talked about turning back, but it didn't make sense having gone that far.

Zahi remembered looking out from the mouth of the cave at the stars above and the lights of the city shimmering below, with the Nile beyond snaking away to left and right, and then the great Arabian desert. And he remembered hearing chanting coming from behind; he knew it must be Abanoub praying, but it sounded alien to Zahi. His friend, you see, was not a Muslim, but a Coptic Christian. When he went back inside, Zahi asked him if he was saying his prayers, and Abanoub replied rather proudly that he had asked the Lord Jesus to deliver them both from danger. Zahi wasn't sure how he felt being placed under the protection of an infidel God, but assumed it wouldn't work anyway. He slept poorly.

They woke early, ate most of their remaining food, and set out while the day was still cool. They climbed the next ridges, and along a defile to a fold of hills set back from the others. It felt different from what had gone before. More remote. Untrod. It sounded different, too. Tiny birds were darting in and out of the rocks, filling the air with chirrups. Abanoub was finding it easier, because these crags were so turned in on themselves that one shaded another. They passed a tiny spring bubbling out of the rocks. And then, almost hidden between two ridges as sharp as blades, they saw an opening in the depths of the rock. A slit opening to a cave. There had to be a mummified wolf in there if there was one anywhere. Probably a selection of them. They could have one each, and others to sell to the fancy antique dealers in Asyūṭ. To the highest bidder!

As the older of the two, Abanoub decided he should go first. But it was a narrow, narrow slit. Hard as he tried, Abanoub could not get through the gap. He shone their torch in, but could see nothing. Just an inner rock face blocking the way. And then the boys realised that it did not close the opening completely; there was a tiny crack within and to the side. It would take someone very skinny indeed to enter. Zahi was probably thin enough, but reluctant and a little scared. He didn't like the idea of going into that unknown without his friend Abanoub. Abanoub dragged his heels when he walked, and he huffed and puffed a lot, all of which was good for scaring away snakes. And any wild beast would see all that flesh on him and choose him over Zahi. And then, supposing Zahi got in, but couldn't get out? He wasn't sure Abanoub could get back on his own to get help. Did he even know the way?

Abanoub seemed untroubled by any of that. His only worry was if the opening was too narrow to get the mummified wolves out. Let's hope, he said, they aren't as fat as me. Off you go Zahi. And tell me everything you see.

What Zahi saw changed his life.

He breathed in, and went instantly from light to dark, from heat to chill, from birdsong and boyish banter to dead silence. Beyond those outer lips Zahi's way became tortuous, forcing him to twist through a maze of rock seemingly compressed on itself. If the initial gaps had been too narrow for Abanoub, the subsequent ones almost stopped Zahi. Then, after scrapes to skin and tears to clothing, the passage opened into a bigger chamber whose floor was littered with stones, many of them shaped like bricks. Shining his torch up he saw an opening six feet from the ground, narrower even than the rest, and above it a colony of bats, hanging from the rock ceiling. From the fact that the stones lay on a thick layer of guano with few droppings on top of them, Zahi deduced that this barrier had only recently come down, probably as a result of the earth tremors. It was six feet above him now, but what depth of bat guano was he standing on? It might once have been twice that. Indeed, he could only reach this internal cave mouth by stacking the fallen stones into steps until he could haul himself up. He stood in the fissure and shone his torch into nothingness.

He expected to be frightened by what he saw, but he wasn't. He was amazed. Up to the height of a man, the cave had been hollowed into a succession of recesses, even in size and depth. And they were filled with writings. Books in some, scrolls in others, piles of papyri, manuscript upon manuscript. And it had been arranged with great care, for each compartment was labelled in faded paint on what looked like a square of animal hide hanging on a peg. Zahi could not make out the language – had no idea if he was looking at words or numbers. The writings were neatly piled, many of them tied with ribbons. It was a vast hidden library. Young Zahi barely managed to squeeze through the gap. Gashed and bleeding he climbed down the other side and stepped gingerly across the floor, leaving the first footprints in the dust for two thousand years. No bats had taken up residence there yet, and there were certainly no wolves, mummified or alive. Abanoub would be sorely disappointed. But Zahi was not. He was gripped.

Egypt's past had been around him, inescapably, all his life - but it had always felt monumental, dead. Here was a kind he hadn't seen. The past in human scale. Whose books were these? What was in them? Stories of battle, perhaps? Of great kings, powerful queens? Of gods and goddesses? Whatever they told, they showed the hand of man in every incomprehensible line. Someone would be able to read them. Someone would unlock them, freeing again the ideas of the people who had written them. Up till now he had day-dreamed through school, but something at the sight stirred him. He knew he wanted to get them out of that cave to learned men who would read them, so he could learn what it was they contained which was so precious it had to be preserved from enemies and destruction. He took several ancient books and some sheets of papyrus, just ones that were on the tops of their piles, and made his way back to the present.

So, İsmet thought, what happened between that wealth of manuscripts in a cave, and the tiny collection in a Princeton basement? From what Cosmopolitan had said he didn't think the Chief Rabbi had any inkling of the size of the original find. Maybe Zahi was now saying things he had not spoken of before. But he had warned İsmet that he would not tell him the whole story. Had there already been omissions? Part of the skill with which the Mufti of Naples was censoring his own account was that İsmet had no sense of any gap in the narrative, much less what once filled it.

So Zahi went back and, as he foresaw, Abanoub was highly irritated. The books looked so old they must be worthless. Who'd ever want to read them, even if anyone could? He stomped off down the hill, convinced that Zahi had found mummies and treasures galore but was keeping them all to himself so he could go back later and make himself a million. Then he slipped and fell, and started howling with pain mixed with anger, and the result of that was the search party that had come out from Asyūṭ to look for the two boys now found them. It was led by Abanoub's and Zahi's fathers. The two men were neighbours rather than friends, and they were as unalike as their sons. Abanoub's father was a butcher, and Zahi's was a schoolteacher. Both were relieved to see their sons again. While Yared Da'oub fussed over Abanoub's grazes, Haroun Suyuti studied the manuscripts which his son Zahi excitedly showed him. He remembered the fuss over the books discovered at Nag Hammadi, and how important they had turned out to be. Perhaps these were also early church scriptures. At which point Yared Da'oub – a devout Christian - pricked up his ears. He said they must take them to the church. Father Matta would know best what to do with them. He would take them round there that evening. Zahi's father said they should all go, given that only Zahi had actually been in the cave.

So they went. Zahi sat with the others in the priest's cold, bare anteroom with its wooden crucifix on the wall. He could sense how uncomfortable his own father – an equally devout Muslim - was, being in that place. Abanoub described how they found the cave, and the leading role he had played in the proceedings. It was just a shame for him that he had not been able to get through the first opening, because he then had to hand over to Zahi. Zahi told Father Matta as simply and briefly as possible how he had found the writings. The old priest listened and nodded and said both boys had done very well. He was sure there were scholars at the Monastery of the Virgin Mary at Durunkah who would know what it all meant. The boys were not to worry; he would handle everything from there. And he gave them each a boiled sweet and the next thing Zahi knew he was on one side of the door with his father and Abanoub and Yared Da'oub, and his precious manuscripts were on the other side with Father Matta.

Very early in the morning two days later there was a knocking on the Suyuti family's front door. Zahi's mother opened it to two monks. Tall men, in black with black velvet cowls. They asked her very politely if she could spare her son to show them the way to the cave. They looked a little frightening, but had kind smiles, and Zahi was excited at the chance to return. Much to Zahi's relief, Abanoub did not accompany them; he was still recovering from his injuries. And to his delight his own father joined them. Zahi found himself staring at him as they climbed the lower slopes, wondering if he was slim enough to go with Zahi into the innermost chamber. Hoping he was. He longed to show him the recesses with their labels and their books and scrolls. Longed for him to see it all as Zahi had seen it: not as ancient manuscripts transported into the modern world but as a complete, intact library. His father would love that. And perhaps he would realise how much it meant to Zahi, which would please him, after years of school reports in which his son had failed to show any real sign of academic interest.

The monks were certainly very fit and strong. For men of God, they climbed like goats, but they would be much too big to get through even the first gap. For the first time in Zahi's life he felt good about being so skinny. Maybe only he would ever be able to get all the way into the cave. Maybe it was really his and his alone. What then would it matter if they asked him to bring out every single manuscript, if all he had to say was: here they are! - when in fact he had only emptied one recess. They may be Christian writings, he thought as he climbed ever closer to them, but he was on their side in all this. He was their protector.

Everything changed when they reached the tomb where he and Abanoub had spent the night. For there, waiting for them, were three men in shirtsleeves. One had a map. Another had a big torch. The third had a scowl. They did not look kindly. They told the monks they were from some Institute of Antiquities, and they'd heard all about this find in the hills. They said it fell under their jurisdiction. The monks had no choice but to let them join the party. Zahi now led the column up the defile. And now, with these strangers in tow, he felt the sympathy of the monks. As if sides had been taken.

When they reached the two blade-sharp ridges, the procession stopped. The men peered through the slit opening while Zahi and his father went to one side to sit in the shade by the spring. Only one of the officials stood a chance of getting even part way in, but Zahi kept his thoughts to himself and waited. His father patted him on the back, proud at the way his son was handling himself among strangers. But inside, Zahi felt very uneasy.

The thinnest official tore his shirt and gave up. And then one of the monks did something strange: he stripped off. Underneath he wore loose white underpants, almost like a loincloth. Standing in front of the cave he looked like a figure from ancient times. Zahi tried not to stare, but realised he was in fact a lot slimmer than he had appeared under all those folds. And from his garment he produced a small bottle of oil which he smeared over himself. Then he handed the bottle to the other monk who rubbed it on his back until his body was slippery and shining. He got through the first gap more easily than Zahi thought he would, but the next bit held him up for an age. Then, with encouragement from his fellow monk and a stream of advice from the officials, he edged round the corner and out of sight.

Zahi started counting.

For some reason, when he had started back from the innermost recess, Zahi decided to measure the time it took to reach daylight. He counted two hundred and seventy four. Admittedly, he was carrying fragile manuscripts which he had to pass carefully through the gaps. But being slimmer than the monk, he reckoned it would even itself out. So if the monk did make it to the inner cave – to the library itself - he was unlikely to return before, say, six hundred. Which would just give him time for a quick look around. In fact, Zahi reached five hundred and ninety when he heard the other monk shout that he could hear his friend coming. At six hundred and twenty seven he could see the monk himself standing in the outer gap.

Now he looked like someone from the garish illustrations in Abanoub's Sunday School Bible. He had cuts and grazes on his arms and shoulders, and a gash in his side. There was blood on the loincloth. Dust, dirt and guano stuck to the oil and in his hair. By Zahi's calculations and from his battle scars, the monk could – just – have got far enough to see into the library cave. He had a brief, whispered conversation with the other monk before coming over to the spring to clean himself up and have a drink. Then he went back to where he had left his habit, and the officials descended on him. Zahi got up to join them, but his father stopped him, saying they should hang back. The men were too far off and spoke too low for Zahi to hear what they were saying, but it looked as if the monk was telling them he hadn't managed to get in all the way. He made hand gestures as if one of the slits in the rock was just too tight to get through. He pointed to the bloody gash and the cuts on his shoulders. But as he was pulling on his monk's habit, he caught Zahi's eye in a look that seemed to Zahi to be conspiratorial. As if the monk had not told the officials the truth which only he and Zahi knew.

And then the officials, in frustration, rounded on Zahi, wanting chapter and verse on what he had seen. And Zahi surprised himself by telling them almost nothing. As if he had seen very little in there. As if he had brought out all he had found. As if he were, perhaps, a little dim-witted. His father misread his son's obtuseness for fright and protected him from their aggressive questioning. It was almost, his father said, as if you don't believe my son. At one point during the spat, the monk caught Zahi's eye again and gave the faintest nod of his head. In the end, the officials gave up and the party came down from the hills in silence.

The exercise yard was now cold and clammy. İsmet's kitchen shift had long since come and gone. Neapolitan straightened his back and stretched. It had felt as if the story was finished. But there was more.

Zahi never saw the officials again. The next evening, however, the two monks knocked on the Suyutis' front door again, and this time they brought with them a much older monk who did most of the talking. They sat almost in silence in the living-room with Zahi and his father, while Zahi's mother made tea. Then, when they were all seated, the old monk spoke. He had a deep, almost musical voice, although he looked frail. He said the Church wanted to thank Zahi for all he had done for her – apparently the Church was female - but she must now ask him one final favour. That sounded a little frightening to Zahi: "one final favour". It sounded like something to do with death. He had to swear never to return to the cave. Never to take anyone there. Not to tell anyone about it or its whereabouts. To make no marks on any maps indicating its location. And, most important of all, he must never ever talk about what he had found in the cave or what he had seen. His friend Abanoub had already given his word earlier in the evening, but he of course had done so on the Bible. Perhaps Teacher Suyuti had a Qur'ān his son could use? Was this, Zahi's mother asked, really necessary? At which point the monk who had gone some or all the way into the cave spoke for the first and only time. Yes he said, looking right into Zahi's eyes as he had done twice before, it is. Zahi threw his father a look of appeal. His father shrugged. It is not, he said to Zahi, really our business. And he fetched the family Qur'ān.

'Is that it?' İsmet asked softly.

The Mufti said there was a strange twist to the tale. About two weeks later there was a huge explosion in the Asyūṭ hills. They often heard distant blasting from the stone quarries, but this was different. Zahi ran up onto the roof and looked back. A column of smoke and dust rose from the crags above the highest level of tombs. From the place he had sworn to forget. Huge rocks were tumbling down the hillside. Then came the echoes, and they felt personal - as if they meant something only to him. And maybe one other person.

There was talk about it in school the next day. It was said bad people had tried to dynamite an opening in the rocks to get at hidden treasure. But they had used too much explosive, and the detonation had brought down part of the ridge above. Two men had been killed. Nothing was left of the treasure. His treasure.

Dr Zahi Suyuti fell silent.

'I have three questions for you, Zahi.'

Neapolitan looked shattered, as if he had lived it all again in the telling.

'Just three, İsmet? I have a hundred…'.

'Do you believe the manuscripts Josef worked on in Princeton to be the ones you brought out of the cave?'

Zahi nodded. He did. Josef said they had four codices and three sheets of papyrus to work from. And that was exactly the number he had picked out of the recesses.

'What effect did this have on you spiritually? It clearly didn't turn you into a Christian.'

No, it did not. He was already on the way to being a good Muslim. Maybe not good, but not a bad one. But the effect? Perhaps the whole experience had made him passionate about the integrity of a text. And about preserving the word, whether we understand it now or not, because someone may come along after we are dead to whom it will mean something. Maybe even something important.

'My last question, Zahi, is: does this extraordinary story of yours have anything to do with Mary and her son?'

Neapolitan frowned a little.

'You mean, beyond anything within the content of the manuscripts - which Josef and His Eminence would know more about than I do?'

Yes, said İsmet, wondering if Zahi were playing for time. Beyond that.

Zahi stood up and stretched again. Then he abruptly sat down.

'As far as the manuscripts in the cave are concerned, academics believe them to have been sacred to a group of people almost contemporary with Mary and Jesus who saw themselves as Jews believing in Christ. People who bridged the gap between the old world of Abraham and Moses, and the new world of the Gospels. This explains why there were Old Testament as well as very early Christian texts in there. Of course the sample is very small; too small for the experts to be certain. After all, it was just what I happened to pick up in a hurry, all those years ago. But that's what their thinking is.

More specifically, the group – persecuted, in fear for their lives - may have chosen the cave as a safe repository for these writings not only because it was so remote and secure, but because it had particular significance for them. It constituted a direct, vital link to the Holy Family itself.'

İsmet almost had to remind himself to breathe, so gripped was he by Zahi's story.

'According to the Gospel of Matthew, İsmet, an angel appeared to Mary's husband Joseph and told him to take his family to Egypt to escape King Herod who wanted to kill the child Jesus. He did as he was told, and they waited in Egypt until an angel appeared to them again to say that Herod was dead and it was safe to return to Israel. Well, according to strong local tradition – it isn't in the Christian Bible - the southernmost place Mary, Jesus and Joseph reached and where they rested was Asyūṭ. To be more precise, in the hills behind Asyūṭ. In a cave, it is said, with a narrow, almost impenetrable entrance. Unless Joseph was a very slim man he could not have got into the cave himself; he may have stayed elsewhere and brought food up to them. But certainly the family would have been safe there. High up. Hidden.'

The whistle blew to clear the exercise yard. Zahi and İsmet joined the small knot of men queuing at the gateway to re-enter the prison buildings. And then Zahi had an after-thought.

'Interestingly, there's something in the Holy Qur'ān that may refer to the Asyūṭ cave. You remember I said that while the monk was in the cave my father and I sat to the side by a spring in the rocks. Where the monk then bathed his cuts. Well, in Sūra 23:50, it says:

> "We made the son of Mary and his mother a sign
> and lodged them on a height,
> where there was security and a spring."

Chapter Fifteen

Auntie Gül Seren was worried about Saljan.

Her niece had taken to locking herself away in her bedroom. She would have supper with the family, during which she'd speak even less than usual. She'd do the washing-up without having to be asked, as she always did because she really was the best of girls. But then she'd slip away and not be seen until breakfast. Her aunt started to wonder if she was climbing out of her window and going off to see Beyrek the Coppersmith. To find out, she finally accepted an invitation from the Hoja's wife to take evening tea and play cards. She really did not like Emine Hanım, who was thoroughly stuck-up. As if the lazy, narrow-minded Hoja were the Vali himself. As if no one in town could remember she was the daughter of Yiğit the Street Sweeper. But Emine Hanım did have one thing going for her: her "ladies' parlour" – for that is what she termed the fussily draped room in which she entertained – faced the side of the coffee house where Saljan slept. Or did not sleep.

So, after supper, Gül Seren followed Saljan upstairs to run a brush through her hair and find some earrings. Hearing her auntie's step behind her, Saljan turned and gave one of her dazzling smiles before closing her door. There was no point in Gül Seren studying the toiletries in the bathroom; her niece was far too discreet to flaunt new make-up or perfume to entice the coppersmith. And her taking a shower meant nothing special as she did that every night. No, this would be settled not by close-up forensic scrutiny, but by vigilance from afar. Gül Seren having dallied with gaudy earrings Emine Hanım would envy, plumped for tiny chased silver studs whose impeccable taste would be utterly lost on her. Much more satisfaction that way. She slipped a pair of silk slippers into her bag and set out for the Hoja's house.

HURRYING ANGEL

The path led around the garden of the coffee house and past the corner of the waste ground beyond. She noted the clearness of the evening, which was good. And she reassured herself that Othman's tree was not going to block her view of Saljan's window, which was very good. The donkey himself was asleep by the wall, which was also good. But the Hoja's mule Safraz was still cropping, which might not be so good. It is to be hoped, she thought as she opened the Hoja's back gate, that the intractable beast does not munch his way into my line of sight.

There were two other guests: the widow Enç, who had once been extremely pretty and acceptably silly and was now very faded and unbearably silly, and an expensively dressed but dumpy woman Gül Seren had never met before who turned out to be the wife of the Governor of the prison. Reşid Hanım made so much of the utter perfection of her marriage to the Pasha that Gül Seren was tempted to ask why her husband spent so many early evenings at a certain address off Atabay Street instead of racing home to her ever-open arms. But she had more pressing needs. The first was to secure a seat at the card-table facing the parlour's French windows, with their excellent view of the coffee house and her niece's all-important window. Unfortunately that was exactly where the widow Enç placed her bony posterior, with the Pasha's wife plumping herself down opposite. This did not suit at all. Not only did it mean Gül Seren having to partner Emine Hanım; it would require her to spend the evening craning her head round to see if her niece made a move down the drain-pipe. The Pasha's wife would probably think she was trying to peer at her cards. This called for flattery, footwork and a little luck.

'What a gorgeous gown you're wearing this evening!' Gül Seren oozed at the vain old lady. 'I couldn't help notice how beautifully it shimmers when you move...Of course you have the perfect figure for it.'

It was more than the widow Enç could withstand.

'My dear! Do you really think so?'

The next moment she was on her feet, dancing over to the standard lamp, the better to catch the light.

'I only wish I could get away with something as figure-hugging. Ah, here's Emine Hanım! Shall we cut for partners?'

And with a deft back-step, Gül Seren placed herself between the widow and the card-table and, in a seamless continuation of the move, fanned the pack in an arc across the baize. Her gambit forced her hostess to avoid the pirouetting widow by going the other way around the room which in turn brought the Pasha's wife to her feet to allow Emine Hanım to reach the sideboard with the tea tray. Next, and this did not carry the risks it appeared to, she turned over a card. After all, it didn't really matter much with whom she was partnered, but it was critical where she sat.

It was the two of Swords.

The Pasha's wife drew the Viceroy of Polo Sticks.

The widow drew the four of Cups.

Emine Hanım, trying not to seem flustered, turned over the King of Coins.

'How lovely,' Gül Seren said to the widow Enç, now stranded mid-twirl on the other side of the room. 'We are to be partners!'

And down Gül Seren sat, firmly facing the French windows with the coffee house beyond. You should be thoroughly ashamed of yourself, she thought as she was handed her tea, but family always comes first.

Play was delayed by the entrance of the Hoja with a tray of sweetmeats. Mahmoud's finest, of course! Gül Seren flattered the old fool and accepted his compliments on the coated nut dragées, the clove *lokum* and the chocolate *halva*, all of which he had tasted in the kitchen just to make sure they were up to standard. Which, he was pleased to say, they were. How Gül Seren kept her figure so trim with such temptations on every side he could not guess. Her waist could not be more than… At which point his wife steered him out of the room, and then commiserated with the Pasha's wife on the burden of having husbands who had not altogether grown up. The widow Enç, who had never come to terms with no longer having a husband - adult or juvenile - looked a little wistful. Gül Seren needed them all to settle down so she could concentrate on Saljan's window and its adjacent drain-pipe, so she handed the shuffled pack to her partner to deal, and the game began.

It was as well that Gül Seren was fairly good at cards, because she could barely concentrate on anything happening in the room. Saljan had switched her bedroom light on, which should have made it easier to spot her making a secret flit, but unfortunately the wind had got up and the branches of the trees were swaying, casting flickering shadows on the walls of the coffee house. At one point, when the widow Enç was on the point of capturing the entire discard pile, Gül Seren became convinced Saljan had opened the window and was about to slip out. The squinting widow misread her partner's horrified stare for some sort of high-low signal, did not play the winning card, and they lost the hand. Then, two rounds later, there again seemed to be movement up at the window only this time Safraz the Mule, as feared, ambled into the foreground and blocked Gül Seren's view. Was that window open or closed? She was so agitated the others asked her if she was feeling unwell. She quickly said she didn't want to speak out of turn, but was Safraz allowed to eat Emine Hanım's jasmine? From the speed with which their hostess moved, the answer was no. The mule was seen off, seats resumed, and then to her horror Gül Seren realised that at some point in the kerfuffle Saljan had switched off her bedroom light.

She could do nothing. If she left the game now on some pretext, it would be too late anyway. It wasn't as if she wanted to stop Saljan, not that she could. She just wanted to know that she was all right. Not being pressured in any way. After all, she was the closest thing the darling girl had to a mother, and if she didn't worry about her, nobody would. Well, certainly not her own father. Jafar, dear man, was too busy running the coffee house to fret over his niece. So that left her. She looked across towards Saljan's window, but Safraz, stubborn as ever, was back. And this time he really was gobbling the jasmine.

Fine. Forget it. Whose turn is it to deal?

Gül Seren returned to the coffee house fairly late. She and the widow had a winning streak and actually the other two women weren't that intolerable after a glass or two of Emine Hanım's hibiscus liqueur. Jafar was already in bed; he said she'd missed a lovely evening. Beyrek the Coppersmith had come over, and they'd all played cards. Even Mahmoud. The two brothers had played the kids. They'd started with *Pişti*, then *Papaz Kacti* and finally *Blöf*, which Beyrek was hopeless at. Couldn't bluff to save his life. Seems a nice lad. He couldn't stay late, because he's got an early start. He's landed a big contract to supply all the kitchen copperware for the new hotel. And he's had the decency to give Old Ragıp all the pot-lids to make.

And where's Saljan?

Gone to bed. She said to tell you she's got Minoş in her room with her, but not to worry. She can't get out. The window's closed.

***

Beyrek was also worried about Saljan, but with more foundation than her aunt. He knew what she was doing. One early evening after work they took persimmons, white cheese and walnuts to the ruins and sat on the fallen blocks of stone amid Egyptian bean-lily and bear's breeches, rustic nard and wild briar. Damselflies darted about them as they ate. Beyrek was curious to know what she and the man in prison found to talk about every week. So she told him. That they pretended to chat about nothing very much so the guards wouldn't get suspicious, but in fact he was dictating a film script to her. Then she'd write it down from memory that night, and revise and correct it over the following evenings. It wasn't just a script; he was simultaneously telling her what each scene should look and feel like. He called it the Director's Notes. The script said what happened in each scene, and what the characters said to one another. The Notes explained more about the look and feel of the scene, the way relationships and themes were developing, details of casting or appearance which were very important to Turali Efendi. There were some things he was happy to leave to the imagination of the people who would actually make the film. And then there were things he felt very strongly about, and was giving very precise instructions which had to be followed.

It was a tiny bit like the relationship between the Holy Qur'ān and the Hadith. He was dictating two documents to her: the Word, and how to bring the Word to life.

What, Beyrek asked, is this film about exactly?

Saljan didn't have to think about this. She said she couldn't tell him. It was Turali Efendi's secret. She was just the messenger. She didn't have the authority to deliver it to anyone other than the intended recipient.

And who was this intended recipient?

She didn't know yet. He hadn't told her. And when he did, that would probably be part of the secret as well.

Beyrek was troubled. He wasn't sure Saljan knew the danger in what she was doing. He had asked Dr Dumrul about this Turali person and he had replied at some length. The more he told him, the more anxious Beyrek became. The man had spent most of his life behind bars for subversion. The courts had branded him as "a dangerous enemy of the state". Now maybe, as Dr Dumrul said, he was on the side of ordinary people. Maybe, as Scheherazade Hanım said, he was a genius with his heart in the right place. But it wasn't fair to endanger Saljan. If he was driven by conviction to make films and write books to stir up opposition to the authorities, that was his affair. But by using Saljan as a go-between, he was exposing her to the charge of conspiracy to commit sedition. Beyrek had gone into the library and looked it up. If she were caught, no one would be able to help her. And Beyrek couldn't see how she could avoid getting caught. As soon as this film came out, the secret police would immediately go looking for anyone who had had sustained contact with İsmet Turali. And given he was in solitary confinement, the list of suspects wasn't exactly long.

But that wasn't all. Things were getting tougher. A big clamp-down was in progress. There were more police and army on the streets. More arrests. More martial music on the radio. Web-sites were being blocked. No phones were safe. It was a really bad time to be smuggling a film script out of prison for an enemy of the state.

There was no point in keeping these fears to himself, so Beyrek shared them with Saljan. She was touched he was so concerned. But there really was nothing to worry about.

He shrugged, got up and looked around for half a dozen flattish stones which he then stacked up as a target on top of a plinth about thirty feet away from Saljan. Then he gathered ten small round pebbles as missiles for her and ten for him. But before he reached her side she had knocked the stones off the plinth. He put them back. She knocked them over again. Then she said she would give him a chance. He set them up, sat next to her and threw. With his seventh pebble he hit the base of the pile. It wobbled but did not fall. The last three missed. So Saljan handed him three of her pebbles, and with his very next throw he sent the stack flying.

She clapped her hands, and then, reaching behind his head with her fingers in his hair, pulled him towards her. She kissed him for the first time. She ran the tip of her tongue slowly over and around the tip of his. She held him, between her mouth and her palm. She smelled of mimosa. She tasted of persimmon.

It was a moment he was at first too worried to enjoy. Then, as the moment went deliciously on, the worry slipped away. But the closer the kiss connected them, the quicker his anxiety for her returned. And not just for her. The kiss created a third entity amid the ruins: us. Beyrek could almost feel the tendrils of responsibility for them as a couple grow out of their embrace.

She rested her head on his shoulder, and he rested his head on her head. They sat like that as the sun dipped below the arch at the far end of the ruined colonnade.

'Why are you doing it, Saljan?'

'Because he asked me. Because if I can carry more than coffee, then I should. Because this won't go on forever, and I don't want to feel ashamed of myself afterwards.'

She said nothing about the remarkable calm, the self-containment of the man, which she found very appealing. Or the fact that he had eyes like conkers. Not that she fancied Turali Efendi. She didn't. But sometimes tiny things become big deciders.

'Besides, the film script isn't about anything political. It's not against the state. And no one knows I'm carrying it.'

'Not between the prison and the coffee house, they don't. But you are writing it down, and presumably at some point you're going to have to deliver it somewhere.'

'Yes,' she replied, after a moment's thought. 'I am. And at that point you can come with me to make sure we are both safe. Me and the script.'

Beyrek wasn't sure this was going the way he'd planned. He seemed to have joined the conspiracy. Funny that.

And another thing. At the start of the picnic there had been just the two of them: Saljan and me. Then, with that amazing, wonderful kiss, two became three: Saljan, me and us. Now she was bringing this man Turali's script into it as if it was part of her, as if she were carrying his baby. So now Beyrek was having to worry for four. If they stayed any longer in those ruins, he'd have enough to form his own football team.

When the shadows were at their longest, and the bats began scouting the twilight, Saljan and Beyrek played another of their games in the ruins: racing one another to the arch from pillar to pillar, without touching the ground. She won, of course. She always did. Only this time he didn't try to compete. He stopped and watched her dart over the fallen columns, silhouetted against the copper sunset. She was still, for all that kiss, as unattainable as she was tantalising. And another thing: she looked for all the world as if she were flying.

Saljan thought about what Beyrek had said about the tightening up. The next day she looked for the signs – and found them. She had a delivery to the dry-cleaners in Atabay Street and noticed soldiers on guard outside the newspaper offices. The doors had been locked with chains looped through the handles. On her way to the Mayor with four medium sweets and some *kunafa*, she turned the corner by the *dolmuş* stand and ran into a police barricade. Luckily the tray was in a high swing, which she simply followed-through to bring it spiralling safely down. The whole street had been closed off. They said it was to stop car bombers. One of the policemen recognised her and let her pass.

The most upsetting sight of the day was on her way back from taking Abdul Bey his afternoon tea, when she passed the Kilim Merchants' Association. She saw men in plain clothes frogmarching Abulfaz Efendi out of the building with his wife who worked as his secretary. Saljan couldn't remember her name, but she would never forget the look on her face as they were manhandled into the back of a van. Almost as upsetting was the fact that everyone in the street pretended nothing was happening. Saljan started forward, opening her mouth to protest, but felt a hand on her shoulder, pulling her away. It was the policeman from the morning's roadblock. With a face full of sadness, he gave her an almost imperceptible shake of the head and then asked to be remembered to her father.

Next Monday she realised prison was not immune to the increasing repression. The queue she was escorted past with her tray was longer than ever. The corridors and walkways were full of inmates on the move. There were guards whose faces she did not recognise. Şevket the Bald whispered to her that, with all the arrests, the prison was now full to bursting. And there were changes afoot, as she would see.

For the first time, she and İsmet were not alone in his cell. An electrician was standing on the table, baldly fixing a microphone to the light. Turali Efendi did not look the slightest bit perturbed, but carried on as if the man were not present. As if he were telling Saljan Bible stories. The electrician ran the microphone cable up into a junction box screwed to the ceiling, nearly kicking over İsmet's coffee cup as he clambered down and left the cell. İsmet rolled his eyes upwards fleetingly and brushed his finger vertically down the centre of his lips to counsel silence. The electrician appeared just as she was leaving, to say they could hear İsmet loud and clear, and that he had a cousin who became a Christian. But she found it all a bit implausible and didn't stick at it.

It was only as Saljan was queuing up to leave that she realised, for the first time, that Turali Efendi had not given her any Director's Notes. And, with that microphone dangling over them, he never did so openly again. Character back-histories, advice on casting and descriptions of how the sets should be dressed would have instantly given the game away. Sometimes he buried instructions within his story, as when he specified, remembering *Kanli*, what the shepherds were wearing when the angel announced the birth of Christ to them. He took particular care to describe each of the Wise Men in detail – character and appearance - to ensure they would resemble the three Politans as closely as possible.

Both their tasks became more challenging. Saljan had to work extra hard in the evenings sifting the script to extract these scattered, hidden directives. And İsmet had to prepare each slug of the story in advance to be certain it would not sound in any way suspicious. From now on, they had to assume someone was listening to everything they said to one another. They were over half way through at this stage, but shaping the remainder of the material became a much more tortuous process.

İsmet started to lose heart. Three weeks later, for the first time, he sat almost in silence throughout her visit, and when he did speak it was not about Mary and her son. The week after, he was very irritable. Why just one cup of coffee? When he was a free man he'd have as many as he wanted. He'd have to dance his cup to stop them coming. How funny, Saljan thought. It was an old expression of her grandfather's. It meant tilting your cup from side to side to show you'd had enough. She remembered Uncle Jafar as a young man calling out from behind the counter, does Hoja Iz want another? No, Grandpa would say. He's danced his cup.

'Would you like me to bring in two next week, Turali Efendi?' Saljan asked him gently. 'Because I'm sure I could.'

'What would be the point? he asked sulkily. 'The second cup would only be cold.'

She didn't tell anyone Turali Efendi was not being his usual self, but her family knew something in her life was different because she didn't take to her room in the evenings. She had nothing to write down. She worried about him instead. He had always been so courteous to her, with never a hint of self-pity. What had changed? She fetched the copy of *Dear Yazmira* from its hiding-place behind the sacks of finest Yemeni Arabica beans in the coffee store and re-read the piece about Turali Efendi on the back, alongside the author's photograph: that face of a boy. She needed a pencil and paper to do the maths, but the information was all there. When she finished, she replaced the book and went to see Othman. He was standing with his ears at ten past ten. Saljan walked along the wall and sat down by him, tickling his flanks with her toes.

'He's been in prison on and off since he was twenty-seven,' she told the donkey. 'He's now nearly sixty. That's over thirty years of his life behind bars. I wouldn't like it. And neither would you.'

Othman glanced across to make sure Safraz the mule was safely in the distance and advanced his ears to twenty to four. Then he put his head down and came up with a huge clump of grass in his mouth. It seemed like as good a plan as any.

The next week Saljan brought İsmet a slightly bigger cup of coffee and a saucer full of pistachio *pişmaniye*, which was the closest substitute she could find for grass. She had no idea that it had been a childhood favourite of his, although in his family they knew it as *tel tel*, or else just "whiskers". He looked up from the tray and smiled at Saljan. He apologised to her for his recent moods. They were unforgivable. He had no right to take anything out on her. She gave him one of her day-breaking grins and said he hadn't been half as grumpy as her father could be. And would he mind getting on with his story because it had just reached a particularly interesting bit, when they all fled to Egypt. He rolled his eyes skywards in the direction of the microphone, winked at her with his left eye so the guards couldn't see, took a pinch of sugary whiskers and a swig of coffee, and resumed.

It was only a matter of time before her aunt found out that Saljan was writing something. It involved no stealth on Gül Seren's part, just a stray current of air and a door that failed to latch. One evening she was putting sheets into the airing cupboard on the landing, thinking about Jafar's first wife. Ayşe had come into Gül Seren's mind because she noticed that one of the sheets had an entwined "A" and "J" embroidered in red thread in one corner. She didn't know there were any still in circulation, and seeing this one threw her a little.

When she married Jafar, he had told her that it was entirely up to her what she kept of Ayşe's and what she got rid of. Given, as he put it, that Gül Seren's choices did not extend to him, the two boys Hussein and Salih, Othman the donkey or Minoş the cat, he could hardly complain if she wanted to sling out his late wife's saucepans. In fact the saucepans were at the bottom of her list, made by Old Ragıp at the height of his powers: thick of base, tight of lid; quick to boil, long to simmer. The sheets were something else: Jafar and Ayşe had not made love in the saucepans.

'You been through the airing cupboard yet?' Jafar called up to her on her third morning in his house.

'Not yet,' she replied, struggling to get boys wary of premature intimacy ready for school. 'Maybe later.'

It was a chore she'd been dreading. They had been given sheets and pillow-cases for a wedding present by her brother and his wife, and Gül Seren made sure they were what was on her marital bed. But she did not want to open that door on the landing. What underwear drawers are to lovers, married or otherwise, airing cupboards are to house-wives. Repositories of shared memories. Revealers of taste and husbandry, good and poor. All those moth-holes, stains and clumsy darns laid out in neat piles. At least she did not have to worry about Ayşe's clothes. Her sister and mother removed them from the house immediately after the funeral. Jafar wasn't ever asked, but it was what he wanted. He had Ayşe's memory to grieve over; he didn't need her blouses or socks.

In the event, the cupboard was almost dysfunctionally impersonal. Nothing that wasn't white. Not an unravelled seam to be seen. Spotless. No signs of the life before the death - except for those embroidered letters. It wouldn't have mattered so much, perhaps, had they not been interlaced. When she saw them, Gül Seren couldn't get out of her mind a picture of Ayşe and Jafar entwined. That was, after all, their message. That was Ayşe's purpose in sewing them onto their pillow-cases as well as sheets. She never sent them to a laundry, so they were not distinguishing marks of ownership. Except they were. They made Gül Seren, who was not a jealous woman, feel like an interloper. What couples did they know, she wondered, whose names began with "A" and "J" whom they could give the whole set to? But she couldn't think of any. So she made sure her brother-in-law Mahmoud had the pillow-cases on his bed, because his hair gel guaranteed them a short, sticky life. The sheets she split into singles and used on the boys' beds until they too went beyond hope.

So what, years after Ayşe's death, was this rogue sheet with its intimate blazon still doing in her - Gül Seren's – airing cupboard? Which is why she slammed the door in irritation at the perversity of inanimate objects and at herself for being caught off-guard after so long. The cupboard being windowless, the air inside was pushed out by the closing door, and a tiny wave of pressure passed down the corridor until it reached the point of least resistance: Saljan's door, which being only half on the latch, yielded to the fugitive puff of wind and swung open. Inside Gül Seren saw her beloved niece at the table. She had an oddly flat pencil in her hand and two stacks of paper in front of her. One clean, one covered with writing. Hearing the hinges creak, Saljan looked up at her aunt, before curling her arm around what she was writing, in that age-old gesture of children at school who do not want their neighbour to copy their work.

'I now know what Saljan does in the evenings,' Gül Seren whispered to Jafar as he climbed into bed. 'She's writing something.'

Jafar looked surprised, but had learned never to underestimate his niece.

'Writing what? What's it about?'

His wife didn't know. But she was worried it might have something to do with the "medium man". That was how they referred to İsmet: by the amount of sugar he took in his coffee. Was she writing his biography? Jafar wanted to know. Because if so, he couldn't see it being very interesting. What had he done, most of his life, but rot in gaol? That was the tragedy of the medium man. Such talent - wasted. Jafar admitted that all he really knew about in the world was running a coffee house, but try as he might, he personally couldn't see a book in it. At this, Gül Seren became a little impatient with her husband, and had difficulty keeping her voice to a whisper. She said it wasn't the potential sales figures that should be bothering Jafar, but the danger to his darling niece if she were caught writing the life of a State enemy.

Jafar wasn't a stupid man, and he adored his niece. He quickly became more agitated than Gül Seren. And as usual when he became agitated, which wasn't very often, he took it out on his wife. Had she asked Saljan what she was writing about? Why hadn't she insisted on knowing? Saljan was putting them all in danger by this selfish act. She must be writing about the medium man, else why would she be so secretive about it? Gül Seren had done quite wrong not to ask. It was a serious mistake of judgment.

Gül Seren rolled away from her husband out of exasperation, and then found herself checking the corner of the sheets on her side to make sure her fingers felt no embroidery. She really wasn't having a very pleasant evening. After a few minutes the pompous, misguided rant blew itself out. Love him as she did, she wasn't going to let Jafar dump the problem on her.

'If you want to know what Saljan's writing about, why don't you go and ask her.'

There was a heavy, hard-done-by sigh from the other side of the bed, and then she felt the springs shift and heard his bare feet scrabbling for his slippers. Then the sound of him putting on his dressing-gown. Then a question.

'Well? Don't you want to know the answer too?'

She thought about asking Jafar if it was beyond his intellectual capabilities to remember Saljan's answer for the five seconds it would take him to get back from her bedroom, but her curiosity won over her snippiness. She slipped on her nightgown, and saw that Jafar was wearing the dressing gown with the sleeves that were too short. The one he looked silly in. She hoped it wouldn't weaken his authority over his unbiddable niece.

She didn't have to worry. They never actually opened Saljan's door. Jafar left their bedroom boldly, but arrived at hers hesitant. He and his wife had a hurried whisper about whether they had the right to ask, which ended with Gül Seren flashing her eyes at him and a sharp inclination of her head towards her niece's door. Jafar knocked on it, quietly at first, and then with some vigour.

'Yes, Uncle Jafar?'

There was no way of telling from Saljan's voice whether she was in bed or still at her table, jeopardising the family with her literary ambitions.

'Auntie says you are writing something.'

'Yes, Uncle Jafar.'

'What….is it about, Saljan?'

'It's a story, Uncle Jafar.'

'Is it a story about…anyone you know? About anyone you deliver coffee to on a Monday?'

'No, Uncle Jafar. It's about things that happened thousands of years ago.'

'Oh.'

He turned to Gül Seren, who gave a relieved shrug. But Jafar still had a gap to fill.

'I have to ask you Saljan, is it for publication?'

'I am not writing a book, Uncle Jafar.'

He looked at Gül Seren, who mouthed the word "fine!" at him.

'Goodnight Saljan. Sorry to disturb you. Sleep well.'

'Goodnight Uncle Jafar. Goodnight Auntie Gül Seren.'

How did Saljan know Gül Seren was also outside the door? They had no idea, but no matter; they got back to their bedroom considerably relieved. Gül Seren felt she had been absolutely right to raise the matter, and Jafar felt he had handled the whole thing masterfully. She took off her nightgown. He took off the dressing gown with the short sleeves. She took off her nightdress. He never wore pyjamas. She got into bed on his side, so he would have to climb over her to get to hers. Except he never got there.

Chapter Sixteen

"They say our mother bore the Messiah. Maybe she did – it's not for us to decide. But she also bore tolerance and in doing so, saved our family. Let us all bear tolerance, and save our world."

With these words of James at his mother Mary's funeral, İsmet finished dictating the script to Saljan with one Monday in hand.

If they had not, there was no hope of an extension. The Pasha made that clear to İsmet in a meeting in his office. The guards dumped İsmet in the chair opposite the desk and left. But the Pasha was not at his desk; he was sitting at a new table piled high with amplifiers, switchers and recording machines. He was smoking a cheroot and wearing headphones. He did not react to the entrance of his most distinguished inmate. He was too absorbed in eavesdropping on his unfortunate charges. From the expressions on his face, he might have been listening to a torrid scene of sexual passion. When he eventually noticed İsmet it was with a forced double-take.

'Ah, İsmet Efendi! Here you are!' he said. 'We had all quite lost track of you.'

And me in the same cell these seven years, thought İsmet.

The Pasha nodded towards his array of sound equipment.

'You know how it is, old friend - new technology that is meant to make our lives easier?'

The Pasha shook his heavily groomed, regularly massaged head.

'My workload has doubled, tripled even! Still, we are all prisoners of the system are we not? Ha! What can I do for you?'

The Pasha did not wait for an answer.

'Your Annual Prison Report read very well. Very well indeed. The only part I was moved to improve on was the "Rehabilitation within Custody" section, but then I realised you were merely echoing my own thoughts on the subject. So I sent it as was, and they are very pleased with it. The talk at the Prison Governors' Conference went better than even I could have hoped. The Chairman summed up the mood of the delegates best, I think, when he said…let me see if I can remember the gist of it… "Governor Reşid understands our enemies better than they do themselves. Those who believe the Devil always has the best tunes should remind themselves that we have Osman Reşid."'

İsmet had not the slightest idea what this meant, but clapped his hands silently and gave a little bow of his head.

'So thank you for your assistance with that also. Now, to business.'

He dropped his cheroot into a half-drunk glass of tea.

'Following my little triumph at the conference, I confidently anticipate being in some demand for my keynote speeches. And they now seem to want an Annual Prison Report every year…'

İsmet glanced at the Pasha, but this was not one of his little jokes.

'…so I had intended to put our discreet little arrangement on a regular footing, so to say. But unfortunately we live in darkening times, and the entire country is on maximum security alert. There is talk of further restrictions: movement constraints, curfews. We here are now, like everyone else, full to the brim. So if someone came up, someone we really wanted, we simply couldn't offer him a place. Worse, they've been sending me riff-raff. Absolute riff-raff. I will tell you, my old friend, in absolute confidence: I believe we are the victims of a clearing-house system. We are getting men in here without any qualifications. I gave them fair warning that, in institutions like this, once you let standards drop you never get them back. We may be the flagship now, but come back in five years' time. Then what, eh? I said to them, if the Ministry were to peg my pension to the aggregated IQ level of the inmates, the way things are going I will retire a pauper!'

The Pasha lit another cheroot and sat back in silence. İsmet waited for him to continue, but he just sat shaking his head from time to time and blowing the occasional smoke-ring. Then he leaned forward and started moving the papers on his desk into his out-tray. After a while, he glanced up, half-surprised to see İsmet still there.

'Heavens, İsmet Efendi! We mustn't keep you! I am sure you have more important things to do.'

He pressed the buzzer for the guards.

'By the by, I was most impressed by the religious stories with which you've been entertaining my friend Mahmoud's rather fetching daughter. Only caught a snatch, mind, but fascinating stuff. A bit over her head I should have thought, but you and I really must make time to discuss the theology of it all at greater length. Yes, after next Monday I fancy you'll rather miss your little coffee mornings.'

Then the guards blundered in and whisked İsmet back to solitary.

***

The entire coffee house was involved in planning the medium man's last tray. Jafar thought of giving him six flavours of *lokum*: plain, rose pistachio, hazelnut, cream with cinnamon, sour cherry and apricot. Hussein voted for a plate of different kinds of pastry: *baklava* with nuts, *baklava* with cream, syrup-soaked *kadayıf*, small round *maamoul* with nut and date stuffing. Gül Seren made a strong case for *halva*, chocolate and pistachio, which Saljan had said he was always pleased to see. Tarık, the coffee and tea maker, suggested he might care for some *aşure* – the pudding Noah's wife made on the Ark from forty ingredients in her store cupboard. Sami the sweets and pudding-maker said maybe they should let the poor man down gently by not giving him anything too special. Otherwise it would be to rub his nose in his loss.

Then Salih, the younger of Jafar's boys, wondered if the medium man might simply like a little of each, and they thought that an excellent idea. Only no quince, Saljan said. Bad enough it being his last tray without upsetting him with quince.

Saljan polished the tray till it glowed. Gül Seren picked sprays of Zambuc jessamine from the garden to adorn it. Jafar prepared the saucers. Sami filled them. Tarık ground a handful of his best Yemeni beans. Saljan stood outside looking down the hill, preparing her route, spotting any camels bound for market that looked as if they might suddenly change their minds.

'Saljan! Ready!'

She heard Uncle Jafar's anxious voice and dashed inside to collect her tray.

One last vertiginous glance for route confirmation.

And she was gone.

For the first time in their fifty-two meetings, Saljan did almost all the talking. İsmet began it though, by saying how very easy she had been to talk to. How enjoyable he'd found it. Her father must take great delight in her company.

She said her relationship with her father barely merited the word. He was closed-off to her and to his family. He had never kicked a football with his nephews, the way his brother Jafar had with her. Yes, he'd sit with his cronies in the garden, but there was always this distance around him. As if he had been pasted into the scene from somewhere else. He didn't really belong with them. He never tried to connect to her. She might have thought, before these Monday mornings, that her father was like a man in solitary confinement, but now she had met such a man, she did not think the parallel apt. By which she meant: the situations might be similar – one can no doubt feel as trapped within oneself as by walls and bars – but the difference lies in how one faces the imprisonment. The difference between outward-looking creativity and vain indolence.

It may simply be, said İsmet gently in a rare intervention, the difference between the tortoise and the hare.

'But what a world of a difference that is,' Saljan replied a little sadly.

Then she remembered herself, and that it was her last time with Turali Efendi, and she decided to brighten the mood and tell him about everyone at the coffee house other than her father. What their names were, what they looked like and what they all did. She talked about how lovely her Auntie

Gül Seren was, and about the way Tarık's beard wiggled as he dashed about the kitchen, and her uncle Jafar always pretending to be shocked at finding Minoş the cat asleep on the sacks of coffee beans. İsmet was most intrigued by Othman and his ears that told the time. He wanted to know how the donkey knew when the clocks went forward and back, and Saljan told him that when she said Othman's ears told the time, she did not necessarily mean the right time. Though inevitably they did sometimes.

They heard the scrape of Şevket the Bald's chair outside. Saljan stood and carefully slid the uneaten sweets and pastries onto a paper napkin which she placed on İsmet's shelf. She put the jessamine sprigs in his glass of water and left it on his table. He watched her doing these tiny, tranquil, enchanting acts of domesticity, and was filled with the pain of realization at what he had missed over the years. Then she looked at him and smiled, and her smile almost made up for it all.

'Please thank them all for their kindness, and Tarık and Sami for their great skills. And thank you, Saljan, most of all.'

Şevket the Bald escorted her out, leaving İsmet sitting as he had been the very first time they met. So that, had she looked back, she would have seen a man who, for all his paleness did not have the air of being beaten down by imprisonment. His own man. Not scared and not defiant. A free man.

But she did not look back. She did not want him to see her crying.

And when the cell-door clanged shut and the lock tumbled home, his conker eyes too filled with tears. As if Saljan had brought him a tureen of poached quince on her dazzling tray.

***

Saljan's only remaining obligation was to get the film script to Murat. Not that she had been told his name, or anything about him. Indeed, it was only a fortnight before her final prison run that she had learned what to do with the hundred and seventy six pages she had filled with her compact hand-writing. She had been wondering how to ask Turali Efendi the question safely, and then her uncle handed her an envelope. She had just returned to the coffee house after a day of non-stop deliveries. She took it into the garden and opened it. Inside was a piece of rice paper. Written on it in pencil was an email address. She looked at the envelope; it simply bore her name. No stamp. She re-read the email address, swallowed the rice paper and went inside to see Jafar.

'A woman, in her late fifties, I would say. Respectably dressed, not gaudy. She just walked in and asked if you were here. I said no, but you would be later. She wanted to know if I'd be seeing you. I laughed and said you were my niece - of course I would. She said I had to put the envelope into your hands in person. Then she left. I think she must have come in a car, but then the phone rang and….why? What was in the envelope? Is there any problem?'

Saljan told Jafar there was no problem. She did not tell him what was in the envelope. And he did not tell her that the woman had the prettiest ankles he had seen in a long while. Not that Gül Seren's were anything but delightful, but he still had eyes in his head and he couldn't help noticing them as she walked to the door. Before the town surveyor phoned about his son's wedding…

Saljan found Beyrek in deep discussion with Old Ragıp about how to make sure his lids would exactly fit Beyrek's pans. There was talk of standardization and making up templates. She didn't really understand what they were talking about, and whiled away the time dropping pinches of metal filings into the small hearth and watching the flames turn different colours. There was a particular combination which produced a livid greeny-blue she really liked. Eventually Old Ragıp left. She hoped Beyrek would not try to explain the science to her, but he just handed her some matchboxes he had been putting copper, phosphor bronze and other filings into for her to play with. He was getting to know her. He knew she didn't care for science and technology, though she sometimes appreciated what they did. Like the dull grey dust in one of the matchboxes which produced a shower of sparks and a crackling noise. Like a long word on a piece of rice paper which would somehow carry Turali Efendi's film script to the other side of the world.

The answer to all her questions was, Beyrek assured her, Dr Berent Dumrul. Beyrek said that first the script would have to be scanned page by page which would transfer the words to a computer file. That would then be sent as an email attachment to the address the woman had given her. The government had been severing links to the outside world by jamming radio and TV stations, and by blocking access to the web. It was unlikely Saljan's friend Yaprak, whom she had wondered about asking, would have the know-how to get the script past the Web Police. But Berent Dumrul was very clever, and very discreet. And it was good that he lived a way away from prying eyes. Let us hope, Beyrek added, that he is sympathetic.

Saljan thought he would be. It was Dr Dumrul, after all, who had brought her Turali Efendi's book *Dear Yazmira*. Which he had already taken the risk of smuggling in from Switzerland. Reading that was what won the coffee house over to the medium man. Of all people, Dr Dumrul would be sympathetic. But his remoteness turned out not to be the advantage Beyrek had assumed.

As often as she could, Saljan tried to be outside the school when the children arrived and left, in the hope of bumping into Scheherazade, but the week went by with no glimpse of her. Saljan wasn't worried because she knew she could catch Dr Dumrul when he popped into Mahmoud's to buy ground coffee and *baklava* which he did every Friday around 6pm. Suddenly at 5.50pm, with no deliveries on the board, an order came in for six sweet coffees to Police Headquarters. It couldn't be delayed. Her cousins had already left to play football. Saljan had to go. By the time she got back, Dr Dumrul had been and gone.

She flopped down, a little frustrated, on the divan. Perhaps she should have taken her uncle and aunt into her confidence, told them she needed to ask Dr Dumrul something, but it would have been so out of character for her, she knew it would worry them. Bloody policemen! And what was the piece of paper she had been handed by one of them who, like everyone else in the entire world, asked to be remembered to his dear friend, her father? She was by the front desk on her way out, when the sergeant on duty called her over and gave her a handbill of some sort. She might have to adapt her routes and deliveries, he said. He was giving her these hours of advanced warning because of who she was. And please to give my very best to…

She had folded it up without looking at it. Now she opened it, and was appalled. From midnight, the country would come under martial law. The list of regulations was stringent: dusk to dawn curfew, prohibition of assembly except for prayer, prohibition of non-permitted movement, prohibition of communication with foreigners, prohibition of receiving or circulating forbidden materials whether by hand, transmitting/receiving/texting devices including radio sets, mobile phones and computers. Use of the internet forbidden. Closure until further notice of all universities, colleges and schools. Closure until further notice of sporting venues and places of entertainment. No hoarding. No black-marketeering. No challenging of authority. No redress against damage caused by the military or police in pursuance of their duties. Suspension of the civil legal system. Binding obligation on all to denounce immediately to the authorities anyone suspected of breaching these regulations. Summary punishment, including the death sentence, for breaches of these regulations. Then, below, were the local ordinances: road closures, confiscation of private vehicles, demarcation of town limits beyond which no unauthorised movements would be permitted.

She looked at the clock. She had five hours and twenty two minutes.

First, she went to fetch Beyrek. It wouldn't be safe to leave before it got dark and, anyway, she'd promised him that he could go with her to deliver the film script. To make sure she and it were safe. He was delighted to see her. He was about to grill some little fishes over the small hearth. He had been going to have them all, which would have been a bit greedy. Lovely, she said. Let's eat, and then we're going out somewhere. He nodded and oiled the grill. He'd seen the way the seriousness chased the smile from her face. He guessed it had something to do with the prisoner's film script, but he kept quiet. He spread a cloth on the table. He put out coarse salt, fine pepper, chopped parsley, a loaf of sesame bread, a jug of ice cold water. The lemon juice sizzled as it hit the blackened skins of the little fishes. Fingers licked, hands washed, lights out. A bit rushed, he thought as he locked up the smithy, but she seemed to like it.

That evening, Beyrek the Coppersmith set himself the challenge of asking her no questions.

Next, she and Beyrek went back to Mahmoud's Coffee House. She formally introduced him to Auntie Gül Seren and asked Uncle Jafar if he minded them borrowing Othman for the evening. She and Beyrek wanted to get a bit of fresh air; it was so close outside. Jafar said it would be good for the donkey to get some exercise. Saljan went upstairs to change, and the others made small-talk during which they worked out that Jafar had done his military service with Beyrek's uncle. Saljan's reappearance at the top of the stairs reduced them to silence. She was wearing a long gown in blue cotton that had belonged to her mother. It was very plain and loose. Her hair, which she had been growing, was now touching her shoulders. She looked very tall, and very, very beautiful as she glided down the stairs. Beyrek was speechless, and so was her uncle. Jafar was the only person present who had known her mother, and the resemblance was so close that he felt it probably just as well his brother Mahmoud was playing backgammon at Abdul Bey's house. He might think he was seeing a ghost.

'You look glorious, Saljan darling,' Gül Seren whispered as she gave her niece a hug.

'Well children', said Jafar. 'Don't be too late. Oh, and I think Othman's tail light may be out.'

'It's a family joke', Gül Seren said, rolling her eyes as she bundled them out of the door. 'Or so Jafar tells me.'

I can't think why she was dressed like that, Jafar said as he made them both tea. Gül Seren, leaning on the counter, was a little taken aback. She told him she thought Saljan looked absolutely lovely. Didn't he? Certainly, Jafar replied. That, he said, was his point. The boy was already besotted with her. Why pile on any more agony? Gül Seren thought for a moment or two, and then said that it wasn't in Saljan's character to lead anyone on. She was as straight as a die. The sooner Beyrek realised how amazing she was, the better. Well, Jafar suggested, pouring boiling water over the fresh mint leaves, perhaps tonight's the night she'll propose to him. And he flipped the lights out.

Saljan did not take Beyrek across the garden to the waste ground where the donkey lived. Instead, she led him around the side of the coffee house. Hanging down from her window was a cord with a basket tied to the end, almost touching the ground, motionless in the still air. In the basket was a sealed packet with tapes attached. She turned slightly away from Beyrek and lifting her dress, slipped the tapes around her waist and tied them so the packet rested at her stomach. She did it in a swift, practised action, so all Beyrek saw was a flash of amazing legs, the packet vanish, and the gown float back down. She turned and, catching Beyrek's hand in hers, took him to meet Othman.

It no longer felt like their town. It no longer sounded like their town. Police-cars criss-crossed the streets, blaring the news of imminent martial law. People scurried home. Shopkeepers put up shutters. Saljan rode Othman, and Beyrek walked by their side. They passed bales of barbed wire dumped in the road. Piles of red and white barriers. A stack of sentry-boxes. There were strange anomalies: floodlights had turned the alleys around the station into day, but Hafiz Square was in complete darkness. The Ibrahim Middle School was a blaze of lights with no one in sight, but the Ayoub Street cinema was already dark, with a small crowd outside. Army trucks waited ominously at the Technical Institute, waiting to pounce. Then Saljan and Beyrek rounded a corner and saw their first checkpoint. Ahead of them, soldiers were pulling a car apart. Someone was crying. Someone was shouting. Then two people were led away at gunpoint.

'Oh dear,' Beyrek murmured, almost under his breath. His instincts were to turn, to flee, but instead he was escorting the most precious person in the world into danger, on her old donkey. And with a bump under her gown they might lose their lives for.

'Don't worry,' Saljan replied. 'This has been done before. It works. Watch.'

They waited their turn. Finally the soldiers got round to them: the pregnant girl on the donkey with the man at her side. They looked at their papers. Then back at them. At Saljan, and her bulge. One of the soldiers gave Beyrek a leer.

'Girlfriend going to have a baby, eh? Go on. Off with you!'

Again, Beyrek's instincts were to run, but Saljan gave Othman a gentle nudge and he moved off at his usual unhurried gait. It felt an age before they reached the end of the street and turned out of sight, and when they did, Saljan reached down for Beyrek's hand. It felt clammy, which it never did, and she gave it a squeeze.

They went through one more roadblock at the edge of the town. The soldiers barely glanced at them, but then an officer wandered out of a tent, scratching himself. He asked where they were going. Saljan said they wanted to stretch the donkey's legs one last time before the curfew began. The officer said that if the Army requisitioned the donkey, and these days anything could happen, he'd get his legs stretched all he needed and then some. Saljan did not reply, and something about her made him slightly uncomfortable. Well, he barked at Beyrek, what do you have to say to that? Beyrek said they would naturally comply with whatever was asked of them in the name of national unity. The officer stared at him to see if he was being facetious, but Beyrek just looked open-faced and honest. The officer turned, spat and went back into his tent.

Only when Saljan and Beyrek were out of the soldiers' sight did they breathe again. Only when they passed the last street lamp of all did Othman's ears move from a defensive twenty-five past seven to a semi-confident ten to three. Their next challenge was the darkness. It was absolute. No moon, no stars, no aeroplane lights blinking down. A thick awning of dark cloud stretched from horizon to horizon. Saljan and Beyrek could not see where they were going, and didn't want to use their torch for fear of being spotted by a patrol. They were totally dependent on Othman knowing the way strategically, and, at the tactical level, not tripping over a rock in his path. He showed no sign of fear or hesitation, but trotted on at a steady pace. They didn't see or say anything for twenty minutes. Beyrek was just starting to wonder if they were lost, when he saw a strange gleam, low in the sky ahead. It looked like a very dim sun, one glimpsed through thick fog. He pointed it out to Saljan, but she had seen it already. He stopped himself just in time from asking what she thought it was.

'It means,' she told him, reading his mind, 'that Kazan passed on the message to his parents. I rang the Dumruls from upstairs, while I was changing.'

Whether Othman could see the light, they had no idea. But it lay precisely in the direction he was taking them. Soon they could hear the old sewage pump clatter and suck, and shortly after that, the path became steeper and started to twist. They were climbing Dr Dumrul's hill. Beyrek noticed that the glow was becoming dimmer, and then brighter. Dimmer at the turns, brighter at the centre of the zig-zags. Sometimes when the path went particularly far to one side, the light went out altogether, only to reignite itself when they were back on target. It wasn't behaving like any sun or star he had ever seen. Nor like a lantern, if Berent had hung one up as a beacon. He looked at Saljan, but he couldn't see her face. Never mind, he said to himself. This is one of those nights. All will be revealed.

As the track levelled off, the guiding light grew fainter and fainter until it went out and never came back. But then they saw the glow from the windows of the motor-home. The door opened and the Dumruls rushed out, clapping and waving. Scheherazade gave Saljan a hug and, ushering her inside while the men looked after Othman, asked in a whisper if she was pregnant. Saljan let out a peal of laughter and shaking her head, released the package from under her gown. Then Kazan appeared in his pyjamas and Saljan gave him a hug and thanked him for being a good messenger boy. He wanted to know if she had brought Othman with her, and Saljan told him it was the other way round. Othman had brought her and Beyrek with him, and he'd had to be a very brave donkey. Kazan insisted on taking Othman some carrots, and then Saljan peered at Othman's ears and said, my – was that the time and Kazan really ought to be in bed. Kazan wanted to know how a donkey's ears could tell the time, and Saljan said she didn't know and that was part of what made it so amazing.

When boy and donkey were settled, Saljan explained to Berent and Scheherazade that İsmet Turali had dictated a film script to her which she had written down and now needed to email. Would they be prepared to help? Given the current risks she would quite understand if not. They said straightaway it would be an honour. Dr Dumrul took the package to the scanner and started the process. Scheherazade asked if they had eaten, and even though they said they had, produced delicious bowls of this and that. Then Beyrek remembered how small the little fishes had been and that Saljan had had half of them, and soon they were all eating and drinking tea and helping to scan the script and sort the pages. They had a good time, until Dr Dumrul turned on the news and the President appeared, justifying the martial law and curfew. He said history would never have forgiven him had he not taken these steps to safeguard national unity and civil order. He said that everyone knew he personally stood for fairness, democracy and justice for all. It was to preserve these principles that he had introduced the present measures. It was for all their sakes and for their children's.

The atmosphere was a little sombre after this. The scanning took on a new urgency, and Scheherazade made coffee to keep them awake. How, Beyrek wanted to know, could Dr Dumrul stop the email getting caught by the Web Police? It wouldn't be going anywhere near them, Dr Dumrul replied. He had a satellite phone which would beam the film script straight up, bypassing land lines and ground stations.

'Can we watch it go?' Saljan asked.

'There won't be anything to see, but by all means, go outside and I'll tell you when I press "send", and it will fly up to the satellite and be relayed around the world to wherever the recipient is.'

When everything was ready, she and Beyrek went outside. What they saw amazed them, because the sky had cleared. A billion stars, the smudges of distant galaxies, constellations, planets, the great white Milky Way, a near-full moon – all of them now gleamed and blinked down on them. Saljan saw a satellite slowly arcing westwards and wondered if it was the one Dr Dumrul was aiming at, but Beyrek said that Dr Dumrul's would be in geostationary orbit and she wouldn't see it move. Then he wished he'd not said anything.

'Are you ready?' Scheherazade was at the window relaying messages and orders.

'Ready!' said Saljan staring upwards.

'Berent says you say when, Saljan,' Scheherazade called out.

Saljan waited for a moment, trying to spot what the satellite dish on the roof of the motor-home was pointing at. It appeared to be a patch of darkness, punctuated by five winking stars. She settled on one in particular and said 'Now!' Then Scheherazade turned to her husband and said 'Now!' and he pressed the button on the mouse and launched the email with its priceless attachment heavenwards.

It felt like an anti-climax when they went back inside. Did they want, Scheherazade asked, to spend the night there? They had spare beds. Saljan thanked her, and said they should get back. Thank goodness the cloud had lifted so they could see their way. Then Beyrek remembered the light that had guided them there from afar, and asked Dr Dumrul what it was.

'It was your trays, Beyrek.' Dr Dumrul said. 'The ones we used for the experiment. Kazan and I tied one to a tree on the top of the hill so it pointed down the track and then we bounced a beam of light up at it, using the other trays to get round the corners. It's a tribute to your finish that you could see the glow a long way off. I got the idea from Archimedes…'

At which point Scheherazade interrupted him and said that was nonsense. The idea was Kazan's. She'd been reading to him from *Alice's Adventures in Wonderland*. And she recited the verse:

"Twinkle, twinkle, little bat!
How I wonder what you're at!
Up above the world you fly,
Like a tea-tray in the sky."

Except, of course, in this case it was a coffee tray.

'You know how it is, said Dr Dumrul with a little shrug. 'It often happens in the history of science that a great idea occurs to two people at the same time…'

They took a different way back. Instead of retracing their steps, they decided to circle the town and come in near the old ruins. The moon gave them light and direction, but Othman knew the way. He knew all the ways. His pace was rhythmical and very soothing. Saljan was worried about falling asleep and slipping off him, so she made sure she stayed awake. Beyrek walked by her side, holding her hand. They saw no one, and no one saw them. There was no checkpoint on the track which snaked round the side of the hill to the back of the ruins. They went past the moonlit columns and arch, trotted along the edge of Othman's waste ground and down the path to the blacksmith's stable. Beyrek swung the door open and they slipped inside. The old nag was in her usual place, but Othman's winter stall was empty and clean. Beyrek spread straw for him and Saljan rubbed him down with a twist of hay. You have been very good and brave tonight, she whispered in his ear. In fact you've turned out to be a very great donkey.

The blacksmith had a hayloft, and it was there Beyrek made a bed for Saljan. As they were leaving the Dumruls, he'd formed the distinct impression she'd reattached the script around her waist, but now, looking down on her, he couldn't see it. She bent over to wash her face and hands at the tap. It was odd, he had almost got used to it. Then again, it made her seem fragile, and she was always so strong. She straightened up. No. She definitely wasn't pregnant now. He was about to ask her what she'd done with it, but remembered his covenant just in time.

Beyrek made one other wise decision that night. He did not linger in the hay loft. He didn't try to spend the night with her. He slid down the ladder and made a bed for himself in the blacksmith's tackroom.

You go up, he said to her, and then I'll put the light out.

As she climbed past him, she planted a kiss on the top of his head. For a moment he wondered if he was right to be wise. Then she was gone, out of his reach.

Chapter Seventeen

The following year was the worst of the thirty İsmet had spent in prison.

There was a host of reasons, some of which he had prepared himself for and some he had not. Oddly, the cruel subjugation beyond the high walls barely touched him. In solitary he heard little and saw nothing. The fact that everyone else in the country was now living a version of his own airless, powerless, dank, wretched existence, had no meaning for him. What does a fish in the black frigidity of the ocean deep know or care of the sudden cooling of water at the surface, or the coming of perpetual night? Unless, by the same token, its own environment becomes even more inhospitable – and that was hard for İsmet to imagine. Not for want of trying. Some prisoners planned elaborate feasts in their minds, gorging themselves on roast meats and flagons of wine, losing themselves with insatiable *houris*. İsmet tried to think how much worse his situation could get.

The answer lay in the issue of solitude. At least, he sometimes used to say to himself, I have a room of my own. True, he had enjoyed the company of Farouk the Forger. A discreet, careful man with a good mind, a strong heart, an impish humour and a flair for sharing pain as well as a crust makes an ideal cell-mate. He never spoke unless he sensed İsmet wanted to listen. He never let problems fester. He never protected himself at the expense of others. But how would it have been sharing with some of the others he had met behind bars? With Kerem – fine but demanding. With the corpulent clerk Sıtkı Güneş – fine, but cramped. With all or one of the Politans – fine, but almost too thought-provoking. And they were the decent ones. What if he were forced to share with some of the child murderers and mad axemen? Or in one of the larger cells with half a dozen others. It isn't fair, Farouk said to him once, to expect people to be delightful simply because they are in prison. Some are just not very nice.

On balance, then, İsmet prized his solitude. He did not have to accommodate himself to another's foibles. He did not have to bite his tongue, or be revolted by anyone's bodily functions other than his own. He had come to terms with his imprisonment. He had learned self-containment. But then he had his Saljan year, and that left him almost desperate. He knew that when he had told her the whole of his Mary story, he would feel empty. He remembered the anti-climax upon finishing a film. It's like it is sometimes after sex, the wardrobe mistress on *The Knot Girls* told him when he came to say goodbye on the last day of shooting. She was packing up her ironing-board and sewing-machine. An older, handsome single woman. You feel that same sadness and unease, she said. When she got back, she would pace around her apartment waiting for the phone to ring. Not about a new job, though they were always welcome. No, for a call from someone who had been on the last picture. Rekindling the intimacy for a moment, before time and new faces dissipated the magic forever.

İsmet knew the Mary script would leave a particularly large hole because of the time he had been thinking about it. And because he could not think of it without remembering the dear old faces of the Politans. But he was not prepared for the Saljan factor.

He could tell, even from their brief, intense meetings, how extraordinary she was. How utterly self-determining. He thought that if she ever did something she really didn't want to do, it would be because she cared very much for the person who would benefit. And he couldn't imagine what it would be like to be on the receiving end of that. But it did not stop him from wondering. Not about sex with her. The whole year, he had not fantasised about that once. And whenever he had thought about what he would do when or if he finally got out of prison, which he did less and less, he certainly didn't see himself settling down with someone even half his age. Or in fact with anyone who had not done enough living to allow long silences in their relationship.

No, what Saljan had left him with was a huge vacuum, and it was shaped by two impressions he had formed of her – impressions completely at odds with one another. She had brought into his cell a normality he had never really known. A girl with a family and a job she took seriously and new trainers. A girl with a mole on her right cheek and a necklace her boy-friend had made her. Who smelled of soap. Who arranged the jessamine sprigs in his glass of water. Someone firmly in the here-and-now who, before she was in his cell was somewhere else, and who would shortly be somewhere different, and she'd get there swinging her copper tray laden with great coffee through busy streets without spilling a drop.

And then there was the impression of someone unattainable, someone almost otherworldly. Who couldn't be pinned down or delayed. Couldn't be held, couldn't be touched. Couldn't be wholly understood. Couldn't be made to care. Wouldn't bend. Couldn't snap. Who would walk away from you. Run away from you. Who might not come back next week. Who wasn't coming back next week.

In Saljan's absence, her normality was no less poignant than her intangible remoteness.

It hadn't just been the Mondays. There were the days leading up to them, when he would fill his time thinking through the next section of script and notes, with a little bit over to wonder what would be on that week's saucer. The day after would be spent rationing himself the crumbs of *halva* or flakes of *baklava* he had saved, remembering what they'd said to one another, eking out the taste of her visit in his mouth and mind. Then it would be time to plan the next pages of the script. Thus went the days, the weeks, the year.

Then, nothing. No one. No more summonses from the Pasha. Now they only allowed him to attend the prison mosque once a month, keeping him at the very back, well apart from the rest. He occasionally glimpsed the old political cartoonist Metin Efendi, who would give him a look to ask how he was doing. İsmet always returned a reassuring nod. And Metin would smile back. İsmet started to wonder what the point was of going to the mosque. He still, after all his time with the Politans and thinking about Mary and Jesus and his brothers and sisters, had no faith. So why attend, now he could neither pass messages nor receive them? The answer was, other people. He needed the sight of other people, even if it was just of their bottoms bobbing up and down some way in front of him during prayers.

Just himself. Just İsmet Turali: morning, afternoon and night. He had heard all his jokes. Knew how all his stories ended except for one, and with the passing of time, the less that seemed to matter. He had become like those old prisoners he had seen shuffling down a corridor in his first gaol: lost from the outside, lost on the inside.

Then he woke one morning feeling short of breath.

He sat up and coughed. It hurt, and the pain was in his chest. A sharp, stiletto pain. Not good. The whole time he had been in prison, occasional stomach upsets aside, he had never been ill. He wasn't a hypochondriac, and he didn't know a thing about how the body worked. Was this just a nasty prison cough, or was he having a heart attack? What should he do? He decided to leave it, and see how he felt after breakfast. When breakfast came, he wasn't hungry. Was that because it wasn't appetizing or was loss of appetite itself a symptom? He stared at the aluminium tray, with its four recesses, trying to decide if it was worse than usual. There was a hunk of bread in one, a hard-boiled egg in another, a small square of white cheese in the third, and an apple in the fourth. A mug of tea fitted into a hole in the middle of the tray. What did he have for breakfast yesterday? He wasn't sure. He thought it was the same. Or was there an orange instead of the apple? He was pretty sure the bread and the egg had switched recesses since yesterday. Or maybe the tray had been round the other way. Would that explain the difference? Anyway, this didn't look too terrible. Why didn't he want to eat it? He couldn't remember. He coughed again. His phlegm looked an odd colour. And what was that, dark against the livid? Hard to tell in the gloom of his cell, but it looked like a spot of blood.

Şevket the Bald had the decency to sit with İsmet in his cell while they waited for the call from the prison hospital. It might take a little while, İsmet Efendi, because there had been a knife fight in the refectory. A pair of thieves had fallen out. Some of the new intake, naturally. They weren't nice and peaceful like the prison's normal crowd: the political subversives and dissidents. Not, he hastened to add, that he lumped İsmet Efendi in with them. He had never been sure quite what İsmet Efendi was doing in prison in the first place. He'd been to see *The Knot Girls* twice, and couldn't see anything objectionable in it. Unfortunately for İsmet, laughing hurt more than coughing.

It was late afternoon before they finally got the word to go down to the hospital. By then, İsmet had started to feel hot and cold by turns. Şevket wrapped a blanket around him, and they set off. He had no memory of making the walk through the prison. He'd meant to keep an eye out for Metin Efendi, and for all those thugs who were lowering the tone of the place. In the event he found himself sitting on a hospital trolley outside Dr Aziz's office without a clue as to how he had got there. While he was waiting, he politely asked Şevket the Bald how his daughter was managing with the two children since her no-good husband had left her, but Şevket didn't reply. He wasn't there. He'd presumably dropped İsmet off and immediately returned to his post. The corridor was deserted. Perhaps, İsmet thought to himself, he should escape. Just stroll out the back. There must be a back to stroll out of. Only he'd have to get rid of the blanket; it made him look like a tribal chief. If he put on a white coat, it would cover up his prison uniform and everyone would think he was a doctor, going outside for a smoke. He lifted his hand to remove the blanket, but it wouldn't come. He was handcuffed to the trolley.

'Ah, Prisoner Turali. Feeling a bit peaky, I hear.'

Dr Aziz was a large man with a booming voice, a pencil thin moustache, and a shaky grip at best on the finer points of medicine. He was, however, extremely good at extracting bullets and bomb fragments, and stitching up knife wounds. He had spent twenty years in the army as a battlefield surgeon, and had taken the prison job for a quiet life. He knew little about illness, and nothing about the afflictions of the elderly. Unless an ailment was preceded by an explosion or a swish of steel, Dr Aziz was not your man. Unfortunately he was the only man İsmet had.

Prisoner Turali was made to stand, touch his toes, drop his trousers, cough. Prisoner Turali tried to interest Dr Aziz in what he coughed, but that did not figure on any Aziz check-list. Eventually he reached into a battered army kit-bag and produced a stethoscope. It had, he proudly showed Prisoner Turali, several dents from ricochets, and the rubber tube was held on with parcel tape. But this chrome veteran of mortal conflict did inform Dr Aziz that Prisoner Turali "had something up, in the general chest area". Prisoner Turali had told him that at the very beginning, but the order of things meant much to Dr Aziz. Everything, he said, in its proper place and time. And the place for Prisoner Turali was in a hospital bed, and the proper time for that was right now. He almost added "at the double", but a glance told him "at the half" might be a little much for Prisoner Turali.

The diagnosis was bronchitis. The bed was hard. The window was barred. The door was locked. The only other occupants of the six bed prison hospital ward were the morning's two knife-fighters. They lay unconscious in opposite corners, manacled to the bed-post, one to İsmet's left, one to his right. A colleague from the kitchens who brought in a meal – İsmet had no idea if it was breakfast, lunch or dinner – told İsmet their story. They were brothers, apparently in love with the same girl. They decided to bury their rivalry for as long as it takes to rob a garage. As they were beating up the petrol pump attendant, the police arrived - a misfortune each blamed on the other. In fact it was the object of their joint affections who had made the phone call, in a bid to rid herself of the pair of them. Even though tipping off the police was generally held by inmates to be a cardinal sin, a straw-poll taken in the kitchens had voted resoundingly in her favour, so objectionable were the brothers known to be. Now, however, they were in no state to talk, and neither was İsmet.

He spent most waking hours fighting the coughing and the chest pain. With the little time left over, he did some thinking. Not particularly coherently. In his lucid moments he realised he was suffering from confusion. Indeed, it was the occasional clarity that alerted him to his muddled state the rest of the time. He did not want to lose his mind. He would rather lose his mobility, his sight and his hearing, on condition he could keep his wits. But he increasingly felt he was not being given the choice. What seemed like days later Dr Aziz paid him a visit. Noticed that he had lost weight. Asked him some questions. Listened to his chest again, and this time could hear a raspy, scratchy sound. Decided it wasn't bronchitis, but pleurisy.

***

While İsmet was being examined this second time by Dr Aziz, Mahmoud the Runner was busy having a stroke.

He was sitting in the coffee house garden with his cronies, soaking up sunshine and respect. He hadn't spoken much, but then he rarely did. He listened and smiled and nodded and sipped his coffee. His hair was glossy.

His collar was starched. Everything was normal. Then some question about travelling by air came up, and the mayor's brother-in-law turned to Mahmoud for his opinion. The great man did not appear to hear. The query was repeated. Again the great man did not reply and they noticed his mouth was drooping. The Hoja shook him gently by the shoulder, and Mahmoud mumbled something they couldn't catch. There now seemed to be something wrong with his eyelids. Panic spread among the posse. The shout went up for Jafar. The great man's brother came and went away again almost immediately to call an ambulance. By the time Saljan returned from a delivery to the weighbridge, the coffee house was deserted except for Tarık quietly getting on with everyone's job behind the counter, and a distraught collection of middle-aged loafers out in front who had assumed that Mahmoud was, like all gods, immortal. So many of the antics of professional mourners had they already adopted that Saljan assumed her father was dead. Reassured by Tarık that he was alive when the ambulance took him away, and rejecting all offers from the demented posse to drive her, Saljan ran all the way to the hospital.

There are few things in life worse than those dashes across town or country to attend family calamities. They can be worse than the suffering endured by the victim of the calamity. Saljan was eight when her aunt Ayşe – Jafar's first wife – was killed instantly in an earthquake. The head-teacher came into her writing lesson and told her to run home as fast as possible because there had been a terrible accident. So run Saljan did, tears streaming down her face, little heart pounding, big imagination racing, convinced by the time she reached the coffee house that she was the only person in her family still alive.

It was no relief to learn that only Ayşe had died; Saljan loved Ayşe. It was Ayşe who had looked after Saljan since her mother died. Not just tending her grazed knees and cooking her meals, but holding her at night as she cried, which Saljan did often. Saljan was four at the time and her aunt was pregnant with Hussein. She had the wisdom to get Saljan involved with the baby without for a moment giving her the impression she was anything other than number one in her heart. It was a difficult balancing act which Ayşe managed fairly faultlessly. After all, she told Jafar, baby Hussein has no idea of the situation or Saljan's needs, and by the time he does the situation will have changed.

She was right. Saljan by six was self-possessed. By seven: self-reliant. By eight, after the death of Ayşe: self-contained. It was inevitable, with a father like hers and Uncle Jafar so busy. Saljan was the only female under the coffee house roof, apart from Minoş the cat, for six years until Gül Seren arrived. It was Saljan's great fortune that her uncle Jafar had impeccable taste when it came to choosing her aunts.

Gül Seren was waiting for Saljan on the steps of the hospital. She enfolded her niece in as big a hug as a small woman can give and reassured her that her father was still alive. He had had a stroke. They thought it was something called an embolism: a blockage to an artery supplying blood to the brain. They didn't know how severe; they were doing the tests now. It was very good that he had got to hospital so quickly. Apparently minutes counted dramatically in terms of preventing the loss of brain cells. Saljan wouldn't be able to see him yet, but they could go and join Uncle Jafar at the Intensive Care Unit and wait until the doctors knew more. Perhaps she would then be allowed to see her father.

Niece and aunt walked through the hospital. It was odd, Saljan thought, but bad as this was, it didn't feel the same as when Ayşe died. Then she felt utter, devastating panic as she ran home. Pounding across town this time, Saljan simply hoped her father wasn't dead. Not because she adored him to pieces, or because she couldn't face life without him, but because he mustn't die before she had a chance to get to know him. She had been, she decided, as lazy as he had. They had let each other off the hook, waived the responsibilities which that closest of relationships – parent and child - demands and rewards. Worse, the death of his wife and her mother, instead of bringing them, forcing them, into the centre of one another's lives, had somehow untethered them.

She remembered that last day in the cell with Turali Efendi, and how disparaging about her father she had been. Maybe he deserved it, but she couldn't be sure he did. Not till she took the trouble to find out. And it couldn't be one-sided. Her father would have to make the effort to find out about her. And now here was this embolism getting in the way. Keeping them apart. By the time she and Gül Seren reached the Intensive Care Unit,

Saljan had decided she wouldn't let it. Indeed, the embolism would be made to pay for its evil deed by enabling the very thing it had tried to prevent: her becoming her father's daughter and him becoming her father.

Getting to see him was another problem. She was at the back of a queue of men in suits who had just stepped out of air-conditioned limousines. Some had shiny black bags, some had several assistants, some just had their own genius. Here then was a little irony. The country's two most famous sons, with Saljan in common to both, lay in hospital beds fighting for their lives barely a thousand paces from one another. The Olympian and the Oscar-winner. Only whereas İsmet was stuck with the bluff survivor of border skirmishes who could amputate a leg faster than he could diagnose hiccups, Mahmoud the Runner was the lodestone drawing the nation's finest neurologists, brain surgeons, diagnosticians and anaesthetists to his bedside. The country's own Chief Medical Officer was due any second by helicopter. But was it possible in the meantime, Saljan asked the head of the hospital who was acting as master of ceremonies, to see her father? Absolutely not. The great man was being wheeled into surgery even as they spoke. And how, Jafar asked, were things looking?

'It is too early to say,' the head of the hospital declared grandly. 'But everything is being done that can be done. It is the least his country can do for him.'

By evening, Mahmoud was stable and the medical luminaries had repaired to the town's most expensive restaurant which had been kept open for them. No curfew for the mighty. Saljan tiptoed into his room with Jafar behind. Her father looked very handsome, and very still. She wondered for a moment if he had died when no one was looking. Then she saw his chest gently rise and fall, and heard the regular, reassuring blips from a battery of machines stacked by his side. His hair looked blacker and shinier than ever, set off against the white pillows. She realised that she had not seen him in bed since she was a little girl. Since she stopped going in to him to say goodnight. When was that? She couldn't remember. Jafar kissed his brother on both cheeks, which made Saljan feel a bit guilty, so she did the same and felt better. Then they sat together by his bedside. After a while, Jafar started to talk.

He told Saljan things she had never heard.

About her father when he was a boy. About how kind he had been to Jafar. How Mahmoud looked after him. How safe Jafar felt in school not just because Mahmoud kept an eye out for him but because, as the kid brother of the greatest athlete the school had ever known, Jafar enjoyed protected status. When Mahmoud started running, Jafar would act as paceman for him, until he could no longer even begin to keep up. He would always watch his brother run though. Not once in those early years did Mahmoud fail to go up to Jafar at the end of a race and hug him. Ask him what he thought. Should he have taken the first lap a few seconds faster? Had he made his break a bit early? Did Jafar have any ideas for improvement? It was partly because Mahmoud was still inexperienced, but there was more to it than that. It was almost as if Mahmoud was uncomfortable that this remarkable gift had been given only to him, and he wanted to share it somehow with his little brother.

A nurse came in to check on Mahmoud the Runner. She looked at each machine in turn. She adjusted the drip in his arm. She moved a pillow. She inclined her head towards Jafar and Saljan as if they too were royalty. Saljan half expected her to walk out backwards.

The picture Jafar painted of his brother was unrecognizable. Was he talking like that in the way one never speaks ill of the dead? Or was this what he had always thought, but kept to himself? Saljan wanted to ask her uncle, but was reluctant to interrupt his flow: the moment was so fragile. The time for it had never been right before, and might never come round again. So she kept silent and waited. He didn't speak for a while. When he did, it was about her mother, Safiye. And Jafar never spoke about Safiye.

'She was a treasure among women. Your father saw her, and was lost. We had never known him passionate about anything other than running until they met, and we all feared – delightful, beautiful, extraordinary as she was – he would start skipping training to be with her. And if he didn't train, he wouldn't win. Next thing we'd know, he'd stop running. But that wasn't what happened. If anything, he trained harder. Wanting to win became determined to win. She took over from me at the track. I can still see her, stop-watch in hand and a tiny worried frown on that remarkable face. When he won, which became pretty much always, he'd ask her all the questions he used to ask me: pace, break-point timings, wind-strength, choice of shoe, all that. She would just hug him, and kiss him, and then put her head on his chest and hold him. She didn't wrap him in blankets. She didn't mop his brow. She didn't become his trainer or his manager or his mother. She just adored him, and he adored her. I said he was lost when he met her, but the truth is he was found. The loss came later.'

Mahmoud the Runner stirred in his hospital bed. Saljan and Jafar caught one another's eye. He - hopeful that it meant he wasn't totally paralysed. She - worried that he had heard what Jafar was saying and was upset. She stood, and stroked his cheek. Neatened the bedclothes. Her father looked fast asleep. A machine which had responded to his movement with quicker blips, calmed down. Saljan sat again, but a little closer so she could hold her father's hand. Then Jafar resumed his story.

'They were married at eighteen. The next year your father ran his first Olympics in Los Angeles. It was the first time either of them had ever been abroad, and they were inseparable. The press loved them, this handsome young couple going everywhere hand in hand. The other runners wrote him off, because they assumed he wasn't training enough, his mind was elsewhere... That, and the fact they had never heard of our country. Well, they soon heard of it loud and clear. It was as if the whole town was crammed into the coffee house. From the Vali himself to Yiğit the Street Sweeper. Everyone was there. We had just opened. We didn't have a television, we didn't even have a telephone. Just an old radio. All of us listening, listening. It was as if the only things in the place were ears and cups of stone-cold coffee. No one moved. No one spoke. We were frozen. There was Mahmoud on the other side of the world running faster than any man had ever done, and all the people who knew him were motionless. And he won! Then we moved! It was something fantastic, something unbelievable. It's hard to imagine now, Saljan, especially seeing him lying here like this. But it is true. After that, more world records. More medals. People talk about golden years; well - they were golden. Until...'

Jafar shook his head. His eyes filled with tears. She wanted to comfort him, but didn't want to stop him from talking. She was desperate to hear the rest. She had to hear it. But she couldn't stand to see Jafar crying. She let go her father's hand, and gave her uncle a tight hug. Then she found a box of tissues and put them on the bed near him. She made some more pointless rearrangements to her father's sheets and blankets, and then asked Jafar if he would like her to find him some tea. He smiled and shook his head.

'No, dear Saljan,' he said. 'Thank you, but I'd like to finish the story. If I don't tell you now, I never will.'

After a minute or two of blowing his nose and sorting himself out, Jafar carried on. He explained something Saljan had never understood. Why, in every photograph she had ever seen of her father standing on a podium to receive a medal, he always looked so sombre. So distant. The answer was he had decided when they got married to dedicate every win to Safiye, marking it with a prayer for her long and happy life. That was why you never saw him jump up and down with delight on the winner's stand, or even just smiling. It was how he was about her. She was the most treasured person in his life, and the one thing he was terrified of was that something would happen to her. And one day it did.

'They had gone to train in the Çeşme Hills. Your father was running marathons by then. He had won pretty much everything else. In fact, he had decided that the only event he would enter at the Atlanta Olympics would be the marathon. He had just turned thirty-one, and he reckoned he wouldn't have many more chances to get under the two hour mark. That was his dream. So she drove him into the hills, dropped him off at the big waterfall, and drove to Firuz to wait for him. But she never got there. It's thought she had a heart attack on one of the hairpin bends coming down from the summit and he found her, twenty-five minutes later, hanging half out of the car. The odd thing was she barely had a bruise on her; she must have been driving very slowly. But she was clearly in a very bad way. Still breathing, just. And - this is so hard to tell you, Saljan - she was pregnant. With you...'.

Saljan had never been told the exact circumstances of her mother's death. Still less the circumstances of her own birth.

'Afterwards people said she shouldn't have been driving, so far gone. But it was barely eight months, and she seemed so very healthy... Anyway, the car was in the ditch and hard as he tried, poor Mahmoud couldn't get it out. So he picked her up, and carried her. And carried you. He ran with the two of you all the way to Taşmak. That's nearly three miles. He'd just reached the edge of the town when he collapsed. A farmer in a truck found them by the roadside. Your father was lying absolutely shattered, with your mother in his arms. The farmer didn't know who was dead and who alive, but drove all three of you to the hospital and there they – somehow – got you out, alive. The terrible thing was, although the rest of the family rejoiced at the miracle of your birth, dear little Saljan, Mahmoud could never see past the loss of your mother.'

Jafar had been meaning to tell her this for years. Every time he noticed her disappointment at her father's shallowness, saw her rebuffed by his disinterest, he'd wanted to explain why. There was no excuse for Mahmoud's self-absorption at the expense of others. For his choice of strangers over family. But there was a reason, and his daughter deserved to hear it.

'It isn't that he didn't – doesn't love you, Saljan. I know it looks like that, but it isn't true. It's rather that he's had the heart ripped out of him once already, and is petrified of ever being close to anyone ever again. Even his own daughter. That's the only reason he'd rather sit drinking coffee with those fools in the garden, than spend time with you. When Safiye died, he took a public decision never to run again. But I think he made another, private, resolution: to go into hiding.'

They sat silently by his bedside until the doctors trooped in to check on their patient. They smelled of grilled meat, red wine, cigars. Jafar lingered for their verdict; Saljan went outside for fresh air. It was a wonderfully cool, clear evening. Sitting at the top of the steps was Beyrek. She was amazed to see him. He had brought food for her and her uncle, and an apology.

'I'm sorry Saljan. I told them we were betrothed. That Mahmoud the Runner was my father-in-law. Otherwise I would have been arrested for breaking curfew.'

To his surprise, she fell into his arms and burst into tears.

Chapter Eighteen

They kept Mahmoud in hospital, adding experts on rehabilitation and therapy to the team that – between lavish meals - fussed around him. An ambulance brought him home with a pharmacy of medication. He was paralysed on one side. He had difficulty understanding and even more difficulty talking. Bright sunlight hurt his eyes. He couldn't sleep at night. He appeared sad and anxious.

Saljan took her father in hand. And the first thing she did was to push his wheelchair into the bathroom, spin it round and wash his hair. She told him that he didn't need that gel all over himself any longer and that the natural look would suit him much better. He seemed bothered, but wasn't in much of a position to protest. At first she tried the spray from the shower head on him, but the water just glanced off the grease. She had bought some industrial strength shampoo for the occasion, took a deep breath, and worked it in to her father's scalp. She remembered just in time to keep smiling, so she didn't look disgusted and he wasn't made to feel ashamed at what she was having to do for him. After a while, she felt his hand lightly touch her waist. He held on to her like that until she turned him round at the very end so he could see himself in the mirror. He stared for an age, and then he looked questioningly at her. She answered him by kissing him on the top of his cleanest of heads, and for the first time since his stroke and on one side of his face only, Mahmoud the Runner smiled.

His rehabilitation was very slow and only partial. What made it complex was that he wasn't just recovering from a stroke. Certainly his understanding of what was said to him improved. But he also had to learn how to engage with the people around him. Saljan coaxed and encouraged him into helping Jafar and Tarık with the coffee tasting. Choosing new *lokum* flavours with Sami. Watching Gül Seren and her give Othman a bath.

Listening to little Kazan Dumrul doing his reading. Sitting in the shade after lunch with Minoş the cat on his lap. In time he slept better, and stopped feeling quite so anxious. He could still be sad, but that wasn't surprising given he had blocked out so much grieving during his years of retreat into vain indolence. And given the shame he felt about the way he had behaved. The old cronies came round very rarely. He said as little in their company as he had ever done, but he only tolerated them now - he did not need or want them. He had his family. And most of all, he had his daughter.

It was a bit like washing his hair. She never gave him a choice in the matter. And he was clearly delighted by her decision. He'd sit in the window where he could see her leave the coffee house on a delivery. While she was away he looked…not anxious exactly, but somehow incomplete. Then she'd appear over the brow of the hill with her tray of empty cups and glasses, and he'd smile and his eyes would light up. She'd put the tray down on the counter and race over to him and tell him where she'd been, and what people had said, and he'd stroke her hand and smile. Jafar had never seen Mahmoud like that since the day he tenderly eased his pregnant wife into the car and drove her away into the Çeşme Hills. Father and daughter could never make up for the time lost since then; too much had passed to be recovered. Instead they started anew, as if Saljan had been an orphan who had then traced her real father. And he was as pleased to have been tracked-down as she was to reclaim him.

Then, early one autumn morning, three policemen came for Mahmoud the Runner's daughter. They were sorry they said, but they had to take her in for questioning and they also had a warrant for her tray. Oh, and their very best wishes to her father for his continuing recovery. It was as well Mahmoud was still asleep and did not see Saljan being bundled into the police car.

They did not take her to the police station, but through an archway into the inner courtyard of a gaunt grey building Saljan had seen but never delivered to. She was signed in. Her identity card checked. Fingerprints and photograph taken. Her tray was whisked away by a man and woman in white coats. She asked for, and was not given, a receipt for it. Then she was led down glossy grey-walled corridors to an interrogation room. She sat there for nearly an hour, being stared at by an unsmiling woman in a uniform Saljan did not recognize. Then two short, burly men came in and the grilling began.

They wanted to know about her exact relationship with İsmet Turali. She looked puzzled. Who was İsmet Turali? The man she used to take coffee to in the prison. Oh, she said, was that his name? The two men exchanged tiny glances. So what was her relationship with him? Saljan said she didn't have a relationship with him. She just delivered his coffee, once a week. For a whole year. She rolled her eyes just remembering the tedium of it. Not just that, but she had to wait while he drank it so she could take the cup away with her. And listen to all his talk!

'What did he talk to you about?' one of them asked.

'Oh, a lot of boring drivel about some old Christians. I didn't listen most of the time, and when I did I didn't understand a word he was saying.'

'Why would he talk to you about that?' the other wanted to know. The cleverer of the two.

'Do you know,' Saljan said, looking him straight in the eye, 'I often wondered that myself.' She shrugged. 'I figured he was just some lonely old religious fanatic who suddenly found himself with a captive audience.'

'Did he ever give you anything to take out of the prison?' the dimmer interrogator asked.

'Yes,' she said. 'His dirty coffee cup.'

The man looked slightly irritated.

'Apart from his cup! Anything apart from his cup?'

Saljan looked a little bewildered.

'What would he have to give me? He didn't have anything I would want.'

And she wrinkled her nose primly. Then a phone went. The stupid one picked it up, listened, then whispered in his colleague's ear. Then they turned again to Saljan.

'Your tray, Saljan. It has a secret compartment.'

'I know', she said. 'Isn't it amazing? It's so clever. And have they looked inside it? Because it's full of mercury which is what helps me swing it so fast round corners. Only, please don't let the other coffee houses in town find out. Because they are dying to know how Mahmoud's can deliver so far and keep the drinks so hot. By the way, if they want to look inside, they'll have to remove the seal which the security guards put over the cap when I started delivering to the prison. To make sure no one removed it and tried to sneak something out in the mercury compartment.'

The two men had another whisper, and the stupider one picked up the phone and asked a question. There was a pause. When the answer came back, he looked a bit disappointed.

At this point the cleverer of the two men changed tack. Here's the thing, Saljan, he said in a friendlier, older brother tone. A film has just come out in the West. It's called *The Bearer*, and it's about Mary the mother of Jesus, and how she deals with the fact that some members of her family believe Jesus is the son of God, and others do not. It's a very powerful piece of work which is causing a considerable stir. And making a great deal of money, I should add. None of which would be our business, neither yours nor ours, were the name of the man who made this film not İsmet Turali.

'So they let him out then?' asked Saljan without sounding as if the answer mattered to her in the slightest.

'No' the cleverer one replied. 'He's still in prison. He's been in prison the whole time.'

'Then how could he have made this film if he's in prison?'

'Our question in a nutshell, Saljan. We can only think he found someone to smuggle the script out of his cell and put it into the hands of collaborators overseas who carried out his instructions.'

'How amazing!' Saljan sounded as if she was really impressed. 'Because he seemed like a really nothing little man to me.'

The clever interrogator held her gaze, but she did not waiver.

'Can you remember anything of what Prisoner Turali told you? So we can compare it to what happens in the film.'

Saljan furrowed her brow and thought for a bit.

'Well,' she said. 'There was definitely something about some shepherds looking after their flocks, and an angel appearing to them. Or maybe lots of angels. But I can't remember what they said. Maybe something about a baby. Or God or something. I'm not sure. Sorry.'

Saljan looked a bit hopeless and the two interrogators looked very frustrated. They were about to get tough with her, when her face suddenly brightened.

'Hold on! I've just thought of something! I'm not the only person who had to sit through his fairy-stories.'

The stupider one shook his head.

'We've questioned the guards,' he said, 'and they say he spoke too quietly for them to hear. They told us they knew it was something religious but more than that they couldn't say.'

'No, not them. The people listening to the microphone.'

The clever one tried not to look too interested.

'What microphone?'

'The microphone the man wired up in his cell. I came in one day and there he was, standing on the table with a microphone and loads of wire. I don't know, maybe they even recorded it.' Then her eyes widened as if she had stumbled on the answer to the whole mystery. 'Maybe that's how they got it out of the prison!'

There was a moment of dead silence, and then both men reached for telephones. Two simultaneous exchanges followed - one heated, the other staccato - after which the phones were replaced and the men gathered their papers. But the clever one had a last question for her.

'Are you a good Muslim girl, Saljan?'

'That,' she replied earnestly, 'is for me to learn only on the day the trumpet sounds. When heaven and earth are split asunder, and I am given the final reckoning by my recording angels: the good deeds into my right hand and the bad into my left.'

At which point Saljan put on a particularly pious face.

'Should we three then find ourselves sent to the same place, then you will see me and know the answer to your question.'

The two interrogators weren't sure quite what to say to this, so they let her go.

***

'İsmet.'

Someone was calling his name. Why couldn't they leave him alone? Couldn't they see he was ill?

'İsmet. İsmet!'

Hold on! He knew that voice. It was Adnan. Adnan the shepherd boy – hero of *Kanli*. He'd been wondering only the other day what had happened to him. Hoping he had made something of his life. Hoping he hadn't been tempted by a little fame and money. İsmet had recalled that conversation with Adnan's mother forty years before, when she wanted to know what would happen to her son after the film, and İsmet couldn't answer her.

'İsmet!'

No matter. Adnan was here, calling him. İsmet could ask him now, could find out exactly what had happened to him.

'İsmet, my old friend. Wake up. It's me, Zahi Suyuti.'

İsmet slowly opened his eyes. There, head down by the pillow at his eye-level, was the unmistakeably elegant Neapolitan, now in his seventies. Indeed, no longer eligible to be called Neapolitan. He was the Chief Mufti of Rome, also a Visiting Professor of Theology at the University of Basel. Zahi Suyuti had taken the considerable risk of travelling back to the country which had imprisoned him without cause for so many years. He would not, though travel there by air again. He had been accompanied in his hot and dusty journey across the Kara Peski Desert and over the Bulakty Mountains by a Swiss doctor who was the Medical Director of the Red Crescent and a distinguished Norwegian physicist. But even if their protection availed him nothing and he were clapped in chains once more, Zahi felt he had no choice but to make the trip. There was something he must ask his old friend İsmet, and it could only be done in person.

Dr Aziz had previously explained to the three foreign gentlemen that Prisoner Turali was now very weak. He feared pleurisy had led, via complications, to pneumonia. The patient was often confused, and might have difficulty understanding what was said to him. He was also short of breath, so long answers were unlikely. Patience was essential. He must not be upset. Zahi Suyuti reassured Dr Aziz that there was nothing upsetting in what he had to ask İsmet Turali. As he had explained when he applied for his visa and as he had told the government representatives who met them at the airport, the issues his visit sought to resolve concerned matters of faith alone.

Dr Aziz turned to the Pasha and conferred with him - the Pasha not being one to miss this sort of excitement. Dr Aziz then spoke again to the three distinguished visitors. If questions had to be put to the prisoner, he said, it would be best one to one. Two of the men would have to wait outside. This led to a discussion among the visitors, as this would provide easier conditions for Professor Suyuti to be snatched away. In the end, the Professor insisted that if this was the only way, then he would have to agree.

At this point, Dr Aziz slipped into the ward to check on the prisoner's condition. When he came back he looked very grave. It was as well they had come when they did, he said in sombre tones, as it was not certain Prisoner Turali would find the inner strength to recover. Professor Suyuti looked very distressed at the thought, and no one said anything for a while. Then Professor Suyuti said that, in that case, he would like to give İsmet Turali whatever spiritual comfort he asked for. As this was an addition to the grounds upon which permission for their visit was based, he hoped that the gentleman from the Ministry of the Interior would give his consent. Dr Aziz turned to the sallow, cadaverous individual leaning against the doorjamb who gave a dismissive nod of his head. As if to say, who do you take us for? Barbarians?

So Dr Aziz took Professor Zahi Suyuti into the ward, and left him at İsmet's bedside. İsmet was now the sole patient, the two thieves on either side of him having already died of their wounds. Zahi looked at his old friend. He was very thin. He was very pale. His hair was now grey. His face was twisted in pain. He looked as if he were barely alive. Zahi prepared himself so that İsmet would hear no anxiety in his voice.

'İsmet.'

***

When Zahi identified himself, a number of thoughts came into İsmet's mind. The first was that he had somehow been transported back to that night he had spent in the Politans' cell, when His Eminence gave his great monologue on faith. İsmet must have nodded off, and here was Zahi making sure His Eminence didn't catch him snoring. But Zahi had aged so! It couldn't be that night. They were all young then – apart from His Eminence, of course. İsmet's next thought was that he must have been mistaken in his belief that Zahi had been released and deported home to Italy; clearly Zahi had been in prison with him all along. Being in solitary confinement, it wasn't surprising he hadn't seen him. Odd that he had never noticed him at prayers, but then, if Zahi had also been in solitary, the chances of bumping into one another were negligible. That must mean Zahi had fallen ill, and they'd put him in the prison hospital. Which explained why his first words to his old friend were:

'Poor Zahi! But at least you're in the next bed!'

Zahi tried to keep it as simple as possible. He told İsmet he had just seen *The Bearer*. It was a wonderful film. Beautiful, moving, profound, and incredibly thought-provoking. It was brilliant the way İsmet had made each one of Jesus's family take a different position about him: some believing in him, some holding to their old faith, some changing their minds, some not knowing what to believe, and one believing in nothing. It was like seeing the inter-faith strife of today at the moment of birth. And the depiction of his mother Mary, fighting to hold her splintering family together, learning amid the pain and grief that it can only be done by humanity and tolerance – extraordinary!

It didn't matter if you were a Christian or a Muslim or a Jew or a Hindu or a Buddhist or an agnostic or an atheist or a pagan. The film spoke to everyone. And somehow united everyone. There had been marches through the streets in Cairo, in Jerusalem, in Amman, Damascus, Istanbul, Islamabad, Rio de Janeiro, New York, Rome, Paris, London, Belfast,

Rangoon and Beijing. Even P'yongyang. Peaceful assemblies of people of every denomination and none, with banners echoing the last line of the film "We bear tolerance". Faced with the power of this tide of popular feeling, several dictatorships had fallen, and more were wobbling. Peace and reconciliation talks around the world that had broken down were restarting, and new ones were being initiated.

İsmet didn't say anything, and the only parts of him that moved were the tears rolling down his cheeks. Zahi wiped them dry and told his old friend he had done an extraordinary thing. But he wanted to ask him some questions about the film. Did İsmet mind? İsmet shook his head and in a whisper said he would answer what he could.

'In your film, İsmet, there are a number of scenes which really interest me. There is one in which the Archangel Gabriel visits Mary. There is one in which the baby Jesus is born. In another, his family flees to Egypt. Then he changes the water into wine. And a bit later he is in the olive grove of Gethsemane, in agony before the crucifixion. Then the crucifixion itself.'

İsmet nods and whispered something. Zahi leaning closer, had to ask him to repeat it.

'I said, you have the advantage of me. You've seen the film; I have not.'

Zahi smiled.

'Absolutely, İsmet. Absolutely. Now let's just take one of those scenes. The one with Gabriel and Mary. In this scene, Mary is wearing a blue gown tied with a black cord and with a stitch-patterned white hem. She has black shoes on. And she is sitting in a yard with animals around her. A cow, some sheep. In a pen behind.

İsmet was looking puzzled.

'You can't see what Gabriel is wearing, because you have surrounded the Archangel's body in a sort of undulating cloud. But from the face, Gabriel is definitely female.'

İsmet looked even more puzzled.

'And then, İsmet, and this has caused considerable controversy, you show Mary as already being pregnant when the Archangel comes to see her....'

It took a moment or two before İsmet could collect his thoughts.

'Some of that, was in the script...' He stopped to get his breath. 'And some was not.'

The suspense was almost more than Zahi could take. It was, though, imperative to keep İsmet as calm as possible. He rested his hand on İsmet's.

'Take your time, old friend, and tell me which bits were in your script.'

There was another pause.

'Mary's robe – blue in the script. The animals – script. But the black shoes and white hem, and Gabriel being female, and the cloud around Gabriel's face, and Mary pregnant...'

İsmet shook his head. Zahi waited, but that was all he said.

So where, Zahi asked gently, did these other elements come from? İsmet shrugged. He said he had no idea. He hadn't seen the film, remember? But he always gave his team leeway about some things. He had to. He couldn't decide everything. Anyway, he asked Zahi, why did any of this matter? If the film worked so well.

This was the question Zahi had been preparing himself for. Because to answer it – and he had to answer it – he would have to break a promise he had made on his father's Holy Qur'ān sixty years before.

'You remember what I told you that day in the exercise yard in our old prison? About climbing the hills behind Asyūṭ with Abanoub, and finding the cave full of manuscripts and papyri? The day I swore not to talk about?'

İsmet nodded, intrigued. Something about him struck Zahi as being more alert. A fraction of the old gleam had come back into İsmet's eye.

'Well, I didn't tell you all the story. I warned you I wasn't going to. And the stuff I didn't tell you, was what I had to give my word over...'

Zahi looked like a man split in two. He wavered, then plunged in.

'I said the recesses containing the library were as high as a man. So they were. But the cave was twice as high again. And on the walls above the recesses there were paintings. Incredible pictures. As fresh as the day they had been done. The first one showed Mary in a yard with animals behind her, in a blue gown with a stitch-patterned white hem. She had black shoes on. And in front of her was an angelic woman's face in a sort of mist that flowed down and around her. And Mary was pregnant. Very pregnant, it looked like.'

The two men sat in silence for a bit. And then Zahi described the other paintings on the walls of the cave, and how İsmet's film contained details from each. Details known only to Zahi and that monk. The odds of guessing them being so remote as to be impossible.

The four shepherds each bearing a lamb over both shoulders at the Nativity. Exactly as they were in the film.

The family living in the Asyūṭ cave itself: Mary with her two sons and baby daughter. Exactly as they were in the film.

The Jesus who turned water into wine at the wedding feast in Cana, still a boy in a blue and gold tunic with yellow sandals. Exactly as he was in the film.

And then two paintings, perhaps by a different – or older – hand. The first showed Jesus at Gethsemane with another man kneeling before him who could have been his twin, and whose red robe was the identical colour to that worn by Jesus's brother in the painting of the family in the cave. Exactly as they were in the film.

Above the Gethsemane painting was a panel in which something had been written in an ancient tongue. Young Zahi had not been able to read it. But the way it was set out had made it look like a poem. Or a prayer. And there, in İsmet's film, was Jesus kneeling in prayer with his brother. And the prayer he was saying was the one the Chief Rabbi of Bessarabia had translated all those years ago in Princeton from one of the three sheets of papyrus Zahi had brought out of the cave:

"My God and Father,

who saved me from despair,

who gave me life through the gift of His great glory,

do not let my days in this world be prolonged,

but let your light, in which no night remains,

shine upon me."

And the Crucifixion, with Mary and all Jesus's brothers and sisters together, standing in front of the cross looking up at him, with an outer semi-circle of people beyond, kneeling with their heads bowed. Exactly as it was staged in İsmet's film.

There was one last panel in the cave. Zahi had not seen it till he turned to go out. It was over the doorway, and was probably the most extraordinary. It showed Mary, watched by Jesus, actually painting the other panels, recording key moments in the life of her son. The Annunciation and the Nativity and the Wedding Feast at Cana and the Flight to Egypt, but not Gethsemane and the Crucifixion. Where those scenes would later be painted – and the panel above containing Jesus's prayer as he faced death - were still blank, awaiting events to come.

Zahi fell silent. But İsmet had found new strength.

'The only two people who saw the paintings in the cave were you and the monk?'

Zahi nodded.

'Could he still be alive? And have briefed the film crew?'

Zahi shook his head. It was impossible. He had told İsmet that two men had been killed in the explosion that destroyed the cave. They were the two monks whom he had escorted up there, one of whom had seen what Zahi had seen, and realised the import of the images. After all, they challenged the entire edifice constructed over two thousand years around Mary and the birth of Jesus. The monk must also have been very moved by the paintings. They were incredibly powerful and immediate. Then, when he turned to leave the inner cave, he'd have seen that last, remarkable panel. What he thought when he realised that the painter of those scenes was Mary herself... Zahi shook his head.

Something else he had kept from İsmet was the look in the monk's eye as he emerged into the light. It was only there for a second, but it managed to be both ecstatic and petrified. Zahi didn't understand it at the time, but he did now. And he also now understood the conspiratorial looks the monk had given him. He was begging for Zahi's silence in the hope that, if no one else ever found out what was in the cave, the paintings might be allowed to survive. But they had to tell the abbot of their monastery - the older monk who swore Zahi to silence - and that sealed the fate of the paintings and the library. The explosion was no accident. Neither was the death of the monks. Thinking back, Zahi was amazed he had not himself met with a fatal fall down those same cliffs a few weeks later. Presumably they assumed that a little Muslim boy would have no idea of the significance of what he had seen in the cave – images which would remain etched in his mind alone for sixty years. Alone, that is, until İsmet's film.

İsmet thought back to Maminou. To the Sunday she took him into the chapel dedicated to the Sainte Vierge Perpétuelle. There was Mary, bowed head ringed with cherubs, hands clasped, beautiful, beatific, impossible.

'Tell me, mon P'tit Ischou, what do you know of sex?'

İsmet knew enough about it to know how to answer his grandmother's question.

'Nothing, Maminou.'

'Ah – and neither did she, Ischou. The greatest woman who ever lived had the innocence of a child – all her life! From her own sinless conception to the moment when her perfect soul was reunited in heaven with her perfect body. Who else could be pure enough to bear Our Saviour?'

Hmm. Try telling Maminou that Mary was six months gone when Gabriel appeared to her. Try telling Maminou that, indeed, Mary had sex on more than one occasion: that Jesus had brothers and a sister to play with in the long dusty days of Egyptian exile. Try telling Maminou that the Holy Bible is mistaken: Jesus was not alone in the olive grove of Gethsemane; he had his beloved brother James to pray with. That James knelt at the foot of the cross alongside their mother. Try telling Maminou that church teaching which seeks to diminish Jesus's human family so as to privilege his status as the Son of God misses the whole point of the story: that Christ embodied both humanity and godliness – and his family witnessed, split apart over, came to terms with and supported the transition from the one to the other. Tell her all that, and you may find briefing the Pope on the same subject the easier option…

'We are not, then, looking for a third person who saw the paintings, are we? We are looking rather for a common source for the images in the cave and in my film.'

Zahi looked up, surprised at how coherent and analytical İsmet suddenly sounded.

'The simplest assumption is that the common source is the truth itself. That Mary's paintings depict what actually happened. She was pregnant, the shepherds each had a lamb around their necks, Jesus had brothers and sisters, James wore red…If so, Zahi, we are looking for someone two thousand years later who also knew the truth.'

Zahi nodded.

'I am sorry to disappoint you,' İsmet went on. 'But it is not me.'

Zahi nodded again, and smiled. He had not thought it would be as simple as that. But as a man of faith he needed to know if they were dealing with some kind of extraordinary coincidence…or divine intervention. And in that connection, he had one last thing else to tell İsmet.

'There have been a succession of sightings of the Virgin Mary in Asyūṭ. Witnessed by thousands of people. The newspapers have been full of it. There are videos on *YouTube*, showing a dazzling white light over the town…'

İsmet barely heard him. He was thinking too hard. Trying to work out who could have added elements to the script to make the film correspond to the truth depicted in those paintings? It wouldn't have been one of the department heads: camera, art, wardrobe, because they cut across and above individual craft areas. That left Murat who was his 'realiser' on the ground. Except that he couldn't quite picture Murat as the 'bearer of the truth'. It could have been whoever Murat used to type the script. Or maybe the rewriting, the transformation of those scenes took place before the script and Director's Notes even reached Murat…

Now it was İsmet's turn to put his hand on Zahi's.

'What are angels?' İsmet asked his old friend. 'Can they be people, like us?'

'They can be people,' Zahi replied, 'but not like us.'

Chapter Nineteen

The other members of the three-man team then took turns to see İsmet. First the Medical Director of the Red Crescent examined him carefully, studied his chart and medication, and then came out and quizzed Dr Aziz at some length. Then he addressed the cadaverous representative from the Minister of the Interior with vigorous authority. Meanwhile the distinguished Norwegian gentleman had gone in to tell İsmet what he had come so far to say to him. But by then, İsmet was falling asleep and did not take in the great honour he was being given. The Ministry of the Interior's skeleton on the other hand, to whom the Norwegian repeated his words, understood them loud and clear.

Within a matter of hours, Prisoner Turali was whisked onto a helicopter, but the patient carried gently from it into the air-conditioned hospital for the ruling elites was referred to as His Excellency İsmet Turali. In place of the bluff soldier Aziz was a squad of the nation's finest medics, several of whom had by chance attended the bedside of Mahmoud the Runner. The President's own physician was now personally responsible for İsmet's return to health. Domestic supplies of amantadine and rimantadine were rounded up. Some counselled oseltamivir, others corticosteroids. An air force jet was despatched to well-disposed neighbouring countries in search of neuraminidase inhibitors. Advice was sought discreetly from experts in Oslo and at the John Hopkins Hospital in Baltimore. It was bad enough being a pariah country few had heard of. For their first ever Nobel Peace Prize Laureate to die in prison squalor would invoke universal condemnation. The glory days of Mahmoud the Runner belonged to another era. Time, perhaps, for a new national incarnation on the world stage.

It was significant that the regime's mind was turning to appearances. Insiders sensed a loss of authority. Of grip. Posters proclaiming "We bear tolerance" started to appear on walls overnight and were not torn down by day. Soon other voices started to be heard. Words like 'pluralism' and 'governance' and even 'democracy' were spoken without the usual postscript from a firing squad. The wise planned their exit strategies. His Excellency İsmet Turalı was sitting up in bed finishing his beautifully prepared lunch, having made steady progress for a fortnight, when who should walk in but Talya Begüm Demir.

Two years had passed since he last saw her, when she came to get him to sign the divorce papers. She looked a little older, which was not surprising. But she was not so coiffed and made-up. She seemed less formal, more natural. İsmet had never seen her like that. She had lost some of her haughtiness, too. She approached İsmet with a tender expression and soft voice. She had heard he was ill. That he had been fighting for his life. She couldn't stand it if anything happened to him. He must get fit and strong to attend the Nobel ceremony. She would of course go with him. She would look after him. But, he asked her, wouldn't that disrupt her Ministerial schedule? She said she no longer had a Ministerial schedule. She had resigned. She was now just an ordinary private citizen. A lot of regrettable things had gone on in the country, including the way she and İsmet had drifted apart. She wanted to change that. She wanted them to be together. She wanted to nurse him back to health so that they could be together again. So they could be lovers again. And this time, it would be different. Better in every way.

She reached into her bag and brought out a book, just as she had done once before, but this looked fatter, less glossy, more serious. She handed it to him. It was called *'The Cinema of Absence – The Secret Films of İsmet Turalı'*. He glanced at it, and put it down on the bed. She knew, she told him in almost devotional tones, she could lay no claim to the secret films. But she had read the book, and with its help she had begun to understand what he had achieved. Who he was. She knew it was very late, but…

İsmet dodged her embrace. She turned aside, offended. He watched her wrestle irritation into a semblance of humility.

'You said you were now just an ordinary private citizen?'

She looked up at him, nodding, upset.

'This clinic is inside a closed air force base, ninety miles from the nearest town. Just before you walked in, I heard a small jet land. For the past few days I've been sitting at the window, watching the planes come and go. This sounded like one of those twin-engine business jets that chauffeur the elites around. My bet is that shortly after you walk out of here, I'll hear one take off.'

He pressed his buzzer. A nurse came in to take his tray away, and to settle him down for his afternoon nap.

When he awoke, Talya Begüm Demir was gone. And so was her regime.

***

When he was better, they took İsmet back to the prison to collect his belongings. The place was empty. Barrier gates swung open. Corridors dusty and echoing. His cell already felt like something from another era. Had he really lived there, alone, for seven years? How had he endured it? He looked at where he had sat. Where Saljan had sat. At the table between them where her tray had sat, every Monday morning for a year.

All İsmet took from his cell were the two books on the shelf: the Bible given him by his dear old friend Metropolitan: the Patriarch of Aleppo, and Baba's old Qur'ān. The Pasha, when he became Governor, had ordered the confiscation of all İsmet's books, but İsmet argued the case for being allowed to keep both the Qur'ān and the Bible on the grounds that his father had been a Muslim, and his mother a Roman Catholic. Then İsmet walked back through the prison, half-expecting the Pasha to pop out and bid him a pompous farewell.

In fact the Pasha had prepared a little piece for the moment when İsmet was released, and the TV crews came knocking on his door for an informed overview. I like to think, he would say wearing his tweeds, that if we taught İsmet Turali anything here, we taught him self-discipline. So important for artists, I find. Of course, he'll have to stand on his own two feet now, but he is welcome back here any time - in a post-graduate capacity, so to say. Ha!

Only there were no TV crews. And, more to the point, there was no Pasha. A while before, two short, burly men had come knocking on his door, asking for his informed overview on the bugging of Prisoner Turali's cell; who had listened to what Prisoner Turali had told the girl Saljan; whether all or any of his religious fables had been recorded and transcribed; what light the Pasha could cast upon the re-appearance of this self-same material in a movie as acclaimed around the world as it was successful. And to give the Pasha a quiet environment in which to mull over the answers to these little brain-teasers, the two burly men had locked him in their own dungeons, underneath the gaunt grey building in which they had interrogated Saljan.

The Pasha being a born survivor could spot regime change even from a basement cell. He smelled burning paper: the scent of secret policemen denying their files to posterity. He heard the clanging of the phones, the running of feet, the revving of car engines, the silence. He used the time before the next incumbents arrived to shape an account uncannily close to the one Saljan had given the same burly men. He could not, he would say, deny that he had played a part – some would say a pivotal role - in the smuggling from prison of his dear friend and collaborator İsmet Turali's magnificent script of *The Bearer*, but he must say no more than that. It was essential, he would add in lowered tones, to protect the underground networks on which freedom of expression and thought always depend during times of oppression.

The Pasha was not worried about being forgotten down in the dungeons. He had a tap, laid on to facilitate water-boarding torture. He knew the headquarters of the secret police and the radio station were always the last to be evacuated but the first to be liberated. And if he lost an inch round the waist in the interim, it would only support his tale of being maltreated by the outgoing thugs to reveal his part in the covert operation to carry dear İsmet's script to the outside world. Which unspeakable cruelties, naturally, he bore in absolute silence, divulging nothing.

Waiting for İsmet outside the prison was Reyhan. They embraced. They shed tears. They looked at one another to see how each had fared. She easily had the edge, they decided, but considering his illness, he came in a good second. Where was Murat he wanted to know? His dearest friend

Murat. Reyhan told him that Murat would be joining them a little later. Had he got everything from his cell? Yes, he told her, everything. But there was something he wanted from the second prison he had been in. He didn't know if it would be possible. Reyhan said she would try. What was it? There was a bench in the exercise yard. The one he had sat on with each of the three Politans in turn. If it could be managed, he would like it picked up and moved to his garden. And put alongside the hedge opposite the quince tree.

And, of course, he wanted a cup of coffee. He wanted, more than anything, to sit in Mahmoud's Coffee House with Saljan. To meet everyone there finally, and have a cup of their wonderful coffee, medium sweet. That's exactly what we thought you'd say, Reyhan replied with her old, winning smile. And that's where Murat's going to meet us. We guessed, she said taking İsmet's arm and carrying the two books for him, you would prefer to walk. So off they went, strolling across the town.

Almost immediately, at Zeki's handcart, İsmet saw two men drinking pomegranate juice who reminded him a little of the cameraman and focus-puller who had worked on the Steppe Westerns. But Reyhan kept the pace up and soon they were passing Pelin's flower stall. There, someone else looked familiar. A tall man buying a bunch of caper bush flowers. His art director on *The Knot Girls* had that same, hunched way of standing. And wasn't there a scene in the film when the handsomest boy in the village picks a caper bush flower for each of the girls? Strange. He must be imagining things.

And then something really odd happened. A bus stopped in front of İsmet, and an old woman got off, with a huge bundle. İsmet saw that in the bundle was a baby goat. The kind with very soft, black fur. He recalled the woman and goat he had been with all those years before, on the journey that had inspired *The Bus Ride*. And then, if that were not coincidence enough, the old woman looked into İsmet's face and said:

'It's good to know they actually let people out.'

İsmet glanced at Reyhan, but she obviously hadn't heard. They walked on.

Then he saw a couple coming towards them arm in arm who looked like the actor and actress who had played his parents in *The Librarian and his Wife*. Considerably older, but completely recognizable. The man even had on the same kind of dark red, lumberjack's shirt that Baba used to wear. It was a little shocking. He glanced again at Reyhan, whose expression was inscrutable. Suspiciously so.

The next tableau was a clincher: a limousine with one wheel jacked up and its driver hunched over the tyre. İsmet did not have to stare to see that it was Özkan with whom he had criss-crossed the high steppes looking for locations. Özkan, who had picked him up from his first prison. And his glamorous but giggly passengers? The three stars of *The Knot Girls* signing autographs for the corpulent clerk Sıtkı Güneş Efendi and his white-haired old mother.

He wanted to stop and talk to them, but Reyhan moved him on. We mustn't, she said under her breath. The secret police may still be watching. We don't want them to spot our hidden friends. But they all wanted to be here. For you to see them. For them to see you for themselves. To honour you.

İsmet smiled and cried a little tear at the same time. He'd assumed the secret police had all fled back to their villages in time for the harvest. That they had listened carefully to the old men's accounts of storms and droughts gone by, so that they could pretend convincingly they had spent the cruel decades as simple farmers. But who knows? It was best, İsmet could see, for the good to remain in the shadows. For their own safety. And for the next time.

Now, though, the sun shone and virtually everyone İsmet had ever known or put in a film was in the streets that lay between the prison and the coffee house on the top of the hill. They were like celebrity crowd extras. He had to look carefully: over there were two of the surviving jut-jawed heroes of the Steppe Westerns sitting in the sun with a bottle of champagne and two girls young enough to know better. At a corner stall, Kerem was buying an ice-cream for a very handsome woman who had to be, İsmet decided correctly, Dear Yazmira herself.

Then they passed two old men arm-wrestling at a tea-room table whom, at a second glance, İsmet recognised as the stuntmen with whom he had swum the Amal Gorge.

Next a high-cheeked grandmother shopping with her daughters. Once the lissome make-up girl with whom İsmet had kept warm at night during a fortnight's filming on the Yurt foothills in the depths of winter. Something one of her daughters said made her laugh, and she tipped her head back and to the side in a way which arced the memory of those fifteen nights across four decades like a spark.

There were a few İsmet had forgotten, a handful he did not spot, and some he did not know, because he had not yet seen *The Bearer*: the young woman who cycled alongside him for a while had lit up the screen playing Mary and was now on her way to Hollywood. The lads playing football in a car park were Jesus's disciples, and Jesus himself was sawing wood outside the carpenter's shop.

Then there were the hidden friends: the slippers of schedules under doors at night, the smugglers of film cans in and out of the country. Lorry-drivers and herdsmen, crossing frontiers unseen. Men and women who hitherto perhaps thought of İsmet as a mythical figure. As just an idea. And now they looked at this frail man in his sixties who had walked further in ten minutes than he had in ten years. And his eyes were bright, and he was smiling. Every now and then he stopped for a little breather by a crowd gathered around some backgammon players or a pavement barber, and he would hear a whisper of his name ripple through the air and the words "*al-hamdu lillah 'al as-salaama*" - "thank God you have arrived safely". Though hard as he looked, İsmet never saw any lips move.

He was deeply touched. He was also becoming tired. Reyhan asked if he wouldn't prefer to be driven up the hill, but he said he didn't want to miss anyone. They paused a while on the bridge. They watched the camels being led to market. Then they started to climb. Their way wound past traders' stalls, between merchants' bales of cottons, drums of spice, bundles of liquorice. During increasingly frequent stops for İsmet to get his breath, Reyhan filled in the gaps: the people who could not be there. Metropolitan – the Patriarch of Aleppo - had died in his nineties at peace in his study. There were already moves by his community to seek his beatification.

Cosmopolitan – the Chief Rabbi of Bessarabia - was now in his mid-eighties, living with his children, grandchildren and great-grandchildren in Israel. He sent İsmet his love, and invited him to visit the Holy Land. Not just his Holy Land. Everybody's Holy Land! And Neapolitan – now the Chief Mufti himself – was back in Rome but would see İsmet at the Nobel ceremony in Oslo. Chef Erdal sent his heartiest greetings but, although nearly eighty, was unfortunately just beginning another prison sentence and could not get time off. İsmet was, however, always welcome in his kitchen and particularly at Ramadan.

The other key missing person was Farouk the Forger. According to Reyhan and to İsmet's considerable amusement, he was now the Senior Curator of Oriental Miniature Art at the Louvre, a post offered on condition Farouk identify all the fakes for which he was personally responsible. He had readily agreed, keeping quiet only about the Louvre's own *Princess Khadijeh Asleep in her Garden* – a picture of which he was rather proud, and which he felt sure the great Bihzad would have painted if only he'd had the idea.

Lastly, when İsmet and Reyhan were almost at the top, their path was blocked by a man with his dog and a flock of sheep so clean they looked shampooed. He turned to apologise: 'You know, sir, what sheep are like,' he said with a grin. It was Adnan, the boy from *Kanlı*, now middle-aged but looking, to İsmet's considerable relief, fit and well. And judging by his weather-beaten face, he had stayed a shepherd.

It was the perfect tribute to a secret filmmaker: his whole life in one vast, unfolding panorama. In a single take.

'You see,' he said to Reyhan. 'Murat really can direct!'

But it was even more than that. It was as if this life, which he had given others to carry, which they had led vicariously for him in films and books, was now being returned. His own life given back to him.

They reached the top. İsmet rested on the cool stone edge of the old water trough and looked back across the town. It was a good view.

'My,' he said to Reyhan. 'We have come a long way. Can't see the prison from here, thank goodness.'

She didn't reply. He turned, but couldn't see her anywhere. She must have gone on ahead into the white clapboard coffee house with its blue shutters. Perhaps to tell them all he was coming. And so he was, but he thought he would sit there just a moment longer. He could hardly believe he'd walked so far. It really was very high up. It was like being in the heavens, looking down on earth. All those people and beasts teeming far below, each with their own lives. Their own untold stories. Good stories, too, and so many of them unfinished. Were they perhaps the best, he wondered, the unfinished ones?

Then he felt a touch on his shoulder. It was Saljan, standing at his side. She looked as she had always done: the striking, willowy girl with a penetrating stare, a tiny mole on her right cheek and an odd necklace with teeth marks.

'It's so good to see you again, Turali Efendi.'

Saljan! The person İsmet needed to see most of all. To thank most of all. He put his hand on hers and told her how very grateful he was. There was something he had wanted to ask her, but he couldn't remember what it was. It can't have been important. Then he stood up beside her. He didn't feel quite so tired now. She was as fit and resolute as ever. Poised, about to fly.

'You look, Saljan, as if you are about to make another delivery.'

She looked at him, and nodded.

'I am.'

'Where is it to, Saljan?'

'You'll see, Turali Efendi.'

She waited a moment until the wind dropped; until the clouds cleared the sun.

She took him by the hand. And they were gone.

Acknowledgements

My first and greatest debt of thanks is to the late Professor Geoffrey Lewis and his wife Raphaela Lewis. Not only did they write books which proved invaluable to me; they also happen to have been my parents. In that capacity, they took me to Turkey from an early age, introducing me to dancing bears, *ayran* and the call of the muezzin across Rumeli Hisarı. Hurrying Angel is set in an imaginary Central Asian republic, but I hope it reflects the love they instilled in me for Turkic people, their ways and food. Their books – from my father's Turkish Grammar and his delightful translation of *The Book of Dede Korkut* to my mother's *Everyday Life in Ottoman Turkey* have been a precious source of language, names, colour and detail.

I am indebted also to a number of other authors for opening the texts and tenets of Islam and Christianity to me. Alan Jones's translation of the *Qur'an* heads the list, and it is a particular pleasure to me that Alan is one of my father's most distinguished ex-pupils. That I did not slavishly follow his translation is a function of my own fictional needs, not a bid to improve his masterly text. *Mary: The Complete Resource* edited by Sarah Jane Boss was of great help, as were Raymond E. Brown's *The Birth of the Messiah* and Geza Vermes's *The Nativity*. Other reference works among the many were Marvin Meyer's edition of T*he Nag Hammadi Scriptures* and Leo Rosten's *The Joys of Yiddish*.

None of the authors I read, however, bear any responsibility for what I wrote in Hurrying Angel. Its text, its characters, its flights of fancy, its interpretations, glosses and connections are mine alone. I share with İsmet Turali the notion that I am the sole author of my work. It is a belief that took a slight knock when, with the first draft complete, I looked up Asyūṭ on the internet.

Printed in Great Britain
by Amazon

Printed in Great Britain
by Amazon

ABOUT THE AUTHOR

Erlend Sletvevold is a first time fiction author from Norway.

I am not your son?"

"Look to the moon, young Narwynn."

And Narwynn looked up at the moon, but could not see it. The Dragon was wholly eclipsing it and casting a shadow over Oaktown. Narwynn stood up, took a few steps forward and met Dreumar's gaze for the first time.

"Narwynn..." the eagle whispered and met his gaze.

Narwynn was not surprised, as he had spoken with an animal before.

"What do you want?" he asked.

"Have you learned who you are?"

"No, they won't tell me. I don't even know what to believe anymore."

"Good."

"Why is that good? What am I to do now?"

"Because, young Narwynn, who you are is not for anyone to tell you, especially not those who claim authority or wisdom. You must find that out on your own."

"I thought for a moment that I might be the son of Sawynn, but Ludazar told me I am not."

"What did they tell you about Sawynn?"

"That Dreumar killed him and that they never found his body."

"And do you believe them?"

"I told you. I don't know what to believe anymore."

"What if I told you I know everything there is to know about Sawynn?"

"How come?"

"I am Sawynn."

Narwynn stared at the eagle for a moment.

"B-but how?" he stammered.

"You will find out when the time is right."

"Sawynn..." Narwynn mumbled to himself before he continued. "Then where do I come from if

"Could it be... am I related to the third hero, Sawynn? You told me he also had a different colour."

"I am afraid you have guessed wrong, Narwynn. Sawynn was not related to you."

Narwynn felt disappointed.

"So I am not destined to be a hero after all."

"We shall see. When the time comes, we shall see. You have abilities I have never seen before. You now need to do what no other hero could. You must kill Dreumar."

Narwynn walked backwards and turned around. He heard Ludazar laugh to himself in the background as he walked out of the white tent.

He started around the roots of the white oak towards his tent. When he was halfway there, he decided to sit down on one of the roots to think for a while. He sat and wondered while the sun set behind the mountains and the moon rose. While he sat there in the light of the night, he thought he could hear whispering. He listened to what they were saying.

"Narwynn..." the whispers said.

Narwynn lowered his gaze and sighed. Not again, he thought.

"Narwynn..."

They sounded closer this time. Narwynn looked around but saw no one. Then he noticed a bird sitting close to the end of one of the white oak's branches. It looked like a hawk but much bigger. Could it be an eagle? Yes, it must be, he thought.

"The King spoke of my father's wolf. It had been seen in the woods."

"Oh yes, Kranox. We always knew he was out there somewhere. Taming a wolf is no easy task. I am sure your father is the only one to have ever done so, unless..."

"Unless what?" Kraus insisted.

"Unless Kritar has done it by now."

Kraus clenched his fists and teeth.

Kritar? Narwynn thought. Who was this Kritar?

"Yes, we do not know how strong your older brother has grown since he betrayed us all," Ludazar continued.

Narwynn gasped. Kraus looked down and took a step back.

"I will find my father's wolf," he said and walked out.

Narwynn saw Kraus walk out before he turned back to Ludazar.

"Well, seems it is just you and I now," said Ludazar.

Narwynn felt confused. Everything he had heard was just too much to take in. Were they really destined to become heroes?

"Ludazar," Narwynn mumbled, "you say that Elna is Elmar's granddaughter, and I know that Kraus is Krucar's son. But what about me? Do you know where I come from as well?"

Ludazar's smile had never been broader. "I have my suspicions, young Narwynn," he said.

prevent that from happening by slaying the dragon himself. But you already have a pet that is stronger than his. The snow-lynx, Elnax, that once belonged to the hero Elmar..."

"Your grandfather."

Elna gasped. She took another step backwards in confusion.

"Elmar was my grandfather?"

"Yes"

Suddenly, Edgar stormed into the tent with Buddy on his tail.

"Ludazar! She's not ready!" he said.

Ludazar looked at Edgar with a clever smile.

"She has Elnax, Edgar. That means she is already stronger than you."

"Elnax might be stronger but she is not. She is still a youngling!"

Edgar walked over to Elna and placed his hand on her shoulder.

"Come, Elna, we're going home."

They walked out.

Narwynn looked at the scene with wide eyes. Kraus seemed careless and turned back to Ludazar.

"I knew it was my destiny to be a hero one day," he said.

"I know, Kraus, and you will finally get a chance to avenge your father."

Kraus smiled.

"But you will need to find a new pet, and the blue-crystal arrow-head will not be enough to take on Dreumar," Ludazar continued.

heard all about Elrud's lost daughter?"

"Yes," said Narwynn.

"Well, you must not listen to him. As I have told you once before, Princess Nari is long dead, and so there is no need to go looking for her."

"How do you know?" Elna asked.

"I know because I am wise. The King has gone mad with grief, and therefore you must listen to me and not him.

"It is a rare thing to see heroes rise in the Green Lands, but it has always been your destiny."

"Destiny?" Elna asked. "How can it be our destiny?"

"Elna, my dear, have you never wondered why Elmar's snow-lynx is loyal to you?"

Elna looked at the lynx beside her before Ludazar continued.

"Have you never wondered why Edgar told you the tales about our past heroes every night when you were little?"

Elna took a step back and looked confused.

"Have you never wondered why Edgar is working for me, but refuses to let you listen to my tales?"

Silence filled the air for a few moments before he made his point.

"The snow-lynx recognised you in the woods because it knew you when you were a little nose-elf baby. Edgar told you the stories because he knew that you might one day have to face the dragon yourself. He supports my cause because he wants to

kept walking.

When they reached the marketplace, Kraus nodded to the hunter with a kestrel on her shoulder. She said to them: "So you are heroes now, I hear. Come to me when you need to track down creatures in the woods. With my kestrel, I can help you hunt down anything out there."

They thanked her and kept walking until they reached a tall white tent by the roots of the white oak, opposite Narwynn's tent. Outside the tent stood the white-cloaked nose-elf with a starling on his shoulder, supporting himself on his staff.

"Heroes of Oaktown," he greeted them. "Ludazar awaits you inside. You three have great adventures ahead of you. If you find that you need magic on your path, come to me."

"Magic…" Narwynn mumbled to himself.

"Oh yes, what did you think the Seven Wise concern themselves with if not magic?"

Narwynn was intrigued. Then he remembered something he had heard a long time ago next to the fire among the workers. He had heard someone say that placing a troll somewhere could only be done by magic and wizardry. And hadn't the whispers of the woods told him not to trust the wizard? Something did not make sense here.

"Thank you for the offer," said Kraus and waved Narwynn and Elna with him into the white tent.

"Greetings, young ones," Ludazar said when he saw them coming in, "I take it you have now

Then the King and his guards turned and started into the woods.

"What just happened?" Elna asked and turned to Narwynn and then to Kraus.

"It seems like the King and Ludazar are not very good friends," said Narwynn.

"I wonder what Ludazar wants us to do," said Kraus and turned back towards the field.

"Shall we go and speak to him?" Elna asked.

"No," said Narwynn. "You heard the King. He told us to be wary about Ludazar."

"Don't be stupid again, Greeny," said Kraus. "Ludazar has always looked after us, and everyone else in Oaktown. The King has not even shown himself here before today. Why should we trust him all of a sudden?"

"But..." Narwynn began but Kraus interrupted him.

"No 'buts'! C'mon, let's go and see what Ludazar has to say."

Kraus started crossing the field. Elna looked at Narwynn for a moment before she walked after Kraus with the white lynx by her side. Narwynn sighed and walked after them.

When they reached the workers' area, Narwynn saw the blacksmith hammering on a glowing piece of metal. The blacksmith looked up at them and said: "Young heroes! Come to me when you need your weapons forged or mended. I will always be of service to the heroes of Oaktown." They nodded their gratitude to the blacksmith and

Narwynn. Dreumar does not stand alone. His followers are helping him and you must get past them first. They are dangerous, and I have lost many of my guards to their ruthlessness."

Kraus clenched his teeth and fists when he heard about Dreumar's followers.

Suddenly, the King looked up towards Oaktown with terror in his eyes. His stag stalled, and his guards drew their white crystal swords. Narwynn turned to see what they had seen. He saw a nose-elf in a white robe and a pointed hat standing on the other side of the field with a long staff to hand. The crystal orb on his staff glowed red, and his cloak moved with the breeze. It was Ludazar.

"Have you come to mislead the minds of our young heroes, Your Majesty?" said Ludazar, his words somehow echoing in the air. "Your daughter is gone. You must give her up and move on. You must continue to rule your lands."

The terror in the King's eyes turned to rage.

"Never!" he shouted back. "You should remember that I am your ruler too, and you cannot tell me what to do. You are no longer my advisor!"

"Very well, but I have a mind of my own, and not even a king can rule over people's minds," said Ludazar before he turned around and walked back towards town.

The King looked down at the three heroes.

"Do not trust the wizard, young ones, and remember what I have told you. Save Nari, save my daughter!"

since Krucar passed away. When you find it, you must become its new master. It will be a helpful companion on your journey to save Nari."

Kraus widened his eyes with interest and was about to say something before Narwynn broke in.

"How do we find the Princess?" Narwynn asked.

The King looked at Narwynn and thought for a moment.

"As I have already said, you must stay out of the dragon's sight. However, you must keep a close eye on him. You must follow him to the place he returns to after his flights across the lands. That must be where he has hidden away Nari and the gold."

"So we will not have to fight him?" Elna asked.

The King looked at them and raised his chin.

"No," said the King. "It has not served any of the previous heroes to stand up to him. You must not fight him. It will end in certain death."

Narwynn felt a shiver down his spine.

"What about after you have the Princess and we have the gold?" Kraus asked. "Can I kill him then? I want to kill him!"

"As long as you save Nari first, you can try if you so wish. But if Dreumar dies before that, we will never find Nari."

"But surely anyone could find her if they don't need to fight him?" said Narwynn.

"That's where you are wrong, young

eyes. How did the King know his name? He had not introduced himself yet.

"Why have you come?" Narwynn asked.

"I am here because I have waited for new heroes to rise and you have now risen. My beloved daughter, Nari, and half of my gold were taken from me twelve years ago. I do not care about the gold, but I need a hero to save my daughter. After killing the troll, you three have achieved what only a hero could achieve. Save my daughter, and you will get the gold."

"I'm sorry the dragon took your daughter," said Elna with compassion in her eyes.

The King looked at Elna but said nothing. Then he looked at Elna's lynx with worry in his eyes.

"What about Dreumar?" Kraus asked.

The King stayed silent for a moment before he spoke.

"You must not let him see you until you have found my daughter."

"I want to kill him," said Kraus.

The King looked at Kraus. "So you are the one they spoke of," he said . "You are the offspring of Krucar, the wolf-tamer."

Elna placed a hand on Kraus's shoulder.

"I am," said Kraus.

"Then the wolf will be loyal to you."

"What do you mean?"

"You should know that Krucar's wolf still lurks around in the Green Lands, looking for its master. It has scared many nose-elves over the years

why the King had stared at him but assumed it was because of the colour of his fur. Many other grown-ups had done the same when they saw him for the first time.

"Good day, young ones," said the King.

"Good day, Your Majesty," said Narwynn, Elna and Kraus in unison.

"I hear you three have killed a troll."

"We have," said Kraus and looked down.

"Then why do you all look so sad? You should be dancing and singing after such an achievement."

None of them answered.

"You will answer the King when spoken to!" a guard shouted and drew his white crystal sword.

Elna's lynx stepped closer to them from behind with his body low, ready to charge at the guard.

"Now, now, Sir Delmur," said the King and raised his hand, signalling for the guard to stand down. "These three shall answer only when they wish to do so."

"The troll ate my Susy," said Elna and started crying.

"It killed my fox as well," said Kraus but did not cry.

"I see," said the King, "I gather that killing a troll could not have been possible without sacrifice. But killing the troll saved a life as well, did it not, Narwynn?"

Narwynn raised his gaze and widened his

Narwynn and said: "Don't ever speak his name!"

Narwynn and Elna stopped and looked at Kraus with their eyes wide open. Kraus turned back around and kept walking.

When they reached the field, they saw that someone riding a large animal, and six guards in red capes, were standing on the other side by the trees.

"That must be the King," Elna pointed out.

"Well spotted, Elna," said Kraus.

"What is the gigantic animal he is riding?" Narwynn asked.

"I'm not sure," said Kraus. "We will see when we get closer."

They walked on a path of trodden grass, feeling a light breeze against their fur. The closer they got, the clearer they saw the King. He rode an animal many times his size, with antlers that stretched far up in the air. Narwynn thought it was almost as large as Rutha had been.

"It is a stag," Kraus pointed out. "They are rare, and usually stay high up in the mountains."

"Woah, it is so big!" said Elna.

Narwynn had never seen a more majestic animal. It was fit for a King to ride, he thought.

When they walked up to the King and his guards, the stag stalled and seemed frightened at the sight of the Elna's lynx. The lynx seemed to notice and kept at a distance while Narwynn, Elna and Kraus faced the King.

The King stared at Narwynn for a moment before he turned to Kraus. Narwynn did not know

youngling answered, "and then Kritar disappeared. The old nose-elf told me it was all the King's fault, and that the King would try and take Kraus as well. My sister and I can't lose Kraus. He needs to be here and take care of us."

The lynx stopped snarling and stepped over to the youngling who was now crying. It licked his tears, as if to comfort him. Then Narwynn and Elna heard someone else approaching from behind. It was Kraus.

"Kumar," said Kraus and looked at the youngling, "it is time for you to go and make some breakfast for you and your sister. I need to be somewhere today."

"Don't go," said the youngling. "I know what you are up to."

"Did you not hear me? Go in and feed your sister. Now!"

The youngling did as Kraus said and ran in. Kraus turned to Narwynn and Elna.

"Are you guys ready to go, or are you going to stand here all day?" said Kraus.

"We are ready," said Narwynn.

Narwynn thought it was strange seeing Kraus without Charky. It felt as if something was missing from him.

Kraus took the lead as they walked towards the field. They walked through the outskirts and past the mines and caves.

"Kraus, who is Kritar?" Narwynn asked.

Kraus turned around, pointed the finger at

outskirts of town. On either side of the path were stone houses and little nose-elves were playing in the gardens.

Neither Narwynn nor Elna had ever been to Kraus's house before and realised they had no idea which one was his. They decided to ask one of the younglings who was waving a stick around in the air, pretending it was a sword.

"Excuse me, young one," said Narwynn. "Do you know Kraus?"

The youngling lowered his stick and looked at Narwynn and Elna.

"What do you two want with my big brother?"

His brother? Narwynn thought.

"We all have a meeting with the King this morning," said Elna. "We thought Kraus might want to walk with us."

"The King, huh!" said the youngling. "I will not let you take him to the King!"

The youngling swung his stick at them. Narwynn backed away in time, but the stick hit Elna's nose.

"Ow!" Elna screamed while the lynx jumped between her and the youngling, snarling. "What did you do that for?"

"I will not let the King take any more of my family!"

"What do you mean?" Narwynn asked.

A tear ran down the youngling's cheek.

"First, my father was taken from us," the

the King before, nor had felt so important. But he knew that the meeting would also include Elna and Kraus. After all, Narwynn had not defeated Rutha on his own. He would never have made it without Kraus and Elna.

Narwynn stepped out of his tent and saw that green leaves had sprouted on the branches of the white oak. The grass was green, and the sun had already risen. His cape felt warm when he put it on. He did not need his spear, and so he left it leaning against the tent.

He walked the pathway to Elna's house. Elna was already waiting for him outside on the steps when he arrived. The white lynx was sitting next to her, looking patient and calm. The lynx was bigger than Elna, and Narwynn couldn't understand how it had become her pet. Yet, Elna's face was sad, no doubt because she missed Susy, Narwynn thought.

"Hello, Elna," said Narwynn.

"Hello, Narwynn."

"Are you ready to go?"

"Yes."

Elna got up and walked down to Narwynn with her head low. The lynx followed her, and Narwynn could not help feeling nervous in its presence. He remembered all too well the night when he had fought against it.

They walked towards the area where Kraus lived, passed the shared storage house, walked through the market place, the workers' area, and turned onto a new pathway before they reached the

9 DESTINY

The word spread fast across Oaktown. Soon everyone had heard the new tale about how Narwynn, Elna and Kraus had freed them from Rutha the Troll. The days were bright and filled with hope, and the snow from a long winter melted away.

A traveller came back to Oaktown with news that word had spread even further. He told the nose-elves in Oaktown that word about the young heroes had reached Cedartown, where King Elrud himself lived.

It did not take long before Narwynn, Elna and Kraus learned that the King was on his way to Oaktown to meet them. They were to meet at the eastern edges of the woods when he arrived. Why they would meet there and not inside Oaktown remained a mystery.

The day arrived when the meeting was to take place, and Narwynn felt nervous. He had never met

spell of silence, he uttered it.

"Aunt Milnu…" he said. "It was all my fault. I took the blue crystal from her and gave it to you."

Narwynn noticed an angry look from Aunt Milnu and expected the worst. He even wanted the worst. He wanted her to hate him because he hated himself.

"Narwynn…" said Aunt Milnu, "you need to grow up. How can you say it was your fault when it was not? Rutha has killed many nose-elves and haunted the woods for years. This whole time, we have feared the woods in the winter because of her. You found the crystal because you wanted to protect us from her. You tried to tame the lynx because you wanted to protect us. You wanted to learn how to ride so that you could protect us. Despite how most of the nose-elves here have treated you all your life, you still wanted to protect them. You only gave me the crystal because no one dared to help you."

"Aunt Milnu…"

"If only you knew who you are. If only I had not promised to keep it a secret."

"What do you mean?"

Aunt Milnu paused for a moment. "I won't tell a secret I have promised to keep, but I will give you a hint… What do you need to be to kill a troll?"

Narwynn could not hold back a smile. Then he raised his gaze and looked at Aunt Milnu, whose eyes sparkled in the moonlight.

"A   hero."

around Kraus. Then they saw four nose-elves running into the clearing below from the woods. Although they were far away, Narwynn recognised them immediately. The one in front was Edgar, who hurried towards the start of the path up to the cave. The hunter with a kestrel and the blacksmith walked over to Rutha's body. The final one was Ludazar in his white robe, with his staff to support him. Ludazar remained where he stood and looked up. Narwynn thought for a moment that he could see Ludazar smiling, but then he thought better of it. Why would anyone smile at such a scene.

"Elna!" Edgar suddenly sounded from behind, panting.

Elna turned as Edgar threw his arms around her and squeezed her tightly to his chest. After a while, he opened his eyes and saw the lynx that was standing next to them. His eyes widened, and his jaw dropped.

"Elnax..." he mumbled to the lynx, "no..."

They all turned around and started walking down the path along the mountainside. Few words were spoken that night. When they got back, they all went home with their heads low. Although the Green Lands were now free of Rutha, they had lost two close friends. And they had almost lost Aunt Milnu too.

When they reached their broken tent, Narwynn and Aunt Milnu sat down next to the dying glows in the fireplace. Narwynn had one thought in his mind that tormented him. After a

"N-Narwynn…" Aunt Milnu stammered from one side. Kraus and Elna stared with wide eyes from the other.

In the blink of an eye, Narwynn charged across the ledge straight towards Rutha. He roared as he jumped up in the air. The lynx let go of Rutha's throat and moved out of the way. Narwynn's head reached the level of Rutha's, and for a moment, he could see the fear in her eyes. He butted into her forehead so hard it sounded like thunder, shoving the blue crystal through her skull, and sending her back to the edge of the ledge.

Narwynn landed on his hooves and saw Rutha's eyes close before she fell over the edge and to a certain death.

He stood still for a moment before walking over to Aunt Milnu to free her from the ropes. She looked at him with her eyes wide. She looked at his horns and then at his hooves.

"Narwynn…" she said.

Narwynn did not answer her but turned around. He saw Kraus and Elna standing on the edge and looked down below. The lynx stood next to Elna. Narwynn walked over to them and looked where they were looking. Down there on the ground between all the melted rocks was Rutha's body. Next to Rutha was Charky, lying still and lifeless. Narwynn realised that both Elna and Kraus had lost their pets in the fight.

Aunt Milnu came over to them and placed her right arm around Narwynn and Elna and her left one

They were right on the edge of the ledge, and if Rutha managed to get the lynx off, she would surely throw it over. Kraus grabbed an arrow in haste, and fumbled with the thread that held the white crystal arrowhead attached to it. He took it off and started joining the one Narwynn had thrown to him.

Kraus stood up and drew the arrow far back in his bow before he released it. The arrow flew through the air like a lightning strike and hit Rutha right in the middle of her forehead. Rutha groaned and took a step back to regain her balance. The blue crystal was stuck halfway into her forehead. She grabbed the arrow and broke it off, but the crystal remained stuck.

"No..." Kraus said. "It is over."

Narwynn saw that the lynx was getting tired. It now hung from Rutha's throat like a piece of cloth hanging up to dry. Then he looked at Aunt Milnu, who was still struggling to free herself from the ropes with terror in her eyes and the fire blazing next to her.

No, Narwynn thought. This could not be happening. The fear and despair intensified. Then a rush of anger and rage built up inside him. Intense energy filled his body that raised him to his feet. He stood up straight and stared at the horrific troll who wanted to eat his beloved aunt. He felt a familiar pain building up in his legs and forehead, but did not flinch from it. He felt how he had grown taller under the opening of the cave as his feet turned to hooves and he felt his horns reaching the ceiling.

being crushed between Rutha's teeth.

"Nooooo!" Elna screamed and fell to her knees.

Rutha stepped towards Elna. Elna cried as she half-heartedly crawled back on the ground. There was nothing they could do. Rutha was far too strong for any of them. Narwynn desperately tried to get to his feet as Rutha grabbed Elna by the waist and lifted her.

But then, out of nowhere, the snow-lynx jumped at Rutha's throat and Elna was dropped to the ground again. Narwynn did not understand why the snow-lynx suddenly intervened nor where it had come from, but he felt relieved that Elna had been saved, for now.

Narwynn looked over at Kraus, who had opened his eyes and looked around in confusion. Then he looked at Aunt Milnu and noticed that she was trying to get his attention.

"Narwynn!" she shouted. "Look!"

Although she couldn't point with her tied hands, she nodded towards something on the ground next to Narwynn. It was the blue-crystal arrowhead. Narwynn reached for it and picked it up. Then he looked at Kraus, who was now getting back onto his feet.

"Kraus!" he shouted and threw the crystal to him.

Kraus grabbed it and looked at it for a moment. Rutha was still struggling to get the snow-lynx off, but it had locked its teeth to her throat.

"Charky!" Kraus shouted.

Then Narwynn saw Rutha continuing to tie Aunt Milnu to the spit. He could not bear the thought of what would happen if they failed to stop her. He started crawling on the cave floor, through old bones and sheep carcasses. When he reached the opening, he saw Kraus hanging around Rutha's neck trying to strangle her, but then he was thrown against the cliff wall and knocked unconscious.

Suddenly Narwynn heard someone else approaching from the path. When he turned to see who it was, he felt a cold shiver his spine. It was Elna.

"Elna, what are you doing here?" Narwynn shouted. "Where is Edgar?"

"I couldn't find him, so I told the blacksmith to go and look for him, and then I ran after you to help."

Then Rutha took a step towards Elna, and Elna took a step back.

"Narwynn?" said Elna in a shaken voice, "I am scared."

"Run Elna! Run!"

Elna was about to run, but then Susy jumped off her shoulder and ran towards the cave. She was probably terrified too and wanted to hide inside it. But before Susy reached the opening, Rutha picked her up between two fingers.

"Little nose-elf brought snack for I," Rutha said and put Susy in her mouth.

Narwynn felt sick when he heard Susy's bones

"No!" Narwynn shouted and got on his feet.

He ran after them and held his spear ready.

"Narwynn, wait!" an out-of-breath voice sounded from behind. "Let Charky distract her."

It was Kraus, and before Narwynn knew it, Charky ran past him and up along the path. Rutha was about mid-way when Charky reached her. He jumped onto her back and started biting into it. But Rutha kept walking, twitching only slightly to throw Charky off, as if he were just an annoying bug.

"Let's go!" said Narwynn and pulled Kraus with him.

Kraus was exhausted and could not run very fast. Narwynn had to drag him along up the path. When they eventually arrived there, they saw a fire burning on the ledge in front of the cave. Rutha was tying Aunt Milnu to a spit next to it. Poor Aunt Milnu struggled and twitched, but it was no use.

Kraus stopped at a distance and started firing arrows at Rutha while trying to avoid hitting Charky, but Rutha hardly noticed. Then Narwynn ran in front of Rutha and stabbed her nose with his spear. The stab made Rutha groan with pain and rise. Then Rutha grabbed Narwynn around the waist and threw him into the cave where he landed on a rock.

"Aaargh!" Narwynn screamed.

His leg and shoulder felt crushed, and he struggled to get back up, only to find that he could not stand. He looked out and saw that Rutha had grabbled Charky by the tail. She then threw him off the ledge, and he disappeared below.

path leading to it alongside the mountain wall. There was smoke rising from the ledge in front of the cave. Narwynn kicked the sheep's sides once more and rode alongside the mountain wall towards the start of the path.

There were trees and shrubbery everywhere, and it was clear that Rutha had not taken the same path as he had. He pushed his way through the shrubbery as he rode, moving branches and sticks aside with his spear. Eventually, he came out on the other side, where the path to the cliff started. And right in front of him was a giant troll, hair full of sticks and skin covered in moss, and to Narwynn's terror, a screaming Aunt Milnu under one arm.

Narwynn rode straight up to them and took the spear off his back. He was just about to stab Rutha in the back when the sheep grew scared and stalled. Rutha heard them and turned around. She took a step towards them and waved her free arm at Narwynn but did not reach him.

"Narwynn!" Aunt Milnu suddenly shouted. "No Narwynn, run!"

But Narwynn did not listen; he was too busy trying to get his sheep to calm down. Then Rutha managed to grab the sheep by its head and pull it towards her. Narwynn fell off and heard Rutha snapping the sheep's neck with a twitch. The sheep went limp and fell to the ground. Rutha turned back around and continued onto the path, mumbling to herself, "Nose-elf takes nice stone from I. I takes nice stone back and makes nose-elf for dinner.".

Narwynn did not think twice.

"No time," he said, and rode off through the trail of broken planks and tents, towards the woods.

It was not hard to track where Rutha had gone. The trail was full of giant footsteps and broken branches. The branches on the ground were so large that it would have been difficult to travel on foot, but the sheep quickly jumped over them, and Narwynn was now used to holding onto the sheep's back whenever it jumped. All those days trying to learn how to ride in the snow had strengthened his grip and given him balance. Now that he and the sheep were moving as one it was impossible for Narwynn to fall off.

Night fell while Narwynn rode. Had it not been for the full moon, neither Narwynn nor the sheep would have been able to see anything. Eventually, he caught up with Kraus and Charky who ran and jumped over the branches on the path.

"Kraus!" said Narwynn.

"Greeny," Kraus answered, "we have to hurry. She has your aunt."

"I know," said Narwynn and rode ahead.

It seemed to have taken forever, but he finally reached the clearing where he had once faced Rutha. He saw the eleven, half-melted rocks, and the one that was broken into pieces next to Rutha's fireplace. But he saw neither Rutha nor Aunt Milnu. He rode into the middle of the clearing and looked around. No one was there. Then he looked up at the cliffs above. There in the mountainside was a cave, and a

Narwynn continued towards the centre.

As he got closer, he noticed that something was not quite right. Some of the nose-elves were running around, looking frightened. Others lay on the ground, sobbing. Then he noticed that many of the tents and small houses lay trashed in a trail of enormous footsteps.

"What has happened here?" Narwynn asked one of the nose-elves who was running.

"S-she came from the woods," she stammered. "S-she came straight through, trashing our houses and tents."

Then Narwynn noticed where the trail of footsteps led. They continued in the direction he was heading, towards his tent where Aunt Milnu was. Narwynn immediately kicked the sides of his sheep and rode in haste towards home. It did not take long until he was there. To his terror, he found that their tent had been trashed as well, and he could not see Aunt Milnu.

"Narwynn!" a familiar voice sounded.

Elna came running towards him with Susy by her side.

"Elna! Where is Aunt Milnu?"

"She took her. Rutha took her!" said Elna with tears in her voice.

Narwynn's heart sank. His jaw dropped as he stared at Elna.

"No…" he said, almost speechless.

"We must find Daddy! Kraus has already gone after them."

that surrounded Oaktown, and smell the smoke they made.

When they reached the edge of the woods, Narwynn saw that some of the shepherds carried wood to the bonfires. The shepherds looked tired and grumpy as Edgar and Narwynn walked past them.

"Out in the woods at this time of night?" said one of them. "You must be asking to get eaten! Rutha has been all over the place lately."

"At least that would have saved me the bother of listening to your nagging, Ajunn," said Edgar with a skewed smile on his face.

Narwynn grinned. It felt good to hear the shepherds being mocked. They were always grumpy, complaining about what everyone else did or did not do. They were probably tired of staying out late all the time, tending to the fires and the sheep. In fact, this evening in particular they looked more tired than usual, and their fires were hardly burning.

When Narwynn and Edgar reached the outskirts of town, Edgar picked the two silver keys out of his pouch.

"I need to get these to Ludazar," he said.

"Are you going there now?"

"Yes. I am already late. I will see you later, Narwynn. It has been a pleasure travelling with you."

"It has been a pleasure travelling with you too, Edgar. Thank you… for everything."

Edgar gave Narwynn a wink before he turned and rode towards the other end of town while

moments. Narwynn knew then that he would miss her, and that she would miss him too. He turned his sheep around, and the woods seemed darker and less colourful than before. The trees looked more lifeless, and small patches of snow covered the dead, muddy leaves on the ground. The path to Oaktown looked rocky and uneven, and shrubbery had grown across it in many places.

"Well, that was awkward," said Edgar, as they started up the path. "You really don't know how to say goodbye, do you?"

"What did you expect me to say?"

"How about 'Goodbye'?" Edgar shrugged his shoulders and looked at Narwynn. "Or 'Farewell'?"

"Nah. Did not need to."

"Well, if you say so."

They walked for a few hours. The shrubbery was painful, and they and their sheep had scrapes and small wounds by the time they reached a clearer path. Narwynn looked at the ground as he rode, and feelings of sadness came over him.

"Why so sad?" said Edgar.

"I don't know," said Narwynn.

"You don't want to go home, do you?"

"No."

"Don't be sad, my green friend. You will be going on another journey soon enough."

Buddy walked ahead on his own. Narwynn and Edgar saw the white oak in the distance. They were getting close as twilight took over from the light of day. They could see the bonfires in the field

"At last!" said Edgar, relieved that they were getting back into familiar terrain.

Narwynn did not feel relieved. For some reason, he had no urge to go home. He had enjoyed the time in Willowtown. And he did not want to lose the feeling of butterflies in his stomach.

They reached a path-crossing. A sign showed that the path they were on led to Aldertown, whereas the new path led to Oaktown.

"Here we are," said Melifer. "This is where I must leave you."

Narwynn felt as if he had been punched in the chest.

"Well, thank you for everything, young Melifer," said Edgar, and placed a gold piece in her pouch while she was looking the other way. "You have been truly kind to us."

"My pleasure." She looked at Narwynn. Narwynn looked back at her and tried to find words, but nothing came to mind. A moment went by before the silence broke.

"Well?" said Edgar. "Are you two going to say goodbye or what?"

Melifer seemed not to mind. She sat still on Gemmy's back and kept her eyes on Narwynn, waiting for him to say something.

"Until next time…" said Narwynn.

"When will that be?" said Melifer.

"I don't know."

"Very well. Until next time then."

They looked at each other for a few more

home. I suspect he will never agree to let you leave."

"He won't," Melifer interrupted and smiled at Narwynn. "We need to leave before he wakes up. I will lead you to the path back to Oaktown. You can each borrow a sheep from the stables. That will give you a reason to come back to visit soon."

"Thank you, Melifer," said Edgar. "That's very kind of you."

As they rode into the woods, Narwynn tried to explain to Edgar what had happened to him on the cliffs. He started by telling him about how difficult it had been to climb them. While Edgar had no problem believing that part, he seemed less convinced when Narwynn told him about the talking goat and how he had magically grown horns and hooves, and had fought it.

"It is true, I'm telling you!" he said.

"If you say so," said Edgar.

Melifer rode ahead and could not hear it while Narwynn kept trying to explain. Narwynn would prefer talking with Melifer than Edgar. At least she didn't make fun of him. Edgar however, could make anyone feel as if they made no sense at all.

Buddy stayed close to them while they were riding. He seemed to be on guard, looking over his shoulder now and again. Sometimes he jumped and turned around. Narwynn and Edgar would jump too. They knew that if anything were to come after them in the woods, Buddy would be the first to notice.

"We are nearly there," said Melifer over her shoulder.

talked for hours without noticing the time going by. It seemed like they would never run out of things to talk about. Narwynn thought he had never met anyone like Melifer.

He woke early one morning and could not get back to sleep. He felt like his body could not bear another day in bed. He thought that perhaps the healer was still asleep and that maybe if he was quiet, he could sneak out as he had done back in Oaktown.

He lay still for a few hours, looking out through the window where the moon sometimes appeared between the clouds. It was nearly full moon, and he wondered if this were magical. Many of the tales he had heard involved the full moon. It seemed to be a time of the month when tales would reach their end, and when something great would happen.

After a few hours the sun was about to rise, and Narwynn heard someone knock on his window, but could not see anyone there. He walked over to it and looked outside. He saw Edgar and Melifer standing outside, waving for him to come out. He did not think twice before he opened the window, stepped back, and dived out. Once more, he hit the all too familiar ground nose first.

"Good, you are out," said Edgar. "We need to leave today. I need to get back to complete my quest."

"What about the healer?"

Edgar shook his head and rolled his eyes.

"The healer here is just like the one back

8 THE RISE OF HEROES

Narwynn had been in bed for a week. The healer in Willowtown insisted that he needed to get plenty of rest before he was ready for the journey back to Oaktown. Edgar was kind enough to wait for him. It seemed as if Edgar did not mind spending some extra time in Willowtown, probably because Emelda would be angry at him when he got back. Besides, he had plenty of gold to spend on anything he wanted in Willowtown.

Being confined to bed the whole time made Narwynn restless. He thought he needed to get out of bed to return to Oaktown, but every time Narwynn tried to leave, the healer stopped him in the door and pointed a finger at him.

"You need to stay in bed for another few days so you can heal fully," the healer would say.

But Narwynn felt healed already. A part of him did not mind staying in bed at the healer's house. Melifer visited him every day, and they often

forever.

"You slammed into the ground like a bag of potatoes," said Melifer, "we were so scared."

"She's right," said Edgar. "No one should survive a fall like that. It is impossible."

Narwynn touched his forehead and looked down at his feet. He had neither hooves nor horns any more.

"Let's get you back to Willowtown," said Edgar. "We need to get you to the healer."

Narwynn reached into his pouch and pulled out a handful of crooked stalks with broken flowers.

"For you Melifer," he said.

"Oh, thank you very much Narwynn," said Melifer. "They are, erm, beautiful."

By midnight, they entered the field of Willowtown. Narwynn lay across Gemmy's back and Melifer, Edgar and Buddy walked next to them. Narwynn had brought no falcon with him, and falcons were the last thing on his mind. Something else haunted his mind entirely. He now knew that there was more to the green colour on his fur than he had previously thought. He really was different.

goat had awakened something in Narwynn that he would never have found on his own. However, the goat was much larger than Narwynn and still stronger. Narwynn got pushed further and further out onto the edge of the rock.

The sun was at its highest in the sky, and shone onto the cliff and the rock, making the smooth surfaces shine. Narwynn felt the edge of the rock under his hoof and did not take another step.

"So this is it, huh?" he said to the goat.

"Yes, it has failed the test and must die."

"What if the prophecy is true?" Narwynn asked, even though he did not know what the prophecy was.

"Then it would not have needed any mercy from me," said the goat and charged towards Narwynn for the last time. It butted its head into him and pushed him over the edge. Narwynn flew into the open air, not realising that he was falling. All he saw was darkness and stars.

Narwynn heard the crackling of a bonfire. He opened his eyes and saw that Edgar and Melifer sat next to him. They had wrapped him up in his cape and placed him close to the heat.

"Oh, look! Look, Edgar, he's awake!" said Melifer.

"Thank heavens."

They both leaned over him and waited for him to speak, but Narwynn did not answer right away. He felt relieved. He had survived after all. But what he had just experienced would change him

goat who was coming towards him.

"Strange... very strange..." the goat whispered. "I have never seen a nose-elf changing like this before."

"What do you mean?" said Narwynn and grabbed his forehead with both hands.

He felt two short horns, pointing out of each side of his forehead. Then he looked at his feet, but saw that they had turned into hooves. His jaw dropped, then he turned towards the goat.

"What has happened to me?"

"It seems to have shape-shifted, but not completely. The yellow nose-elves always shift fully into their new form."

"Yellow nose-elves? Shape-shifters? What are you talking about?"

"The shape-shifters shift only when they need to or choose to."

Narwynn took a step with his new hooves and almost fell over at first, but then got used to it. He looked at the goat and saw that it prepared for the final blow. Then he felt enraged in a way he had never experienced before.

They both charged forwards and butted their heads into each other. It sounded like thunder, and perhaps it was thunder. They took a step back before butting against each other again. And again.

Narwynn could feel the rage of battle driving him, giving him strength. He hated the goat now, and thought the goat hated him. They were now of the same species and yet they were enemies. The

Narwynn again.

This time Narwynn fell onto a long rock that stretched out from the cliff wall. He felt beaten, weak and could barely move. Thoughts of hopelessness ran through his mind. He tried to get back up on his feet, but he could not stand up. His whole body felt crushed, cold and out of energy.

He saw the goat making its way along the mountainside towards him. He realised that there was no escape. The goat could easily walk where he could barely climb. It had hooves that gripped the rock perfectly. It was large and robust, and its forehead, from which its long horns stretched backwards, was hard enough to crush Narwynn's body. There was nowhere to go.

Narwynn crawled back along the rock he was on. It was so far down that he could not see the ground below. There was only the mountain wall and, ironically, he thought, several falcons hovering in the air. The talking goat approached him once again, ready to butt him to his doom. As Narwynn reached the edge of the rock, the goat stepped onto it at the other end.

Then something strange happened. Suddenly Narwynn felt an unfamiliar flow of energy through him. It flowed through his whole body until it stopped in his forehead and feet. It became painful, and he wanted to scream. It felt like two rocks crushed his feet between them, and the inside of his head sucked out on each side of his forehead. Then it stopped and he was back on his feet facing the

"I see…" the goat whispered and paused for a moment. "So the wizard's prophecy may have been true after all. He must have made sure this green youngling came to face me. How else could he make sure he was right?"

"What prophecy?"

"It does not need to know."

Suddenly the goat took a few steps back and aimed its forehead at Narwynn.

"Erm, w-what are you doing?" Narwynn stuttered while clinging to the stone wall behind him.

Narwynn did not think twice when the goat charged at him. He jumped up against the wall next to him and tried to climb away, but it was too late. The goat butted into him from below. Narwynn flew up in the air and landed on a ledge further up the cliff. He gasped desperately for air. He looked down and saw that the goat was making its way up towards him.

Narwynn threw himself around and started climbing again.

"It seems scared already," the goat sounded from behind him. "It cannot be the nose-elf in the prophecy."

Narwynn could no longer climb. He clung to the wall behind him and stared at the goat as it approached.

"What are you talking about?" he said. "I only came up here to look for falcons. What have I done to deserve this?"

The goat did not answer but butted into

and closed his eyes. There was nothing he could do.

"Green. I have never seen a green nose-elf before," something whispered into Narwynn's ear. "They are blue on one side of the mountain and yellow on the other, but never are they green."

Narwynn opened his eyes and stared straight into the goat's eyes. The goat looked at him with its yellow, empty eyes. Narwynn's heart pounded even harder than before, and he started sweating.

"I wonder what its name is..." the goat whispered.

"Woah! What in Nightwood?" Narwynn shouted. "You can talk!"

The goat took a step back. It looked confused, but then it took a step forward to face Narwynn again.

"So, it can speak too," the goat whispered.

"Sure, I can speak. How can you speak?"

"Interesting. It is green, and it can speak. I thought only the yellow nose-elves could speak."

"What do you want?"

"I am not the one who intrudes here. Why is it up here on my cliff? No nose-elf has been up here since that blue one who used to steal my flowers long ago."

Narwynn thought twice before he spoke.

"I am here to look at the view. I can see all of the Green Lands from up here. It is beautiful," he said.

"What is its name?"

"My name is Narwynn."

two long sticks pointing up from behind the ledge. They could not be sticks, he thought. They were too thick and had not been there earlier. Then they started to move, and Narwynn jumped for a second when he realised that they were horns.

A giant goat, at least three times Narwynn's size, with horns longer than Narwynn himself, walked upon the ledge. Narwynn's heart pounded in his chest, but then he remembered that goats were plant-eaters. He sat down and watched it while it sniffed around on the ledge. It was a majestic creature, he thought.

Suddenly the goat saw Narwynn. Perhaps he had climbed into its territory, though he did not worry about it. There was no way for the goat to reach Narwynn anyway. The wall between them was so steep that anything without fingers to hang from could not get across.

But then, to Narwynn's astonishment, the goat started to walk towards him. It leaned against the almost vertical wall and stepped on it. This looked impossible. There was nothing on the wall to stand on, and yet the goat's hooves did not slip. It came closer and closer, and Narwynn did not know what to do.

He looked for an escape down the cliff wall, but he would fall if he tried. Then he looked upwards but soon realised that he would not be able to lift himself fast enough to escape. The goat came closer and closer. He wondered if it would push him off the cliff wall. He clung to the wall behind him

from the nest, he could raise it without having to go to the trouble of fighting a fully grown falcon.

He started to climb sideways towards the ledge where he had spotted the nest. The wall was almost vertical, and Narwynn was more hanging than standing. Had he slipped, he would have fallen to the ground. When he reached the ledge, he looked into the nest only to be disappointed. It was empty, except for a bouquet of blue flowers swaying in the wind. He thought he could give them to Melifer, picked them all and put them in his pouch. Then he sat down on the little ledge and admired the view and hoped that a falcon would show up.

He could see Willowtown close by, and Oaktown looked like a small patch in the distance. He also saw five other towns. The one furthest north seemed like a tiny dot because it was so far away. Although Narwynn was quite high up, he was still surrounded by mountains in all direction. And the tallest one was the one furthest away from him, the northern peak.

Narwynn had been sitting for a while when he decided that waiting for a falcon was a waste of time. Then he looked for a way down and realised that climbing down would be far more complicated than climbing up. He started climbing back where he had come from, and hoped that he would find a way down from where he had taken the first break.

When he got there, he looked back at the nest. Nothing moved inside it any more. But he could see something else there now. It looked like

looked up, fearful of the endless amount of cliff wall. They were so steep that one mistake up there could mean a fall. He had no chance, he thought.

"Narwynn?" Melifer asked, "Are you listening?"

"Oh sorry, I am just calculating my route, that's all," said Narwynn.

"I see."

Narwynn stepped up to the cliff wall and placed one hand on it. He could see a possible path up, but he did not know how far he would go. Nor did he know how he would get back down. He found a grip, pulled himself up and found another grip. He climbed slowly but steadily for a while. The rock was ice cold, and Narwynn's grip weakened. He soon realised that he needed a break and found a small ledge where he could sit and rest.

As soon as Narwynn turned around to sit, he realised how high up he was. A cold shiver ran down his spine, and he clung to the wall behind him. What am I doing? he asked himself. Melifer and Edgar looked like small beetles down on the ground. Narwynn envied them. He longed to be down there with them, safe and warm.

His hands warmed up again, and he was ready to continue. Before he started upward, he looked around for falcons. It was difficult to see. He pulled himself up a few more lengths, where the view was better. There, on a small ledge some distance to his left, he saw a large nest with something moving inside it. Chicks, he thought. If he could steal a chick

Narwynn caught up with Edgar and Melifer by the edge of the woods where Buddy jumped in among the trees right away, and Gemmy seemed obedient and eager to walk further south now that the sun rose in the horizon.

The trees in the south looked different from the ones around Oaktown. They stretched taller, and their branches stretched more upwards than sideways. Long-stalked blossoms stretched up from the frozen ground all around them, defying the cold. There was no snow at all, and it felt like winter was further away there.

Melifer led them on a path that stretched upwards towards the mountains. She seemed to sit comfortably on Gemmy's back and peeked back over her shoulder now and again. Edgar looked around and held an arrow drawn in his bow, ready to aim at any approaching threat. Narwynn held his spear ready, with the sharpened white crystal up in front.

It did not take long until they reached the cliffs. They stretched so high up that Narwynn could not see the top. All he saw was a gigantic, almost vertical wall of rock. How would he get up to the falcons? he thought.

"Well, well, well, here we are. The falcons are probably up there somewhere," said Edgar, trying not to laugh.

"How are you going to climb up to them, Narwynn?" Melifer asked.

Narwynn hardly paid attention to them. He

"I am going to tame a falcon," he said.

"But the cliffs are dangerous. There are dangerous creatures up there."

"That's all right, we have a predator pet with us," said Edgar, just as Buddy walked in from the side and sat down next to them. Melifer's eyes widened, and then they mellowed.

"Oh, he is so cute!" she said.

"Yes," said Edgar, "but we have to leave now if we are to make it back before dark. Come, Narwynn."

Narwynn jumped off Gemmy's back and walked over to Edgar. Suddenly he wanted to stay a little longer and keep riding with Melifer. But he needed a pet, and this was his best chance of finding a predator thus far. He had to go to the cliffs with Edgar.

"I'll be happy to show you the quickest way there," said Melifer.

"Well, if that is not too much trouble," said Edgar.

"Not at all. This will give me a chance to ride in the woods again. I haven't since the summer."

"Very well, then," said Edgar, and turned around, walking south.

Melifer looked at Narwynn and smiled. Narwynn returned the smile at first, but then he looked to the side. Melifer rode after Edgar and caught up with him.

"Wait," said Narwynn when he realised that he was far behind them.

Melifer walked over and jumped up on Gemmy's back behind Narwynn. He felt the warm rush again, and the butterfly whirlwind.

"Now, use your left leg to push carefully on this side..." said Melifer and pushed Narwynn's leg against Gemmy's side. "See how she turns right?"

Narwynn was too concentrated to answer but kept following the instructions. Throughout the night, Melifer continued teaching Narwynn how to ride. She told Narwynn about how she had known nothing but riding since she had been little. Narwynn enjoyed listening to her voice and found her story fascinating. He told her about the trip from Oaktown and the goblins in the forest. She seemed a bit shocked at first, but then she said she thought Narwynn was brave. They forgot about the time and place, the sun rose, and then it was a new day.

"There you are!" Edgar's voice sounded from behind, "I have been looking all over for you."

Narwynn realised that the sun was up and the time of day it was.

"I am sorry!" he said. "I met Melifer and forgot the time. And look, she has taught me how to ride!"

"Well done, my friend. But hurry up now if you want to go to the cliffs. We need to find a guide."

"The cliffs?" Melifer interrupted.

"Yes," Narwynn answered.

"Why are you going there?"

Narwynn smiled and raised his chin.

before he responded.

"Yes, yes, of course! I'm fine. That was on purpose. I just wanted to see how strong her hind legs were. I must say I am impressed," said Narwynn, as he got up and placed his hands on his hips.

Melifer giggled a little. Then she took Narwynn's hand and led him back to Gemmy. Narwynn felt warmth flowing through him. Melifer placed his hand on Gemmy's neck and stood close behind him. The butterflies in Narwynn's stomach created a whirlwind.

"Feel her heartbeat, Narwynn... Listen to her breath... Follow it with your own... She will only let you ride her if you are confident... She needs to know that she can trust you," said Melifer, "Now, try again, but don't fight her, just follow her movements."

Narwynn carefully jumped on Gemmy's back. She was a bit uneasy at first, twitching and kicking with her hind legs. But this time, Narwynn focused on following her movements and remaining calm. Soon, Gemmy was calm too and walked around without trying to throw Narwynn off.

"She likes you," said Melifer. "Do you know how to steer?"

"Em... am I not steering her right now?" Narwynn asked, just as Gemmy made a half turn to the right and a full turn to the left before walking backwards. Melifer giggled again.

"Here, let me show you."

"Narwynn. What's yours?"

"I'm Melifer. Do you ride, Narwynn?"

Narwynn felt a sudden panic coming over him.

"Sure, yes, I ride sometimes," he said, and then he regretted it to his bones.

"Come on over, you need to try and ride little Gemmy here. She's a gem, just a little nervous. The Troll has been lurking around in the woods here lately, and Gemmy is afraid of trolls."

Narwynn thought he was far more nervous than the sheep was. But there was no way out now. He had to do it, although he knew it would end in catastrophe. He would make an utter fool of himself, that much he already knew.

"It will be my pleasure," he said and walked over.

Stupid! he thought to himself. What is wrong with you?

Melifer jumped off Gemmy and handed Narwynn the leash. Narwynn's knees were trembling, but he tried to act casual. He placed one hand on the sheep's back and took a moment. Then he threw himself on top of her and grabbed hold of her neck. Gemmy immediately turned and succeeded in throwing Narwynn off. Narwynn was bounced up in the air where he screamed for a short moment before diving onto the ground nose first.

"Oh, Narwynn, are you all right?" said Melifer and came over to him.

Narwynn raised his head from the icy snow

high and bright now and shone its blue, glowing light onto the snow and ice. And there, in the field, Narwynn spotted a young nose-elf riding a sheep. She looked beautiful, he thought.

Although the sheep tried to throw her off, it did not succeed, and she stayed on its back, swaying up and down, following its movements. Narwynn walked over to her where she rode. Then he watched how she steered her sheep round and round in the field.

"Hello there!" he said. "You are out here late."

He thought he had sounded stupid as soon as the words had passed his lips. Why would he point out that she was out late? She already knew that.

She turned her head and smiled at Narwynn. He thought he had never seen anyone so beautiful. And she did not seem bothered by his colour when she looked at him.

"Hello!" she answered, with a soft voice that filled Narwynn's stomach with butterflies. "I am not out late. I am out early."

"Have you already slept and woken up?"

"Yes."

"How in Nightwood did you manage that?"

"I love riding, and I love riding under the moon and the stars. So I wake when everyone else is sleeping to go riding at night."

"I see."

She made it look so easy, as if she had done nothing but ride all her life.

"What's your name?" she asked.

woods are only sounds. They do not speak to anyone. And if the dragon were here, we would have been dead by now."

"No, you are wrong, Edgar! I heard them, and I saw the dragon!"

Narwynn could tell by Edgar's face that he would never believe him. He got to his feet and wrapped his cape tightly around him.

"Why are you here, Edgar?" Narwynn asked, "Have you finished with your secret quests yet?"

"I was looking for you. I spoke to one of the wise who has just travelled across the mountain from the south. He said he had seen several falcons flying around the cliffs. I thought you might be interested in trying to tame one? I suspect even Kraus would be jealous if you came back with one of the fastest birds in Nightwood."

Narwynn gasped. He forgot all about the whispers and the dragon.

"Yes!" he said. "Show me where!"

"Now, now, my green friend. It is far too late to start wandering through the woods. And besides, we will need a guide who knows where the cliffs are. Meet me at the inn in the morning. We will find someone there who can show us where to go."

"All right, Edgar. I will see you in the morning."

Edgar smiled and nodded goodnight to Narwynn before he headed off.

Narwynn stayed for a moment and looked back at the woods and the moon. The moon was

"I am different."

"Exactly..."

Narwynn sobbed on the icy ground. He did not understand what the whispers meant nor why they spoke to him. He figured they just wanted to frighten him and remind him of his failures.

"Look to the moon Narwynn..."

Narwynn raised his gaze to the moon and saw the dragon once more. It flew closer this time, and Narwynn could see its features in the moonlight. He could see its wings, horns and long tail. It looked enormous up there in the sky, gliding across the lands.

Narwynn got to his feet and walked backwards, before he turned and ran back towards Willowtown, still looking over his shoulder. Suddenly he slammed into something and fell to the ground.

"Who were you talking to?" a voice asked.

Narwynn looked up at the nose-elf he had slammed into. It was Edgar. Then he turned on the ground and pointed at the moon to show Edgar the dragon, but it was no longer there.

"I-I don't know," he said. "The whispers... could you not hear them? They showed me the dragon."

"Whispers?" said Edgar, and looked bewildered.

"The whispers of the woods. They spoke to me, and they have spoken to me before too."

"Don't be silly, Narwynn. The whispers of the

and night gradually took over from day. He stepped beyond the shepherds and their bonfires, all the way up to the edge of the woods. There he stood for a while, looking up at the stars. The night sky was beautiful, he thought.

Suddenly his thoughts were interrupted by a familiar voice, whispering in the dark.

"Narwynn..." the woods whispered.

Narwynn jumped but did not fall to the ground this time.

"What do you want?" he said.

"Tell me Narwynn, do you still think about what you saw that night?..."

"I don't want to think about the dragon anymore. I don't know what to believe about him."

"You should believe only what you can see for yourself."

"But I don't want to see him. I don't want anything to do with him."

"You cannot avoid it Narwynn... the dragon will face you one way or another..."

"You're lying! I cannot do anything about him!"

"You do not know who you are..."

"Don't say that!" Narwynn felt angry now. "I know who I am. I am a useless green nose-elf who cannot do what others can. I cannot tame animals, I cannot ride, and I am weak. I am..."

Narwynn dropped to his knees and tears ran down his cheeks.

"Continue, Narwynn..."

7 THE TALKING GOAT

Narwynn and Edgar stayed in Willowtown for three days. Narwynn thought the days were long as he did not have much to do. Edgar was gone most of the time and did not tell Narwynn where he went every day. It was as though Narwynn was brought along only to be left alone in a strange town.

Narwynn tried to speak to the nose-elves in Willowtown, but they all looked at him with disgust. They even shied away from him as soon as he approached them. He figured they were more repulsed by his colour because they had never met him before. Therefore, Narwynn had spent most of his time in Willowtown wandering on the outskirts and the field. He found himself longing to go back home where things were familiar and where he had at least some friends. He decided he would save his gold until he got back home.

In the evening of the third day, Narwynn walked to the field while the moon rose in the sky

spells of the day were turning more and more orange. The ground felt colder under Narwynn's feet, and the wet snow turned to ice. The night was taking over from the day, and the frozen ground was blue under the moonlight, while at the same time the trees and branches were glowing orange in the light from the sunset.

"It's getting dark, Edgar," Narwynn pointed out.

"I know, my friend," Edgar answered, "but look ahead now."

Ahead was a willow, stretching high up towards the sky. Narwynn could see that they were approaching a field filled with bonfires, just like the ones surrounding Oaktown to keep the creatures away. As they started across the field towards Willowtown, Buddy came to walk with them.

"I think you should be proud of yourself," said Edgar and smiled.

"Why do you say that?" Narwynn asked.

"Because you have now travelled to a new town. You can now call yourself a traveller if you wish to."

Narwynn grinned and felt a rush of excitement. It was true. He had never before travelled this far from Oaktown. And he could not wait to see what this new place had to offer, especially now that his pouch was filled with gold.

and Dreumar is the only one who can lead us to her."

"Yes, that is what the King would like you to think. What else have you heard?"

"On the other, Dreumar killed the princess and must be defeated before he kills again."

Edgar looked up and smiled for a moment before he spoke again.

"You have heard what I have heard, my green friend, and you will need to make your mind up about what you believe."

"But what if the princess is still alive? Would it be wrong to help Ludazar then?"

"I'm afraid I don't have all the answers. And you should be careful about those who claim they do. All I know is that the dragon puts all of us in danger, including you and Elna, and therefore I choose to help Ludazar. Now, let's talk about something else."

Narwynn was still confused but did not argue with Edgar. After a while, his thoughts turned back to the goblins.

"Why did we need to steal the gold from the goblins?" Narwynn asked.

"Oh, it is not their gold. Goblins are slimy thieves, the lot of them. All we did was to steal some of the gold back."

"I see."

Buddy wandered off again, and it was just Edgar and Narwynn. They kept their guards up and scouted for movement among the trees. The sunny

"Yes."

"Then why did you not tell me before?"

"And spoil the surprise? Hah, I don't think so."

Edgar had a strange sense of humour, Narwynn thought. How did Elna put up with this every day?

"How did you know they were here?" Narwynn asked.

"A traveller told me that he had seen a pack of goblins in the south," Edgar answered. "They had stolen some keys he was meant to bring to Ludazar. Goblins will take anything that looks shiny."

"But why does Ludazar need the keys?"

"Hmmm..." said Edgar and rubbed his chin, "let's just say he needs them to deal with a certain dragon problem... and so do I..."

"Will you use the keys to kill Dreumar for Ludazar?"

"Hah! Now, that would just be silly, wouldn't it? Why would anyone fight a dragon with a pair of keys?"

Narwynn thought for a moment.

"Edgar... there is something I don't understand about the dragon."

Edgar sighed and rolled his eyes.

"All right, tell me what you don't understand."

"Well, it's just that I've heard two different versions of what Dreumar did to the lost princess."

"Carry on."

"On the one hand, the princess is still alive,

Edgar stopped by a small wooden box that the goblins had left when they ran after Buddy. He opened it, and inside were gold pieces and two silver keys. Edgar grabbed the silver keys and a handful of gold pieces.

"Go on, take some," said Edgar, "they will come back soon."

"But what about Buddy?" Narwynn asked.

"He knows what he is doing. Don't worry about him."

"But isn't this stealing? I am not a thief."

"Just grab some. I'll explain later," said Edgar before he turned around and ran towards the shrubs again. Narwynn grabbed some gold pieces and ran after Edgar. They jumped back over the bushes and started in through the woods for a little while, and then slowed down and walked silently while catching their breath.

"I think we should be safe for now," said Edgar.

"What about Buddy?" said Narwynn, but as soon as the words had slipped past his lips, he saw that Buddy came in from one side and started walking with them. Buddy did not have a single scratch on him.   He must have outrun the goblins easily, Narwynn thought.

"Buddy's job was to distract the goblins," said Edgar, "and they could never have caught up with him. He is too fast."

"So this was all part of a plan?" Narwynn asked.

They were disgusting creatures, Narwynn thought, and he could not wait to get far away from them.

Then Narwynn noticed some movement in the shrubs on the other side of the clearing. As he looked closer, he could see that something was moving through them, towards the goblins. When it had reached the clearing, Narwynn saw that it was Buddy, sticking his head out through the shrubs.

"Edgar!" Narwynn whispered, and nipped Edgar in the fur again.

Edgar said nothing but raised his hand and pointed towards Buddy. Then Buddy jumped out of the shrubs and into the clearing. He snatched a dead rabbit that the goblins had saved for later before he shot back into the bushes and trees. The Goblins screamed with rage and grabbed their clubs and maces from the ground and chased after Buddy. One after another, they shoved themselves through the shrubs scratching up their skin and deepening the clefts in their ears even more. They were very angry with Buddy for stealing their food.

"Now!" said Edgar, just as the last goblin had left the clearing, and then jumped over the shrubs. "Come on!"

Narwynn did not know what Edgar was doing, but jumped after him and landed inside the clearing. He saw that it was full of carcasses and bones. Goblin-slime covered everything. Narwynn tried to avoid stepping in it as he ran after Edgar, but then realised that it was no use, as he would get goblin slime on his feet no matter what.

hand so as to tell Narwynn to slow down and be extra quiet. Narwynn had figured out the signs Edgar had given by then. The smell became stronger and stronger as they got closer to the clearing, and then Narwynn started to hear something as well. It sounded like growling, but not like the growling of a hound. It was almost like the growls were voices, talking to each other.

The shrubbery blocked Narwynn's view of the clearing. He felt curious and nipped Edgar's fur to get his attention.

"What is that sound?" he asked.

"Shhh!" Edgar answered, "they must not hear us."

"But what are 'they'?"

"They are goblins, and they will eat us alive if they see us."

Narwynn felt an ice-cold shiver down his spine.

"So why are we going closer to them?"

"Shhh! Just wait and see."

"But I can't see!"

Then Edgar pointed at a small opening through the shrubs where Narwynn could look through. Narwynn looked, and then wished he had not. It was a terrifying sight that Narwynn had never seen before or had even imagined. The goblins had green, slimy skins and long pointed teeth. Their ears were long too, with holes and clefts in them. The sound of them growling to each other gave Narwynn the creeps, and their smell made him want to be sick.

from far away. We will need to be quiet and keep our guard up. Buddy will stay ahead and look out for Rutha."

"I understand," said Narwynn.

Narwynn followed Edgar in among the trees. They walked with their guards up and their eyes wide open, ready to detect anything that moved. Occasionally they both jumped from spotting something, but every time it was just Buddy lurking around in the distance.

The trees were naked, and the icy snow on the ground crunched under Narwynn and Edgar's feet every step they took. They did not see many animals, except for the occasional white rabbit that would run and hide as soon as it saw them. The rabbits were jumpy little creatures, Narwynn thought. And they had reason to be, as they were nourishing to eat, and all the hungry predators and creatures out there were probably looking for them at that very moment.

Narwynn and Edgar walked and walked, and they did not talk much, except for the odd occasion where Edgar would stop, raise his hand and whisper "Quiet, I heard something." Narwynn did as Edgar said, even though he never heard anything that made him wary. Edgar must have good ears, Narwynn thought; he must have gained a lot of experience travelling in the woods in winter. How else would he be able to detect all these sounds that Narwynn could not?

They approached a clearing in the forest, and Narwynn noticed a nasty smell. Edgar raised his

Narwynn reached the outskirts of town. There, he saw all the miners pushing their wheelbarrows and carrying their chopping tools in and out of the caves. Their tools were almost entirely worn down and needed mending, but the blacksmith probably struggled to keep up with all the worn down items that were brought in. Narwynn felt a twinge of pity for the miners, but was then distracted by the sight of Edgar who was already waiting for him on the other side of the field.

Narwynn felt eager and ran across the field. He ran past a sheep and its shepherd, who tried to ride it but kept falling off. Serves him right, Narwynn thought. He is not laughing anymore now that he is the one falling off. Narwynn's resentment for the shepherds had grown since he had tried to ride the sheep. They were impolite and grumpy, and were always looking for somebody to complain about.

"Hello," said Edgar, as Narwynn approached, "you should not waste energy on running. You will need all your strength on this trip."

Narwynn stopped and bent forward while catching his breath. Buddy was sitting next to Edgar when Narwynn arrived, but rose and started into the woods on his own. When Narwynn had caught his breath, he stood up straight and answered Edgar.

"I have plenty of energy," he said.

"I see," said Edgar. "Well, there will be no more running now. In winter there are no leaves on the trees, and all the creatures out there can see you

"Pssst!" someone said from behind.

Narwynn and Elna turned and saw that Edgar had been hiding behind the door.

"Narwynn," Edgar whispered, "run home and get your things, and tell Aunt Milnu that we will be gone for a while. Then meet me by the edge of the woods."

Narwynn smiled and nodded. Elna held up a finger and moved it back and forth in front of Edgar with a stern look on her face, as if to tell him that he had been naughty. Then she smiled and turned to Narwynn.

"I'll help Aunt Milnu out when you have gone."

Narwynn thanked Elna and ran back to the tent. Aunt Milnu seemed to appreciate that Narwynn was going away with Edgar. She knew that he was one of the strongest nose-elves in the Green Lands and that Narwynn would be safe with him. She also seemed excited when Narwynn told her that Elna would help her out while he was gone. Aunt Milnu liked Elna and appreciated spending time with her.

Narwynn hurried through town. Some of the workers were already out busy. The tailor could be seen through his window, sitting comfortably inside his little house, sewing and mending capes and hats of cloth. Some of the shepherds were over by the stables, tending to the sheep. The blacksmith was outside under his shed hammering down on a glowing piece of iron that would become either an arrowhead or a small knife.

what Elna had told him.

"Don't listen to Edgar, my dear. He will not go on any more journeys this winter. He will stay here with his family where he belongs."

"I see."

"Are you not supposed to be resting at the healer's place still? I heard you had slipped and hit your head on the ice."

Narwynn suddenly felt guilty about having left the healer's house.

"Yes," he said.

"Edgar!" Emelda shouted after Edgar, who had now left the room before she looked back at Narwynn. "Well, you will go back to the healer's place. Elna will walk you."

"Of course, Emelda."

"And Narwynn…"

"Yes, Emelda?"

"Your…No… don't worry. Off you go."

Narwynn and Elna walked out of the room and up to the front door.

"What was that about?" said Narwynn.

"I don't know. She probably just thought of something and then forgot about it. She is usually like that. Like she always has something on her mind."

"I see."

Narwynn opened the front door and looked outside. He wondered where Edgar had gone. Then they stepped outside and closed the door behind them.

85

had always wanted to go on a journey to another town. He tried not to seem too excited.

"Will it be dangerous?"

"It will, but I figured you might need to gain some experience so that Kraus can't bully you so much," said Edgar and smiled at Narwynn.

They heard the entrance door open. Elna ran back across the map and almost stumbled on the edge. Edgar rolled his eyes again, then swallowed and looked down at it. Narwynn looked over to the living room door. Elna's mother came through, holding Elna's hand behind her. She looked angry.

"Edgar," she said, and looked at the map on the floor and then at Edgar, "don't even think about it."

Edgar had already started to roll up the map. Narwynn thought he was acting like a naughty little boy who was being told off by his mother.

"But I was just going to… Why won't you let me? You have gone away so often lately while I hardly ever get to…" he started.

"No."

"Yes, dear."

Edgar continued to roll up the map. Then he lifted it off the floor and placed it in the corner of the room, opposite to where his arrows were.

"Oh, hello there," said Elna's mother and looked at Narwynn. "I didn't see you there."

"Hello, Emelda," said Narwynn.

Although this was the first time he had ever spoken to Emelda, he knew a lot about her from

"Daddy!" Elna interrupted. "Don't be silly. You painted it yesterday."

"Very well then, clever little Princess."

Edgar gave Elna another pat on her head, but instead of her head, his hand patted Susy, who had sneaked up there while they were talking. He jumped and pulled his hand back, and Susy jumped down on the floor. Then Edgar smiled again and turned around to grab something from the corner of the room. He grabbed an arrow that had an arrowhead missing. As Edgar turned back towards the map, he swished the arrow around without looking. Edgar would have hit Elna on the head had she not bent down to pick Susy up again.

"So, my friend. Oaktown is here," said Edgar and pointed at the image of an oak tree on the map.

Narwynn had never realised how far west Oaktown was in the Green Lands.

"I see," said Narwynn, and tried to look fascinated.

Then Edgar pointed slightly further down at the image of a willow tree.

"This is where we are heading."

"Mhm, I see…"

"The journey there will take all day."

"Very well…"

Narwynn wondered what Edgar was getting at.

"We will have to stay there for a while."

It was as if Edgar expected Narwynn to be reluctant to go because of this. However, Narwynn

quiet. They approached Elna's family's house and saw that torches were lit inside. As soon as they opened the door, they heard Edgar greet them from the living room.

"Did you free him?" said Edgar, then appearing from around a corner. "Oh good, you did. How are you feeling Narwynn?"

"I feel fine," said Narwynn, touching the big bump on his forehead.

"He jumped out of the window and landed on his nose in the snow," said Elna and giggled.

"I see. I'm afraid the healer underestimates us, my friend. Sometimes he will not let us leave the bed for days."

"Oh."

"Come here. I want to show you something."

Edgar walked back to the living room, and Narwynn followed him. In the living room was a map that had been rolled out on the floor. The map depicted the Green Lands from above. Edgar walked around the map as Narwynn walked up to it. Then Elna came after them and walked straight over it across to Edgar. Edgar rolled his eyes at first, but then smiled at Narwynn and patted Elna on the head.

"That's incredible," said Narwynn. "Where did you get it?"

"This map is a magical treasure that has been passed down from generation to generation for longer than anyone can remember," said Edgar with a serious look.

Narwynn.

"Daddy told me to come and get you," said Elna. "He said he needed to speak with you."

"But I have not spoken to the healer yet."

"Daddy said that the healer is strange and that we do not need to listen to what he says."

"I see," said Narwynn, and felt relieved that he did not have to speak to the healer. "But how do I get out?"

"Daddy said the best way to escape from the healer is to jump out of the window."

"Really? How does he know?"

"I don't know."

"Very well then, I'll come out."

Narwynn walked over to a chair in the corner of the room where his cape occupied a stool. He placed his cape over his shoulders, so it hung down across his back. Then he walked over to the middle of the room, faced the window, and took a deep breath before he started towards it and jumped out head first. He dived through the air for a short moment and landed face first in the snow on the ground. It somehow felt familiar, but he did not realise why.

"I'm out," he said as he pulled his nose out of the snow.

"Well done," said Elna and smiled. "Now let's go and see Daddy."

They walked out of the workers' area. It felt great to breathe the cold, morning air. No one else was outside, and except for the howling wind, it was

Narwynn woke up in a house he thought was unfamiliar at first, but then remembered being there before. Aunt Milnu had brought him there once when he had been ill. It was the healer's house. There was a window in the room, and Narwynn could see that the sun was about to rise outside. The horizon had a pink aura in the promise of a new day.

He felt his head and found a large sore bump in the middle of his forehead. His nose felt sore too. He thought he must have hit his head on the ice and been brought to the healer by Edgar. But he could not stay at the healer's house. He had to go and meet Edgar so that he could come along on the journey to Willowtown.

He thought that perhaps the healer was still asleep. If he were quiet he could sneak out. He thought about it for a while, but then he thought better of it. It would not be wise to leave before hearing what the healer had to say. He decided to stay in bed and wait for the healer to wake up, and ask if it would be all right if he left.

After a while, he heard someone knock on his window, but could not see anyone there. Then a hand appeared, knocking on it again before it disappeared below. He rose from the bed and felt the cold floor under his feet. Then he walked over to the window and looked outside. The hand appeared again, and Narwynn saw that it was Elna jumping up to knock as she was just too short to reach it. He opened the window and leaned out.

"Elna, what are you doing here?" said

rabbit over his shoulders.

"Still have only mushrooms to bring home, Greeny?" Kraus asked with a smirk on his face. "I knew it would be no use teaching you taming. You are too useless to do anything, and you always will be."

Narwynn looked to the ground and forgot all about the exciting thoughts from earlier. Then he looked up again and saw that Edgar had stopped and turned back around.

"Kraus..." said Edgar, "Narwynn has just waited for the right opportunity. He is coming with me on a secret quest in Willowtown tomorrow. As Narwynn wants a more exotic pet, he has been waiting for us to go there before taming one."

Narwynn was astonished. Was he really being invited to come along on one of Edgar's journeys? He had never even been to another town.

"I see," said Kraus, and the smirk faded from his face. "If you say so, Edgar."

Kraus seemed to have great respect for Edgar. He said nothing more, but nodded to Edgar and went inside the storage house to hang up his rabbit.

Edgar turned to Narwynn.

"Come by my house in the morning," he said. "I need to show you something."

Narwynn raised his eyebrows and opened his mouth. He said nothing but took a step towards Edgar. As he did, his feet slipped on the icy, wet snow underneath. He fell to the ground nose first and soon saw nothing but stars.

in. His mushroom supply was running short. If he and Aunt Milnu ran out before mushrooms started growing in the woods again, they would have to spend the last of their copper savings on food from the market.

He noticed someone standing in the corner of the room, taking down smoked squirrel meat from a rail of hooks; it was Edgar. Narwynn thought he would say hi at first, but then he was shy and did not. But as soon as Narwynn was on his way out of the door, a voice sounded from behind.

"Shouldn't you be picking up red meat from here by now, my green friend?"

Narwynn turned around and saw that it was Edgar speaking to him.

"Not had much luck taming an animal yet, have we?" Edgar continued.

"No."

"I see. It is a challenging game. Well, good seeing you, Narwynn."

Edgar started past Narwynn and out of the door.

"Shouldn't you be out on your journey by now?" Narwynn asked.

Edgar did not turn around but answered over his shoulder.

"I'm off tomorrow."

Narwynn wondered what Edgar's journeys were. He had told Narwynn that he was going on a secret quest. But why was it a secret?

Suddenly Kraus showed up with a snow

6 GOBLINS LOVE GOLD

The snow had started melting in Oaktown, and everything was wet. As Narwynn walked towards the storage house, he almost slipped on the slush that covered the pathways. He decided to walk on the sides where the snow had not been hardened to ice by everyone walking on it.

It had been several months since the night in the field and the whispering from the woods. Narwynn had persevered in trying to ride the sheep, but without success. At least he had learned how to do so, he thought. He just needed to keep practising.

He looked forward to when the snow would be gone, and he would be able to go deep into the woods again. Rutha would be asleep in the summer, so he could look for an animal to tame. Then he could be a hunter in the woods until winter came once more, and with a predator pet by his side, he would feel safer in the woods.

Narwynn reached the storage house and went

seen. You do not know me any better than you know yourself..."

Narwynn felt his heart pounding in his chest.

"What do you mean by that?" he said.

"You think you know who you are, but you do not. You listen to twisted tales and put your trust in simple workers, arrogant hunters and wicked wizards. There is more to you and this world than can be learned from that which is spoken."

"What in Nightwood are you talking about?"

"Look to the moon, young Narwynn."

And Narwynn raised his gaze to the moon, where he saw what he had never seen before. Up there in the distance before the moon, was the shadow of a dragon, flapping its giant wings in the sky. Then Narwynn rushed to his feet and ran home as fast as his legs could carry him.

who could make sense of the words. He tried to listen carefully, but it was hard to hear at first. They were only whispers, and whispers can be hard to hear. Then Narwynn thought he might try to get closer so he could listen to them better, but he knew Rutha the Troll was probably waiting there somewhere in the dark.

Although he knew it was dangerous, Narwynn got up and walked towards the edge of the woods. The sheep did not follow him but started to walk in the opposite direction. The sheep seemed even more anxious when it was alone. It would probably walk back to the stables, Narwynn thought.

Narwynn could feel his heart beating faster as he approached the edge of the woods. He had not brought his spear. He knew that if he took another step, he would be easy prey for Rutha and whatever else that lurked among the trees. He stopped and tried to listen, but his heartbeat sounded loud from his chest, and his knees had started to tremble. Thin, pointed spikes of ice covered his wet fur, and his nose felt as if it would break if something were to touch it.

Suddenly the whispers from the woods became clearer.

"Narwynn..." they whispered.

Narwynn felt a cold shiver down his spine once again and fell back onto it.

"W-who's there?" he stammered, "A-are you Rutha?"

"I am not a troll nor anything else you have

Everyone laughed. Narwynn did not look down, but looked straight at Kraus instead.

"I will show you!" said Narwynn while the sheep jumped around behind him.

"You are too soft," said Kraus, looking more serious now.

Narwynn said no more but turned around and ran towards the sheep, jumped on top of it, and grabbed hold of its wool. The sheep started twitching as soon as Narwynn had mounted it. After a few moments, Narwynn was bounced high into the air, where he waved his arms and legs before diving into the all too familiar mud nose first. He heard all the shepherds laughing as he raised his face from the mud, but did not hear Kraus laughing this time.

"You see?" said Kraus.

Narwynn kept jumping on the sheep's back, only to be bounced off for the rest of the day.

When the light from the moon and the stars had taken over from the sun, Kraus and all the shepherds went home. Narwynn knew it was time to take the sheep back to the stables, but he was still sitting in the mud, having been thrown into it a while earlier. His whole body felt numb, sore and beaten up. He needed some time to gather his strength before he could get up and go back to town.

While he sat there by starlight and moonlight, Narwynn listened to the woods. They were whispering, whispering tales in the night. Narwynn had heard many nose-elves talk about the whispering of the woods, but never had he heard of someone

Narwynn was already waiting in the field when the shepherd arrived the next morning. He was eager to see if the next sheep was better behaved than the one from the day before. He would soon learn that it was not. This day and many days to come would be more challenging than he had imagined.

Challenging days turned into challenging weeks. Weeks in the cold snow, hot from the battles with the sheep, wet with sweat, melted snow and mud. He had thrown himself on their backs so many times that he could now do it with hardly any thought. His grip was getting stronger every day, and his balance on the sheep's backs was so skilful that it felt like the ground was moving whenever he was not mounted on them. Yet he only managed to stay on them for a few moments longer than when he had first he started.

Shepherds stood and watched him sometimes. They seemed fascinated by his persistence. "Well done! You held on for almost three seconds," they would say as he crashed onto the muddy ground. "You will get it right next time."

Narwynn felt more and more hopeless. Was there no end to his failures and the other nose-elves' mockery? He had almost decided to give up for the day when he saw a familiar face among the crowd of shepherds. It was Kraus.

"Trying to learn new skills, are we?" Kraus shouted without even trying to hide the laughter in his voice. "Seems to be going well for you."

time and again, but every time he threw himself on, he was thrown off again in an instant.

At the end of the day, Narwynn found himself soaked in sweat, mud and melted snow. The sheep was soaked too. Narwynn was so exhausted that the few times he managed to get onto the sheep's back, he fell off as soon as it moved. Eventually, he could barely get back on his own feet.

He thought he had to make it.

"Still at it, are we?" a voice sounded.

The shepherd had returned.

"I can't do it..." said Narwynn, "he throws me off every time."

"At least he got some exercise," said the shepherd, pleased, "and it seems you got some exercise as well."

Narwynn looked into the ground, and sad thoughts ran through his mind. But then he clenched his teeth and looked up again.

"Let me keep trying!" he said.

"Now-now, little green nose-elf," the shepherd said, "it will be dark soon, and then it will be dangerous for the sheep and you to be this close to the woods. Especially in the state you are in now. Come back tomorrow. The other sheep will need exercise as well."

The shepherd attached a leash to the sheep and led it towards town. Narwynn stayed for a few moments until he had caught his breath. Then he walked back in the twilight of the evening through the falling snow.

change strategy, he thought.

Then Narwynn thought about the shepherd's words: "He will never go close to the woods."

He walked after the sheep towards the edge of the woods. The sheep tried to walk in other directions, but every time it did, Narwynn made sure that he blocked its path.

They were getting close to the edge of the woods, and Narwynn saw that the sheep was getting more and more nervous. Only a few more moments now, and the sheep would be forced to come closer. Its attempts to slip by Narwynn were in vain, and as they were coming up to the dark edge of the woods, the sheep slowed down and stopped.

Suddenly the sheep panicked and ran straight towards Narwynn. Narwynn held his arms out to the sides to show that he would not let it past. When the sheep was close enough, Narwynn jumped to the side and threw himself onto its back, and then grabbed hold of its wool.

The sheep was not happy. It jumped around, twitching to throw Narwynn off, and it did not take long to work. Narwynn's grip loosened, and he bounced up in the air and smashed onto the ground nose first.

"AAAAARGH, stupid sheep!" Narwynn shouted after the sheep as he raised his face from the snow.

The sheep jumped around again, looking pleased with itself.

The day went on, and Narwynn kept trying

"Oh, but then it seems we are in luck!" said the shepherd.

"What do you mean?"

"Well, this sheep is acting out. Perhaps you can practise by teaching it to behave."

"But, I don't even know how to ride one that behaves."

"You don't know much, do you?"

Narwynn was lost for words.

"Exactly, before you can know, you must learn."

Narwynn felt butterflies in his tummy. Was the shepherd serious? Did the shepherd think that practising on this sheep would be a good idea?

"I need to get home for dinner, anyway," said the shepherd.

"What?" said Narwynn.

"You don't expect me to stand here and watch, do you?"

"Oh, um, no, I suppose not."

"Well, good luck then. And don't worry if the sheep runs away. He will never go close to the woods. Rutha is probably lurking around the edges at this very moment."

The shepherd walked off and left Narwynn in the middle of the field with a sheep jumping around him.

Narwynn tried to approach the sheep, but every time he got close, it walked further away. For what seemed like an eternity, Narwynn chased after the sheep, unable even to touch it. He needed to

twitch. The shepherd slammed onto the ground next to the sheep, and then the sheep started jumping around, looking pleased with itself.

"Fool!" said the shepherd. "Are you trying to have me killed?"

"No," Narwynn answered. "I just recognised you from some time ago and thought I'd say hello."

"Well, you should know better than to distract a nose-elf while he is riding a sheep these days. The sheep are all nervous and misbehaved."

"Why are they nervous? They did not seem nervous before."

"That was before and not now. Sheep are afraid, like all the animals now, and they do not want to be out in the open. They know that Rutha's second favourite dish is sheep."

"What is her first favourite?"

"Nose-elf."

Narwynn felt a shiver down his spine.

"So why do you take them out here?" he asked.

"They need exercise," said the shepherd and looked startled. "What are you doing out here? Should you not be at home in the warm like everyone else?"

Narwynn smiled. He liked it when someone assumed he was like everyone else, but he was not. He loved it when others saw that the cold weather and the falling snow did not stop him.

"I want to learn how to ride," he said. "I need to find a sheep that is not busy and start practising."

What was he talking about, Narwynn thought?

Narwynn brought some dried mushrooms back to Aunt Milnu on his way home. He decided to stay with her for the rest of the day, but he could not stop thinking about the tale about Sawynn. He thought about how incredible it would be to ride through the sky on an eagle's back, even though he doubted he ever would.

But there was something he could do. He could learn to ride a sheep. Then he would move better through the snow in the woods while looking for small predators to tame, and he would not worry so much about Rutha out there.

The next morning, Narwynn walked to the outskirts of town before he saw anybody else. On the outskirts were several workers who were working hard and steady. The miners were digging in their caves as usual, but this time none of them noticed Narwynn as he walked by. He thought the miners were always digging, being some of the most hard-working nose-elves he had ever seen.

As he reached the fields, Narwynn noticed that one of the shepherds was there, riding in circles on a sheep. It looked rather challenging, as the sheep sometimes threw the shepherd off its back. As Narwynn got closer, he saw that it was the same shepherd he had met by the fire some time ago.

"Hi there, shepherd!" said Narwynn.

The shepherd turned his head to see who had greeted him. But as he turned his head, the sheep took the opportunity to throw him off with a sharp

from her if she came after you."

It was a brilliant idea, Narwynn thought.

Suddenly, Edgar appeared with Buddy by his side.

"What's going on here?" he asked, "I told you to leave her out of all this!"

"Edgar…" said Ludazar and gave him a smile, "we have just been telling tales; nothing more, I assure you."

Edgar looked at Elna.

"Come, Elna," he said, "you should not be here."

"But, Daddy, why not?"

"Because I said so."

Elna got up and walked over to her father.

"You too, Narwynn."

There was something different about Edgar. He had always seemed so relaxed and jolly before. But now, he was serious.

Narwynn got up as well and walked after Edgar and Elna, who were already walking away from the seven cloaked nose-elves. Just as Narwynn caught up with them, he heard Ludazar's cold voice from behind.

"You cannot protect her from her destiny, Edgar. Even if you get to the dragon first, you would not be strong enough. Only the master of Elnax would stand a chance…"

Narwynn turned to look back and met Ludazar's gaze. Ludazar grinned back at him in a manner that sent shivers down Narwynn's spine.

Narwynn did not know what to say. He felt a sense of hopelessness. If not even Sawynn could kill Dreumar, then surely nobody could, he thought.

"I think the Green Lands need a new hero who is even stronger than Sawynn was," he said.

"Exactly..." said Ludazar with his skewed smile.

"Is it possible to ride an eagle if you tame it?" Narwynn asked.

All the cloaked nose-elves burst into laughter, except for Ludazar.

"Yes, I believe so..." he said.

The laughter stopped.

"Don't be silly, Ludazar," said a cloaked nose-elf with a sparrow on her shoulder. "The tales about eagle riders are all made up by the travellers. We all know they are not true. Sawynn is surely the only one who has ever been on an eagle's back."

Ludazar waited for a moment before he spoke again.

"Believe what you wish, but riding is a skill that one can develop. The only reason most nose-elves ride sheep is that they are the easiest to manage. I'm sure a skilled rider could manage to ride all sorts of animals after practicing well enough."

Elna nipped the fur on Narwynn's arm to get his attention.

"Narwynn, Narwynn," she whispered, "perhaps if you learn to ride, you would be able to run faster in the woods, and then you wouldn't have to be so worried about Rutha. You could ride away

he had chosen for this fight.

"The fight drove them further and further up the mountain. It was not long before Dreumar and Sawynn disappeared from sight. I waited all night and saw no more of them. At sunrise, however, I heard the roar of a dragon. When I looked up, I saw Dreumar circling the mountain, and I knew who had won."

The story entranced Narwynn. He looked at Elna, who smiled back at him. Then he looked at the six other cloaked nose-elves, who seemed bored by the story.

"You missed one important detail, Ludazar," said one of them as he offered his starling a pinch of seeds.

Ludazar gazed at him and shook his head. But the nose-elf with the starling ignored it and continued.

"No one ever found the remains of Sawynn after the fight. And we know that they are not there. For King Elrud's guards went there many times while Dreumar was busy flying across the lands. They did not stop until they had found the spear and brought it back to the King's dungeon. The King keeps all the heroes' weapons there, locked away from anyone who would try to wield them against Dreumar.

Ludazar shook his head once more. But then he smiled and looked at Narwynn.

"I wonder… what does our young Narwynn here think of these tales?"

"Dreumar had only just risen in the Green Lands at the time, and I knew we needed to stop him. A dragon will kill anyone in his path and breathe fire onto the lands. I also knew that Sawynn was the strongest nose-elf in the Green Lands, and therefore I ordered him to rid us of the dragon plague.

"King Elrud disagreed as Dreumar had hidden his one and only daughter somewhere in the mountains, and only he knew where she was. When I sent Sawynn to kill Dreumar, the King did everything he could to stop me. But I knew that the lost princess had not been hidden; she was dead. Therefore, I had to disobey the King for his own sake and lead Sawynn to Dreumar.

"I journeyed to the Northern peak where I faced Dreumar myself. As soon as he saw me, Dreumar flew towards me with a raging fire in his breath. It was then that Sawynn dived from the sky on an eagle's back straight down at Dreumar."

"Eagle's back?" Narwynn interrupted. "I thought you said that Sawynn had no pet."

Narwynn thought of the shepherds who sometimes rode their sheep. Then he tried to imagine someone riding an eagle, but he had never seen an eagle, so he could not.

"Oh, young Narwynn… Sawynn had no pet, and nor did he need one. For he could control any animal he had ever come across. He could see through their eyes, listen through their ears, and control their movements. The eagle was the predator

elf with the pointy hat.

Narwynn raised his gaze. "How do you know my name?"

"I know many things, Narwynn. For I am Ludazar, head of the Seven Wise."

"Ludazar?" Elna interrupted. "The wizard who led the third hero to Dreumar?"

"Indeed, young Elna," said Ludazar. "I trust you have enjoyed the tales Edgar has told you about our heroes?"

Elna paused. Then she turned to Narwynn with a serious expression.

"I think this nose-elf knows everything," she whispered.

Some of the others chuckled. Narwynn turned back to Ludazar.

"Did you know the third hero?" he asked.

"I sure did. And I will tell you all about Sawynn. For what are tales worth if they remain untold to the young?" said Ludazar with a clever smile.

Susy suddenly jumped out from underneath Elna's hat and sat down on her shoulder, as if she knew that a fascinating story was about to be told.

Narwynn felt confused but leaned forward to listen to Ludazar.

"Sawynn was the strongest hero in the Green Lands, and yet, he was not of the Green Lands. He had brown fur with no pet by his side. His weapon was a spear with a red crystal, sharper than any other.

"What journey are you going on?" he asked.

"To Willowtown. I have a secret quest in a few months when the snow starts thawing"

"I see."

Elna turned to Narwynn again and grabbed his hand.

"Let's go."

And then they walked together through the melting snow between the torches. As they approached the storage house, Narwynn and Elna noticed that there were seven nose-elves sitting around the fireplace next to it. They were all wearing white woollen cloaks, and some of them had long staffs with crystal orbs attached to the top ends. Each of them had a different kind of bird for a pet, except for one. He had no pet, but a tall hat on his head, pointing towards the open sky above.

"Look, Narwynn," said Elna.

"I see them," said Narwynn.

"Can we go over to them and listen to their tales?"

Just as Elna had asked, the cloaked nose-elf wearing the pointy hat rose, looked over at them and waved. It was an invitation to come and sit with them by the fire.

"er…" Narwynn hesitated. "Very well".

Narwynn and Elna walked over to the fire and sat down with the seven nose-elves. They were all quiet, and they all looked at Narwynn. He lowered his gaze and regretted walking over to them.

"Raise your gaze, Narwynn…" said the nose-

Elna noticed Narwynn when she handed the arrows to her father.

"Narwynn!" Elna said, "I thought you had already left."

"Hello Elna," Narwynn said, "I just have to pick up some mushrooms from the storage house first."

"Oh? Can I come with you?"

Elna turned to Edgar.

"Can I go with Narwynn to the storage house, Daddy?"

"Sure, you can. Just don't go out in the woods again. I was terrified last time when you did not come home. I went looking for you all night."

Narwynn noticed that Edgar was looking at something behind him. Narwynn turned around to see what it was. As he turned around, he saw that a bobcat, bigger than himself, was passing him, before it circled Edgar and sat down next to him.

"There you are, Buddy," said Edgar and tickled Buddy under the chin. "I was just looking for you."

Elna walked over to Buddy and hugged him. It was hard to tell whether Buddy liked hugs or not. Susy had taken refuge under Elna's hat. She did not seem to appreciate being that close to a bobcat.

"Will you take Buddy with you on your journey, Daddy?" Elna asked.

"Of course I will, Princess. I would not feel safe travelling without him."

Narwynn grew curious.

had no choice but to run through the cold and come back to the tent shivering.

Narwynn met someone on his way to the storage house. It was Edgar, Elna's father.

"Hello there," Edgar said.

"Hello," Narwynn answered.

"I hear that you are trying to tame a pet."

"Who told you that?"

"Elna told me."

"I see," said Narwynn and looked to one side. "It does not look as if I can do that after all."

"And why is that?"

"It's because I can't find any animals. And I keep thinking that I can hear Rutha, and then I have to run back."

"I see," said Edgar. "It sure is harsh out there in the woods this time of year. One can't be too careful."

Elna came towards them from the market place, wearing the same oversized cape she had borrowed from Edgar to follow Narwynn and Kraus into the woods. She carried something in her arms that covered her whole face. Narwynn could not see what it was at first, but when she came closer, he saw that it was a bundle of arrows with white crystal heads.

"Daddy," said Elna as she approached, "are these the right ones?"

"Yes, they are, Princess," said Edgar. "I hope the arrow-maker did not charge too much for them?"

everyone else. All he needed to do was to find a smaller predator. He thought about small owls and weasels. After taming one, it would be his pet, and he could hunt instead of gathering mushrooms.

"Are you going out there again already?" Aunt Milnu asked.

"Yes," Narwynn answered, and threw his cape over his back and grabbed his spear.

"I worry about you when you are away, you know."

"I know."

"You are careful out there, aren't you?"

Narwynn turned around and looked at Aunt Milnu.

"I am as careful as I can be. But with Rutha lurking around out there, it is difficult."

Milnu lowered her gaze. Then she raised it again and smiled.

"Well, you will go nowhere before you have picked up some dried mushrooms for me at the storage house. I will have supper ready for us when you get back."

Without another word, Narwynn walked out of the tent and down the path towards the storage house. He did not feel like running errands for Aunt Milnu. All he wanted was to go to the woods and find a predator he could tame. But he knew that they needed more food and he wanted to spare Aunt Milnu the cold walk through the snow. She did not have a cape unlike him, so he ran the outdoor errands this winter. During previous winters, they

5 THE WIZARD'S WISDOM

It was mid-winter. The snow was deep, and the air cold. Only a few nose-elves with thick fur capes were outdoors in Oaktown. Some of them shovelled the snow away from their houses. Others walked around with burning sticks, lighting blue-flame torches to melt the snow that covered the footpaths.

Narwynn found it more and more challenging to venture into the woods. He had not had much luck in finding animals since the night he had fought the white lynx. His walks in the woods often ended up with his rushing back to Oaktown as he kept thinking he could hear Rutha the Troll somewhere in the distance. He would not want to face her out there in the deep snow when it would hinder him but not her.

But Narwynn did not give up. He wanted to become a hunter and told himself that he would not stop looking until he found a predator he could tame. His new skill would make him a little more like

thought about it that way until Elna had said it. Despite his failure to tame the lynx, he had got off to a good start at learning taming skills. Perhaps he could find a smaller animal and tame it on his own.

The sun rose as they stepped into the field of Oaktown. The white oak looked red in the morning light, and the town was waking up. Elna and Kraus were so tired they looked as if they were sleep-walking. Narwynn, on the other hand, felt wide awake. He was excited to practicing taming further and becoming a hunter.

trees.

"What was that about?" Kraus shouted, confused at what had just happened.

"I don't know," said Elna, "it just looked at me and then left."

"Yes, we saw that much," Narwynn interrupted, "but why?"

"I don't know!"

After they had gathered and talked, it turned out that Elna had worried about Narwynn the whole night before. She had woken early, borrowed her father's cape, and followed them into the woods without their knowing, as she had feared they would tell her to go back home. Charky knew she was there the whole time and went over to sit with her while they waited for the lynx to appear.

They walked back through the woods, confused after what had happened. Narwynn was disappointed that he had failed to tame the lynx. Kraus kept talking about how it made no sense that the lynx had not killed Elna when it had the chance.

"What a waste of a journey," said Narwynn. "I am sorry I couldn't do it."

"Hah, you are so stupid!" said Kraus. "Did you really think you would be able to tame a lynx the first time you tried? You endured far longer than I expected."

"I think you did great, Narwynn," said Elna. "And now you know how to do it next time you get a chance."

Narwynn raised his eyebrows. He had not

Then, out of nowhere, someone screamed: "Nooo!"

The lynx looked up and stepped off Narwynn. He turned his head to see who had screamed. Wearing an oversized fur cape and hat, and a stick in her hand, Elna came running towards them with Susy on her shoulder.

"No, Elna! Stop!" Narwynn shouted.

Elna stopped, and Kraus and Charky hurried into the clearing from the other side.

"Run! It's dangerous!" Narwynn continued.

"But I won't let it kill you," said Elna.

Narwynn thought she had a point.

"We have this under control, Elna," said Kraus. "I was ready to step in."

"But…"

They were distracted by the lynx stepping towards Elna. Krauss drew an arrow but lowered it for fear of hitting Elna. Narwynn desperately tried to get to his feet but fell down again. His body felt crushed. Charky ran to the rescue, but the lynx turned towards him and snarled, which made Charky stop and lower his head and put his tail between his legs.

There was nothing they could do as the lynx stepped up to Elna, who stood frozen and stared back at it. The lynx stopped in front of Elna, sniffed her, and looked down at her for a moment. Then, to Narwynn and Kraus's astonishment, it lowered its head as if to bow, and took a few steps backward, before turning around and disappearing among the

Narwynn felt focused. Nothing else existed but him and the lynx on the blanket of snow under the stars. Suddenly, the lynx jumped after Narwynn. Narwynn rolled over onto his side, and got back on his feet with his spear raised towards the lynx. He walked towards it and stabbed after it with his spear, but the lynx moved out of the way.

When the lynx charged at Narwynn once again, he could not get away in time. He held his spear with both hands and shoved the shaft into the lynx's mouth as he fell to the ground. The lynx bit wildly at the spear shaft while trying to reach Narwynn's head. It got so close that Narwynn could smell its breath. Then he pushed the spear to the side and hurried back onto his feet. He felt helpless. How was he going to defeat this beast?

The lynx came for Narwynn again, but this time he pointed his spear towards it. The lynx stopped and then started circling him. He followed the lynx's movements with the tip of his spear. Then he tried to stab it, but missed and lost balance. The lynx jumped at Narwynn's back instantly and pushed him to the ground. It tried to bite into his back but ripped his cape off instead.

Narwynn rolled around and held up his spear with both hands. The lynx jumped on top of him and snatched at his head, only stopped by the shaft of his spear. He suddenly felt the lynx's claws digging into his skin. He groaned and pushed desperately, but it was no use. The lynx pulled itself towards Narwynn's head until its teeth scratched his face.

night he would spend in the woods.

Then, finally, something stepped out from among the trees on the left edge of the clearing. With snow-white fur and large paws, the snow-lynx somehow walked on the surface of the snow without falling through. It took steady steps towards the bones in the centre of the clearing. It was enormous, Narwynn thought.

"How about that?" Kraus whispered, "It's one big cat."

"What do we do now?" Narwynn whispered back.

"You have to defeat it without killing it. If you fail, I will shoot an arrow at it and send Charky to distract it while we run away."

Narwynn saw Kraus loading an arrow in his bow and noticed that Charky stood ready next to them. The snow-lynx reached the bones and sniffed for a moment.

"Go!" said Kraus and tapped Narwynn on the shoulder.

Narwynn was confused and frightened but grabbed his spear and got on his feet. His fur cape had frozen to the ground, so he had to jerk it loose. With hesitation he stepped into the clearing. The lynx looked at him and snarled. Narwynn could feel his heart pounding in his chest but kept stepping out through the snow towards the lynx. The lynx was larger than Narwynn, and its mouth was so vast it could easily fit the head of a nose-elf between its teeth.

some smoked meat. Then he rose and threw the bones into the clearing.

"Smell that, stupid cat," said Kraus.

"What do you mean by that?" Narwynn asked.

"Predators are always looking for food. Bones are good bait."

"Then why didn't you throw them out there sooner?"

"The wind wasn't right."

Kraus pulled a few strands of fur from his shoulder and held them up in front of Narwynn. When he dropped them, the wind carried them to the side and away from the clearing.

"Predators will walk into the wind when they hunt so that they can smell everything ahead of them. If the cat comes for the bones, it will enter the clearing from the left side."

Narwynn looked over to where Krauss pointed but saw nothing there. Then he looked to the other side and saw something moving between the trees.

"What's that?" Narwynn asked.

"Oh, that's just Charky. He has found something over there, but I can't see what it is. You stay focused now."

Narwynn and Kraus sat still and gazed at the left side of the clearing until the moon and stars had taken over from the sun. The snow glowed blue in the moonlight, and the frost on the trees glittered. Narwynn thought it was beautiful, but he was so cold he could barely stay focused. This was the first

Kraus turned and gave Narwynn an angry look. Then he turned back to the clearing.

"We will wait here for a while and see if the cat appears. It is always best to start looking from the place where you last saw it."

Narwynn saw Charky stumbling his way through the snow around the edges of the clearing, sniffing for snow-lynx.

"Won't it get too late?" Narwynn asked. "It is already past midday. We will never make it back before dark if we stay any longer."

"We will not go back tonight, Greeny. If we are to have any chance of finding the cat, we need to be patient. Hunting is all about patience."

"But it will be dangerous. And cold!"

"What did you expect? Taming predators is dangerous in itself. You will try it for the first time on a snow-lynx deep inside the woods. The night is the least of your worries now, I'm telling you."

Narwynn raised his eyebrows, and thoughts of regret ran through his mind, but he tried to stay calm and casual.

Time went by, and the sun was sinking lower and lower towards the horizon. The white light of day turned orange as the sun set even deeper. Eventually, the sun disappeared behind the trees whose shadows stretched far along the snow on the ground. The meagre warmth the sun had provided during the day faded, and then it was cold and dark.

Narwynn shivered. He grabbed some dried mushrooms from his pouch and ate them. Kraus ate

"I will only tell you what to do. The rest will be up to you and the cat. You will need to fight it until it is defeated. Only that way will you have tamed it."

"What if I can't defeat it?"

"Then it might eat you."

Narwynn felt a shiver down his spine.

They continued west while the sun reached its highest point in the sky. The snow was deep, which made it harder and harder to walk. It was challenging to keep the pace up, and their feet were getting cold. They had not seen a single animal since they entered the woods. The only things they could see were bare trees and snow. The snow looked smooth and undisturbed until they reached a strange track that crossed their path. The track was made from giant footsteps, which could only mean one thing.

"She was here," Kraus whispered. "Keep your guard up."

Narwynn raised his spear higher and looked around, but he saw nothing but the tracks disappearing between the trees.

Eventually, they reached a clearing. It stretched across to a mountain wall, and Narwynn realised that they had reached the foot of the western peak. Kraus raised a hand, signalling to Narwynn and Charky to wait. They stopped and looked at the clearing.

"This is it," Krauss whispered. "This is where Dreumar defeated Elmar."

"I reckoned," said Narwynn.

someone were watching him whom he could not see. He shook his head and continued through the workers' area and into the western outskirts of town.

He noticed a few miners who had already started their work for the day. Or had they worked through the night? One of them stopped with his wheelbarrow and gazed after Narwynn as he walked past him. Narwynn gave the miner a nod, but the miner did not return the gesture.

As Narwynn entered the field and headed towards the western edges of the woods, he thought he saw someone from the corner of his eye. Yet when he turned, there was no one there, just a rock with a stick leaning against it. Narwynn continued across the field and saw that Kraus and Charky were waiting by the trees.

"Hey, Greeny," Kraus shouted, "you're late!"

"What do you mean I'm late?" said Narwynn. "The sun has just risen. I'm early."

"You are late if I'm here before you. Now c'mon before I freeze to the ground."

Kraus and Charky started walking in among the trees just as Narwynn reached them. Narwynn glanced back across the field and saw a small shadow in the light of the morning sun. He could not see what it was before he turned back around and hurried after Kraus and Charky.

"Let's track this cat down so it can teach you something," said Kraus.

"I thought you were the one who would teach me something," said Narwynn.

"Are you not glad to hear it, Aunt Milnu?" he asked.

"Of course I am, Narwynn. It's just, I don't know much about taming animals, but I know that it can be dangerous. You will be careful, won't you?"

"Of course, I will."

"Very well. Now eat your mushrooms. As you said, you will need all the energy you can get for tomorrow."

Narwynn ate and felt nearly full when he had finished the mushrooms. The mushrooms made him tired, and he fell asleep as soon as he lay down. That night he dreamt of heroes fighting a dragon, with their coloured crystal weapons and large predator pets.

He woke before sunrise. He thought he would go back to sleep at first but did not. Instead, he threw his pelt over his back and tied it around his neck. Then he grabbed his spear and went outside.

The fireplace was still warm from the night before, but it no longer glowed. Narwynn sat down next to it and held his hands over the heated stones surrounding the ashes. The night faded, and sunlight appeared on the horizon. When the sun rose, it was still cold but warm enough for Narwynn to get going.

No snow had fallen overnight, and Narwynn followed a trail between the torches from the day before. It was quiet in Oaktown as most nose-elves had not yet risen from their beds. Yet for some reason, Narwynn felt like he was not alone. As if

on her chest on a string. Narwynn thought it looked good on her, and she deserved to have it.

"Hello, Narwynn," she said, "good that you are home early. I have just heated the leftover mushrooms from yesterday. Are you hungry?"

"Thank you, Aunt Milnu," Narwynn answered. "I am starving, and I will need to eat so that I have lots of energy for tomorrow. And look, I brought some more mushrooms from the storage house for you to have while I'm away."

Narwynn handed Aunt Milnu the dried mushrooms he had picked up from the shared storage house.

"What is happening tomorrow? You are not going into the woods on your own again, are you? I was so scared last time when you were gone until after dark. Please don't scare me like that again."

"I am going to the woods, but don't worry Aunt Milnu. Kraus will come with me, and he has a fox."

"I see. And what will you two be doing out there this time of year when there are no mushrooms to pick?"

Narwynn smiled.

"Elna persuaded Kraus to teach me how to tame animals. Isn't that wonderful, Aunt Milnu? Soon I might have a pet that I can go hunting with, bring home meat and earn more copper, perhaps even silver, and..."

Narwynn noticed that Aunt Milnu was looking down instead of at him.

"B-but, isn't it..." Narwynn stammered before he was interrupted by Kraus.

"Well then! it's settled. Meet me by the western edges of the woods at sunrise. The last traveller who said he saw the lynx had been on his way to the western peak when he came across it."

Kraus got up and grabbed his things. Then he nodded the other hunters goodbye as he stepped past them. Charky followed him.

The other hunters looked tired. Most of them had been half asleep since Elna told the bedtime tale. The hunter who used his possum for a pillow was asleep and would probably spend the night there by the dying fire.

Narwynn did not feel tired. He was excited about the next day and could not wait for it to come. Elna, however, yawned, and Susy seemed to have fallen asleep under her hat.

"I want to go home now, Narwynn," said Elna.

"I will walk you," said Narwynn and got up.

As they walked towards Elna's house, Narwynn thanked her for persuading Kraus to teach him how to tame. He walked her to her door where they said goodnight before parting. Edgar was not waiting at the door this time. He was probably out in the woods on some mission, Narwynn thought.

Narwynn walked back to the path of trodden snow between the blue-flame torches. The path took him back to his tent, where Aunt Milnu was sitting by the fire outside. She had the blue crystal hanging

"Why don't you teach Narwynn how to tame animals, Kraus?" Elna asked.

"Me?" Kraus answered "You must be joking. He is too stupid to learn anything at all."

The other hunters laughed, and Narwynn looked down once more.

"Narwynn is not stupid," Elna interrupted. "Perhaps it is just you who is a bad teacher and refuse to do it because you will look stupid yourself."

Narwynn raised his eyebrows. He was astonished that Elna, who always seemed so gentle and innocent, could speak to Kraus this way.

"Fine!" said Kraus. "I'll teach him. But don't blame me if he gets hurt."

Elna leaned back in her seat and smiled. Narwynn smiled too. He could not wait to learn how to tame animals, even if it was from Kraus. Finally, he would be able to get a pet of his own.

"So, are you going to find the lynx then?" asked the hunter with a weasel across his lap."

Kraus smiled before he spoke.

"Well," he said and turned to Narwynn, "that's what you wanted, wasn't it?"

Narwynn swallowed. He had not expected them to suggest that he, a beginner, would try and tame the lynx.

"Er, would that not be too dangerous for me?" he asked.

"Oh, no," Kraus answered, "not at all. Let's go and search for it. If we find it, I promise you I will tell you how to tame it."

"The fight drove them deeper and deeper into the woods until no one knew where they were. After seven days had passed, a traveller came across Elmar's green crystal sword, lying in a pile of glowing ashes, and a lynx as white as snow sitting next to it. The traveller saw the remaining glow in the ashes fading, and the lynx walking among the trees.

"Some say that Elmar's lynx still wanders the woods, searching for its master. Some even claim they have seen it return to the spot where Elmar's sword and ashes were found.

"The lynx is probably still out there somewhere, lying comfortably on a pillow of moss in the deepest corners of the woods. And wherever he is on this starry night, he is probably, at this very moment, falling into a deep, peaceful sleep."

Narwynn noticed that Elna's bedtime tale entranced the hunters. Some of them were staring at her with their mouths open. Others looked as if they were drifting into sleep. One had even laid down on the ground, using his possum as a pillow.

"Where was Elmar's lynx last seen?" Narwynn asked.

"Hah! You are not seriously thinking of searching for it, are you?" Kraus laughed.

"Why not? If we found it, then someone could tame it to protect us from Rutha."

"Oh, for a moment there, I thought you were going to try taming it yourself. That would have been a disaster."

elves know that, and for a good reason."

"What tale?" Narwynn asked.

Everyone looked at Narwynn as if he had spoken out of turn. Even the pets stared at him for an instant. Narwynn lowered his gaze, but then looked up again and repeated himself.

"What tale?"

Kraus sighed and poked the burning firewood with an arrow, pushing it closer to the centre.

"Why don't you tell the tale, Elna?" asked the hunter with a kestrel on her shoulder. "I'm sure your version is better than the one we know."

"Very well then," said Elna, and half-closed her eyes and raised her chin. "I'm sure Daddy's version is the best of all.

"Elmar was a hero like no other. His pet was a lynx as white as snow, and his weapon was a green crystal sword so sharp it could cut through steel. The cape he wore was cut from the most delicate pelt known to nose-elves, but no one knew what animal it came from.

"One day, Elmar received a letter from King Elrud himself. In the letter were words of desperation and despair, begging for help to find the lost princess. The words made Elmar feel sympathy for his King, and he made it his duty to find the princess.

"Elmar did not search long before Dreumar dived from the sky and confronted him. Dreumar blocked Elmar's path, and therefore Elmar had no choice but to fight."

"You are not to poke fun of Narwynn that way!" said Elna and pointed a finger at Kraus. "He knows how to do many things."

"As you wish," said Kraus and held his palms up. "It's just, you know, he does not even have a pet."

Everyone laughed again, and Narwynn lowered his head and looked into the ground.

"Just stop it!" Elna finished with a stern voice that sent a chill through the crowd.

"Very well, Elna," said Kraus.

"You are Edgar's daughter, aren't you?" said the nose-elf with a weasel on his lap.

"Yes, how do you know him?"

"Went hunting with him once."

I see, so these guys are hunters, Narwynn thought to himself but did not say it out loud. That's why they all have predator pets.

"Impressive that bobcat of his," said another hunter. "I hear they are even harder to tame than foxes, aren't they Kraus?"

Kraus looked at the other hunter but did not answer him.

"His bobcat is nothing like the snow-lynx that good old Elmar tamed though," said an older hunter. "A pity he is no longer with us."

"Elmar?" Elna interrupted. "He was the hero who fought Dreumar for seven days, wasn't he?"

All the hunters fell silent and looked at Elna.

"I suppose Edgar must have told you the tale, huh?" said the old hunter. "Not many young nose-

from Kraus.

"Very well, Elna, but only for a little while."

Elna smiled as she did when she was excited.

"Perhaps they are telling tales as the workers did before," she said.

Narwynn suddenly looked up at Elna. She had aroused his curiosity.

They walked out of the shared storage house and looked over at the nose-elves and their pets by the fire. Narwynn hesitated at first but noticed that Elna was already going towards them. He sighed and walked after her.

"Hello, Kraus!" said Elna as if she already considered Kraus as her friend.

Charky trotted over to Elna as soon as he saw her and started licking her face.

"Hello, little one," said Kraus. "I did not catch your name before."

"My name is Elna."

"Have a seat, Elna," said the nose-elf with a kestrel on her shoulder, "but watch your mouse. Our pets here could be hungry."

As if she understood the words, Susy jumped from Elna's shoulder and scurried under her hat.

"Hey, Greeny!" Kraus shouted when he saw that Narwynn approached them too. "You can sit down too if you know how to do such things as sitting."

Everyone laughed. Narwynn lowered his gaze and crunched his shoulders as he walked over and sat down next to Elna.

41

He gave the crystal to Aunt Milnu instead. She thought it was beautiful and wore it as a charm.

One evening, Narwynn and Elna walked to the shared storage house together to pick up some food. Susy sat on Elna's shoulder as she usually did, enjoying the view while they walked on the thin layer of snow between the blue-flame torches that lit up the path to the shared storage house. They walked past a few grown-ups who carried carrots on their shoulders and potatoes on their heads. Some of them smiled at Elna as they crossed paths, but no one smiled at Narwynn. He did not mind, as he had never known otherwise.

When they reached the shared storage house, they saw that the fire was burning at the bonfire spot, with several nose-elves sitting around it. They were not workers. They all had predator pets sitting beside them or on their laps. One had a kestrel perched on her shoulder, and another a weasel lying across his leg. The biggest pet was Charky, who was sitting next to Kraus on the other side of the fire.

Narwynn pulled Elna into the shared storage house as soon as he saw Kraus and Charky. For some reason, he did not want them to see them.

"Shall we go over and sit with them, Narwynn?" Elna asked while she grabbed a piece of squirrel meat and put it into her pouch.

"No, I don't want to," Narwynn answered.

"Why?"

Narwynn tried to come up with a reason but failed to do so. He did not know why he shied away

4 THE ART OF TAMING

The first few snowflakes fell over Oaktown, leaving a thin white coat on the ground and the rooftops. The town was quiet, as most nose-elves preferred to stay inside at this time of year. Smoke rose from the chimneys upstream against the falling snow. It was almost dark, except for occasional spells of light that broke between the dark clouds above.

Narwynn had not been in the woods since the night he had encountered Rutha the Troll. Instead, he had tried to find someone who would use the crystal he had brought back to destroy her. However, neither the blacksmith nor the shepherd had shown any interest in it. They had both told Narwynn that he had been a fool to go looking for it and for bringing it back.

Eventually, Narwynn had given up trying to convince them to use it. He realised that they were scared and cowardly for talking about using it to kill Rutha but shying away when they had the chance to.

of sniffing from behind. The sound sent a shiver down Narwynn's spine, and his legs started running before he even thought about running.

Finally, just after the sun had set, Narwynn stumbled into the field of Oaktown. Although he kept trying to run, his legs could no longer carry him, and he stumbled across the field. When he reached the outskirts of town, he sat down on a bench and looked back while catching his breath once more.

Then, by the edge of the woods, Narwynn thought he could see the shape of two eyes staring longingly after him, but not daring to cross the field. Although the sight still frightened him, Narwynn smiled a little and looked down at his shivering hand. There, he was holding a sharp, blue crystal arrowhead.

behind the stone. He stepped out a little further to see better, but could not see her. He thought she must have gone back into the woods to look for him. He sighed with relief and turned back around. Then he faced the enormous face once again, so close their noses almost touched.

"UUUUAAAH!" Narwynn screamed.

Rutha tried to grab him, but he jumped out of her reach just in time. Then Narwynn thrust at her with his spear and hit her on the nose.

"AAU!" Rutha screamed and grabbed her nose with both hands.

Then Narwynn saw that the crystal was about to fall out of her belt. He swung his spear at it, and it fell out and onto the ground. Before Rutha could let go of her nose, Narwynn jumped forward, snatched the crystal from the ground beneath her and ran as fast as his legs could carry him towards the trees.

When he reached the trees, he looked over his shoulder and saw Rutha coming after him, but she was too slow. Narwynn thought he could easily outrun her and started in between the trees. He ran and ran. After a while, he could taste blood in his mouth and knew he could not run any more. He had to take a break and found a rock to sit down on while catching his breath. He thought Rutha must be way behind him.

After sitting on the rock for a while, Narwynn noticed that the sun was setting in the distance. Oh no, he thought, not again. He decided to keep moving and got back up. Then he heard the sound

"Smell I nose-elf flesh?" a deep, dark voice sounded from right in front of Narwynn.

Narwynn jumped so much that he screamed and fell onto his back. Then he looked up and saw two round eyes, each as large as his head, staring down at him, and a nose that stretched almost to the ground. It was Rutha. She was difficult to see because her long, frizzy hair was full of sticks and tree bark, with her skin covered in moss.

Narwynn crawled backwards on his back in terror. Rutha took a step after him but did not move very fast. As she stepped out from the trees, something shiny became visible on her waist. It was a blue crystal that she had strapped into her belt. Narwynn saw it but was too busy crawling away from her to think any more of it.

He got to his feet and started running back towards the rock. As soon as he reached it, he jumped behind it while looking out to the side. He saw Rutha moving slowly after him and felt the panic building up within him. It was difficult to breathe and to stay calm. What was he going to do?

He turned around to look for a place he could hide where Rutha would not find him. He saw that the next rock was close and out of sight for Ruth but not him. He ran towards it, took his spear off his back and held it while he sat down behind the rock. He waited and hoped that Rutha would not find him there.

He had waited for a while, and Rutha had not found him. He found it a challenge to peek out from a nose-elf camp. It was also far too greasy!

Suddenly he heard a familiar sound from the woods where he had come from earlier. He heard sticks cracking and branches breaking. He turned around to see what it was and saw the treetops trembling in the distance. Then he noticed that whatever it was out there between the trees, it was moving towards him!

In an instant, he jumped off the rock and hid behind it. His knees were shaking, and his fur stood on end. Although he was hiding, he could not help but peek out on the side of the rock in anticipation. After some time, Narwynn could see the trees at the edge of the clearing trembling and even their branches breaking, but then it suddenly stopped, and he could not see any creature.

Where the branches had broken, he could only see something covered in sticks and moss, but it was too far away to see what it was. He waited, but nothing happened. The movement in the trees had stopped and did not start again.

After waiting for a while, Narwynn realised that he needed to go back. The sun had already started setting, and he did not want to return to Oaktown after dark. He hesitated at first, but then walked towards the trees. He would have to come back to look for the crystal another day, he thought.

As Narwynn approached the trees, he suddenly heard a loud, sniffing sound. He jumped and looked around in all directions, but could not see anything.

had fought Dreumar first. Just as the thought had entered his mind, he saw another clearing ahead. It seemed much larger than the one before.

As he reached it, he saw that it was clear all the way across to the mountain wall. All the trees and the grass were gone. There was only dry dirt and several large rocks scattered across the ground. Some of the rocks looked as if their tops had once been melted. As if drops were running down their sides. Narwynn figured that Dreumar's dragon breath must have melted them, and he chilled at the thought.

Narwynn walked towards the closest rock and looked carefully in all directions. He knew he was in potential danger as long as he walked in plain sight. As soon as he reached the rock, he leaned his back up against it and looked back to see that nothing was following him. Then he thought that the arrow must have fallen into one of the rocks from above, so he would need to search the top of each one for the crystal. He climbed on top of the first one, only to find a smooth surface with nothing blue penetrating it.

He looked around at the other rocks and noticed that there were at least a dozen. And then he saw another rock at the far end of the clearing that was broken into several pieces. Next to it was a large circle of smaller rocks with burnt firewood inside and a spit above it. The circle of rocks was surrounded by animal carcasses, some old and rotten, and others new and fresh.

Narwynn thought it looked far too large to be

walked, but he did not hear anything.

By midday, Narwynn reached a clearing, but did not walk into it. He knew better than to walk into places where he was vulnerable from every angle. Instead, he walked around it. While doing so, he heard something in the distance from across the clearing. It sounded like the cracking of sticks and branches, like nothing he had ever heard before.

He walked slower and felt his knees trembling. Suddenly he regretted going alone. He would have felt safer if someone else were by his side. To his relief, the sound seemed to move away from him, and it eventually faded. He continued moving slowly around the clearing until he reached the trail he had walked along before.

Narwynn looked back to see if he could catch a glimpse of what he had heard, but all he could see were trembling treetops beyond the other side of the clearing. Then the treetops stopped trembling.

Could it have been her, he thought? For a long time he had not believed in the tales about the Rutha the Troll. He had never even imagined what she looked like. Was she big or small? Did she have a long nose like the nose-elves, or did she look completely different from them? He did not know, and he hoped he never would. He just longed to find the blue crystal arrowhead so the workers could get rid of her.

Narwynn eventually reached the woods in the north. He felt exhausted and needed a break, but he thought he needed to find the place where Krucar

the door behind him.

Narwynn walked home to his tent and found Aunt Milnu cooking supper on the fireplace outside. They had some late dinner together before they both went to bed. It took Narwynn some time to fall asleep. He could not stop thinking about the tales about the dragon and about Rutha the troll, and the blue crystal that the workers needed to protect them from her.

The next morning was unusually cold for the time of year. Narwynn woke early, but Aunt Milnu did not. Narwynn got up and walked outside, and past the dying fire. He threw on his hare pelt, grabbed his spear from the side of the tent and started walking.

He walked north, past the workers' area and the outskirts of town. The field was still green with grass, but the woods beyond were yellow and red, and dying leaves were falling from the trees.

Narwynn had thought about the tales and the blue crystal arrowhead all night. He had hardly slept, yet felt full of energy and excitement. He had decided not to ask Elna to come with him, as he did not want to put her in harm's way. She was not as fast or as strong as him, nor did she have a cape to keep her warm. He had to go alone.

He entered the woods and took the trail that led north. The trees and their branches formed a tunnel around the path, glowing orange in the morning sunlight. It was quiet, and Narwynn listened for the sounds of creatures approaching as he

"So, you think it is still there?"

"I don't know. I thought it was just a bedtime tale that was not true. But the workers told the story again tonight in a way that seemed true."

"Then we need to go and find it, so they can use it to protect us from Rutha."

"No, Narwynn. They said it was too dangerous to go into the woods now when the winter is approaching. We are not allowed."

"I know..." said Narwynn and sighed while he looked at the ground.

He did not even know whether the crystal would be there. All he knew was that Elna's bedtime tales and the tales the workers had told were different. One thing was certain: no one had found the last crystal, so it had to be somewhere.

They reached Elna's house, and Narwynn walked her to the steps by the front door. Someone stood waiting for her on the doorstep. It was Edgar, her father.

"There you are, princess," said Edgar, as Elna ran up to him and gave him a big hug. "You have been out late tonight. Say good night to your friend now. Then you must hurry to bed."

"OK, Daddy," Elna said before she turned to Narwynn, "Night-night, Narwynn."

"Good night, Elna," said Narwynn.

Narwynn was surprised to see that Edgar smiled at him. Few grown-ups ever did.

"Sleep well, my green friend," said Edgar and winked at Narwynn before he went inside and closed

the traveller, "how Rutha suddenly appeared when we had no heroes left in the Green Lands? As if she were here as a test for any rising heroes to prove themselves worthy."

"It is rather suspicious," said the blacksmith, "but I can't think of anyone who would be able place a troll anywhere it does not want to be. That would require magic and wizardry."

"Magic?" asked Narwynn just as the shepherd and the other workers rose from their seats.

"But now it's getting cold and late, and it's time to go home," said the shepherd.

Narwynn noticed that it was completely dark, the moon was up, and the stars glittered across the sky. It was late, indeed, and Aunt Milnu was probably getting worried. He got up, and then helped Elna to her feet. As Elna and Narwynn walked home, Elna had more to say.

"Narwynn?" she said.

"Yes, Elna?"

"You know, when Daddy told me the bedtime tale about Krucar, he said something about the last arrowhead that the workers did not mention."

Elna had Narwynn's attention.

"What was that?"

"According to the tale he told me, Krucar had fired only one arrow at Dreumar. The arrow had hit Dreumar but bounced off his dragon scales. It had fallen through the air and penetrated a rock on the ground. And then the blue crystal had been stuck in the rock ever since."

"No, little nose-elf, but she is…"

She? Narwynn thought.

"Rutha the Troll has woken from her summer sleep once more, and it is no longer safe to travel in the woods. That horrid creature. She has been around ever since Krucar died. Only those with great experience, strong weapons and strong predator pets and capes to keep them warm can go out there now. Rutha is too large to be killed by a normal nose-elf, and only a hero with coloured crystal weapons and a strong pet could stand up to her."

"Then why can experienced nose-elves still go out in the woods when she is there and it is not safe?" asked Elna with her eyes wide open. "Why is it not too dangerous for them?"

"Because they are wise enough to run as soon as they see her," said the shepherd before the blacksmith had a chance to answer, "and send their pets to distract her while they get a head start."

"What if we were able to find the last of Krucar's crystals?" Narwynn interrupted.

"Hah! That's a fool's errand, green one," said the healer. "Many have gone to look for them up there, but no one has yet found it. Don't get any ideas now. I am a good healer, but I will not be able to help you once Rutha has finished with you. Even if she decides not to eat you, she will crush your bones and squeeze the breath from your body.

Narwynn felt a shiver down his spine.

"He's right," the shepherd added.

"Don't you think it is rather convenient," said

"A real shame about his children," the healer broke in. "Ironic really. There he went to save the King's daughter, and now he is not here to take care of his own. Such a tragedy."

All the workers nodded. They all seemed to know about Kraus's family.

The workers continued to talk about Krucar and his wolf. Narwynn learned that Krucar had been a hero who had travelled to the northern peak with his wolf to find the princess and kill Dreumar. It had been the King who had commanded him to do so. Krucar had carried a bow and seven blue crystal arrows. Everyone had waited in the hope that the dragon would finally be gone, but Krucar had never returned. A traveller had later found six of Krucar's arrowheads in a pile of ashes up in the northern woods. For some unknown reason, the King had commanded that the arrowheads be brought to him.

Narwynn thought of what the guard had preached in the market place before. The guard had told the crowd not to kill the dragon before they knew where the princess was.

"I wish we had some of those arrowheads now," said the shepherd.

"So do I," the blacksmith sighed. "They would have been handy."

"Why would they be handy now?" Elna asked. "The dragon is not here at the moment."

Everyone looked at Elna once more. The blacksmith leaned towards her with a serious look on his face.

the dragon. The dragon Dreumar."

Suddenly the workers fell silent again. They all looked at Elna this time.

"How in Nightwood does a young nose-elf like you know his name?" asked the blacksmith.

"My mummy and daddy told me the tale every night when I was little. I don't need bedtime tales anymore. I'm a big nose-elf now."

"I'm sure you are," said the traveller and smiled. "May I ask who your mummy and daddy are?"

"Their names are Emelda and Edgar."

"Aaah…" said the traveller. "Well, I shan't argue with them."

"Argh, that Edgar," said the blacksmith, "carefree as always. Turning horrible events into cosy little bedtime tales. Sounds just like him!"

Narwynn looked at Elna and saw her smiling when the workers talked about her parents. But then she looked like she had thought of something else, and stopped smiling.

"But is it true that Kraus's father is dead?" Elna asked.

"I'm afraid so, little one," said the traveller, "but Krucar was a true hero."

"He was indeed," the blacksmith admitted. "He and his wolf fought Dreumar for three days and three nights. But by the end of the third night, Dreumar's fiery breath blew Krucar to the ground."

"It is said that Krucar's wolf still lurks around in the woods and the peaks, looking for its master."

laughter had died down. "Hope will drive you mad. There is no hope."

Narwynn grew more and more curious while the workers discussed. Was this indestructible monster the dragon he had heard about before? Why was there no hope? He needed to know.

"There is always hope," the healer said, "Krucar nearly got him."

Krucar? Narwynn thought. He was sure he had heard this name somewhere.

"And then he got burned," the shepherd added.

"Krucar and his wolf gave him a hard time, I'll admit to that," the blacksmith said, "but he had no chance in the end."

Krucar and his wolf? Narwynn realised it now. He had thought it was a lie.

"Narwynn, Narwynn," Elna whispered and poked Narwynn in the side to get his attention. "They are talking about Krucar, the wolf-tamer. Kraus's father!"

"Shhh! I know, but be quiet. I want to find out what he was fighting against." Narwynn hissed.

"But don't you know, Narwynn?"

"Know what?" he asked and turned towards Elna. Suddenly he was interested in what she had to say.

"Well, it sounds like that bedtime tale Mummy and Daddy used to tell."

"What tale?"

"The one about the three heroes who fought

back. "The animals are moving towards the north. They can sense that he is in the south, and they are moving away from him."

Narwynn got curious. Were they talking about the same dragon he had heard about in the market place?

"What are you talking about?" he asked.

He regretted asking as soon as the words had slipped past his lips. Everyone around the fire stopped talking and stared at Narwynn. He looked down and waited for them to keep ignoring him and go on with their argument.

"Why don't you explain it to them?" a traveller asked the blacksmith.

"Explain it to them? Hah!" the blacksmith laughed. "How could anyone who has not seen it possibly understand it?"

"He's right," the shepherd interrupted.

"I think they should know," said the traveller. "Otherwise they will be worse off, not knowing what to do when they eventually cross his path. If they know, then at least they will be wise enough to run."

"Go ahead and tell them then," said the blacksmith. "If you so wish to scare the young ones, telling them about the indestructible monster that plagues our lands."

"Indestructible?" the healer interrupted. "Surely, there is still hope."

All the other workers laughed, as if they had heard a funny joke.

"Hope, huh?" The blacksmith said when the

"Did you just come from the storage house?" Elna asked.

"Yes," Narwynn answered.

"Do you have enough supplies to keep you and Aunt Milnu through the winter?"

Aunt Milnu was not really Elna's aunt, but Elna felt as if she were, and so she referred to her as Aunt Milnu. However, Narwynn had never spoken to Elna's parents. He thought they didn't want to talk to him like so many of the other grown-ups.

"Yes, I have dried a lot of mushrooms, and Aunt Milnu has gathered firewood for us."

"Good."

"What about you? Did you hang up the mushrooms we gathered last week?"

"Yes, I did. And my father has smoked plenty of squirrel meat for us. He and his bobcat, Buddy, have been out hunting squirrels for several months. Squirrel meat tastes good when smoked."

Narwynn looked down.

"You are lucky," he said.

"Why?" Elna answered.

"Because your father is a hunter. I don't even have a…"

Narwynn was interrupted by the blacksmith who raised his voice at one of the shepherds.

"He is lurking around up north, I know it!" the blacksmith shouted. "I saw smoke rising from the woods up there, and I know it was him burning his victims."

"No! You are wrong!" the shepherd shouted

storage house, which was open to everyone who lived in Oaktown.

One day, Narwynn walked down to the storage house with his hands full of mushrooms to be hung up. He saw that a group of nose-elves had gathered around a fire next to the storage house. Elna was among them, with Susy looking comfortable on her shoulder. There were workers and younglings there, and they all seemed to have a good time talking and telling tales.

Narwynn hurried into the storage house and hung his mushrooms up so that he could go and sit by the fire with Elna and the others. Perhaps he could even speak to some of the workers if he sat there for long enough. Not likely though. They would probably ignore him as they always did. Narwynn walked back outside and ran over to Elna and the others.

"Elna!" he said.

Elna turned around and saw that it was him.

"Narwynn!" she answered. "Come and join us."

The workers gave Narwynn scornful looks when he came over. Narwynn ignored them and sat down next to Elna. When he sat down, a scrubby looking shepherd spat at his feet.

"Stranger..." said the shepherd.

Narwynn pretended not to notice. Elna could not have seen or heard. Had she done so, she would have given the shepherd a hard time about his behaviour.

3 RUTHA THE TROLL

It was autumn in the Green Lands. Yellow leaves from the white oak now covered the ground in Oaktown. The woods looked gloomy in the distance, and few nose-elves wanted to go there at this time of year.

The winter preparations kept the nose-elves busy, and now and then they even forgot about the dragon. Everyone had to make sure they had gathered enough firewood and food to keep them through the winter. As winter was rough, having enough firewood and food would be crucial to surviving it.

Narwynn was confident about the approaching winter. He had been hanging up his leftover mushrooms to dry for months, and Aunt Milnu had been chopping enough firewood to last them through this winter and the next. She liked to stay warm, she had said. Narwynn and Aunt Milnu had stored all their food and firewood in the shared

wanted a hare pelt for a long time.

When Narwynn came home to his tent, his Aunt Milnu was still awake.

"There you are," she said. "I almost started to worry about you. Did you and Elna find mushrooms today?"

"We found many, but few wanted to buy them. I have brought some for our dinner," Narwynn answered.

"Suits me just right, I'm starving! What is that around your neck, Narwynn? Is that... is that?"

"Even better, Aunt Milnu. This is not a piece of a rabbit pelt. This is a whole hare pelt. You know what that means?"

"It means you can keep warm outside this winter," Aunt Milnu said and gave Narwynn a warm hug.

"Yes, Aunt Milnu. I can finally explore the woods in the winter. I cannot wait!"

"Yes, yes, but you will do nothing before we have had dinner together. Let's see what we can make of these mushrooms."

Aunt Milnu put a few mushrooms on a spit and placed them over the fire inside the tent. Narwynn sat down and held his hands up in front of the flames. All the tales he had heard about the woods in the winter. It sounded magical.

Elna had worked hard to gather all these mushrooms? And now most of them would go to waste as they would not stay edible for more than two or three days. He would need to hang them up to dry in the shared storage house for them to last longer.

"Oh well, I suppose I could have a few mushrooms with my hare leg tonight. Tell me, how would you like to trade them for a hare pelt? I have so many that I don't know what to do with them."

Narwynn raised his gaze with his eyes wide open. He had been trying to save up for a piece of rabbit pelt for years, and now he was being offered a whole hare. He swallowed and tried to sound casual.

"Sure. Why not? How many do you want?"

"I'll take half of them. That way, I'll have enough for the rest of the family as well. Here is your pelt."

Kraus swayed one of the hare pelts off his shoulders and handed it over to Narwynn. Narwynn, in return, poured half the mushrooms into Kraus's large silver pouch, which became so heavy that even Kraus could barely lift it.

"Thank you, Kraus," Narwynn said.

"Save your thanks for someone who cares, stupid..." said Kraus and started through the market place. "C'mon boy!"

Kraus and Charky walked away. There was something odd about Kraus, Narwynn thought. He could not quite put his finger on it. But Narwynn's thoughts soon returned to his hare pelt. He had

"Susy and I need to go home to my mummy and daddy now, Narwynn," said Elna as she grabbed a few mushrooms to take home. "You can borrow my hat to keep the mushrooms in if you want to."

"Thank you, Elna. Thank you for your help today."

Elna walked off towards her family's wooden house, and Susy climbed up her back and onto her shoulder. Narwynn remained standing in the background of the crowd that surrounded Kraus's stall. He watched as nose-elves from the crowd bought their meat and walked off without even noticing his mushrooms. Eventually, there was almost nobody left in the market. It was time for Narwynn to go home to his aunt and eat some mushrooms with her.

"Hey, Greeny," someone said as Narwynn was getting ready to go home, "have you got any mushrooms left?"

Narwynn turned around and saw Kraus and Charky coming over. Kraus was holding three hare pelts over his shoulders and the meat he had kept for dinner in his hand. It looked like he had sold everything else, even the bones of the three hares.

"I have almost all of them left, unfortunately," Narwynn answered and looked down.

"Haha!" Kraus laughed, "you really are a useless little nose-elf, aren't you?"

Narwynn got so angry that he could barely restrain himself. How could Kraus make fun of him like that? Did he not understand that Narwynn and

When they reached the centre of the market place, Narwynn and Elna noticed that everyone was crowding around one of the stalls where a dark-furred fox stood on one side. Something seemed to draw everyone's attention to this one stall. Someone is getting rich tonight, Narwynn thought.

He was curious to see what they were selling at the stall. Perhaps he could start to gather or grow whatever they gathered or grew, and then he too could get rich. He tried to peek through the crowd in front of the stall, but he could not see who it was or what they were selling.

"Look, Narwynn! It's Charky!" Elna said and pointed at the fox.

Narwynn then realised that this was Kraus's stall and that he was selling meat from his catch of the day. Hunters rarely brought back any catch at all, but when they did, everyone wanted a piece of whatever animal they had killed. Kraus and Charky had had a good hunt, and now they were reaping the rewards.

It was unfair, Narwynn thought. He and Elna also had had a successful day, but hardly any buyers were interested in their mushrooms. If only he had a father who could teach him taming, he too could have been a hunter.

He felt annoyed where he stood, holding a hat full of mushrooms that nobody wanted. He had to work so hard for next to nothing, while arrogant nose-elves like Kraus could hunt with their pets and earn enough in one day to keep them for weeks.

As they continued walking into the market place, Narwynn noticed two nose-elves who were not selling anything. They stood on tall stools at opposite ends of the market place. The closest one was wearing a long white cloak.

"We must destroy the dragon!" the white-cloaked nose-elf shouted to a crowd in front of him. "He has killed our princess and will kill again if we don't stop him."

The one on the other side wore a long red cape. Narwynn could tell that he was from the King's guard. The King's guard all wore red woollen capes.

"We must find the lost princess!" the guard shouted to the crowd in front of him. "We must not kill the dragon before we find her. She is still alive and only the dragon can lead us to her."

Narwynn was confused by these messages. He thought about what they might have meant for a moment, but this made him even more confused. Then he decided to think no more of it. There were more important things to think about for now.

"Mushrooms for sale!" Narwynn shouted as they moved closer to the centre of the market place. "Only one copper piece per mushroom!"

Nobody seemed interested, except for an occasional buyer who would buy one from Elna. As usual, the buyers avoided Narwynn, and some looked at him with disgust as they walked by, repelled by the colour of his fur. Luckily, Elna shared half her copper pieces with Narwynn.

"Rutha has woken from her summer sleep, ye know," another shepherd said. "We have seen her between the trees at night, staring at the sheep with hungry eyes."

Narwynn had heard the tales about Rutha the Troll before, but he did not believe trolls existed. He thought the grown-ups told such tales to keep the young ones from entering the woods during winter when it was dangerous to wander between the bare trees. And why in Nightwood would any creature sleep during summer when it was warm and wake up in the winter when it was cold? It made no sense, but perhaps there was more to the tale than he thought.

"What did he mean by that?" Elna asked. "Could we have been eaten?"

"Don't listen to him, Elna. We were fine, and I would never let anything eat you. Especially not a stupid winter-troll."

"Very well then."

Narwynn and Elna walked away from the shepherds and into Oaktown. They went towards the market place where the nose-elves would gather in the evenings to trade their goods. Blue-flamed torches surrounded the market place. Some of the traders had small stalls where they displayed the vegetables and seeds they had grown. Others were standing in open areas holding tools while shouting, "Tools for sale! Look at this item, little nose-elves; it's a good one!" It was now time to find someone who wanted to buy mushrooms.

before dark, but Elna was tired and struggling.

The sun sank lower and lower in the sky, the shadows cast by the trees stretched further and further along the ground, and a howling breeze sounded louder and louder. The sky turned pink as the sun was setting, and the cirrus clouds looked like glowing firewood in the sky as the sunlight gradually disappeared below the horizon.

Narwynn heard creatures growling and howling in the distance and felt his heart beating. He feared that they would not make it. Elna was out of breath and so tired that she could barely walk.

Eventually, they saw the white oak of Oaktown in the distance.

"Look, Narwynn!" Elna said. "We are nearly there."

Narwynn smiled and felt a sudden relief that they had made it back in time. They passed through an opening between the trees and started to cross the field. The field was full of sheep and lambs, and nose-elf shepherds sat by little bonfires close to the edges of the woods. They had to keep the fires going all night to protect the sheep from the creatures in the woods.

"Out in the woods late, are we?" one of the shepherds shouted after Narwynn and Elna as they passed one of the bonfires. "Lucky you didn't get eaten."

Although Narwynn knew that the shepherd was right, hearing this annoyed him, and he did not respond.

They pushed their way through the remaining shrubbery and crawled over and under a few more branches. Past the pine tree was a clearing in the forest, filled with flowers of every colour and hundreds of mushrooms.

"Wooah!" Elna gasped. "So many mushrooms!"

"I know, right?" said Narwynn. "This is one of the best places in the eastern woods to gather mushrooms. Now take your hat off so we can fill it up."

Elna took her hat off, and they both started filling it with mushrooms. Susy ran around in the grass between the mushrooms and flowers. She stopped now and again to eat seeds that she found on the ground.

By the time Elna's hat was full it was midday, and Narwynn knew it was time to head back. If they waited too long they risked reaching home only after dark, and that would be dangerous. All sorts of harmful creatures could easily sneak up on them in the dark.

They headed back. Elna had insisted on taking the easy route without any more shortcuts. She wanted a safe and comfortable journey home, she said. Narwynn eventually agreed to take the easier route, and then they walked while holding Elna's hat full of mushrooms between them.

Narwynn knew that this route was longer than the shortcut, which worried him. He told Elna many times that they had to keep up the pace to get back

Charky stopped licking Elna's face and started walking after Kraus. They walked side by side into the mist until they disappeared.

"Can you get a fox, Narwynn? I like foxes," said Elna.

"You know I can't, Elna," Narwynn answered. "My aunt cannot teach me the art of taming animals."

"I know! We can ask my daddy to teach you."

Narwynn lowered his head, looked into the ground, and said: "He will probably not go near me. Nobody will. They all think I am strange because I am green instead of blue like them. Nobody will ever teach me anything. I can barely get anyone to buy the mushrooms I bring back to town."

"I don't think you are strange. I like you very much, and I think green looks great on you."

Narwynn could not hold back a little smile when he heard these words.

"Thank you, Elna."

They continued walking along the dark path and noticed the mist gradually disappearing, and the trees and shrubbery growing further and further apart. Again, beams of sunlight filled the space between the trees.

"Look, Narwynn! Mushrooms!" said Elna.

Narwynn saw small clusters of mushrooms on the ground.

"Yes, Elna. Just wait until you see what lies beyond that pine tree," said Narwynn pointing at it ahead.

"Who are you?"

"My name is Kraus, son of Krucar, the wolf-tamer."

Wolf-tamer, Narwynn thought but did not say it. What a load of nonsense!

"Alright then, Kraus, son of Krucar, you gave my friend Elna such a fright. You should apologise."

Then Narwynn turned towards Elna, and what he saw made him feel silly. Elna now smiled and laughed. She was petting the dark fox while it licked her face.

"Apologise?" Kraus asked. "Seems like you are the only one who is scared here."

Narwynn was angry now. He stared at Kraus, thinking that he wanted to hit that ugly, scarred face. It looked like someone had already roughed him up quite badly.

"How did you get that scar across your eye?" Narwynn asked.

"Oh, this?" Kraus said. "Just a scratch from when I tamed Charky. You wouldn't know anything about taming animals, of course. I see you don't have a pet of your own. Fox- taming is tough. Most who try are killed in the process and only the toughest nose-elves can do it. Fought Charky for three days and three nights, and then I became the youngest hunter ever to have tamed a fox.

"But now I have to go and hunt some rabbits. Good luck with your... whatever childish game you guys are playing out here. Remember to get back to mummy before it gets dark... C'mon boy!"

appeared right in front of her, snarling. Narwynn felt his heart pumping. He would not let anything hurt Elna, he thought.

He jumped in between Elna and the fox. The fox was larger than him and could have killed him in an instant had he not pointed the sharp crystal towards it. It started to move back and forth, and Narwynn followed its movements with the crystal.

Then Narwynn heard sticks cracking on the ground somewhere behind the fox. Something was approaching, and it sounded at least as big as the beast that already threatened them. Narwynn felt his heart pumping even more, and a drop of sweat ran down his fur. How would he get out of this? Whatever walked in the mist behind the fox came closer and closer.

A slight puff of wind came through the bushes and stirred up the mist. The walker finally became visible. To Narwynn's astonishment and relief, it was not a dangerous creature after all. He lowered his spear and sighed as the walker approached.

"Hah! Bet you got properly scared now!" The walker laughed at Narwynn and Elna.

"What is so funny? I could have hurt your fox," Narwynn answered.

"Oh, don't worry. You could never hurt Charky. He is much more dangerous than you are."

Narwynn recognised the walker with the fox. He had seen him in Oaktown before, but had never spoken to him. He wondered who he was.

they were not careful. Narwynn held his spear out in front, and Elna held hers ready at the rear.

They had walked for a while when they first stopped. Narwynn suggested a shortcut that went off the pathway.

"Is that not dangerous?" Elna asked.

"A little, but I have done it many times," Narwynn answered.

"Very well then."

They walked in between the trees and shrubbery that surrounded the shortcut. It was not an easy trail to hike. In some places they had to climb over and under branches that were in the way. Elna felt Susy shaking on her shoulder, and then she started feeling a little scared herself. Narwynn, on the other hand, loved to travel off the road, and he wished there were even more hurdles in their way.

As they walked deeper into the woods, the trees and shrubbery grew closer and closer together, and less and less sunlight got through. It grew colder and colder, and a mist started to appear around them. Elna clung to her little stick, and Susy had taken refuge inside her hat, only to peek out now and again.

"Are we getting close to where the mushrooms are, Narwynn?" Elna asked.

"Yes, just a little longer," Narwynn answered.

Suddenly Elna screamed. Narwynn jumped and turned around, and saw that Elna stood frozen in the mist, trembling. She seemed to be staring at something. As the mist moved, a dark-furred fox

mouse Susy, and Elna stood laughing behind him.

He grabbed Susy by the tail and held her up in front of Elna.

"Do you know this little crawler?" he asked although he knew the answer.

"She woke you up quicker than I ever do," Elna chuckled.

Narwynn could see that Elna was ready to go mushroom-gathering. She had her oversize hat on, and held a short willow stick with a pointy end. Susy had crawled back on Elna's shoulder, where she usually sat when they went for walks together. It was time for Narwynn to get ready too.

Narwynn did not have a hat as Elna did, but his stick was far better than hers. It was long and made of solid oak into which he had carved beautiful patterns. At the end of it, he had attached a pointy, white crystal. Narwynn and Elna had to bring their sticks to protect themselves from creatures in the woods.

Narwynn took the lead while they walked towards the western edges of Oaktown and crossed the field before stepping in among the trees. The light from the morning sun appeared in yellow spells between the branches, leaves and trunks. Brown and orange leaves crunched under their feet with every step they took on the path.

Both of them were on guard and looked out for anything that could spell danger. They knew that there were dangerous creatures around, some bigger than both of them combined that could find them if

the woods during winter. Most of the younglings did not believe them, as they had never seen anything that looked like a troll before.

Narwynn was a young nose-elf, and like many young nose-elves, he was full of beans. He loved spending summer days in the woods. However, in winter it was too cold to go there without a cape, and he could not afford one. He often dreamed that one day he would be able to buy one and explore the woods in the winter.

Narwynn lived in a tent right next to the thickest root of the white oak with his aunt. He had never known his parents. In fact, he had no idea who they were. Whenever he asked his aunt about them, she said that it was not for her to tell. But she told him that she promised to take good care of him long ago and she would never break a promise.

Although Narwynn had few friends, he appreciated the ones he had. His best friend was Elna. She was a younger nose-elf who sometimes accompanied Narwynn on his walks in the woods. They often gathered mushrooms together that they would trade for copper pieces. Narwynn saved for a rabbit pelt cape but was still far from able to afford one. Elna saved for a new hat, although she liked the one she already had.

One morning, Narwynn was suddenly woken up by something big and hairy crawling on his neck. He jumped to his feet, shook his head, and waved his arm around, trying to grab the crawler. When he finally managed to grab it, he saw it was Elna's white

2 INTO THE WOODS

Years went by with no word about the dragon, yet the nose-elves worried that no one knew where he was. Had they known where he was, they would have made sure to stay away from him. All they could do was to hope not to cross his path wherever they went.

Many of Oaktown's inhabitants prepared for the next time Dreumar would pass by. Some built stone walls around their houses. Others were running in circles in the fields, unable to decide what to do. The miners dug caves deep into the ground, and the blacksmith worked day and night, making weapons and tools for cave-digging and wall-building. Few nose-elves could banish the fear and worry from their minds.

The younglings, however, did not know about the dragon. The grown-ups had made sure the younglings were afraid of other dangers instead. They had told them there was a troll that lurked in

promise. But can I ask why?"

"Because knowledge is power, and power must belong to the wise."

now, and take the baby back home. Nobody will take him away from you. I am Ludazar, head of the Seven Wise, and I will let everyone know that he belongs here and nowhere else. A prophecy has been told about such a nose-elf. It said that a green hero would rise in the Green Lands. I suspect the hero in the prophecy is the baby you hold in your arms. May I ask your name, dear?"

"M-my name is Milnu," she stammered.

"Very well, my dear Milnu. You shall raise this little nose-elf as your own, and you shall tell everyone that he is your nephew. No one will question your words, nor will they blame you for raising him. Now, let me walk you home."

Milnu felt confused and relieved at the same time. She was grateful that she would be able to raise him in Oaktown, just as she had promised some time ago.

Ludazar and Milnu walked side by side on the pathway of trodden grass towards the white oak. Milnu told Ludazar that her tent was close to the centre, right where the thickest root of the white oak sank into the ground. Ludazar told her that he was heading the same way. When they got there, the glows of a dying fire still shed some light on Milnu's tent.

Before Milnu went inside, Ludazar had one last thing to tell her.

"Milnu, no one must know about the prophecy," he said.

"Of course, Ludazar," Milnu answered. "I

running from?" he said.

"Oh, please let us pass, something terrible has happened, and I must get this baby away, fast," the nose-elf with the baby answered.

"Of course, you may pass, but may I first know what you are running away from? You see, if there is danger where you came from, I do not want to go there."

"No, no. Nothing like that. My friend gave birth to this baby a while ago, and now his fur has grown. I thought it was all right at first, but then, then…" She choked on her words and wiped tears from her cheeks.

"Then what?"

"It was as I have feared. The baby's fur is not blue like ours," she said, and turned him around so the old nose-elf could see. "It is green."

The old nose-elf raised his eyebrows for a moment before lowering them with a broad smile across his face.

"And what is the problem with that?"

"Do you not understand?" she shouted. "They will think he has been stolen from another land where their fur is green, and then they will take him away from me."

"And what of his mother and father?"

The nose-elf with the baby lowered her gaze and shook her head. She did not answer the question, and nor did she want to.

The old nose-elf lowered his staff, put his hat back on his head, and said: "My dear, you can relax

many dreamed that one day a new hero would be born, who would grow strong enough to kill the dragon Dreumar and bring back the lost princess.

Oaktown surrounded a white oak close to the centre of the Green Land woods. An open grass field surrounded Oaktown, and beyond the grass field deep woods stretched through the valley and up the mountainsides. Mountain peaks could be seen in all directions from Oaktown, and the northern mountain peak was particularly tall and famous. It was called Dragon Peak, as this was where Dreumar returned after his flights over the Green Lands.

One starry night, on the outskirts of Oaktown, an old nose-elf wearing a white cloak and a pointy hat walked under the moon and stars. When he saw an eagle watching him from a tree branch close by, he gave it a skewed smile. When he saw a troll staring at him from between the trees, he pointed his staff towards it, causing it to turn back into the darkness. He felt a cool breeze against his long fur and fresh grass under his feet. He loved going for starlight walks late at night, listening to the whispering of the woods, and thinking of times long gone and of times soon to come.

His thoughts were suddenly interrupted when he saw another nose-elf running towards him. The other nose-elf was carrying a baby nose-elf on her arm and looked frightened. As she came closer, the old nose-elf held out his staff to one side and his hat to the other.

"Stop, young one. What dragons are you

and find the stolen princess, but none had yet succeeded. Every time they challenged Dreumar, he fought them ruthlessly and burned them with his breath of fire.

No one knew where Dreumar came from. Nor did they understand why he had stolen the princess. Some said he was angry with the King. Others said he was jealous of him because he did not have a kingdom of his own. The tales were many, but where the dragon had come from remained a mystery.

The nose-elves were peculiar creatures, neither larger than foxes, nor smaller than hares. They had long noses, pointy ears, and large round eyes. Some wore hats or capes, and others wore nothing at all. In the Green Lands, the nose-elves had blue fur. In other lands, their fur had different colours.

They lived close to the animals, and in the Green Lands they were known for their skills in taming and hunting them. Those who were really good could tame an animal larger than themselves. Some of the hunters, for instance, took fox cubs and raised them to help with rat- and rabbit-hunting. This was a dangerous game, and therefore most hunters tamed falcons or weasels instead.

Sometimes tales were told of heroes who had tamed wolves to hunt large prey, and had even tamed eagles to fly through the sky between the lands. These were, of course, only tales, and most nose-elves doubted they were really true. However,

1 THE PROPHECY

The nose-elves lived in the lands of Nightwood among many other strange creatures. Nightwood was divided into four nose-elf kingdoms, and although exciting tales could be told about all four, this particular tale took place in the Green Lands.

The Green Lands were ruled by an old nose-elf king whose name was Elrud. To King Elrud's despair, a dragon had risen in the Green Lands. The dragon was known as Dreumar among the nose-elves who knew about him. Dreumar had stolen the King's one and only daughter and hidden her away somewhere in the mountains. He had stolen the King's gold too. Since then, Dreumar had flown across the Green Lands and destroyed everyone who crossed his path.

No one knew why Dreumar flew across the lands instead of settling down somewhere in the mountains, as dragons were known to do. Some nose-elves had tried to rid the kingdom of Dreumar

ACKNOWLEDGMENTS

My most sincere thanks to Melanie and Ulla
for helping me develop this story.

CONTENTS

	Acknowledgments	i
1	The Prophecy	1
2	Into the Woods	Pg 6
3	Rutha the Troll	Pg 21
4	The Art of Taming	Pg 38
5	The Wizard's Wisdom	Pg 56
6	Goblins Love Gold	Pg 75
7	The Talking Goat	Pg 93
8	The Rise of Heroes	Pg 112
9	Destiny	Pg 128

DEDICATION

For Tabby, the most precious little cat who kept me company while writing the first pages of this book.

Copyright © 2020 Erlend Slettevold

All rights reserved.

ISBN: 9798563347984

Narwynn
Rise of Heroes

Erlend Slettevold